THE HUNTING TOWN

BROTHERS, VOLUME I
ELIZABETH STEPHENS

Contents

Part I
The Fighting Pit

Knox

Echoes of pain and pleasure sear the night, and the sheer magnitude of the sound is absorbed by nothing. Not the rotting wooden walls or the packed earth under my boots in place of floorboards. The barn is overfull, bodies crammed into every inch of the light and trickling out into the darkness.

Somewhere in between our town and the next, Clifton stumbled upon this shack. Large enough to house a hundred comfortably, we're more than twice that by now. I stand in the center of a loose ring of men across from a guy with a shaved head and a black eye. He wears a mean snarl and snaps one curled fist into his other open hand.

I smirk. I've seen him in the ring before squaring up against one of my brothers. Aiden warned me about a serious left hook, but also ran me through a list of the guy's failings about a mile long. Thanks to him, I'm far from nervous as he takes a first step towards me. Hell, I'm downright relaxed. What are brothers for, right?

"Total obliteration," Dixon whispers into my ear, as if reading my thoughts. He gives my shoulder a tight squeeze and I clench my jaw to keep from wincing.

I click my tongue against the backs of my teeth and shoot him a tight smile. "You're the boss." He grins and his teeth are bright white against his obsidian skin. He might be my brother, but we couldn't look further apart. Growing up, he always made fun of me for being white. Said that blood doesn't show up so easily on his color.

As I move forward, the crowd goes wild. The density of the group is dangerous for them, but they never learn from it – not even after a kid got trampled and hospitalized last year. I recognize a lot of the same faces from the week before – other fighters, friends from Seventh Street bars, and the sycophants from the nearby colleges that make up the bulk of the screaming.

Amid the cries, a chorus breaks out: "Knu-ckles, Knu-ckles, Knu-ckles." A few weak shouts try to break through with the name of my opponent: "Sla-ter, Sla-ter..." In this room, they're quick to fade. I'm the crowd favorite, mostly because I'm easy money if you know how to play the stakes.

My opponent swings for my face with loose, uncalculated aim, but there's power behind the blow. One hit might keep a guy down long enough for Slater to finish them off. Lucky for me, I'm not any guy. He swings for me again and this time, I take the hit to my stomach. Hurts like hell and I'm sure it'll leave a bruise tomorrow, but it gets me close enough to strike at his leg. I nail his quadriceps with lightning quick jabs and pull back. The guy's knee buckles and he looks up at me with momentary panic before I bring my fist down. Once in the cheek and he hits the soil. Both of his hands are down, but only for two seconds. A third and the match would have been called.

I shake my head slowly. "Should have stayed down, big guy." He's disoriented and tries to block, but moves too slowly. Throwing both arms up, I drive straight through them with my left hand and crush his nose. Blood sprays from it and he canters back like a log, staggering into the screaming masses behind him. They do nothing to break his fall.

I don't wait for his people to cart him off the pitch, but carve a path through the crowd. Dixon stays behind to collect my cash – and his – but I've got eyes only for one thing. "Hello sweetheart," I say as I approach the bar. I rub my hands together and Ollie, the bartender, waves a dishrag at one of the college kids. The kid starts talking through his ass until Ollie gestures to me. Seeing me, he tumbles off of his barstool, gestures to it frantically and runs his hands back through his gelled hair so that it sticks up in every direction.

"Aw fuck man, sorry I didn't know that was your spot. No harm, right? No foul?" He chuckles nervously and edges back as I step close enough to really hurt him if I wanted.

"Man?" I say, closing the gap until we're chest to chest.

"Sorry. I meant Knuckles. Sorry! Knox. Knox, sir."

The larger part of me wants to laugh at the moniker, but I manage to keep a straight face. "Scram, kid." I cock my head and he scurries away, disappearing into a crowd of sweaty, shifting bodies that are all gearing up for the next fight.

As I slide onto the barstool, Ollie slams a triple whiskey down in front of me and laughs. "Always the hard ass."

"Got a rep to protect. Can't have some little shit talking down to me like he owns the place." I scan the guy sitting to my left. Another college kid. It takes him about a second to vacate his seat, leaving it free for Clifton.

Clifton pats me on the back hard enough I choke on a sip of my drink. "Fuck you," I cough.

"Sorry," he says and I roll my eyes because he seems to mean it. He might have been the biggest of the brothers – along with Aiden, his twin – but he's damn near the softest man I've ever met. The only biological brothers in the group, he's a one eighty from his twin even though they're identical in every physical aspect – same broad shoulders, pale skin, white blonde hair. They'd been separated at birth and placed in two separate foster homes. Clifton got placed with Marguerite, eventual mom to all of us. Clifton was her first and it was fifteen years before she was able to track down Aiden. By then it was too late. A pattern of systemic abuse had ruined the poor bastard.

"Nice fighting out there today," Clifton says, nursing the beer Ollie places in front of him. Though he may not be much of a drinker, I'm finished with my whiskey and halfway through round two while he watches me, sipping so daintily.

I shrug. "Boring." I slap my hand down onto the stacked crate in front of me – a makeshift counter. "Ollie, find me some real competition next time."

"You'll have some next week." He cocks his chin to the right and I follow the line of his gaze. Instantly, I harden.

"Knox." A Mexican guy about my height is coming towards me wearing a wife beater and a shit-eating grin. "Or should I call you Knuckles? You've been making a name for yourself in my absence, I see."

"Already out of the can and back on the hunt for blood. What's it been, a year?"

"Nine months," he corrects with a confident tilt of his head, exposing stick-and-poke gang tats that I think are meant to intimidate me.

"Congratulations. Anything under a year brings you onto this side of pathetic."

The man's face flushes and he balls his hands to fists. Just under six three, he may rival me in height, but I've got more meat on my bones. Doesn't much matter though. Last time we sparred, it hospitalized us both. Broken ribs, missing teeth, swollen eyelids all around. Ollie had to call a draw because Mario and I were intent on killing each other. Then the kid got locked up for possession and distribution – heroin, I think – and our rematch was postponed indefinitely. Until now. And I'm not the same kid I was back then.

"And how long have you been locked up, Knuckles?" he sneers.

I smirk and drain the rest of my whiskey. "Never been. Unlike you, I'm what some might call intelligent."

Mario steps forward but a shorter man I hadn't seen standing behind him grabs the back of his shirt. He whispers Spanish words under his breath and twists Mario's hand until I hear something pop. I try not to let my surprise show.

"Alright, you've had your fun," the older man seethes, "now go out there and make me some money." He slaps the back of Mario's head and Mario winces when the man raises his hand a second time. The older man meets my gaze listlessly before turning and following Mario into the crowd.

"Who was that?" Clifton says.

Ollie sweeps a dirty rag over the sticky tabletop. "Who?"

"The guy holding Mario's chain."

"Oh him? He's uhh…Mario's dad." Ollie twitches as he reaches into the large metal cooler underneath the bar for a beer. He cracks it and takes a sip.

"Damn." I laugh. "Papa's come to shadow him?"

Ollie leans across the crate between us and drops his tone to a whisper. "By papa I hope you mean *Padre*."

"No shit?" I turn, hoping to catch another glimpse of the infamous Padre, leader of the Mexican mafia around these parts. Not a particularly terrifying bunch, they're still a big deal for a small town and can afford to swing their weight around a little. But hell, in a small town so can we. The Brothers is what they call us.

Ollie says, "You guys want to go up top to watch? Mario's fight's about to start. I'll send the new girl up with y'all's drinks."

Beer sprays from Clifton's lips and I bark out a laugh. "You're kidding."

"You hired a woman?" Clifton lowers his pitch and glances around. "Are you insane?"

"Girl can take care of herself, I'll give her that. Plus, she's reliable, good with the money, and every other guy in here is sweet on her."

"Dixon give you the go ahead?" The moment I get an affirmative, I ask my second, more important, question. "She pretty?"

Ollie's lips curl away from his teeth and he ruffles his lanky brown hair. "Uhh yeah. Pretty." He swallows the word as he speaks, so that it comes out of his mouth sounding like some mutilated bird squawking deep in his stomach.

"What's that supposed to mean?"

I swear, but when Ollie turns away from me it's to conceal a brilliant blush. "Just get the hell upstairs. Fight's starting."

He presses a button beneath the bar, lodged in one of the crates, and a bell sounds. Screams erupt and I hear the first smack of a fist against skin already. I curse under my breath and head for the stairs, throwing Ollie a frustrated glance before trudging up onto the platform. Clifton's close on my ass and Dixon and Charlie are waiting for us at a table overlooking the fight. Aiden sits slightly apart from our other two brothers even closer to the banister. He likes watching the carnage even more than I do. I pause by his arm and though I want to give him a clap on the shoulder, I remember who I'm dealing with. I drop my hand and I don't speak to him at all, noticing how fixed on the fight he is.

"What's the winnings?" I say to Dixon as I collapse into the wicker chair to his right. Every chair in the damn joint is different and most are falling apart. Next to beer and bandages, chairs are low on our list of priorities for the joint. Still, it's not like we'd have trouble affording it. Dixon hands me a stack of cash. Mostly fifties. Even so, feels a bit light.

Dixon doesn't look up from the bills spread on the table in front of him. He's busy organizing them into bricks of varying amounts. "Little more than twenty five hundred for you," he says with a shrug. I whistle. "Nobody worth their salt would bet against you when you're up against Slater. It'll be more next week against Mario."

Irritated, I open my mouth to say something clever when a glass of bourbon drops onto the table in front of Dixon. My brothers all fall silent and even Aiden looks up. By the time my gaze has followed the caramel colored hand up the slender wrist to the woman's face, she's already been talking for ten seconds.

"Name's Mer. I'm the new bargirl around this place. I don't take shit and if one of you hits on me so help me *dios mio*," she crosses her fingers over her full tits and meets the gaze of each one of my brothers bluntly. Not many have the stones for that and adrenaline hits me like a body shot when it's my turn, but the moment's over quickly. "I will piss in all y'all's drinks. Now I got three triple whiskeys and two beers. That'll be twenty bucks even."

"Eighteen for the same order at the bar," Dixon challenges with one eyebrow cocked.

She kicks out a hip and narrows heavy black eyelashes over a blisteringly brutal gaze. "For eighteen you can go get your drinks yourself."

"Fuck," Charlie says, laughing hard. I cover my mouth with my hand, but Clifton and I both crack. Nobody ever talks to Dixon like that. Nobody.

Dixon grins and leans back in his chair – a rocking chair missing an arm. "Where'd you come from Mer?"

"Don't see how that's any of your business."

"It is my business."

"Why?"

"This is my business." He pauses long enough for confusion to play out across her face – the widening of her eyes, the twitch of her mouth, her fingers moving up to sweep through her hair.

"Well then, boss man, I guess you're shit out of luck. I didn't come to make small talk. I came to serve drinks. Now that'll be twenty bucks even."

Dixon's smile falls and I can tell that the girl is coming dangerously close to the limit. His limit. Standing, I pull a twenty out of my pocket and hold it towards her. She watches it shrewdly, but her lips still part and she sucks in a small breath when she finally looks at my face. Really looks. Wonder what the hell she's thinking.

"I'll be back in a bit to check up on you fellas," she says rapidly and with an evidently southern lilt. She reaches out to take the cash and as her fingers graze the crumpled edge of the green, I release the bill and snatch her wrist, holding her with an easy pressure which I harden when she fights against it. Her eyebrows draw together and she opens her mouth, likely to retaliate, but I speak first.

"You can talk to me like that, but not Dixon," I say, keeping my voice calm but the threat implicit. "Never Dixon."

Her gaze widens again in a way that I'm unable to interpret, though I try. It's not quite fear, it's not quite anger, but idles somewhere in between. And Jesus Christ on her, the expression is riveting. Pretty – that's what I'd asked Ollie, wasn't it? Pretty doesn't even touch this woman. She is pure fire and I'm humbled by her sudden, inexplicable docility. She passes that glance to Dixon beside me and a carmine hue touches the tops of her cheeks, running over the bridge of her nose. She's not wearing any makeup.

"Whatever," she grunts, tugging to free her arm. I don't release it. Her gaze flashes to Dixon. "Sorry." Her pitch is deep and honest enough for me to believe it. Smart girl.

Out of the corner of my eye, I see Dixon nod. She nods back and pulls again against my grip, which I'm slow to release. Her skin is satin and smooth, layered over taut, lean muscle. I watch the way the muscles in her thighs flex and soften as she bounds down the stairs and I wonder if she isn't moving so quickly to get away from us. Hell, I don't blame her.

"Damn," Charlie says, breaking the silence hanging between us. "Just damn." I look around and vaguely realize I'm still standing, straining my optic nerve as I try to see through the wooden floorboards of the home team's patio to follow her. "I think that might be the hottest chick I've ever seen."

"You say that about anyone with a snatch," I mutter, slumping back into my seat and turning my attention towards the fight. With purpose. Because I'm searching for her purposefully.

I'm surprised when I find her a few seconds later, emerging at the other side of the barn on a set of steps identical to the ones we just climbed. It leads to the private area roped off for the visiting team's fighters. Slater is seated amidst a group of young guys that quiets the moment Mer plops their drinks down with the same gracelessness she showed us. She's a terrible fucking waitress, and absolutely perfect for the barn.

I smile to myself, resting my elbows on my knees as I watch her lips move without being able to hear anything over the thrashing of the crowd below. Mario's taunting his victim now and it sickens me. Any man who steps into the ring deserves a clean fight, a clean break. No need to resort to barbarism. Then again...my gaze pans over to Aiden who's watching the blood sport with a blank expression that's as close to happy as he ever gets. Barbarism is Aiden's MO.

Mer turns to head for the stairs, but one of Slater's minions steps in front of her and another closes in on her from behind. It's the latter moron that slaps her ass hard enough, her body entirely lifts off of the ground. She pitches forward at the same time that warm whiskey shoots down my throat and turns to fire in my stomach. Like the hammering in my chest, that fire has nothing to do with the liquor's potency.

The urge to fly across the room over the tops of so many heads grips me and I wonder how fast I could get there. How many bones would I have to break? The scratchy splinters of my chair bite into my skin like little teeth and I hear Dixon say my name twice before I finally have the strength to tear my gaze away from the scene and look at him.

"You okay, brother?" Dixon says.

I shake my head once. "Slater's fuckers are giving the new girl a hard time," I growl. Fuckers are closing in on her and though I could blow through them in a minute and a half, they're bigger than she is and she's delicate and feminine and outnumbered.

"Oh geeze." Clifton stands, and I stand with him. At the same time one asshole's hand lights down on her shoulder. As if I needed more of an invitation. "I'll go give Ollie a heads up."

"Don't bother Ollie." The words rip out of me in a breath and the hatred that I feel simmering through every one of my nerve endings reminds me of that very first time I got into a fight when I was a kid. The very first time everything had gone to red.

I head towards the stairs but as two men close in on her, I'm thrown. She reaches up to the hand on her shoulder and forces it away from her skin by the pinky. The man screams as she breaks it. The second guy barring her path raises a fist that could impale her, but Mer kicks the guy in the stomach and as he folds over, she kicks him again in the face. He topples backwards down the stairs, but she doesn't watch to admire her work. Instead, she turns back to face the first guy and drives her fist across his cheek again and again until his whole face is bloodied.

"Ho-ly-shit," Charlie says, and I turn to see that all my brothers are on their feet. All but Aiden. His face is passive and nonplussed.

Some of the spectators watching the current fight are distracted by the commotion and when Mer steps over the writhing body at the base of the steps, a group of them cheer. Ignoring them, she heads to the bar and as the next fight takes the ring, she revisits our table. "You boys need anything else?" she asks, making a face as she glances from my steel-toed shit kickers to my face. Probably wondering why I'm still standing. I'd have thought it obvious: I'm standing because I'm floored by her.

"Another round," I say, though the words don't come easily. I want to ask her something else.

She nods once and turns, but my feet are moving before I can control them. I catch her on the stairs and slip my hand around her upper arm though, the moment I so much as touch her, she rips away from me and puts another few stairs between us. I have to look almost straight down to see her face as she tilts it up. Staggered as we are then, the top of her head comes up to my belly button.

"Don't," she says and her cheeks redden. "You can't just go around grabbing people…"

"Are you okay?" I let her anger go unacknowledged for now. "Those guys give you any trouble I'm happy to handle them."

She runs her fingers back through her hair, pushing it over her shoulder so that it falls in thick raven waves down to her lower back. She's got a thin layer of bangs that cut across her forehead and sweeps them to the side now, albeit unsuccessfully. "Okay?" Her voice doesn't waver, though her glossy brown gaze dodges mine.

"Slater's friends."

"Those guys?" She rolls her eyes. "They're college kids. Harmless."

I smirk, though anger or something like it tickles the base of my spine and I'm reminded again of the red. The Red. "Tough guy, huh?"

"Who? Them?"

"No. You."

Her mouth. Her full, blood red, fucking mouth. It manages to be sexy even when it's this severe. "I don't need you looking out for me. I can handle myself."

"Fuck me for asking." My fists tighten around the railing.

She pivots from me, though I'd meant to turn away first, but damn if she isn't the kind of woman that holds your attention and doesn't let go. Like a noose. "Thanks but I'll pass on the offer," she sneers. Over her shoulder, she adds,

"Oh. And if I did ever want help, you can be damn sure that you're the last person I'd ask."

There it is again. My new friend. Or perhaps my constant companion, resurfaced. Just a pinprick this time, but it's still dangerously scarlet. The Red. "Jesus fucking Christ, you're a real piece of work, aren't you?"

"You have no idea."

She makes it to the base of the stairs, ass filling out those frayed jean shorts in a way that makes my gut throb. Not my gut. My cock. I rearrange it quickly in my jeans, hoping that the black material hides the stretching. She comes to serve us anymore drinks I'm going to end the night with a lethal case of blue balls. "Can I ask why I'm somehow not good enough to help you wail on some assholes, or did you not see my fight earlier?" Damn. Am I feeling wounded or what?

"That's why," she says blandly, as if she doesn't give a rat's ass about me or anyone. "Next week you're fighting my brother."

Shock hits me. *Padre*'s daughter. Mario's sister.

"Well fuck."

Mer

I remind myself again why I'm in this city that god forsook, why I walked into this barn house *de mierda* and begged the shrimpy brown-eyed bartender for this shitty job. Why I'm standing halfway up the staircase that leads to the guest team's landing with my back pressed against the wall, arms crossed, gut tense. It's all for him. It's always only ever been for him and for me and for our collective survival. My no good, dumb ass brother.

I roll my eyes when he takes a hit, blood spraying from his mouth as the one they call Knuckles lays into him. Knuckles is the same height as my brother but fuller in the chest. He's faster too and he cuts clean, with the precision and calm of a much older man though I don't imagine he's over thirty. Blood on his chest catches the gleam from the lights dangling like dice from the cross-beams that cut across the roof. His fists are huge, pale hands carving chunks out of Mario's stamina. Watching him dance around my brother on light feet does something to me. Something animalistic and dark. I'm hungry in ways I haven't been in months and though I know I should be rooting for my brother, I'm not.

Mario pulls a move I've seen him make several times before – a feint to the left before jabbing once with his left hand, twice more with his right. Knuckles dodges the first two strikes easily, but takes the second to the cheek at the same time that he brings his knee up into Mario's stomach. Mario bowls over, arms flailing out and leaving his torso entirely unprotected. Knuckles doesn't hesitate. He hits Mario in the chest with force. I bet he fractures my brother's sternum. *El idiota.*

Mario gasps and tries to recover, but I see him sag, even from all the way over here. I roll my eyes and am about to head down the stairs when the floorboards on the landing above groan. I glance up. My father walks to the railing and stares down at his only son with a fixed expression that I know well. *Carajo.* I wonder how much he put on Mario to win, though judging by the expression on his face, it's probably in the realm of five figures. He already owes Loredo so much, I wonder if this won't finally be the time that Loredo decides to close the register and cash him out. Indefinitely.

A bell dings and I push forward into the crowd as it loosens. Some boys head into the darkness outside the open barn doors, but most flock to the bar. Mario's on his knees in the dirt and Knuckles is clapping hands with the man I came for. The one with the dark skin they call Dixon looks directly at me as if called by something divine and though I can't hear him with all of the sweating, breathing bodies so close to me, I see his lips mouth, "Just a second."

Knuckles shifts around Dixon's body and spots me through the layered frat bros between us. The expression he wears morphs from surprise to a shocking shade of darkness. He glances between Dixon and I. Heat crawls from the back of my neck and inches down my spine until my pussy lips are flaming and it has nothing at all to do with the sweaty male bodies glancing my arms. I shift my weight between my hips and use Dixon's broad body to block the sight of his friend who looks pissed for absolutely no reason I can think of. Still, it's a good look for him.

"Tell your friend he fought a good fight tonight," I say, holding out my hand.

Dixon takes it and the rough weight of his palm is interrupted by something smooth and feathery as money passes between us. I am careful as I slide my hand over the front of my shirt, and hope that the well-rehearsed move is as discreet as it has been in the past. Mario normally doesn't notice, but nothing escapes the man who created us and I can imagine that his eagle eyes are pinned on me now that I'm speaking with the enemy.

Dixon nods and the smell of citrus and ginger wafts from his skin, even in this hot room that smells of horseshit, beer, and sweat. "Your brother stood his ground well...for a while."

"Not for long enough."

"All the better for you." Dixon lifts a brow and glances directly at my tits, though he doesn't seem to be the least bit impressed by them. I respect that he's got eyes only for his money. "The pot had him lasting thirty six minutes against my brother."

I grin carnivorously, but say nothing. We both know that when I put in my bet, I had Mario clocking out at minute twenty three and I was right on the dot. On the money. "I saw your boy fight last week and Mario's only gotten ballsier since prison – not better. Wasn't a hard calculation."

"Not for someone with a little street experience herself."
He gives me an appraising look and for some reason, I feel
pride when I inhale my next breath.

Trying not to let it show, I run my hand back through my
hair and shrug. "Enough to keep me alive in a room full of
thugs."

Dixon smiles at me though there is a guarded air to his
expression, as if he's wearing a mask that won't budge. It
gives me the chills and I'm grateful for Mario's distraction
when he calls my name. He's crouched on the ground and
some skinny ginger is standing over him dripping spittle onto
my brother's back and kicking dirt up onto Mario's face.

I brush past Dixon, walk right up to the kid and shatter
his nose with my fist. I can't help but revel in the sensation of
his bones meeting mine. The slight crunch that reverberates
loudly through the shouting and laughing around me says
that something's given way – something of his, not mine.

"Fuck off, *puto*. You so much as look at my brother again
and I'll meet you in the ring myself."

The kid's friends grab his arms and pull him out from
under me. I mirror the gesture with my own brother, but not
before kicking his boot, bending down and whispering to him
in Spanish, "Get up. *Padre's* watching."

That seems to strike some fear into him because he
manages to stagger up into a vertical position and loop his
right arm over my shoulders. The left he cradles to his chest
and, like his sternum, I gather it's also broken courtesy of the
big guy barring our path.

"Do you mind?" I say and I meet his gaze when really all
I want to do is look anywhere else.

His face is sculpted out of hardened bone, dark hair cropped short against his scalp. He isn't handsome in the way most girls might find men handsome in an ad for cologne or a fancy watch. He's way past rugged for that. Instead, he looks like some kind of Roman mercenary who's come to take me by force unless I fight him to the death. Jesus, how I'd love that fight. Reaching Elysium with those deadly, emerald eyes staring down at me.

"Are you deaf?" My panties are damp and my brother's weight is porcine. The scent of moonshine and weed wafts from Mario's skin and I know my brother was halfway faded when he stepped into the ring. He's a fool to think he could have come into this game anything less than prepared when Knuckles was his opponent.

Knuckles – Knox – grunts in a brutish way and rubs his hand across a stomach so ribbed it looks like he swallowed paint rollers. His palm streaks burgundy from breast to abdomen, and his hip bones are visible above the sagging waist of his pants. No belts in the arena. And I don't see boxers either. Fuck. When he steps out of my way I nearly burst forward, lugging my brother's weight to and up the stairs.

Spade meets me halfway and I wonder if he doesn't use the opportunity to his advantage when his hand 'accidentally' paws across my breasts. I wrench away, but don't dare raise my hand to the *pinche pedejo*. He's a nasty fucker with a proclivity for torture. I can't deny that he's a good fighter though. Far better than Mario. Probably even better than Knuckles, not that he'd ever be able to prove it. Spade's been banned from fighting in every pink slip pit in the South because his opponents only leave in body bags or in comas. I'd say it's because he's Russian and doesn't know any better, but I've seen the look he gets when he hovers over a dead body. The bastard gets off on it and my dad doesn't care because it was Loredo who hired Spade from the Russian mob in the first place.

Padre's still convinced the man is a body guard, but anyone with half a brain or eyes to see would know better. No cartel leader hires a mercenary from the Russian mob to take care of one of their low level employees. And no bodyguard takes orders as poorly as Spade does. In fact, I often catch Spade looking at dear ole' daddy in the same way a hound looks at its prey rather than its master.

"Plumeria," a cool voice calls.

Gritting my teeth, I take the steps one at a time until I've got both feet planted on the landing and am standing directly in front of him. "*Padre?*"

He's seated on a wicker chair watching Mario writhe in pain on the sofa, thin face drawn in disgust and something lethal. In an effort to distract him, I clear my throat. It works and he flicks his gaze to me. The same chocolate brown eyes I have, though everything else I am is my mother's. The eyes are the only things I will concede.

"Plumeria, who was that man you were speaking with?" He says, switching to Spanish. He speaks in a rough brogue that betrays his poor, rural roots. Just a farmer's son trying to make it in the big city. I wish it gave me more sympathy for the man, but the bastard deserves nothing from me.

"Dixon," I answer blandly, "He's Knox's manager. I was congratulating them on the fight."

"Not manager. Brother."

"Brother?" I say. *Padre* nods, opening his mouth to elaborate, but I shake my head. "And why did you bother asking if you already knew?"

"There is evidently a lot I do not know and that I have left to the secondhand information of others." He shoots an icy glare at Mario, curses, and lurches forward to smack my brother in the ear. He hits him so hard, he bleeds. "You said you could beat him. That there was no chance of a loss."

Mario cries out and a flutter of nerves flurries through me. I don't like the kid, but it doesn't change the fact that he's my brother, the last sibling I've got left and the only one to ever stand in my corner against the cartel.

"It's your own fault," I shout, switching back to English automatically.

Padre twists to look at me and passes a hand over his oily hair, bares his teeth. "What did you say to me? Your own father…"

"Don't give me that. If you believed I was your kid too, you'd have asked me what I thought the odds would be. I saw Knox fight last week and I knew he was good…"

"Is that why you bet against your own brother?"

My jaw goes slack and so do most of my muscles. My hand twitches, reaching for the wall to my right. It's dry as bone beneath my fingers and just as brittle. "How…" I cough into my fist and try to recover – failingly. "I didn't…"

Padre glances over my shoulder as Spade saunters around my body. He takes the seat to the right of my father and pulls a crumpled stack of folded bills from his inside jacket pocket. I cup my right tit, shocked to no longer feel the cash's hard edge between my nipple and my bra and while my brother curses me to hell's lowest chamber, a jolt of rage sweeps me. I'm pissed. I sidestep my dad and advance on Spade who does nothing but splay his cheek for me to hit, so I do. Then I grab for his hand. The rest happens too quickly.

Like a boomerang, my hand hits him and he retaliates by slapping me in the face hard enough to whip my head around. As I stumble towards the railing, Spade shoves me from behind. The cool wood cuts into my belly and the whole railing shakes like the legs on a startled colt while, at the same time, knocking the breath clean out of me. Spade comes up against my spine.

He overpowers me, spinning me into the shadows of the back wall and wrenching my shorts down over my ass. He's fumbling with his belt and for a second, I don't know if he's just reminding me how much bigger he is than I am and that he holds power over me in every way imaginable or if he really does mean to rape me right here, right now.

Behind me, my father is shouting, Mario is coughing and much closer than that, Spade drags my hair over my shoulder and shoves his tongue deep into my ear.

"You are mine," he breathes and the scent of his breath — rot and moonshine and the dip he chews — makes my gag reflex kick. He presses himself closer and closer to me. I can't breathe with my injured cheek wedged against the dusty planks and his whole body surrounding mine. Like an eclipse, the whole world is gone in seconds and the hot flesh of his hand on my ass is all I can feel.

Betraying my fear, I yelp, like the little girl that I am. I close my eyes and clench my fists and though I don't stop struggling, I do mentally prepare to take a very short trip to a very faraway place. I can feel my father close by, pushing or pulling on Spade's shirt, though I doubt it makes much of a difference and I'm reminded again that Spade is the one who has the upper hand.

A voice cuts through the chaos like a cleaver. "You've got to the count of three, big man."

The voice is familiar and I struggle to place it in the haze of my confusion. Then I hear the cock of a hammer and when I blink my eyes open, I glance past my father's pathetic, quivering form towards the men on the stairs. All five of them. It isn't Dixon that stands in the front of the pack however, though I thought he was the one in charge, but Knox, and the strangest settling of relief stops the muscles trembling in my arms and legs.

"Thought there was a no carry policy in here," Spade crows, without releasing me. In fact, his hand snakes down to spread my ass cheeks and when Knox's gaze flashes to mine, I look away. I'm embarrassed and I feel like crying, cutting something, someone, me. I fucking hate this. I hate being a girl. I hate crying. I hate Spade. I hate my father, my brother, this man stepping up for me.

"We own the place. We decide who carries." He keeps his pitch low, but the sinister chords carry. "You want to die tonight? We're out in the middle of nowhere. Plenty of places to bury a body."

Spade sneers and I throw my elbow back into his stomach, but only because he lets me. He catches it and the pressure of his chest eases up on my spine. He bends in close and in heavily accented English whispers, "You will be mine very soon, *moya lubov.*"

He releases me and I trip over the leg of the table as I do everything in my power to cover the exposed crotch of my panties and hoist my jean shorts back up over my bare ass. My hands shake badly and Knox mutters a terse order to the others to step aside and let me through.

They obey and I'm running and my vision is blurred and I want so badly just to fix my clothes, flip back my hair and keep on serving drinks, but there's a knot of hysteria in my lungs that's swimming up the length of my throat and in my head it sounds like screaming. A woman screaming. I know her voice, I know her name, I know her face. Is it me? I'm not sure.

Wolf whistles chase me out into the night air and I run into its embrace, and don't stop running until I reach the trees. I collapse against the first one I find. It's a sapling, and shivers under my weight as I brace my shoulder against the slim, coarse trunk and feel for the buttons and the zipper along the front of my shorts. I manage to get both undone, but it seems to take hours.

Like some puzzle I knew how to solve once, but no longer remember, I can't get my clothes to do what I want. My hands are not my own. They're silver. Stained by moonlight. I close my eyes as goosebumps break out across my arms though I'm far from cold.

The wind whispers my name and I jump. "Holy shit. How...how long have you been standing there?" My voice wavers as I drink in the sight of Knox. Standing just a dozen paces away, he's wearing a black tee shirt, black jeans, and a grimace. The moonlight falls across his skin and glints off of the barrel of his gun.

I wonder if my expression betrays fear, because the moment I turn towards him, his crude, near barbaric severity softens. I gasp at the unraveling and he edges back, lifting both hands to shoulder level. "I'm not going to hurt you," he says. Funny, because I hadn't even considered that.

I must look vulnerable enough though for him to say it and needing to correct the impression, I step back into the shadows of the trees so that he cannot see me. From that safety, I stammer, "I fucking know that. I didn't need you to follow me and I didn't need you to stand up for me in there." Jesus, it's a lie. Because I need everything, and nothing. Just the words he said before and his hand against my cheek. A promise I can believe in. A taste of something gentle. A different life.

His eyebrows come together and the hollows beneath his prominent brow make him look demonic. His lips draw back from his clenched teeth and all at once he stows his gun in the back of his jeans, I presume, to keep from shooting me with it. "What the hell is wrong with you?"

"What's wrong with me? What's wrong with you and your constant need to be a man and be in charge and defend the poor and defenseless?" I rebuff lamely. "I don't need you! Just get away from me."

"You know what – I should have just left you. I should have seen you across the bar pinned to that wall being assaulted and just let him fucking..." He doesn't finish his sentence, but his face twists like he's sucking on something sour to the point that he's no longer recognizable. He's vicious and violent and reminds me for a brief and harrowing second of Spade and I remember the bastard's hands on my ass, hear his voice in my ear, taste his salty sweet skin.

These memories, though from moments ago, should be gone by now, locked away, but instead I'm drowning in them and my heart is racing too fast and I'm breathing so damn hard and shivering though it's as warm as an Arabian winter. The sticky heat wraps around me and I imagine that it's the only thing holding me up. I stagger and moonlight cuts across my hand as I reach for the tree, but it's disappeared.

I gasp and everything disappears but two men in the moonlight. No. That's one man twice. His back is turned and he's walking away from me and it's as if he's taken all of the light with him because it's suddenly so dark and I'm afraid and a child and in my ears I hear pounding, like a train, though I know it's a fist on the door coming to take me away.

"Please don't let them take me away," I say, though he can't hear me. "Knox," I gasp and the air comes shorter and harder. I clutch my chest and my right knee wobbles dangerously. "Knox."

He twists and seeing me, hesitates. Suddenly, he's running and I'm hit by a wall even though he's far away. "Mer," he shouts, but I'm lost, falling for hours and days until the grass punches into my spine. It's hard and scratchy against my legs and back and I want to stand, but I can't seem to catch hold of anything to pull me to my feet. There's nothing for a moment, but the sound of me dying, and then in the next there's him.

He rises over the horizon of the grass before dropping to his knees. He grabs me roughly as he takes a seat and drags me onto his lap. He's leaning against something and I'm surprised when his tee shirt comes down over my head. He gathers up my wrists and holds them to my chest and uses his whole body to warm me.

"Shh." His voice is a command and I am able to find solace in that. "Follow my breath." I can feel the rise and fall of his chest but it means nothing to me. "Mer," he barks. He takes my chin between his fingers and forces me to look at him. Envious irises ringed by an even darker green. "Breathe."

"D...d...dying," I rasp and my throat closes entirely or maybe it's just his hand around my neck, cradling my head.

"Plumeria." His voice is a shout that pummels like a jackhammer through me. He calls me by my full name. Not many people call me that and no one has ever spoken those four syllables with such importance. I feel commanded by it. Compelled. Lifted.

I black out but resurface what feels like years later, though I know it was only the span of a much-needed breath. His hand is on my forehead, lifting up my bangs, and my crown rests on the broad pillow his massive shoulder creates. I can't move at all, but I can hear the air coming in and out of my lungs and his deep bass whispering, "Like that. Exactly like that. In and out, even, calm. Nothing's going to hurt you, not while I'm here."

"But...you'll leave." I wish I can take back the words the moment I say them but I can't.

His arms tighten around me and I am rendered immobile by his size and the sheer density of him. But I don't feel threatened. I feel safe. "I'm not going anywhere, Plumeria, and nothing is going to hurt you."

He's true to his word and as a sequence of familiar constellations pass by slowly overhead, he doesn't move except to pull gently on my hair. My breathing is back to normal and I no longer shake, but I still don't get up even though I should. My brain is mud, though I know that's only part of the reason.

The larger part is that seated with him in his heat and his protection is the happiest and safest I can ever remember being and I'm afraid if I so much as flinch and sever the sensation I'll burst into tears. This is the last I can ever see of this man. No one was ever supposed to see this part of me. To erase evidence of this night from my life's history book, he too must go into the box of memories. The box of pain.

The haunting notes of a wind chime sound in the distance and I begin to close my eyes as a sudden fierce sleep grips me. Beneath his breath, Knox curses and a second later those bells become voices.

"Knox!" I don't recognize the speaker, but Knox must because he shifts out from underneath me and sets me gently on the grass.

He glances down at me and must read the obvious intent in my expression because he issues another quiet order. "Don't move." He turns to face the cursing voices without budging from my side. "I'm alright."

"Christ, brother, we were worried that *Padre* and that walking asshole had…"

"Don't come over here," Knox shouts and another heaping of fear freezes my bones at the thought of being discovered here by four other men when I'm already at my most vulnerable.

"Why the hell not?"

"Because I'm fucking Plumeria," he says, holding out his arms as if it were the most obvious explanation. "Now get the fuck back." The grunts and whistles of approval make me smile on the inside, though the grin doesn't quite touch my lips. I had wanted to fuck Knox, hadn't I? Had being the operative word. Not anymore. Sleeping with Knox now would ruin me.

"You know the rules, brother," Dixon chides.

"Yeah, yeah, yeah. No girls at the house. That's why we got a field."

"Good." The jangling of keys.

Knox stretches above his head and snatches something silver from the air. Starlight. "Thanks."

The distant sound of voices fade and when Knox looks down at me, the pressure of his gaze is brutal enough to wound. I wince and try to stand, hoping to move away from him but he's there. He's everywhere. His hands slide around my lower back, pulling me into his heat and after the despicable weakness I just displayed, I don't feel capable of pushing him away.

Fuck it, I think to myself as his fingers cup my ass, he can just have me. I slump against his chest, but instead of lowering me back to the ground and taking me for himself in the way all men seek to take women, he hoists up on the waist of my shorts once, and then again, both times hard enough that my feet leave the ground and I have to hold onto him.

There's a pressure in my chest I'm unable to displace where the numbness is supposed to be and when he fastens the button at my hips and pulls my zipper up to meet it, I cough into my fist. It's all I can do not to cry. And then I wait for it – for him to ask me a barrage of questions that peel the skin back even further though I'm already only flesh and feelings.

He clears his throat and steps away from me. I try to think of something to say but my throat is gooey with saliva that I can't swallow. Finally, he breaks the silence. "I'm not doing anything right now and I'm thinking you are in pretty serious need of sugar…"

"I'm not in shock," I say, but I barely complete the sentence. I flick my gaze up to his face and see that he isn't angry – for once – but is smiling.

He shakes his head. "Of course you aren't. What I meant to say was, I'm feeling hungry and Patty's Place is open late. Care to join me?"

Shock makes me grin, though the expression is as wobbly as my knees are. "You go to Patty's?"

"What? A guy like me isn't allowed to like pie?"

"No. I mean yes." I look down at my sneakers and the patch of disrupted grass peeking up around their dirty white soles. The air smells like earth and pollen, but like sweat, eucalyptus and blood even more. "I mean, you can like whatever you want." The harsh edge I usually hear in my own tone eludes me, and I sound like a kid.

"Good. I'd like for you to come with me." He holds out his hand. I've never held anyone's hand before. I mean, not unless I was trying to hurt them, or stop them from hurting me.

"I'm still on tonight."

"Fight's over and the place is mine. I'll text Ollie from the car and let him know why you can't make it."

"Why can't I make it?" I say skeptically.

He shrugs, still holding his hand flat out between us, like an offering. "Sex, obviously."

I smirk, "Thanks." Funny thing is that I mean it. I place my palm against his and he laces his fingers through mine. I flush at the contact, finding it surprisingly intimate. His hand is warm and dry and covered in calluses from the fights. I wonder if that's how he finds my hand too.

We go the long way around the barn to avoid the smokers hanging out in the shed, opting instead to trek through brambles and immense stretches of ivy to the parking lot. About half of the cars have cleared out so I feel less bad about leaving Ollie all alone. He did me a favor, hiring me on the spot like he did. I'd thought the place was his because when he'd hired me, he hadn't had to call the owner.

My gaze wanders over the back of Knox's head down his thick neck, over his shoulders. The muscles flex beneath them and he still sports dark streaks across his back, from his left shoulder blade to his right hip. It's blood, though the fact that it's my brother's doesn't bother me. The sight of his skin covered in bruises and a few faint abrasions around his right ribs feels like home to me. Home? What the fuck am I saying? I don't even understand the meaning...

"*Pinche idiota*," I shout as his right hand reaches to push aside a curtain of Spanish moss. A flare of aggression lights up his face, but it flickers quickly and fades when I pull his fingers into mine. Now I'm just holding both his hands like the idiot I just accused him of being. "Chiggers. In the moss. Don't look at me like that. *Lo siento.*"

His eyes are huge and his lips are parted. He licks them after a moment and grins. "No reason to apologize."

He ducks under the misty grey curtain, following the path that I show him. When we hit gravel, he leads me to a 1980 Chevy C-10, charcoal metallic. Of course he'd drive a muscle car. I'm smiling at the selection until I realize that his hand is on the passenger door's shiny silver handle. It glints as it catches the moonlight. Guys don't open doors for girls like me and yet here he is, body framing the darkness of the doorway.

He's not looking at me, but at the ground, as if there are diamonds nestled there in the gravel. His brow is tense, lips severe and when he holds his hand towards me, I understand the implicit order. He reels me in until I'm directly in front of him and inhales once, then again.

"I'm going to ask you one question about what happened back there, and no other. Do you understand?"

I want to say no, but he isn't asking and I'm not up for a fight. So instead I nod, hold my breath and pray.

"Did I get there too late?"

"Too late?"

His thumb sweeps the back of my hand, applying a firm pressure that terrifies me, because it betrays how his fingers shake. With rage. He must notice me noticing because he releases me and shoves his hands into his front pockets. "Did he rape you?"

Knox might as well have thrown a bucket of ice water over me. I freeze, moving only my head as I twist it to the side, like when Spade hit me. I'm only just now beginning to feel the makings of a bruise, and evidently he sees it. The moon is strong and I feel it on my skin as a whisper of sunlight. Then his fingers.

They start beneath my eye, following the curve of my cheek back to my ear. He doesn't ask me if it hurts, if I've taken a hit before. Both are obvious. I feel him come close to me. So close I wonder if he's going to kiss me. I'm struck over the head with a brick when he does. His lips are full and they're hot as hell and sinfully smooth as they sweep my hairline. I jerk back, but he's already pulled away and is standing on the other side of the car door, watching me from over its rim.

"Get in."

I pass my hand over the leather bench but hesitate before taking a seat. "I wasn't," I say, letting the heavy curtain of my hair fall between us. "He didn't."

His chest expands...deflates...expands...deflates... His teeth bite down and he grunts something between them.

"What?" I ask.

"Good," he says, and true to his word, it's the last thing he says on the subject.

He only manages to shrug out of the anger he wears like a coat when we're on the road, back in the city. Lights start growing more frequently out of the ground as the first of the storefronts pass. It's late. Most people are inside with their loved ones. City's too small for night owls. But there are some of us. The delinquents and the degenerates, struggling for survival in alleyways, dealing drugs beneath the shady awnings of gas stations, vomiting on street corners as they try to drag themselves home or…eating pie.

He sits across the metallic tabletop with his elbows spread wide, wearing a jersey from his gym bag. Two Irish coffees, two empty plates, four empty glasses, a slice of pecan and a slice of pumpkin rest between us. I didn't realize how hungry I was – how thirsty either. I've been keeping pace with him the whole way and the slices are big, and the whiskeys aren't singles. He pauses halfway through his last slice and leans back against the cracked, plastic leather. It's fire engine red and squeaks beneath his weight as he drapes his arms across the top of the bench seat.

"What?" I say, draining half of my last Irish coffee. I'm lightheaded already. Always been a lightweight. Probably not a good idea with Knox watching me like that. "What?" I say again.

"What." He shrugs, tone so flat and nonchalant it makes me wonder what I'd been asking about in the first place.

I shake my head. "Never mind."

"So your brother fought…" He pauses and seems to consider.

It's that consideration that makes me laugh. "You don't have to lie to me. I've got eyes, and I'm not like the other girls you probably bring to this place so I know what I'm looking at. My brother's a piece of shit. He's got a good arm though. I just wish he would practice – and I don't mean prison brawls. He thought he'd learned something in the can. If anything he's only gotten worse."

I blow air out of the side of my mouth and trail the older waitress behind the counter with my gaze. She's got a yellow apron on. It's stained but she's smiling at the mean looking trucker on one of the red swivel stools and he's smiling back. Next thing, I realize I'm smiling too. So is Knox. And his mouth is distracting.

"I mean, look at you," I blurt, for want of something to say, "If my brother had half your discipline tonight's fight would have gone a lot differently. You've clearly had practice – and not just street fighting. Boxing – probably some martial arts too. My guess is that you've been at this since you were a kid. Probably knocked out a boy's teeth for the first time when you were nine and couldn't believe how good it felt." I point my fork at him and he leans forward so quickly I sit back.

"You're good." He swipes his left arm across the tabletop and clears a path through the dishes so that nothing sits between us but my plate. He's huge, taking up more than his fair share of the space and is watching that plate like a killer, like it's the only thing keeping him from something he wants. I refuse to acknowledge my own body's mirrored response.

"Some dickwad stole Charlie's bike at the foster home, so I went to get it back. He was thirteen and a hell of a lot bigger, but something in me snapped. I don't even remember what happened during the fight – just the before and after. Taking that first hit to the cheek and then waking up with blood on my hands. Kid had two missing teeth."

His eyes grow distant and a small smile plays at the edge of his mouth. The expression is one I understand in its entirety: the stinging guilt-free surge of bloodlust, and the surrender to it. It's a part of him as much as it is a part of me and suddenly I'm beginning to think that Knox and I have more in common than I'd thought.

We're not the only two in the diner, and the loud table of drunks seated two booths behind him should have been distracting, but looking at him, I'm able to block it all out. "He was actually in a boxing class for troubled youth," he continues, "and when his coach saw what happened to him, he came to find me. Enlisted me into his practice. I've been boxing ever since, some MMA on the side. I even tried jujitsu, karate, krav maga. Anything I can, that lets me hit something."

I smile at that. Can't remember ever smiling so much. Can't remember the last time I smiled… "Me too."

He leans even further forward then and drops his tone so that I have to lean forward to hear him. "You know what? I bet you're a better fighter than your brother."

"Of course I'm a better fighter than my brother. I practice. He's a slob."

Knox laughs and it's a contagious thing. I feel unsettled by it, but not displeased. "So," he says, drawing out the word in a way that claims my attention. He's looking down at the table, drawing slow patterns on the outside of his glass with his thumb. Dragging the edge of his finger along the rim of his glass, he wipes cream away, then licks it free with his tongue.

"So." I clear my throat and as I sit up straighter so does he.

Then the strangest thing happens: a schoolboy pink hue surfaces in his cheeks. "I saw you talking to Dixon earlier." He doesn't say more than that and I'm left waiting.

"Yeah. And?"

"Did he ask you out or something?"

Dios fucking *mio.* My jaw drops and Knox looks away from me quickly, massages his neck, burns an even more brilliant pink. "No," I snort, just a touch o' class. "Definitely not."

"I figured as much. Not really his style." His voice is calm, but there's a funny twitch in his cheek.

"What's not? Dating?"

"He doesn't trust women. He's more of a fuck 'em and leave 'em type."

"Well then I guess we've got something in common."

Knox's frown doesn't suit his face and I wonder what I've said this time. "So what were you talking about?" He's no longer asking and I know that I'm treading a very fine line though what I don't know is why or how we got to this point.

I shake my head, chewing thoughtfully on another bite of pumpkin pie. My favorite kind, even if the pudding part is too sweet and the crust is too dry. "I had to collect my winnings."

"Winnings?"

"Don't look so surprised."

He sucks in a breath through his teeth and looks away, giving me a nice bright glimpse of a welt I hadn't noticed near his left temple. Other than that, he'd sustained less damage in the ring than I had outside of it. I wonder if he thinks I'm weak. A cold stone sinks in my stomach. "You bet I'd win?"

"Like I said before, he might be my brother, but I'm not an idiot. It was a pretty easy bet."

"Damn," he says. When he meets my gaze, his eyes are bright as hell and it has nothing to do with the fluorescents overhead and their reflection in his gaze, which is clear enough to see myself in. I look beat, and he's still sitting there staring at me like I'm a regular girl, the kind you take on a date and hold doors for and defend against assholes. But I don't need his help or protection from him or anyone. "How much did you win?"

I shrug. "Nothing, turns out." When his eyebrow lifts and half of his smile dips, I answer the question he hasn't asked out loud. "Spade took it. Pulled it out of my bra before you showed up."

I take another sip of my coffee, wishing the whiskey were stronger so I wouldn't be so hurt by the sudden fierce expression on Knox's face. He thinks I'm weak. Must be. And if I truly weren't I'd have been able to defend myself better. Instead I needed him, and in more ways than one. I fucking fainted... *carajo*...

Knox looks away. "Fucker has an issue with women, huh?"

"Maybe."

"Or is it just you?"

"It's especially me – how about that?"

"Sick fuck," Knox mutters. "Call me if he ever gives you grief."

"I can handle myself."

His gaze stabs into mine like toothpicks to the retinas and the expression contaminates my coffee. It's sour next time I bring it to my lips. "Call me."

I lean back away from him, but the bench has me caged. "Fine," I curse, "I don't want to talk about that *culero* anymore."

A few moments of silence pass between us and I think about just fucking off and finding my own way home until all at once, he clears his throat. "How old were you when you started fighting?" His genuine interest makes the rock in my stomach sink further. If he keeps heading down this road, soon I'll be shitting blood.

"I don't remember," I say quietly.

"Well where were you? You're not from here, or I'd have seen you before two weeks ago." His fingers drum over the pocked metal between us.

"Christ, I don't know."

"You don't know?"

"Why does it even matter?" I drop my fork and it clatters against another empty plate. "I go where *Padre* drags Mario. I hardly like the bastard, but I've got to take care of him."

"Why?"

"*Hijo de tu puta madre.*" I slide towards the booth's exit, but he props his boot up in my seat.

"That's not very nice," he says, all calm. It maddens me and I punch my fingers back through my hair, wishing I could reach across the table and strangle him. "You don't tend to get very close to people, do you?"

I wince again, as if struck, and I swear I hear him hiss very lightly under his breath when I show him my injured cheek. "No. No point in investing in that kind of shit. My dad will be dead soon, me and Mario along with him."

"Why do you think that?"

"Because when you're poor in the cartel you die young. And my dad's made sure we've stayed broke ever since I was born. Since before I was born."

"I thought your dad was some big shot."

I laugh, though there's no pleasure in it. None at all. "What gave you that ridiculous idea?"

Knox shrugs, scratches his chin, drinks more coffee. "Rumors of a reputation travel though I suppose my brothers and I don't deal with too many cartel men so we haven't given it much attention. But what about that ugly mother fucker? He's got a Russian brand. Mafia?"

I nod my assent, though if anyone were in earshot, I could be killed for doing less. It's obvious who he is or rather, what, but no one speaks of it. That's how Loredo likes everything: obviously discreet and perfectly evil.

"If he can afford a guy like that then he must be doing okay."

"I don't want to talk about Spade or my dad or anyone." There's heat on my tongue that doesn't go unnoticed.

Knox sits up straighter and nods once. "Fine. Then we'll start with the easy stuff." He tries to relax again against his seat, but the atmosphere hangs like a starched blanket around us. "What's your favorite color?"

I try to help him relieve the tension, but my thoughts are scrambled. My favorite color. My favorite color? I think of the colors that bring me pleasure: red, blood stains on a tee shirt; black, the color of nothing when I close my eyes; purple, but only when it's got green or yellow in it because then it reminds me of a healing bruise; pink, the color of the inside of a scar. "I don't know," I huff, keeping my eyes closed.

He doesn't say anything for a minute, and I wonder when he eventually gets up and leaves if he'll even bother giving me a ride home. I could probably walk from here, but it'll be cold. "My favorite color's amber."

I lift my gaze, but my eyelids weigh tons. Slowly, I blink. "What?"

"Jurassic Park is the first movie I can remember seeing – at least all the way through. I liked the way the bug looked trapped in that orange rock. My foster mom, Marguerite, told me it was amber, explained how tree sap fossilized over thousands of years and made it look like that. She said it was rare. I did a ton of research on it after that and started saving up all my cash so I could buy a piece. Had almost enough for a tiny bead too, but Marguerite beat me to it. She didn't have much but that Christmas, I got a gift – just one bead of amber on a string." He shakes his head and stares down at his glass, and in the way he speaks so tenderly, I understand he's offering something to me.

"Not six months later, a sixteen year old kid took it from me. I tried to fight him, but he was too big. Beat the shit out of me, and put me in the hospital. And of all the years I've been in the game, that's the only fight I really remember."

I feel trapped, and though it isn't the first time I've been caged, it's the first time the bars have been made out of kindness. He's watching me work my lips, struggling to find something adequate to say in response. I don't, but what I do blurt out is, "More."

"Excuse me, darling?" he smirks.

"Will you tell me more?"

He grins. And he does. He talks until morning's first rays peek in through the crooked blinds and I listen to stories about his brothers, his businesses, his childhood, his dead mom, clinging to his words as his voice rubs me raw. I'm so engrossed, I don't notice exhaustion hit until he laughs at how many times I yawn.

He stands and, laying his hand on the back of my neck, I am warm as he leads me out into the cold. The sky is lavender, each cloud colored in with the most spectacular pink. But around their edges, there's a darkening where the lavender and the pink meet. Amber. Wrapping his tee shirt tight around my legs, which clench together on top of the freezing leather, I lean into him. He doesn't push me away, but lifts his arm around my shoulders and turns on the heaters. They blast against my face, tasting of dust from disuse. Amber, eucalyptus, sweat and blood too. Home. I imagine that this is what home is like.

I'm an idiot. That's all I can think as I brace my hands on either side of the sink and lean onto my arms. My head hangs low so I don't have to look in the mirror, but when I open my eyes I see the horror on my chest in living color. This black button up is fucking ridiculous, but not as ridiculous as the aftershave I'm wearing, or the Rolex.

The guys have been giving me grief all week. Calling me all kinds of ludicrous things — recalcitrant, distrait, aloof — and in all the vocabulary that would have made Marguerite a proud English teacher and an even prouder mother. Shit, throughout the past week I'd forgotten to do half the things Dixon told me to. I don't know why I'm thinking about her on such a perpetual goddamn loop.

Mer. Plumeria.

She features in the darkness at night, hair splayed across my pillow, taking up more than her fair share of my bed. When I wake up, punching through the darkness to the light, my dick is hard as a Louisville Slugger and worse than that, I'm strangely lonely. Never felt so lonely all my goddamn life.

I'd half considered challenging Dixon on the no-women-allowed-in-the-pad-period policy, but in trying to formulate counterarguments to what he'd surely say I come up with nothing. I know nothing about the girl though she knows everything about me. And the way she'd listened to every single thing I'd said like she'd never been more fascinated…a girl couldn't make that up, could she?

Fuck, what couldn't a girl lie about? I groan towards the ceiling. Such a moron. If Dixon only knew the shit I'd told her, he'd skin me alive. Shit nobody was supposed to know outside of the family – about our clubs, properties, and business – and she's in the cartel no less. But with her sleepy gaze watching me so gratefully as I spoke, it had been impossible to stop. And now I'm standing here in a tricked out outfit planning on going to a backwoods barn to hit on the bartender. Fuck me. I straighten up and undo the top button, then let my hand drop. Fuck it.

Without giving myself the chance to back out, I flip the lights, grab my jacket and head to the living room. My plan is to pass through it and into the garage quickly enough that the guys won't see or stop me. There's a fight on. Should be easy enough. But the moment I step out of the hallway, Charlie says, "Thought you left already." Turning, he glances at me from over the top of the couch. "Holy shit. No wonder you took so long."

His dark eyes pass over my outfit once, then he barks out a laugh that makes my pulse throb and my vision flash red. "You look like a beauty queen. I'd have thought you'd want to get there early tonight." My other brothers turn to look, and all but Aiden snigger under their breaths. Dixon switches the TV off and they stand together, reaching for jackets and keys.

I frown, confused as fuck. "What the hell are y'all doing?"

"Waiting for your slow ass," Dixon crows, flipping the collar of his black leather jacket and smoothing it down. He's wearing a tee shirt beneath, and so are the others. I don't know if I've ever even seen a guy in a button up before at the barn and another wash of nausea guts me.

"Why are y'all going tonight? We're not fighting."

It's Charlie who says, "Just because we're not in love with the girl like you are, doesn't mean we don't want to see history being made." He starts for the door, but Dixon grabs his arm at the elbow.

"He doesn't know." Dixon's eyes widen and a slow, carnivorous grin spreads across his face.

"Uh oh," Clifton murmurs.

Charlie slaps his leg and howls, like a caricature I'm about to erase. I can feel the heat building up in my blood and I demand that someone tell me what is going on, but Charlie turns to Dixon and begs, "Please let me tell him. Call it a Christmas present."

"Jesus, Charlie..."

"Tell me what?"

"It's Mer..."

So much as her name in Charlie's mouth makes my whole body shudder. I take a threatening step forward and Dixon holds up a hand. He isn't smiling anymore. "You're getting too volatile, brother, over a girl you barely even know."

"If that Russian bastard touched her I swear to god..."

"Knox, nothing happened," Clifton intervenes, "Ollie didn't call you about the fight is all."

"I'm starting to see why," Charlie mumbles.

"Out with it, Charlie," I shout, "What about the fight?"

"It's Mer!"

"What's Mer?" I run my hand back over my head roughly, feeling hot all over and too constrained by this goddamn button up and the pressure of all of my brothers staring at me like I'm some sort of zoo animal.

"The fighter!" Charlie throws out his arms, color rising in his cheeks. He's a Native, with inky black hair, taunting lips and a muscular, but wiry build. He's got a short temper, and I'm lucky he isn't as good a fighter as I am because the look he flashes me is pure fire. "Mer is fighting tonight."

My right knee turns to cardboard and my lungs threaten collapse. "Who?"

"Mer! Jesus Christ. What's wrong with this man?" He throws out his arm and takes a turn of the room. "You really gonna make me repeat it again?"

"Fuck. Who is she fighting?"

Charlie smiles sheepishly and chuckles once. "Oh. Yeah, about that…"

"Ollie said it was hard to find someone who could stack up relatively evenly in terms of weight and even harder to find a guy willing to do it," Dixon cuts in, voice, like his gaze: cold. "He had to go with Tyler."

"Tyler is a fucking rapist."

"He was never convicted," Clifton finishes with a small, apologetic shrug. He doesn't meet my gaze, but I see his expression without understanding it. He seems to be smiling softly.

"Dixon, you selfish fuck." The temperature in the room plummets and I know I've crossed a line, but I don't step back from it. Not when I'm as juiced as I am. The only person in the house allowed to authorize something like this without consent from any of the rest of us is Dixon. He did this.

Dixon straightens and takes a step towards me – he doesn't fight in the ring often, but when he does, he fights mean. Not that it would have mattered much in this moment. I'm juiced enough to really fucking hurt something. "What did you say to me?"

Aiden stands slowly from the couch and I know that if Aiden comes at me, someone's going to end up in the hospital – likely me – and I can't afford to miss Mer's fight. The bit of my brain that's still functioning tells me to leave and I obey. I find my keys, my car, and the highway and am lost in the darkness until sounds begin to radiate along the horizon. Lights come next. I swing into the parking lot so fast gravel scatters beneath the wheels. The first bite of autumn eats into me because I forgot a coat, but as soon as I get to the door I remember why I don't need it.

The barn is as full as it's ever been – fuller even. I have to nail one guy's spleen and possibly break another kid's knee in order to carve a path through the bodies. They're densely packed together and if so much as one single person lights up in here, more than two hundred living souls are headed straight for the grave, mine and Mer's among them.

The bell emits a quiet ding and the throngs roar. I curse and force my way forward until the perimeter of the ring comes into view. From where I am, I can just make out two distinct shapes shifting in and out of focus in the center of the pit. My chest pulls in air in long draughts, like I'm drowning and I'm reminded of the way she'd called for me out in the field. She'd been drowning then too, and I understand in one small shattering moment that there's a different woman hiding inside Mer's brittle outer shell. Plumeria. Mer might be able to take care of herself, but it's Plumeria that I don't want to see hurt.

I'm feeling my most monstrous self at the thought of somebody hitting her. I should turn back now, head to the bar and down a bottle, but I can't. I'm nailed to the scene, now on the front lines. There is nothing that separates me from the warriors in the pit and nothing to keep me from crossing that space and ripping out Tyler's throat. Nothing but honor. Hers, not mine. To intervene now would be to shame her. So with space at my front and betting, cheering bodies at my back, I remain fixed with my feet planted and my arms crossed over my goddamn button up.

I'm standing behind her so she doesn't see me. I want her to, just so she knows she's safe. So she knows she can bow out any time; at any moment ask me to take her spot in the ring. And fuck, I want to see her face too. I want to know if she's hurting, what she's thinking, why she's doing this, who coerced her. I glance around, but her big brother is nowhere to be found in the crowd, or upstairs in the visitor's section.

While the visitor's section is empty, Tyler's frat boy fuck buddies crowd the home team's landing, undoubtedly pissed out of their minds and feeling themselves because they never get to sit VIP. Why the fuck is she a visitor? She works at the bar and she's here with me, which is just another reason why Ollie should have called. She's mine. Maybe not mine. But she's already starting to feel way too much like she belongs on the home team's seats, not to mention in my bed. Her hair on my pillow. Her sweat on my sheets.

Tyler swings and she switches quickly under his arm. Cheers and new bets rip from mouth-to-mouth, throats going hoarse with how violently they scream when her fists connect twice with Tyler's stomach. Being that he towers over her by no less than a foot, she hits him higher than she should and it leaves her left side open, which Tyler's quick to take.

He brings his fist into the curve of her waist and I expect her to crumble, but the only reaction he wins from her is the spasm that ripples across the muscles in her back. Her skin is vibrant and glistening, dark caramel interrupted only by that black bra and a pair of men's basketball shorts cinched around her hips. They'd probably fit me like spandex, but they drape to her knees, reminding me of how small she is and how stupid this goddamn fight is and how I'm going to throttle Dixon, skin Tyler, and butcher Ollie.

She's got dimples in her lower back and I see her flat, carved stomach when she pivots, but she doesn't come all the way around. Instead, she grabs Tyler's wrist when his right fist hurtles towards her. His left pounds into her upper thigh and when I catch her profile, she's got her teeth clenched. Yanking down hard on his arm, she drags him to her level. Her right arm folds and she jerks up once and then again, cracking her elbow against his face. Blood explodes from his nose and mouth and when she nails him a third time, he canters back, looking stunned and sedated.

Idiot kids around me are cheering, surprised at her sudden win but I know better. Tyler's biggest strength in the ring is that nobody takes a hit better. She'll have to beat him to a bloody pulp and I hope to Mary, Jesus, and whatever gods she prays to that she doesn't take any hits in the process.

She backs up, giving Tyler undeserved space to collect himself. When she stops moving, she's close enough to touch. I could reach out and stroke the long length of braid that runs down the back of her head like a zipper. Better yet, I could grab its thickness, wrench her into my arms, and finish the fight she started.

"When Ollie asked me if I'd fight you, I didn't think it would be this much fun." He spits out a tooth and rubs the back of his hand across his mouth, trailing blood to his right cheek. "When I finally get you pinned down, you little *panocha*, I'm going to fuck that *panocha* bloody."

I close my eyes. I've got all the composure of a bright white scream.

"You might pin me down," she says with easy confidence, "but I've heard you're a limp dick mother fucker so I'm not too worried about that last part, *puto*."

The crowd screams. Tyler blanches. "Fuck you, bitch…"

She cuts him off. "According to the other *panocha* I talked to, probably not."

Roaring, Tyler throws himself at her and lifts her whole body from the ground. He throws her down and my mind is made up. I'll cut off his cock and feed it to him, the fucking prick. We don't have written rules but there are unwritten ones and Tyler just wrote off at least three. If she taps out now, there won't be any shame in it. Tap out. Tap out. Let me in.

She does none of those things. Instead she sucks in air between her teeth and writhes on the earthen pitch. She watches Tyler as he approaches with slow menacing steps. His gaze pans up and down her frame and my fingers flinch towards the scene. I don't know how I remain grounded because in my mind I'm using my whole body to crush him.

He closes in on her and she sweeps his feet. When he hits the ground, she rises and waits for him to find his footing, but Tyler fights cheap. He kicks in her ankle and as she falls with a groan, he cracks a fist against the left side of her face. She lands directly at my feet on hands and knees and spits up blood between the toes of my boots.

She tenses and I wonder what she's thinking because as she rises to stand, heavy braid slipping over her shoulder, she's rigid in ways she wasn't before. Slouched posture now straight as bone, limp fingers balled, she looks at me and a surge of pure electricity chars the air between us. She's got blood on her chin, the bruise on her cheek has already started swelling and pale patches of purple decorate her abs. I want to reach out and touch her, but I keep my arms locked across my chest, wedged underneath my armpits.

"Turn," I grunt. I want to say more, but I can't. Not with Tyler looming over her, looking like he's ready to end it. And more.

She blinks at me and for the split second it takes until she turns, I wonder if I don't imagine her smiling. Tyler's fist is careening for the back of her head but she spins, ducks under his arm while her braid whips around her neck. She clips him in the inner thigh, then in the stomach, and when he doubles down, thrusts her hand up to his nose, breaking what wasn't already broken.

Tyler's torso folds to meet his knees, but he still tries to swipe at her stomach. She jumps out of reach then kicks, spinning in a move only someone her size with impeccable aim and speed would be able to master. She hits him in the gut and as he struggles for breath, she takes out both of his knees. A loud crack, then he's down on one hand, clutching his other to his right kneecap, as if hoping to physically hold the leg together. From the ferocious and uncommonly fast way she moved, she slows and paces in a slow circle around him.

"On your feet or I'll end it now and make you look completely fucking ridiculous," she whispers, and there is no more of that japing condescension I heard earlier. There is only the thirst for blood.

Had I just imagined every moment leading up to this? I think so. Was this fight evenly matched? I'm beginning to think not. She stares down at the brown haired boy as if everything leading up to this moment was only because she had allowed it. Tyler was nothing to her and here I am standing on the tips of my fucking toes, dying with the urge to protect her. She needs protection from nothing.

I'm a fucking fool. She wanted a fight not a win. Fuck 'em and leave 'em. That's what she said and I didn't listen because I didn't want to believe her. She's doing this to teach me a lesson.

Tyler struggles to his feet and the cries of the room have never been louder, nor have they ever felt so distant. Tyler strikes for her chest and when she dodges that in a move that's explosive quick, he kicks for the slit between her legs that he'd wanted so desperately.

Rather than move, she grabs his ankle with both hands, stopping its trajectory and wrenches hard enough to throw him off balance. As he begins to fall, she advances on him, hooks her right arm under his left and, spinning around him, places her left hand between his shoulder blades and forces him to the ground. She straddles his back, takes a fistful of hair in hand and uses that to tilt his face up. For a fraction of a moment, his eyes meet mine.

She has to shout to be heard over the crowd now. "You done, *pinche culero?*"

"Fuck...fuck you..." He's barely got the words off his lips before she slams his face against the earth. A cracking sound fills the space, adding to the chorus of cacophony.

"Let's try that again, piss for brains," she says, "Are we finished?"

Tyler chokes on his own blood. It pours down his chin to his throat, dripping onto the packed soil from his bobbing Adam's apple. "Fu...fuck..."

She punches his face into the ground twice more and when he fails to respond the third time, she releases him. The crowd breaks immediately, bodies moving into the ring to swarm her more than they are to resuscitate Tyler. Money begins changing hands while the captains for the night try to keep tallies and scores.

I don't move. I just watch the girl pull the band from her hair that held back her bangs and wrap it around her wrist. They flop over her forehead, strands adhered there in blood and sweat. Men try to congratulate her, try to offer her beers or other shit excuses to get her into bed but rather than except the freebies, she holds up both hands and pushes through them.

I wonder where she's going and am more determined now more than ever not to follow her. She doesn't need me.

She likely doesn't think of me in the same way I think of her so religiously. Hell, in the past days she's become my fucking religion. And my pornography. I think of her first thing when I wake up and first thing when I hit the sheets at night. Wondering what those tits would feel like around my cock. Wondering how hard her tight little body could take a pounding. And more than that, wondering what it might feel like if she opened up to me. Charlie was right. I'm fucking pathetic.

I glance to the right to see Charlie scrambling through the crowd, chasing the man with the money. I wonder how much he bet. The thought makes me want to rip out his teeth. Clifton and Dixon are chatting at the bar. Aiden's nowhere to be seen. I turn, sparing only one glance back at Mer and it's in that glance that it occurs to me that the distance between us is closing, and getting closer.

Bodies block her from view, but a few moments later she resurfaces directly in front of me. A small circle of space opens up around us and I wonder what my expression must look like because the guys that were on her nuts a second ago seem suddenly so preoccupied with their drinks and their money.

"What took you so long?" Her face is a frown that's far too serious.

"What?"

"You took ages. Had to let him get way too many hits in while I was waiting. And this one even kinda hurts." She points at her foot and I cringe at her swelling ankle. She seems nonplussed by it and is instead, too focused on my response. What the hell is happening? She didn't tell me she was fighting, wouldn't tell me anything about her, doesn't need anyone, let a man beat on her somehow for my benefit, can barely look at me but now...

"You waited for me?" I say, though the words taste wrong coming out of my mouth.

She shrugs, keeping her arms crossed over her chest in my mirror image. "I didn't want you to think I was weak. Plus," she says, swiveling around, "after what happened last week, I didn't want any of these fuckers thinking they could get away with anything. Tyler's always creeping around so when Ollie paired us up, I didn't complain even though I knew it was kind of a joke. Tyler deserved what he had coming." She smiles and blood seeps out from between her teeth. Has there ever been a woman more beautiful? Not one that I've fucking seen.

"You fought for me?"

Her face flares a bright and incriminating red that makes my whole chest tighten, like I've swallowed a stick of lit dynamite and it's gone off in my lungs. "I mean...no. I just...like I said...I...you...I'm just glad you saw it but if you're going to be a dick about it..." She starts to turn and I grab her elbow too hard because my muscles aren't obeying me in the way they were before.

"You wanted me to see you." I don't mean the fight and judging by the tortured expression that crosses her face, she knows it.

"Yes." She bites her bottom lip and my gut is rock solid and the halfie that had been idling in my pants at the sight of her has become a thick shot of bone. I drop my hands to the side and she edges half a step back, angling her body as if she's expecting an attack. She's not half wrong.

"We need to get out of here."

"Okay," she says hesitantly. She puts another couple inches of space between us and the men that hover nearby perk up, hoping to use the distance to their advantage. Anybody so much as breathes on her, I'll break their necks. "I just need to change and get my winnings from Ollie. I'll meet you…"

"No. Now."

Her eyes widen. She licks her lips and rubs at the blood on her chin with her hand. I want to lick it off. She nods and I hold out my arm, urging her under it. She's slow to comply. "Is everything okay?"

"Fine."

"Hey, I can't go that fast. That *pito* did a number on my foot."

"Can I carry you?"

"What?"

I don't wait for her answer, but sweep her legs and cradle her back. She lets out a yelp and circles her arm around my neck, even as she lets out a cry of protest. The faces we pass watch us with a knowing in their eyes that she hasn't caught on to yet.

Ollie's is among them and I hesitate only long enough to bark, "Hold Plumeria's money for her." He nods, tries to offer an explanation, but I don't hear it. "I'm not done with you by a long shot." His face falls and his lips move, but I shove past him. The density of the crowd has released somewhat, making it possible for me to reach the massive, open doorway in a minute, and the near empty parking lot seconds after that.

"What are you...where are we going? Are you going to murder me because I swear to god I'll be really fucking..." I reposition her body in my arms so that she's upright and she gasps when I release her back. Her spine meets the wall of my car, passenger's side window peeking out on either side of her shoulders. With my hands, I spread her thighs around my waist and lean into her, soothing the pressure of my erection in the soft heat of her core.

"Shit," she gasps, realization dawning on her in a breath. Her eyes are wide and she's never looked more ferocious or simultaneously vulnerable. I take her by the back of the neck in a grip that's too hard, but I don't know how to soften it, tilt her head back and crush my mouth to hers, tasting the metallic tang of her blood on her lips. I expect a momentary hesitation on her part but the moment my lips brush hers, her mouth parts and she moans, arching into me.

Her hands find my shoulders, nails digging into my skin through my stupid, fucking button up and I'm blinded by lust. I have to have her, and I could have her pants down and my dick sheathed by her whole body in under a second, but that's not what I want. Correction. That's not all that I want. I want limitless euphoria and her complete surrender.

Her tongue finds mine and her fingers fumble with the buttons studding the front of my shirt, but I don't have the patience to let her undress me. I slide my hand around her back, throw open the car door and fling her carelessly across the bench seat. She grins up at me and the moonlight pours in through the window, illuminating the smooth, elegant curves of her taut, carved frame. Very slowly, she spreads her legs and even though she's still fully clothed, I get the feeling I'm being taunted.

With one swift jerk, I rip my shirt open, sending buttons scattering across the gravel and the floor of the truck. I cover her body with mine, my warmth meeting hers to form one perfect union. My right knee is on the floor and I reach back to slam the door shut behind me. I kiss her deeply, devour her jaw and work my way down her neck. Her skin tastes like salt and metal and earth all I see is caramel and onyx as I pull the tie from her hair and drag my fingers through the braid.

She's breathing hard and everything is in fast forward. Her bra is gone and so are my pants. I reach past her elastic waistband and slide a finger deep into her wet heat. She moans low and arches up so that her perfect mocha nipples meet the wall of my chest. I can't wait any longer. Don't know how I've waited as long as I have to hold her like this.

I hook my arm around the back of her head, cushioning it and simultaneously trapping her between the wall of my body and the back of the seat. I've got a condom on and as I plunge mercilessly into her hot, perfect opening her gaze doesn't break from mine and my gaze doesn't break from hers and we are, like this, connected. The moment seems to last an eternity and seconds. Her eyes at some point close, and she bites the inside of my arm. I growl and my whole body stiffens.

The orgasm comes over me violently, gripping the backs of my thighs and working its way up to my neck. I bury my face in the waves of her thick hair and she combs her fingers across my scalp in a way that's soothing and warm and sensual. I've never felt more grounded anywhere than in my own house, or here, with her in the front seat of my truck. All the doors are unlocked, the moon is bright, and we're sure as hell loud enough to attract spectators, but her hands wrapped around my back are enough.

Now is the moment where I would say somewhere along the lines of, 'thanks, but I won't be needing your number' or 'no, I won't be staying, I have somewhere to be.' To tell her either of those things wouldn't just be an outright lie, it'd be sacrilegious. Her arms fall away from my skin and I feel her begin to shift beneath me, but I lay my palm against her chest and hold her down, moving so that I'm kneeling on the floor of the cab and she's spread before me on the bench like an offering. I take her like one.

Kissing my way down her body, I worship her breasts, tracing the lines of the bruises on her rib cage with my tongue. Her breath, which had slowed, begins to pick up and when I glance up at her face, her eyelids flutter. The muscles in her legs are taut as I bite and blow against them, before finally making my way to the pale brown slit that rests at their provenance. A thatch of soft curls tickles my nose, though I'd have taken her any way she was offered. Taken and devoured.

Her taste is sweet and her lips are smooth fire. I penetrate her with my tongue before suckling her clitoris until her knees begin to clench around my ears. I glance up. Her eyes are closed and her mouth is open and her hands are clutching the back of the seat and the steering wheel. She whispers my name in a curse and a single tear drips from the corner of her eye as I slow.

"Don't," she says, and I obey willingly. I'm a glutton for her.

I pin her legs apart and take her for everything she has, then I take more. Her back is arched up off of the seat and her fingers are pressed against the window. She shakes and then screams. Spanish words fly from her lips in an incoherent stream, but I do hear her say my name half a dozen times and when she's finished, lying limp on the seat before me at her most vulnerable, my halfie turns to stone.

I open the glove compartment box and push aside my gun, finding a condom. I slip it on, letting the used one fall to the floor unceremoniously. I sit on the seat and pull her body onto mine facing me. Her arms are weak but I hold her steady and when she kisses me, I know that she knows what I want.

She slides onto me, moaning as she does. Plumeria's full, perfect lips caress my cheek, my neck, my ear. I grip her thighs in my hands, cupping her ass in my palms and squeezing so hard I know I'll leave bruises. A true sadist, she works me like a torturer, teasing me and taunting me until I have to beg for it and I do beg. In low growls, with my hand yanking hard on her hair, I beg her to let me finish inside of her. She speeds up, twisting and arching and when I come, the world devolves to darkness while my head grows light.

I don't know how long we're in the cab of my truck exactly, but when I surface I can't move. I've been asleep but the sun poses no threat to the horizon. The sounds from tonight's earlier fight are dead and the night is pitch black on the outside of the windows. They're entirely fogged over. I could be in another town, in another city, in another world.

And I wouldn't give a fuck. She's lying on my chest, wedged between me and the back of the bench chair. My knees are crushed against the passenger's side door and her legs are tangled with my legs.

Glancing down, I see her eyes are closed. Her breath is light and even and her hair fans across her back like a blanket, reaching her perfect ass. I reach down and squeeze it, thinking *mine*. The word blankets me and I put up no resistance. Not after what passed between us and I don't just mean the sex.

There was a moment, as I lowered her back down onto the bench after tasting the sweetness of her sex for the third time in which we kissed. The smell of condoms, my dick and balls, and her pussy and ass was on each of our mouths – hell, the whole cab smelled like little else – and she looked at me and I looked at her and in the silence between us we both took the first step towards that most dangerous of words.

Is this what love feels like? If so, I understand why people kill and die for it.

"Shit," she moans, sounding hoarse and for a moment I panic that I spoke those three little words out loud. Then she says, "Damn I'm sorry."

Her voice makes me smile and I hold her still as she begins to move. "You aren't heavy and I'm sure as hell not about to go anywhere."

"Maybe you're not, but I need to." She sits up and coughs into her fist. Pain flashes across her face as she clutches her right ribs, fingers sliding over her full breast and titillating that hardened little nipple. Christ, even after everything, I want her again. Forever. Fuck. I want to take her home.

"You okay?" I ask. My voice is genuine and I hope that she hears that. I took more than she had to offer me this night.

She shakes her head and though she moves slowly, she's reaching for her clothes. I want to burn them. "I thought I was hurting before."

I sit up, though my head spins and my arms and legs and stomach are sore. A euphoria blows through me, but I can feel it dwindle more and more with each garment she puts on. She reaches for her sports bra but, looking at it groans and snatches up my shirt instead. "Would you mind if I borrowed this?"

"It's yours."

"I promise I'll give it back. You can pick it up from Ollie next time you see him."

"It doesn't have buttons anymore."

Pulling her arms through the sleeves, she smoothes her hand down the front of my shirt and blinks brightly. "Oh. You're right."

"So where are you going that's so urgent in the middle of the night?"

She shrugs. "I should just get going."

"Why don't you stay? Let's get a hotel in town. Stay all day tomorrow, maybe Sunday too." I touch her shoulder and she closes her eyes in no reaction that I can interpret, but something is off. "What's wrong?"

"Nothing. I just can't stay. I need to...to go." Her voice masks a very real emotion lodged somewhere in her throat.

I frown as chill from the night air seeps in through the windows to contaminate the warmth we created. Goosebumps break out on my forearms. "Can I have your number at least?"

"I don't think that's a good idea," she says immediately and I chuckle under my breath at the irony of all my traditional tactics used so effortlessly against me.

I lean in towards her, but when I go to kiss her cheek she throws open the passenger's side door and stumbles out into the breeze. It wraps around her and she shudders. I shudder. I hold her gaze steady and watch her from the lit cab, looking so fragile in the darkness. Plumeria. I want to shield her.

In a slow, near patronizing tone, I tell her a truth I've never told any woman. "I want you to stay."

Her lower lip trembles and a very real fear transforms her face and I remember the way she'd called out for me in the field, not far from where we are now. I'd turned and seen her falling and she had looked at me needing me to save her from herself. Plumeria doesn't call for me now. Instead, Mer turns and runs. Her car starts a few seconds later and I barely manage to button my jeans in time to follow her.

At the end of a long, woodland road, she sets her blinker to turn right, away from my house and away from the city. I wonder if she really does live this far out, or if she's just doing whatever she has to, to get away from me. A sudden exhaustion passes through me like a ghost and I decide to make it easy for her. I pull up beside her car, setting my blinker to left and reach across the cab to roll down the passenger's side window. After a pause, she rolls hers down too.

"I know I don't know shit about you, except that you're powerful and smart and beautiful and a fucking dick." I lick my lips. Fuck it. "But I think I'm falling in love with you. Just thought you should know." I give her a second – or rather, I give me a second of hope but I refuse to wait for anything that I know won't happen – then I roll up my window. I pull onto the road and drive back to my own house on autopilot.

I feel like I just made a quick trip from heaven to hell and now I'm back on earth. To make shit worse, Dixon's waiting for me when I open the door. "You're out of line," he says, standing from the living room couch the moment he sees me. "And all for Mer? What is she to you? Your brothers come first. Have you forgotten that – or have you forgotten that I'm your fucking brother too?"

In the darkness his face appears as a shadow against an even blacker shadow. I remember the first time I met him, in Marguerite's house. She'd brought him in and told me and Clifton to be nice. She'd fed him pancakes for dinner and he'd glared at her like he'd been poisoned, but less than a month later, he got me a job washing dishes at Cactus Bar. Now we own it. "Answer me," he roars when I say nothing.

I pause before breaking past him, arms down at my sides, fight gone from my bones. I remember the way he'd looked at those pancakes and imagine that my face mirrors his as it looked then. Some combination of fear, skepticism, betrayal. "It's done."

"What's done?"

"Plumeria and I. I fucked her and left her. She got what she wanted."

Dixon follows me broodingly all the way to my bedroom door. "Don't you mean, you got what you wanted?" He's smarter than I am. He's always been smarter than me.

"Good night brother." I close the door.

Mer

My body is seconds short of complete and total collapse by the time I make it back to the ramshackle, two story house I share with Mario and our padre on the outskirts of town. The lights on the main floor are on when I pull up, which doesn't surprise me. Padre's probably passed out drunk on the living room couch. Mario's probably in his room fucking one of the strippers from Camelot or jacking off – depending on how much cash he still has from the last fight he won. That was a while back.

I hold my shirt closed with one hand and shove the key into the lock. My brain is fried, soul shattered even though my thighs and hip flexors are sore in all the right places. He couldn't have said to me what I thought I heard. Nobody's ever told me anything like that in my life. Nobody but *mi madre*, and she died so long ago the words are only half remembered. My mind probably filled in the rest with hope and delusion. But Knox, the man they call Knuckles, falling in…nah. I refuse to think it.

He could have no reason to say what I thought he did. No reason besides the endorphins shooting through his system. But if he did. If he had. I shake my head as I push open the door. I'd kill for him to tell me that he lo… Everything on my mind and in my heart dies like a bird hitting a glass window and then the ground below it. Thump

thump. Then it's done. DOA. No more reason to ever think or dream about love.

The couches have been pushed against either wall and a single recliner faces me at the far end of the space, positioned right in front of the fireplace. In it, sits Loredo. Spade is sprawled across the couch to the right, some sort of black duffel bag on the ground in front of him. He kicks it beneath the couch and stands when he sees me. I don't breathe, but instead let the door swing shut at my back. I drop the bag I'm carrying.

Mi padre and Mario – the two tragic bits of family I have left – had left – are lying on their sides in the center of the room, blood seeping from wounds to their temples. They've been dead for hours and judging by the abrasions covering Mario's face and arms, and the fact that one of his legs looks very broken, he didn't go down without a fight. Spade has pale pink all over his arms – blood he wiped off but didn't wash – as well as a cut on his face. Other than that he looks unharmed.

"Plumeria," Loredo whispers in his own whispery sort of Spanish, "how have you been?"

I take a few steps forward and cross my arms over my chest. I shrug. "Same as ever, *tio*. I see *padre* finally got what was coming to him."

"You don't seem upset."

The funny thing is that I'm not. The initial upward spike of my heart rate has subsided once more to a dull thump. "Was only a matter of time." I glance at Mario's corpse – not the first family member I've lose to *padre's* vices – and a small pinprick of pain lights up my chest. Then nothing. I glance again to Loredo.

The only evidence of Loredo's age is his sleek silver hair. Otherwise, he looks young, face cut narrow like a hawk's. Black eyes peer out above a long, thin beak. He might have been attractive once if it weren't for his mouth. It's too big for his face, making him look like he's in a constant state of laughter. There's something repulsive about it. About him.

He rubs his palm off on his straight black pants and says gently, "Your brother had a critical disadvantage in his fight against Spade, who was evidently not the first man to beat up on him in recent weeks," he says, switching to English, "I imagine that if you were to try to fight Spade in your condition you'd see a similar fate, having been injured even more recently."

"Probably," I say with a shrug, looking Spade over. There's no denying it. Even in my best form I could never beat Spade and that isn't something I say lightly. I don't know anyone who could. Spade is built like a goddamn eighteen wheeler, every inch of him solid bulk. He's six foot six with hands like baseball mitts and he's trained in about every style of fighting there is. "I was in the ring tonight."

"Looks like that wasn't the only work out you got. Who was the lucky lover?"

I'm distracted from Loredo's iniquitous face by Spade, who shoots towards me so fast I stumble over my feet and slam against the closed behind me. He grabs the collar of my shirt and rips down, pulling the whole shirt free with little resistance.

"Mother fucker." The back of his hand meets my already injured cheek and a heat sears my wrists as I use my arms to break my fall. I groan as Spade drops to his knee beside me. "Who fucked you?" He whispers to my cheek in that stilted, Russian brogue. His body shakes with a rage I hadn't anticipated and I grin, knowing he won't be able to control it. It'll be lights out for me in ten…nine…eight…

"Oh it was a whole truck load of guys. At least seven. College kids. I decided to celebrate after kicking one of their friend's ass and they thought they'd teach me a lesson. Overall I'd have to say it worked out well for everybody…"

He drives his fist into my ribs – the bruised ones – and the breath flees from me entirely. My fingernails catch in the slats between the faded hard wood as I swallow a breath, then his fist comes for me again. He continues this controlled and systematic torture for a few minutes before I hear Loredo calling Spade's name distantly, through a fog.

"Spade, give me a moment to speak to my niece, won't you?" Reluctantly, Spade lets up. He uses his foot to roll me onto my back. My breasts fall to either side while pain and fire splinter across my sternum, consuming my rib cage and working down my spine, one vertebrae at a time.

"Plumeria, can you hear me?" I lift a hand and give him a thumbs up. He laughs quietly. "Such an impressive woman, and in so many ways." I hear shuffling and when I next blink, Loredo is crouching to my left, watching Spade from across my body. He looks to me. "Tell me the man's name."

The answer is fuck off, but curiosity compels me to ask why he even wants it. To this, he responds, "Your father did not pay his debt."

"He paid his debt with his life." I cough, spasms shooting through my stomach like knives.

"I thought so as well, until Spade made me a rather interesting proposition. You see, I am still out the eighty thousand your *padre* owed me, so I figured murdering the last of my brother's pathetic brood would be enough to help me find peace with the money I have lost. But then Spade offered to reimburse me for the total – in full – in exchange for your life. A generous offer until I remembered your dear sweet *padre* mentioning something about a band of brothers coming to your rescue last you were at the bar. I began to wonder if there wasn't someone who might be willing to pay more. They own a great deal of property, these brothers, and if you made half the impression on them you made on my colleague here, then I'm sure the payment will be well worth the wait." His gaze glances down the length of my body, but there is no lecherous intent. Just a passive evaluation of the assets. "Well worth it. So tell me now which one of them stuck his little cock into you and we can all be on our way."

I spit in his face. Spade's fist knocks into my stomach and everything goes blue.

"Doesn't matter. When you don't answer your phone, he'll eventually come by wondering what happened to you."

I grin, suddenly elated that I hadn't given in to that desire to give him my number or leave him with any promises that I'd call.

"Something about that amuses you?" Loredo frowns.

I shake my head stiffly. "He won't come." Better this way. I can survive a life of torture knowing that he's safely removed from this fucked little universe. I'll never see him again. I was dead the moment I stepped through the door.

"Then you'll be Spade's problem soon enough. I'll give the man ten days to come retrieve you. Spade, call Luis and tell him to bring my things. Together, you two can pack up the bodies. Looks like I'll be staying a while in this shit hole."

Spade nods, but his gaze doesn't leave my face and his hands twitch towards me. It's Loredo however, who speaks. "Spade, why don't you take her upstairs and get her cleaned up? She'll want to look her best when her lover shows. And Spade." Loredo reaches out and grabs Spade's forearm as he grabs me by the back of the neck. "I don't want you fucking her until her father's debt has been settled." Spade growls. "She may not be a virgin but I let you at her, you'll lower her purchase price. That said, you are free to do whatever else you'd like with her. She'll be under your care until then."

Care. Price. Debt. Words that mean very different things for ordinary people. I know the real reason Loredo doesn't want Spade to fuck me is because he might not want to keep me after he's had me and Loredo isn't sure that my 'lover' will show. He won't. He may know where I live, but he doesn't know my number and left rejected less than an hour ago. I hang like a rag doll in Spade's arms as he drags me up the stairs, through my bedroom and into my bathroom.

He undresses us both, pushes me into the shower and follows me in, closing the shower door behind him. His hunger oozes out of him like some sickly perfume. I can smell it, like chicory and chewing tobacco, as he approaches. He shoves me forward roughly so that my tits are crushed against the cold wall. My breath fogs the white tiles until he turns the hot water on and lets its stream run over me. He washes me, gripping my tits and sliding his fingers into me aggressively while his other hand works his monstrous cock. The kind to bloody a girl even when moving gently, and Spade is anything but gentle.

"Don't close your eyes," he snarls. A second later, when I fail to acquiesce to his request, he backhands me. My elbow crashes through the glass wall of the shower, but Spade grabs my hair before the shards can take my arm entirely. He throws me to the wet floor and begins to moan. His cum drips onto my stomach and legs and he pushes me flat down with his foot when I go to wipe it off. "This is your life now," he says, "do you understand?"

I nod, right hand closing around a large shard of glass, just in reach. As he stretches down to grab my arm, I cut the glass across his face. He canters back, and the water on the floor does a better job of disabling him than I ever could. He crashes through the other side of the shower wall and clunks his giant head on the lip of the toilet as he comes down. That's a concussion at least. I start to shake with laughter as he tries to stand and fails, again and again. The sound both carries and echoes, consuming me as it pulls me further and further down into its embrace.

So many ironies, and so many unavoidable consequences of actions that I had no part in whose outcomes led to this. My whole birth was a tragedy. My whole life is a joke. And it's funny as hell so I laugh and I'm laughing still as his feet and fists find me and I don't stop laughing until a belly full of blood rushes up into my mouth. And as I pass out, I hope to hell he kills me tonight. A night where I felt, for the first time

in my entire wasted existence, that glimmer of love and hope.
To even taste it was enough.

Knox

I notice Dixon watching me from across the table. He's been on me like moss on a rock ever since I blew up last week. Not that Dixon is dad, by any means, but the guy did get us to where we are now and that comes with a certain amount of respect, well earned. We're a long way from washing dishes. And we're happy because of him. Well, most of us anyways. Not Aiden. Not me. Not now. First time I've been back to the barn in seven days and I'm only here because Charlie's fighting.

I stay focused on my kid brother in the ring, dancing on light feet but not packing punches like he oughta, on the cold beer trapped in my left hand sweating beneath my fingertips, on Dixon's gaze pressing against me like a fucking fist to the throat, on the scratchy arms of the wicker chair that leave splinters behind like scathing little reminders that I'm just a mortal man who can't stomach rejection.

I don't look for her and so far, I've succeeded in avoiding the sight of her perfect shape. The long black hair, caramel skin, those lips... Fuck. Even the smell of this shitty barn has my dick twitching – sweat and beer and blood and hay and dirt – all of it reminds me of her in a painful way that has my balls ready to burst. There are few smells these days that elicit any other reaction.

Clifton curses when Charlie takes a nasty right hook to the shoulder. His opponent is bigger and Charlie is scrappier than the effort he's displaying. He could stand to learn a few things from Plumeria... And in the stroke of a second I'm thinking of her again.

"Hey." I look up at Ollie as he slouches into the empty chair to my right. He's got a black plastic bag in hand and sets it down on the table. "Yours, I believe."

I snatch up the bag and look inside to find a stack of fifties. Flipping through the cash, I quickly calculate that there must be at least ten grand here. "Where the hell did'ya get this?"

Ollie sits back. "What?"

"I said where'd you get it?"

"Mer." He runs a hand back through his greasy hair, eyes darting away from mine quickly. "She said to leave her winnings for you."

"Mer's winnings? She doesn't want the money?"

Ollie stares at me like I'm a fucking madman, though he doesn't say it aloud. Probably still thinks I'm aiming to get his head on a pike. "Look, I don't understand the shit between you two, but since she left I figured you'd want it."

"Left?" I swivel around to face him when I should be looking out for my brother.

"Yeah man. She quit almost a week ago." Ollie's eyebrows draw together and he reaches into his back pocket for his cell. "Last thing she sent was this." He tilts his phone towards me and I see a few strange characters scrawled across the screen. Eventually, I'm able to decipher their meaning: *"I quit. 36428 2 K. Try. M."*

"I think she was trying to write sorry there," he offers with a shrug.

My mouth is dry and a deep sadness fills me as my slow ass finally understands. She quit because of me. Must have left me the money as a tip. Like I'm a goddamn prostitute. And an expensive one at that. Doesn't make sense though. Even if that's what she was getting at, she needs the money more than I do. She'd a kept it. "You try calling the number?"

"I tried but it's disconnected. Sucks too. I didn't realize how much I needed a second set of hands around this place."

"Talk to Dixon about getting a replacement," I say absently. I lean back in my seat, feeling heavy as I weigh the two options I've got in front of me: take the money and accept that there are some battles I'm just not meant to win. Or go after her with everything I've got. A slow smile creeps across my cheeks as I handle the cash. It's dry between my fingers, most of it well creased and well used. Prostitute or not she wouldn't have given it to me if there were no hope. She wouldn't have bet on me either. I slip the money into the inside pocket of my coat.

"She leave town, or you think she's still at the same address?"

"No idea."

"Can you find out?"

Ollie makes a face. "I'm not sure."

"I'm coming to you on hands and knees."

Kid looks down at his hands. They're pale and bit to hell around the nail beds. Then he leans in close and lowers his voice to a whisper like he might not want one of my brothers to know. Weird, but I don't question him as he starts to give me some of the information I'll need as I plunge into my next battle against Mer for Plumeria's heart.

I smile at the thought as Ollie says, "I know one of the girls that works down at Camelot. She's been fucking Mario. I could probably ask her and get a good idea."

"You think you can hit her up by tomorrow?"

"Latest, by Tuesday."

"Thanks, man." I take his hand and he shakes it hesitantly, either surprised or worried, I can't tell which.

"No problem…"

"And I'm sorry, I didn't mean to brush you off," I say, leaning forward to rest an elbow on the rickety wooden table. "Griffin's little brother is a freshman this year and he's been looking for work. I'll send him by tomorrow and you can try him out on an easy night, see how he does. He can hold his own from what I can tell."

Now Ollie just looks shocked. "Thanks."

I laugh, feeling a strange giddiness at the decision that's come over me. I'm going to take this girl through the power of charm – another word for coercion – and in doing so I'll do something I've never done before: I'm going to try. "I'll add more money to the account for your bar back once you've selected him. No reason to let another one get away." I take his shoulder in my hand and give it a light squeeze. "Don't hesitate to come to me for anything."

Dixon and I ride home alone. Aiden has a fight in the city at a different ring. One where there is no mercy rule and where the odds on leaving in a body bag are fifty-fifty – if your opponent doesn't, you do. Charlie's gone to watch to get some pointers after tonight's loss and Clifton joins them as back up. We don't ever let less than three of our own go to the pit in town. As we park in the garage, Dixon asks me about my conversation with Ollie and when I tell him, he slams his car door shut.

"You're different now," he seethes.

I roll my eyes. "Different because I've started taking on more responsibility? It's a responsibility that I should have taken more seriously before now. The clubs aren't just yours, brother. And I spend more time than anyone in the ring. I should be lead on everything concerning the barn."

Dixon clenches his teeth and balls his hands to fists as we wade into the living room. "You're a fucking ingrate. After all the work I put in to build up our assets. To build you up into a man…"

"And men have needs, my brother, and those needs include women." I throw my coat onto the back of the couch and grimace at the empty empire that surrounds us. "That's what this is really about, isn't it?"

"You're getting your head all fucked up because of a chick…"

Pointing at all of the pictures of us and Marguerite that date back to our childhoods, I speak over him. "We are family, brother. But we're also men. Men have women. Men have kids. What did you expect? That we'd all stay your boys forever? I want a family of my own some day, to give my kids what none of us ever got. Don't you?"

Dixon's face is severe in the low light radiating from the kitchen. I flick a lamp on and his frown only grows more pronounced. "No."

I breathe air out of the corner of my mouth. "We may be family, but we are still individuals and I don't always have to agree with you."

"When you make a decision that affects us as a group, it goes by me first," Dixon hisses through his teeth. His eyes have never been so bright a white, or so crazy. "Don't make me throw you out of the house…"

"This is my house too," I roar and the sound echoes off of the high ceilings. "And this no women in the house rule is a fucking insult. You're not my fucking father…" The words break on my next laugh, though I don't recognize it as such. The sound is harsh, mean. "You're fucking terrified, aren't you? Of losing control? Of us no longer needing you? Because when that happens you'll look around and realize your hard ass is fucking lonely. You keep this up, brother, and you might just die that way…"

Dixon comes at me in a burst and slugs me in the ribs. He doesn't hold back either, and that man's always had a good throwing arm. Anticipating the blow is the only reason I can breathe through it. He shoves me against the wall, disrupting a few photos Marguerite took shortly after Aiden joined us. He stands apart, looking anywhere but at the camera in all of them. Glass shatters in the frame as one of the pictures hits the ground.

Dixon is pure fury as he steps back into the center of the living room, as if knowing that distance is the only way he will be able to master the carefully constructed control he's so proud of. But I know as well as he does, we're all the same. All wounded in our own fun, unique little ways. Foster child syndrome. Finding Marguerite and each other saved us. We were the lucky ones and Dixon is still clinging to that. So afraid and proud and angry. I can see each emotion pass across his face like the turning of book pages before he leaves the room and the silence settles around me.

He shouts over his shoulder, "You can have the barn but if I see that girl in this house Knox, I'm going to kill her."

I'm cold, my stomach sore from where I took a hit, though not sore enough to keep me from going after him. I stop myself halfway down the hall. No point in fighting over a girl who probably hates me. Even though I said what needed to be said, the whole argument might be for nothing when it comes to Plumeria. I lay on my bed that night with the curtains open, counting sheep and stars.

I massage the bruise on my stomach and try to plan what I'll say to her if I do manage to track her down. I wonder what sort of expression she'll be wearing – what she'll be wearing. I close my eyes and picture her tits, those thighs and what's waiting for me between them. I jack off to thoughts of her, like the teenager I assured Dixon I wasn't, her name on my tongue whispered to the darkness.

I get up too early and head to the second floor library. I should spend more time here, but I don't. Going to the computer, I draw up the files for the month's coming fights and make a few changes to the schedule. Then I refill the booze order and give Morgan, Griffin's little brother, a call. I share Ollie's number with him and tell him where to go and by when and get a call from Ollie not long after I hang up.

"Hey. How are you?"

I grunt, "I could complain, but I don't want to waste the time. She still at that shitty place outside of town. Exit 29 on the 401?"

"Not sure." His voice is high pitched, off somehow but I'm not interested in him. "Talked to Mindy. She said she hasn't seen Mario in two weeks."

"Fuck." That's a bad sign. I groan and lean back in my chair, then I get up all at once. "Better go see for myself."

"What's that supposed to mean?"

"I'm tired of waiting. I need to see her."

"Could be some shit, Knox. That family isn't exactly notorious for being clean and reliable."

"Yeah, I know."

Ollie lowers his gravelly pitch. "Could be some cartel shit. I'd steer clear unless she contacts you first."

That hadn't occurred to me. But it doesn't matter. I'm already in the car. "Good advice."

"You gonna take it?"

"No."

"You're fucked in the head, man. You know that?"

I laugh hollowly to myself as I pull out of the garage and onto the road. "Tell me something I don't know."

"Shit." Rustling on the other end of the line. "Well good luck, I guess. Give her hell."

"Oh I'm planning on giving her more than that." My dick and my heart.

Her house is in farm country, straddling the farmer district and that of their farmhands and surrounded by apple trees still clinging to a faraway summer. Now all their leaves have changed to brown and the forgotten apples that litter her dusty dirt driveway are dead and rotten.

In the pale light of sunrise the last time I dropped her off, I'd thought the house was grey. Looking closer, I think it might have been painted blue at one point because I see patches of scattered navy paint decorating the façade. Two stories and it doesn't seem to have a basement. Just a porch leading up to an open screen door.

There are two cars in the driveway – one a Rolls Royce, the other a busted Ford. I park behind both of them so no matter which she drives, she won't be able to sneak past me to get away. I can't decide if that makes me psychotic or practical as I turn off the ignition and step out of the car wearing a standard black tee shirt, faded blue jeans, and black shitkickers with the safety toes. No button ups, no cologne. Just me and desperation.

Damn. I'm nervous. Nervous as a fucking dweeb asking the head cheerleader to prom. She's going to say no. I know it, she knows it, and so does the rest of the school. But I'm a proud mother fucker and I'm going to ask even if it peels the paint right off me when she says what we all know she's going to.

My boots thud loudly against the uneven slats leading up to her porch. The screen is open, clacking against the doorframe in the wind. The door behind it is closed and locked so I rap my knuckles across its faded surface firmly, crossing my fingers and hoping to high hell someone's still inside and that she didn't move to another state entirely just to get away from me.

"Plumeria, it's me. I know you're in there, I can hear you moving." There's at least one different set of feet falling across creaking floorboards, though more likely two. Or more. I'm surprised until I remember where Ollie got his information – or lack thereof – and I roll my eyes, fully expecting Mario or one of the strippers from Camelot to open the door as the footsteps draw closer. I'm wrong.

The door opens wide and a Mexican man with grey hair sighs, then grins, as if he's pleased to see me. I can't fucking fathom why. "Welcome. Which of the Cleary brothers are you?" He has silver hair and cinnamon skin and the raven eyes of a fox. I can't tell if he's thirty or sixty but there's something in the set of his jaw and the volatility of his gaze that reminds me of Plumeria. I wonder if they're related.

"Where is Plumeria?" I say, rather than answer.

Glancing past him, the space is empty all the way up to the meager fireplace against the far wall, hidden behind a cracked leather armchair. Wooden floorboards are ancient and rattling, the ceiling is high and the fan that decorates it must be broken because even though it's muggy inside, the fan is covered in dust and cobwebs. There's not a photo or piece of art in sight, not that it would have done much to improve the livability of the place.

Plumeria lives in a shithole and though I know I shouldn't have expected more, it still bothers me in ways that tell me I care too much for a girl who's given me so little.

"She's just in the bathroom, freshening up for you. You know how women are," the man drawls, moving deeper into the house. I follow with reluctance because nothing he's said to me so far is right. Plumeria isn't the kind of woman to freshen up and there was no way for her to know I was coming.

The damp air is stale and smells faintly of air freshener. The rose kind, which increases the feeling that I've just walked into a morgue. My fingers are twitching, and I wish I hadn't left my gun in the car. As it is, I'm the only unarmed man in the room.

The silver-haired serpent has a bulge on the inside of his left ankle that's unmistakable, though the other two men in the room hold their weapons even more conspicuously. They're both carrying Berettas in their left hands, two identical versions of one another leaning against the left wall. The outline of where a sofa used to be rests between them, though that sofa now sits on the right side of the room. The apparent leader of the trio gestures for me to take a seat on it, so I do. A cloud of dust puffs up around me.

"These are my business associates," he says, "don't let them trouble you." A door that I can't see somewhere down the hallway to my right opens and closes and I hear the shuffling of more than two feet. Standing by the chair positioned in front of the fireplace, the man claps his hands together. "Perfect timing. Thank you, Spade. And Plumeria, you have a guest."

Plumeria steps out of the mouth of the hallway into the living room and I remember that I'd been debating whether or not to bring flowers. She doesn't need flowers. She needs mercenaries and gunpowder and automatic weaponry.

Plumeria's naked body is covered in scratches and bruises. She walks with a limp, favoring her left leg, and her right eyelid is entirely swollen shut so that she looks at me with her left. There's a tugging at the thick grey chain locked around her neck, beneath which she wears a symphony of brightly colored abrasions in varying stages of healing. She's got half-healed lacerations on her arms, a white bandage plastered to her left leg that's weeping crimson, and the wound I last saw on her lip has been reopened, what looks like recently, because there's fresh blood on the blackened side of her face. She's been tortured, possibly raped. Blood on the inside of her thighs only confirms it.

I am a shell of who I was before.

Spade steps into the room behind her, holding the other end of the heavy lead connected to her throat. He reels her into his bare chest and slides his hand over her stomach to mark an implicit claim. I rise to stand. No other words are said, or need to be said, between this man and I. Either he is doomed or I am, because one of us will die today. And soon.

"Loredo," Plumeria says and her voice warbles though her pitch is strong. She is muscle and bone and skin and coughs into her fist and I refuse to be distracted by the fact that all of her seems to be a little wilted – not if I'm meant to keep her with me among the living. And I will. This is not just a statement of intent, but a vow. "This isn't the right brother. You've wasted your time. Just let Spade take me and be done with this charade."

The man called Loredo's wide lips twitch. "Spade," he snaps.

In a single moment that's too fast to retract, just like its consequences, Spade slides his hand down Plumeria's stomach and inserts a finger into her all the way up to the palm. Her body pitches forward though she doesn't scream and I know then that it was a mistake to stand, because my knees grow weak and for a moment I wonder if I've keeled over.

Instead, I say quietly, "Enough. I am the brother."

Loredo snaps again and Spade withdraws. He slides his finger into his mouth, licking it clean without breaking the line of my gaze. My stomach pitches and I try to remain relaxed, but fail as he pulls Plumeria towards the couch, closer to me. To torture me. Close enough that I can smell the sweat and blood on her skin. The fever too. He doesn't stop grinning. I could reach out and touch her where she stands, drag just a fingertip over her scarred shoulder, though I don't fucking dare. We are playing a game and in the game of monsters and dead men, everything is sacred and nothing can be revealed. Already, I have given away too much.

"*Muy bien,*" Loredo drawls, stepping away from the fireplace and into the center of the room. It nearly kills me, but I move away from Plumeria to walk with him.

"I assume you want payment for the girl," I say coldly.

There is surprise on Loredo's face that I know is because of Dixon and I feel a momentary guilt for the way I last spoke to him. Everything I said was true, but I did not know just how much I needed him until now. To mimic the mask he wears in perpetuity is one of the many lessons he taught me as a child that has value to adulthood. "You are correct. Unfortunately, her father passed away before he was able to repay his debt. Her brother was unavailable to step in and recover this loss, so it is sadly left to little Plumeria."

"How much do you want?"

"The total remaining is a measly eighty thousand, but Plumeria doesn't have it, so I've been forced to put her on auction." He shakes his head and clicks his tongue against the backs of his teeth, feigning remorse. "I came into town because I heard that there may be another bidder. Plumeria refused to tell me his name, so I had to wait for someone to come calling, and here you are."

The bottom drops out of my stomach and for a moment the world and walls switch places. I am inside out and nothing but pure violence. Red begins to seep into my field of vision, claiming a dangerous amount of space. Wouldn't give up his name. My name. She was here, being tortured for the past nine days because she refused to let Loredo give me a single phone call. She could have ended her own suffering so easily. Why didn't she ask for me? Was it pride? Was it me? Does she hate me so much she won't use me to help her even now?

"Another?" I say, clearing my throat.

"Second to Spade, of course." He gestures to the man and when I turn, Spade grabs the chain and uses it to throw Plumeria onto the ground at his feet. While she coughs up blood spatter onto the floorboards, he takes a seat on the couch and combs his fingers back through her hair, meeting my gaze and succeeding in straining the limits of my composure. But it does not break. It will, but not yet. I'm not ready for The Red to take me. "Spade has agreed to pay the amount in full in exchange for the girl. Can you beat his offer?"

Loredo knows I can, and I gather so does Spade. His eyes watch me hauntingly from the sofa as I turn and begin to make my way towards him. I crouch beside Plumeria's body, keeping about three feet of distance between us. I watch her unseeingly, because I can't afford to focus on her injuries in this moment. Not when it could mean her life. "I'm not sure," I muse.

Loredo's voice catches as he speaks and I hear the first notes of anger begin to warp his tone. "Plumeria tells me that you own a couple of farms. Couldn't you afford to sell them in exchange for the girl? I assure you, she'll be well worth the price." Farms? But Plumeria knows I own much, much more than that. The whole damn city. Hell, I could give the guy half a million of my own or ten times that if I borrowed from my brothers – in cash, today, just to take her home with me. But he thinks we own farms...

And then it hits me. Plumeria let herself be tortured, not for pride, but in the desire to protect me. My chest smolders and I can't speak. It takes me many deep inhalations, which I hope appear contemplative from the outside. "I don't own them on my own. I share them with my brothers," I say, clearing my throat into my fist and ignoring the urge to commit homicide that grips me when she flashes a frightened glance at my face.

I'm sorry, she mouths into the floorboards and I close my eyes to block out the sight of blood on the insides of her lips. If I fall apart now, we both leave this house in body bags and Spade and Loredo leave alive.

Loredo says, "You should know that none of my men have spoiled her since you last saw her. She'll be every bit the eager whore that you remember." Spade clenches up, face burning a brilliant cherry. Finally. I nearly sigh with relief. He's given me the opening I needed.

As our host continues driveling on, I lower my tone and speak just loud enough for Plumeria and, more importantly, Spade to hear. "But it might be worth it to taste that sweet ass again." I place emphasis on the word and the response is immediate. Spade stiffens and clutches the chain tighter to his chest, winding it around his fist as I move closer to her.

"Damn, she might be the tightest pussy I've ever been in and the way she works that mouth on my dick and balls..." I whistle between my teeth. "She could go pro. And she was so eager the first half a dozen times, I wonder if it would be even better to have her all chained up like this to my bed so I can do whatever sick things come to mind." Plumeria's face turns towards mine and I see anger and fear and angry, frightened tears drip down her cheeks. I close my eyes, push through the wall that has formed in the cavity where my heart used to be, and continue. "Maybe I'd even let my brothers take their turns..."

I reach out to touch her bare shoulder and Spade lets out a roar, then tackles me to the ground. My back stings as it hits the floorboards, but it doesn't hurt as much as the sight of her wincing away from my outstretched hand.

Spade sits up on my chest and lifts up a fist while Loredo shouts at him to stand down. Spade can't hear the guy. He can't hear anything but the gushing of blood through his ears, the calling of bloodlust needing to be sated and I understand this man above me because I hear it too, but it doesn't own me anymore like it used to – like it still owns Spade.

I twist my head and let his fist eat up the floor. He roars an angry scream and I punch him in the throat once, twice, a third time, until he loses his grip on me. I kick him off and we both rise to stand, but when he lifts his fists and angles his body towards me, I cede a few feet of ground and hold up my palms.

"I get the feeling that any number Loredo throws at us, you'd match and so would I. Why don't we settle this like men? Fight for Plumeria? Winner leaves with the girl, loser doesn't leave at all." My chest is heaving. That little itch inside of me waiting to unleash the floodgates is loosening, like worn elastic. I need to let go. My left leg is shaking and so are my fingers, but my mind is still a steel knot of harnessed control. For the moment.

Spade cocks his block of a head to the side and squints at me. In a heavy, Russian accent, he asks, "What about money?"

"Not our debt. Not our problem."

Loredo steps between us and cracks the butt of his gun across Spade's cheek. "I paid good money for you, now you listen to me…" Spade rights himself and throws his full weight behind the punch he levels at Loredo's face. It's almost beautiful to watch, the way the man's head cracks backwards, whiplash so severe it severs the top of his spinal column while Spade's fist shatters the full face. Loredo hits the back wall, two goons too slow to catch him, before slumping down onto the floor. He's dead.

"I am *Russkiy mafiozi*," Spade screams, before devolving into a stream of unintelligible Russian curses.

He advances on the corpse and kicks it while the two remaining Mexican men draw their guns. One of them manages to get a round off and though it hits Spade in the right arm, he doesn't slow. He tears the gun away from the second fool and uses it to shoot the first before turning on the second. He tosses the guns aside even though he could have killed me and been done with it. But this man and I are alike in more aspects than I care to acknowledge. We both have too much pride. Spade's gaze passes to Plumeria, still kneeling on the ground, metal shackle wound around her neck. Pride and something stronger. We both have desire.

The thought just about rips me apart but I still hear him through my rage as he says, "Just us men." He grins, unfazed by the blood dribbling down his arm or the welt below his right eye. That doesn't bother me. "Ready?"

I grimace in a way that shows all my teeth. "Ready." And like a ribbon pulled, that fine thread holding me together unravels and the Red monster and I become one.

I see only crimson and limbs and feel nothing but the inside of my own chest as my lungs pull in air less and less evenly. My heart has exploded and when my eyes clear I see my thumbs buried in the eye sockets of a man I know I've met but whose name I can no longer remember.

Spade. The word comes to me along with the realization of where I am and why I'm here and I grab a thicket of his blonde hair and I shatter the back of his head on the linoleum. We are in the kitchen and there is a trail of blood leading around the counter. A block of butcher knives is turned over and I gather that we used them by the fact that there's a knife wound on my chest just over my heart. Below me, Spade is dead and I killed him.

His hands and legs have stopped twitching and as my adrenaline crashes like two school busses full of kids headed straight towards one another driven at full speed by suicidal sociopaths, I hear a voice saying my name though it takes me a moment to recognize it.

"Plumeria," I cough, rolling off of the male body and onto my back. I rise to stand when she does not respond and step out from behind the kitchen counter, returning to the living room to find her naked in its center. Blood and bodies litter the ground around her. She's crying and I shake my head, hoping to clear it and be better able to understand what could have won this reaction. Is it Spade? Does she cry for him?

My body is heavy and the world begins to slip sideways but I still see her as she charges across the space towards me and wraps her arms around my chest tight enough I begin to feel the first of the damage I sustained. Painful, but not irreparable. I pray that the same can be said for her as my hand comes down on the back of her hair and her warmth presses against my tattered tee shirt.

"You killed Spade. That *culero*. That *mama vergas pendeja. Carajo!*" She chokes back sobs, still attempting to marshal her reaction. I'd tell her not to bother. I'd tell her so many things if only I could find the lungs in my chest or the tongue in my mouth. Right now, all I feel is her body tucked against mine where nothing can get to her. Nothing.

"You came for me," she says, "you fought for me."

I tilt her face back so that I can look at it and carefully, I drag my finger underneath the plum colored bruises on her cheeks. "I would have died for you," I say, meaning it for reasons that go beyond logic. I don't know her likes, her tastes, her favorite anything. But I know her. Deep down, The Red knows her too. Like she was and always has been a part of me. I kiss her forehead, but as I bend to meet her mouth, my body lists to the side. I stagger forward and she catches me with a grunt, carefully maneuvering my weight over her similarly broken frame.

"*Mierda*," she says, staggering herself, "you're hurt bad. Fuck. I didn't want you to be in any of this. I've got to get you home."

I hand her my keys and she helps me out into the darkening light, down the porch steps and to the car. I'm not so sure that there's one thing hugely wrong with me, but if everything isn't a little wrong. Everything but the woman sitting next to me. I sit close to her. Close enough to rest my hand on her leg, though she won't let me lie down.

"You've got a concussion," she says as the car bounces down the road, heading towards a peach horizon. "Stay awake with me." When I glance up through the window, I see a blood moon rising.

"Are you okay?" I ask her, lips moving though I can't feel them. I can only feel the blood dripping onto my chin, but I try to focus a little harder when she tells me that she's not. Forcing my eyelids open a little further, I glance down the length of her body perched on the edge of the seat, which is still pulled out to accommodate the length of my legs. My gaze lingers over the bright white bandages that cover her hip.

"What did he do to you?" I say, and I wonder if I really want the answer.

She shakes her head. "Just beat me up. That's all."

I know it isn't, but I'm not in a position to argue, given that the pounding in my ears is growing louder. "How long?"

"Not that long," she whispers.

I slam the side of my fist against the window, trailing blood in the shape of a hand as it falls back onto my lap. "How long?"

She closes her eyes, takes the turn that I tell her and says, "The night we were together."

The night we were together. Nine days. The full extent. I'm still punching the dashboard when she lays down on the horn. A few seconds later, the passenger's side door is being forced open and people are grabbing my hands. They call me brother and though I see their faces, all they present is a wall between me and the one that I came for. I start to thrash against them and they struggle to pin me down. Aiden and Charlie are at my arms and Clifton is reaching into the car and I hear a tight scream. Red. It's coming back, obscuring most of my vision until I can see little else.

"Fuck," Clifton says. "Sorry. You're naked." He states the facts that make me rabid and the boys at my arms wrench back hard enough I'm shocked I keep both shoulders in their sockets.

"Don't fucking touch her," I sneer.

Clifton looks to me and then back at the car before removing his shirt in a simple gesture. "Don't touch me there," she says, though I don't yet see her. "Hurts like hell."

Easing her legs over the edge of the bench seat, she grabs onto Clifton's shoulder and lets him help her out of the car and though I hate the sight of another man touching her when she's in just a tee shirt, the sight of her is enough.

She wraps the chain still attached to the metal clasp at her neck around one arm and shoves the opposite shoulder under my left armpit. When she lifts, she asks my brothers to help her and they do. We walk like atoms forming a single complex molecule towards the door, which opens up before we reach it. Dixon stands there and his eyes go first to Plumeria and then to me.

They narrow. "Take her to the guest house and lock her inside. Take Knox to the lab in the basement."

"Take me to my room. Plumeria stays with me."

"The hell she does," Dixon says through gritted teeth. "Not until we…"

I throw myself forward, dragging half the other bodies with me. I reach Dixon and slam my forearm across his throat. I roar, "If you want me to leave, tell me to fucking leave! If I stay, she stays with me."

Clifton manages to wedge himself between my body and Dixon's. He slams a needle into my thigh and I curse. The arm I've got braced against Dixon's throat slips back to my side and my whole body sways left, and I know I must be crushing Plumeria beneath me. The silence is broken up only by my ragged breath and Plumeria's wheezing.

Then Clifton whispers, "He's not right without her. When he's better you two can hash out the living situation, but until then let him keep her here. You should go walk off steam."

I remind myself to kiss that man on the mouth as my bedroom door assaults my plane of vision and a strange serenity washes over me. For now, however, I think I'll lie down with Plumeria and sleep.

Part II
The Strip Club

Dixon

The wind against my face is cold and hard but neither cold nor hard enough to curb this particular brand of rage. I tend to feel it only when one of my brothers are getting their asses handed to them in the ring, when they gamble away too much of their money, when they drink themselves into stupors and lose themselves to drugs or women or the bottle – when they put themselves at risk. There's a risk now, I'm sure of that, but this time it is my brother. He's going to tear everything that we've worked so hard to build apart and it's our town, our world, our universe. No one else is allowed to breach that, least of all a woman.

I wonder if I'd be so angry if it weren't a woman. If Knox had brought home a man would my hands be this tight around the steering wheel of my Audi? Or is it the fact that she's a lover and that she means so much to him? I take the Lord's name in vain, shouting it into the wind in the hopes that he'll give me answers. He always has until recently and I'm reminded that all fathers at some point abandon their children.

I pull up at Cactus, our favorite bar because it was our first, and slide into the spot I've used in the back since I first took over management some fifteen years ago. I was sixteen and bar manager, and by eighteen I owned it. Since then I've

– we've – built up the streets surrounding it to a six block oasis for residents and out-of-towners and college kids as far as three cities over.

I throw open the back door and the few staff that recognize me, greet me. Most of the newer faces in the kitchen and behind the bar look confused as I pass, but I don't stop to introduce myself. My brothers and I like to keep a low profile, stick to ourselves, do good work and run our businesses right – at least we did until Knox lost his mind and handed his testicles over to a whore named after a flower.

The sight of any woman right now brings up an image of her face in my mind, so when the waitress comes to my corner booth, I tell her to send the guy over. She probably thinks I'm gay, but I don't care. I can't stand the sight of a soft face and a pair of tits right now, even if Mer's face was less than feminine for all the damage that had been done to it. I wonder what sort of mess she got my brother into. If it will kill him. If it will destroy us.

The tables are slightly sticky and I'm staring down at my black reflection against the black, shiny surface when I hear the waiter approach. "I heard you're looking for me? What can I do you for?"

"A coke and a fifth of whiskey. Top shelf. Neat."

"Wow, you celebrating something?" He asks with a laugh, hoping to elicit one out of me.

"No," I sneer, "I'm in mourning."

"Oh," the waiter pauses, fumbling awkwardly with more than just his speech. He drops his pen underneath the table and I see that it's badly chewed. I kick it back to him across the carpet and fold my hands over the sticky gloss, ignoring the low drums beating out some Dance Hall and the sight of ugly women swaying to it just a few feet away on the dance floor. "I'm sorry for your loss."

"Yeah me too. Why I could use a drink." I lift my gaze to the waiter's and recognition flits across his face.

"Oh shit. Sorry. I didn't realize…I'll be right back with your drinks. On the house, of course." His rubicund cheeks quiver as he speaks.

"I have a tab," I grunt. The small town celebrity bit got old when I was twenty one.

The kid nods again and leaves me in a much-needed silence, one that isn't broken by his return. Alone, I drink – not in peace, but in the sort of hazy rapture I'm used to, one shot after the other after the other. The night's still young by the time I stumble out of Cactus and onto the busy street.

People pass me but I don't see faces, only shapes and outlines, a multicolored sea that reeks of vomit and smoke and cheap perfume. It's the latter scent that intensifies when I make my way from the brightly lit streets studded by red velvet rope clubs and throngs of college kids loitering outside of them, hoping to get in and starting fights when they're denied entry. We got standards at my clubs. Standards that I can't meet at the moment.

I pass by the door to Camelot as it swings open and a bachelor party staggers out. The bachelor – at least I assume he is by the way he hangs between two others with his fly down and his belt open – throws up on the street inches from me, chunks of blue and pink spewing from his mouth and onto my tan boots. I see the right one sail up into flesh as if not my own or under my control and the bachelor goes down, the two guys on his arms with him.

One of the bouncers steps from the shadows underneath Camelot's broad, black awning and it takes me a moment to recognize him as Marcel through the haze of the liquor. He looks surprised to see me here and like this and pushes the college kids down the street away from me. He makes an effort to speak to me, but I'm wasted and crippled by shame and the simultaneous desire to burn everything I spent so long creating to the ground.

Camelot's one of the last bars on the Seventh Street strip and as I leave it behind, sound begins to fade. I can't tell if it's because I really am so far off the main road or if it's because I have begun to fade myself. Half a block later, the buildings are already rundown, my face is on fire and I realize I left my jacket somewhere – maybe I didn't bring one at all. The wind is thick with chill, and I can sense that it is cold, but I don't feel it against my flesh. Like the whole world is just on the other side of a thin sheet of glass.

Someone calls my name, but when I glance around, there is no one. Just the darkness of an alleyway, a cab crawling up the street. A group of college kids sit crammed in the back, garbage music wafting out on the breeze, and as a voice shouts my name again one of the blonde sluts in the back seat turns and looks at me.

"You Dixon?" Two white men with vibrant red hair emerge from the dark side of the street, looking like comic book characters or buffoons; one is taller than I am and meaty in the chest though the other is short and lanky.

Together, they make a ballerina and a bear and I laugh for no reason I can think of.

"Dixon," the bear says to the ballerina amidst a sequence of other words I can't replicate. I'm not even sure that they're English.

I reach out for the nearest wall and lean against it. Brick and grout crumble beneath my fingers, the consistency dry and rough like sand but twice as hard. "Mr. Cleary," I choke, "only friends call me Dixon and you ain't no friend of mine." Song lyrics dance through my muddled thoughts. They're old and I can't complete them.

The two men share a glance and more hushed words. Then the bear looks at me with a hooded gaze that reveals very little and states, "You never know. We may be."

"What do you want?"

"Looking for our brother."

"No Weasleys around here," I drawl.

The shorter one glances to the taller, passing him a look of misunderstanding which is not reciprocated. The bear's eyes never leave mine even as the ballerina says, "We look for Spade." His voice is thick with an accent I can't place.

They're closing in on me and the heat behind their requests is starting to wear me thin. I feel myself take in a deep breath and clench my teeth. When I straighten up, I take a handful of brick from the building's dilapidated siding with me. "I don't know a Spade. Now you need to get off my block."

"Our brother missed a meeting tonight. A meeting with a group of Mexicans…"

And there it is. Heat ravages me, shooting up the backs of my thighs and into my chest like splinters or needles. "Mexicans aren't my concern…"

"But you know where they are, yes?" The bear says and he watches me with a knowing that makes me feel as if I've just betrayed my own brother though I haven't said anything at all. He knows me, this man. And I know nothing. I am lost.

"Lots of Mexicans in this town…"

"You know the ones we're looking for."

I do. And I incinerate from the inside out with self-loathing. I can't give her to them because she's in my house. The woman is in my house. With my brother. My brother did this – no, she did this. She lured him in and stripped him of his sanity and I'll take my revenge for what she's done like I will against anything that tries to hurt my family. "You guys have three seconds to get out of here."

"Or what?" The bear eyes me up and down. "You cannot even stand."

"Are you challenging me?"

The bear steps forward, but his shorter comrade holds out his arm. "No. No challenge. We telling you to lead us to the Mexicans who have our brother or we'll tear your town apart."

It's the last word that leaves his lips, but not the last that leaves mine. "You dare threaten my family?"

My fist finds his throat, but I don't punch, I grab. I throw him face first into the building and hear his nose and at least a few of his front teeth shatter. He crumbles to the ground, coughing and spitting up blood while his taller brother comes at me. He hits me in the cheek and the stomach several times with enough force to maim, but not kill me. I can't even feel the pain through the glass wall of the alcohol, though I know he'll leave behind some damage for tomorrow.

I stagger backwards, foot slipping off of the edge of the curb. Unsteadily, I throw myself forward. I grab the tall guy around the waist and my legs give out. We fall together into garbage cans and I hear a thunderous banging sound, shouting that is neither his nor mine, and a cry of pain. Hands grab at my shoulder, wrenching me around and I kick the shorter man when he tries to reach past me for his brother. His head cracks against the brick wall and he slumps down, motionless, while I drunkenly roll back to face the bear.

I kneel on the man's chest, and watch him painfully drag in air. Something stabbed him in the back and there's blood on his hands and mine and a tear in his shirt and his eyes have rolled back into his skull but I drive my fist forward anyways. I crack his eye socket and then his jaw.

"Hey!"

My fist slows, as if weighted down and driving through water. Fingers tug at the back of my shirt, choking my collar. I swing my arms around, intending to drag whoever it is to me and suffocate them to death, but my hands close around her shoulders. It's a her and I'm hit with both a soft guilt and a limitless hatred.

I curse to myself, ready to throw the woman out of here and threaten the hell out of her to keep her slutty mouth shut. It's the whore from the taxi. She's white with blonde hair, wearing a white corset and black jeans. Her stilettos are black lace and I have no idea what she's doing here so close to me with her tiny face contorted in fear. Another woman where she doesn't belong.

"Get out of here," I growl, pushing her to the side.

She falls to the concrete with an "oomph," reaches back and catches herself with her hands. Shaking her head, she pushes her hair out of her face. If she's surprised at the blood on her palms she doesn't show it, but instead looks towards the man on the ground who was defeated not by me, but by a garbage can. It takes me to that moment to notice the jagged, rusted pipe-end protruding from the front of the bear's shoulder.

"No. You get out of here," she says, claiming my attention away from the bloodied man and for a moment it's as if she's also speaking a foreign language.

"What did you say to me?" I rise up onto my haunches so that I'm only half standing. Even then, I still tower over her. The dim light from the street is at my back and with as black as my skin is, I imagine that to this little white over-privileged college brat, I look monstrous.

Her gaze flashes over my shoulder and abruptly she shouts, "Don't!" I turn to see a fat woman duck behind the brick wall and drunkenly, I lurch towards her. "Hey!" The blonde's voice turns my head around. Her jaw has set. She inhales once and exhales slowly. "You need to leave now if you don't want to get arrested."

"Can't get arrested," I slur. And it's true. I know too many people, own too many secrets. Half the cops have been to Camelot where they've received more than just lap dances they don't want their wives to know about. By their infidelities and their addictions, I am protected.

"You will get arrested if one of these guys dies and one or both of them will die if you don't let me get to them. I'm a med student and a paramedic and he needs to be rotated onto his side."

Confusion and adrenaline and booze, the sin of all sins, compete in my blood stream and I feel oddly out of control as she crawls around me to reach the body. She rolls him onto his side and unbuckles her belt, rips it free, then begins to slide it around his back. She whispers small, near inaudible words under her breath that sound either like curses or prayers, working diligently despite the blood on her hands and on her white chest.

Lifting her phone to her ear, she trembles as she shouts into it. "Paul? Hey Paul, I need the bus just off of Seventh street. There was a fight between two guys. They nearly killed each other." Her gaze flashes to me and I notice, as she lies like all women do, that it is very blue. Like the sky I used to stare up at as a kid on very clear days. Knox liked doing that too. He used to say that this was what forever and nothing and everything looked like. I told him that blue was just a color but he didn't care what I said, even then.

I watch the muscles in her throat contract as she swallows hard and shifts a little further away from me. Then she inhales once and turns her attention back to the body. "Yeah I've got at least a concussion on one of them and I think this guy here has a punctured lung. He fell and was impaled by a rusted pipe. Probably will get sepsis and he's having trouble breathing and I don't have any equipment to drain his lungs short of the pointy end of my shoe…exactly…"

She doesn't look again at me and I back away from her towards the mouth of the alley, then stumble out onto Seventh.

Knox

Fuck yes. I come awake with a panic that fades quickly to warmth. It swaddles me like a womb and I am an infant again. Loved without understanding. It is the first emotion a child experiences. If only for an instant. That love of being born. And it may be the drugs or the adrenaline or the endorphins that produce such a feeling in me now, but I yield to it with no resistance.

"Knox?" Fingers trace the line of my spine and I want to touch the hand, but I can't move. "Knox?"

"Love?" The voice whispers back and I realize only seconds later that it was mine. I feel embarrassment as light laughter washes over me like a veil. She's watching me when I open my eyes.

"I told them they gave you too much morphine." Plumeria's voice reaches me clearly but the sight of her mottled black-and-blue face slips too quickly from my grip, like trying to catch smoke.

"Where are you? Why can't I see you?" The words lumber off of my lips laboriously and miles seem to span between each of them.

"I'm right here," she says, mouth finding the lobe of my left ear. She kisses me, her heat sidles up next to mine and she uses herself like a blanket to line my side. "We're both alive and clean and okay." She kisses the side of my head and

I feel overwhelmed by the gesture. My cock is already hard. My right hand crosses my body to find her waist, as if guided there, and I roughly drag her to me. She curses. "Christ, Knox, are you even alive?"

"You just said I was." My lips reach towards hers and find them. I pull her to me, wrapping my hand around the back of her head and then from there, seek her breasts. I squeeze and she shudders and suddenly I'm positioned between her thighs. "I love you," I groan as I enter her sweet, sacred flesh. And it's mine because I fought for her and because she yields to me and because I'm a beggar for it and because I hope that she cares for me back.

We are limbs and lubricant and latex for some indeterminate period of time, and then asleep for some time after that. When I next blink my eyes open, everything is in slightly better focus even under the gaze of the low, orange lights. My hand rests in the dip of her lower back. Her hair is wildly strewn across the pillow like I'd dreamt it so many times. Her eyes are closed and her breath is light. She's asleep and, not wanting to wake her, I twist to face her underneath the sheets, careful as I move because of the pain that ripples across my rib cage suggesting that at least one – but probably more – ribs are broken. And the sex definitely didn't help.

Her left, good cheek is down against the pillow which means that for now I can only see her right. It's swollen, bruised, and discolored and makes my stomach ache in a way that's unfamiliar. This feeling of hatred, of shame, of loss. Of failure. I failed her. For nine days, I failed her, and it was all because of my pride. I should have followed her ass home. I should have stood out on her porch and begged her to take me. I shake my head, unable to picture how things should have gone, but didn't. I didn't even have the balls to pick up the phone and call to check in on her. By the time I did, it was almost too late.

Thoughts of Spade twist my vision to red, so I close my eyes, lay back on the mattress and inhale in long even breaths that match the length of each exhalation. I look at her again only when I've mastered that. Someone's removed the collar from around her neck, though the bruises that linger are like a cruel flashback. She's got cuts on her hands, a deep laceration across her palm, and her sides are a deep brown color that I'm sure spans her full stomach. She's got broken ribs too. Keeping my breath as even as possible, I lift the covers just a little to inspect the rest of her. She's got minor bruising on her lower back and on her legs, but I'm more troubled by the white gauze lining her right leg from her pelvic bone, halfway down her thigh.

Carefully, I lift one corner where the fresh tape seems to be loosest, and pull back the top half of the bandage. Seeing the wound, I slide it back into place and get out of bed. My feet hit the floor and are unsteady, but I make it to the door and then into the hallway, down the hallway and into the living room. Red has claimed my vision and I can't see through it. A voice says my name and my hands find the top of a table and I swipe everything off of it onto the floor.

"Fuck!" I roar. Arms come around me and I'm too weak to fight against them. My legs are slipping out from under me and there's a pain in my chest that I can no longer ignore. I feel the couch come up around me.

"Easy now." I open my eyes. Clifton stands in front of me with his arms crossed. He knows. I can see it in his grey eyes that carry just a hint of sadness.

"I'm sorry, Knox," he says, "we all know how much you care about her."

My head is so heavy, I catch it in my hands. "I failed her."

"You didn't." Clifton drags one of the ottomans over and takes a seat. "Not according to her."

"You talked to her?" That gives me pause.

Clifton nods. "After you passed out," he says, answering my unasked question. "She said you showed up unannounced and blew through Spade like a real killer. Said you gouged his eyes out. That true?"

I nod, but say nothing, feeling guilty and horrible and ashamed that I'm jealous even now that she was awake and talking to my brothers. I'm volatile. On edge. The slightest touch would be enough to unravel me – no, not unravel. Disintegrate.

"Spade got far less than what he deserved. He spent the past nine days beating her and he carved his fucking name into her leg." I choke, struggling through the words.

Clifton says nothing for a long time. Then, "She told me."

"She did?" I look up, stunned and irritated, though I try to mask the latter emotion because there's no place for it here, among family. Clifton nods and I grunt, "She's not much of a sharer."

Clifton smiles crookedly, though it's a patronizing thing, and sweeps his hand back through his blonde hair until it stands up on end. "I think she might be different than you remember after what you did for her. After you blacked out and Dixon left, she made me help her give you a shower, wrap your ribs, and stitch your chest and your ear back together. She wouldn't let me look at her until she sat me, Charlie and Aiden down and walked us through what we needed to know about her dad's dealings with Loredo and how Spade was seconded to his team through an uneasy partnership with the Russian mafia. During that time she was with him, she found a bunch of photos he had taken of the cartel and papers with what looked like copies of their books. She said she always suspected he was a spy, but now she's pretty sure. Looks like you pissed off some pretty serious people."

"Shit," I whisper. "If this puts the family in danger, we'll leave."

Clifton smiles a little bigger and the lightness in his eyes makes it possible to breathe a little easier. "That's what she said. We won't hear it. She's with you and you're family. You guys aren't going anywhere."

I exhale relief and ease back onto the pillows. "Thank you, brother."

"You'd do the same for me."

I nod, meaning it. I'd walk through fire for him. As I would, and did, for her. That's family. "Where's everyone else?"

"Aiden and Charlie are canvassing her old house. They got most of the mess cleaned up yesterday, but wanted to go back today to bleach the hell out of everything."

"Yesterday?" I say, gripping the edges of the couch pillows as I try to sit up. "How long have we been out?"

"You've been asleep for about thirty hours. She's been awake most of the time. Just went to bed a few hours ago." Clifton glances at his wrist though he isn't wearing a watch, and shakes his head. "Tough as nails, that woman. I don't think I've ever come across another woman like her." He pauses. Clicks his tongue against the backs of his teeth. "Another soul."

A swelling of pride fills my chest. "Neither have I."

"For the record, I know Dixon is pissed, but the rest of us like her. I mean, it was unrealistic that nobody would ever find a woman worth seriously being with and I have to say, when it comes to Mer, I don't blame you."

"Don't get any ideas," I grunt.

Clifton laughs hard. "After what happened to the last guy? You've got to be joking."

I smile, though uneasily. I did just kill a man. In the fighting ring I've come close to taking a life and have hospitalized my fair share of opponents, but I've never taken a life – only Aiden fights in the ring for more than money and pink slips – and even though the bastard deserved what I gave him a thousand times over, it still doesn't feel good.

"What about the bodies?" I say, as a distraction from the sight of blood still creasing my fingernails.

Clifton rubs his hands together. "Burned," he answers affirmatively, "To the last tooth. All five of them."

Like I'm jolted by a hundred volt battery, the drugs battering my brain dissolve and I am momentarily lucid.

"Five?" There were only four. Spade and the three Mexicans killed by the fucker.

"Spade, Loredo, Loredo's lackey – some guy called Luis – and Mer's dad and brother."

"Fuck."

Clifton's face falls. "You didn't know. I'm sorry." He shakes his head. "They killed her family eleven days ago, the night she arrived home and Loredo confronted her about repaying her father's debt. We found them buried in the backyard. Figured it was best to burn them too."

I close my eyes and try to breathe but fail, just as I failed her. I failed her whole fucking family.

"Hey," Clifton says, his voice a soothing balm on the raw wound that covers all of me. "You saved her life." Clifton's words pull me through the solid carmine sheet like a rope. I crack through the surface and breathe hungrily, ribs searing with each inhalation.

It's hard to think, to process, to know what to do next. My mind is cloudy, thoughts flying a thousand different directions. "There was a second guy working for Loredo. Not Spade or Luis, somebody else. He must have gotten away."

Clifton nods. "Mer told us. We've scanned for him but so far nothing. Couldn't have gone far though. Aiden's checking the local hospitals."

I nod back, trying to seem coherent and engaged. "To bring him back here?"

Clifton makes a face. "Would be if it were Dixon we sent for him."

"Not really Aiden's style." I cluck. "Where is Dixon?"

"Marcel called to say he's sleeping off some nasty drunk at Camelot."

"Our strip club?"

"The one." Clifton's frown grows more severe. "Our big brother is losing it."

"So am I. I just…I care…"

"I know, man, I know. We all do. And nobody's going to hurt her. The moment you brought her into our house, into your room, she became family. We're all part of this now. Together."

The words fill me with a warmth and a relief I'm not used to feeling. I've never been on such precarious ground before, never risked so much. Never put the people I care about the most in danger. Never been in love. "I appreciate hearing it. I just hope the others feel the same way. I won't have any more harm come to her on a cause of me…"

Clifton groans and kneads his shoulder, visible in one of the white tank tops he's always wearing. "You've got to let it go."

"What go?"

"Everything. Just get better. Dixon will come around." He stands and dusts his palms off on his jeans. "Now, as the man with the most experience actually dating women in this house, I'll tell you that she's probably going to want to see a familiar face when she wakes up in a strange place."

Now that makes me grin. "You know Charlie's pretty ass gets more pussy than you do."

Clifton laughs. "You worry about your own issues. Like getting that woman some food. Mer's only eaten once since she arrived and I don't imagine they fed her right these past days."

Standing, I lick my lips. Like my mouth, they're paper dry. "She tell you anything else about...about what happened to her?"

Clifton looks away, shakes his head. "Nah. She didn't. She was forthcoming about everything else but shut tighter than a vice on what they did to her. Wouldn't even tell me what I already know happened when I bandaged up her leg. If she hadn't been up near twenty hours straight, I doubt she'd have let me help bandage her at all, or let Charlie take the chain off her neck."

I nod, feeling sick again. I'm about to stumble to the kitchen and just make it to the door when Clifton surprises me by snaking his hand around my upper arm. He holds me back and though the guy is taller than me, he doesn't look down at me. He doesn't look at me at all.

"I want you to hear it from me," he says, "but I may have overstepped with Mer."

I hold my breath, and don't speak.

"I offered to drive her to the hospital to see Leanna." His voice is low, pitched as a whisper and I am eased by its gentleness even if the words themselves are cutting. "I asked her if she needed a rape kit or a pelvic examination."

My eyes close. I reach for the wall. Clifton guides me to it.

"She said no, that Loredo wanted to keep her untouched so to speak. I don't know that I believe her. Not with the way Spade kept her all these days, like a doll. He took care of her in his own sick, twisted way. Hey, I'm sorry," he grunts, taking my weight as I begin to slump forward. "I just wanted you to hear it from me."

I nod and sink down onto a barstool until my elbows meet the granite counter of the island. Clifton's still standing near me, with his hand on my shoulder. Supporting me, in more ways than one. The thought of her being raped by Spade hits me brutally, in a lucid visual. I rip away from it, from Clifton, and stumble to the fridge. Food. Food for Plumeria. That I can do. The past I can't fix.

"I'm sorry," Clifton says again.

"Nothing to be sorry for," I murmur, "I'm thinking it too." Pulling out a container of deli meat, mayonnaise and mustard and some other ingredients that together make a sandwich, I head from the room, out from under Clifton's stare. His kindness is difficult to bear, and I can feel it following me down the hall and before I turn down the hall to my bedroom, I pause.

"Thanks, Clifton."

"For what?"

"Being good to her."

Clifton smiles ever so slightly and crosses his bulky arms over his tiny G.I. Joe tank. "What family's for."

Tengo hambre. It's all I can think as wakefulness creeps over me way, way too soon. I feel like I just fell asleep, muscles all soup, bones rickety splinters splintering. I'm fractured shards and a patchwork of stitching. Stitching that spells his name. I shudder, wondering how long I can keep Knox from seeing what he did to me. *El hombre sin nombre.* Brutal bastard. White devil. I still can't believe Knox killed him. No one has ever, ever done anything…*puto,* I can't even finish the fucking thought. I just can't believe what he did. He saved more than just my life. He salvaged the last drop of my hope.

Blankets rise up to the tops of my shoulder blades and my hips slide over the soft sheets, sinking into the depression made by a sudden weight. I reach for him and his hand takes mine.

"*Carajo,*" I whisper sleepily, "you're cold."

"Sorry," he grunts, hissing as he slips under the blankets and my knee brushes up against his leg. He groans again when my arm rests on top of his abs and when he tries to stroke my face, I curse.

I smile, though even that causes me pain. "We are some kind of something, aren't we?"

"By something, I think you mean mess."

Though the drugs aren't enough to keep the act pain-free, I still manage to roll myself onto my back. A stinging radiates out from a single point to the right of my spine. I remember him kicking me there and wonder if I'm ever going to be able to fight again. Or run. Or walk normally. The ache on my back is worse than the one on my stomach. Then I open my eyes and see him – the other him, the real him – propped up on some pillows next to me and remember that none of that other shit matters because we are both alive.

"Is that a sandwich in your hand or are you just happy to see me?"

He smiles, but there's a reservation in his expression that leaves me feeling as ragged on the inside as I probably look. Not that I'd need a mirror to tell me how bad the damage is. I still can't open my right eye all the way. "Clifton says you haven't eaten enough."

"I've had other things on my mind." As I attempt to sit up, he snakes his hand around my upper arm and does most of the work for me. He stacks the pillows up until they are at the same incline as his, draws the blankets to my waist and slides the plate on top of my thighs. I don't hesitate to dig in.

"You've told Clifton a lot," he says. I wince, expecting heat, until he adds, "Thank you."

I pause, mid-chew and look up at him. "For what?"

His gaze flicks quickly to the ham sandwich I'm holding and I wonder if it isn't the sandwich he's looking at, but the abrasions around my wrist from the rope. "For trusting him, even if it was just enough."

"Easy guy to trust," I answer with a light chuckle, more nervous than I wish I was as we head together into uncharted territory. "Look, I…" His eyes open up and I see into their green depths wondering what the hell I've done right in my life to end up here when I should have died at the age of ten. "I don't know where to begin." Honesty. That's a start. "But I am so, so grateful. No one's ever done anything like that for me before and I owe you everything."

His face falls, and I don't see the relief I expect. "I hope that isn't why you're here now." He runs his hand back over his buzzed scalp, making a face as he pulls something in his side that has yet to release.

"*Verdad?* I mean, I didn't owe you before when we slept together and I'm sure as hell not here now only because of what you did to Spade but I can say that it helps." I smile and his frown twists into something ascorbic. "I'm sorry. I know that you probably didn't want to kill anybody and I know that what you did to Spade might bring a shit storm down on you and your brothers and if you want me to leave now then don't think that I won't. I don't want to…"

He cuts me off, not with a shout but with a kiss, and though I can feel the anger radiating out of him, when that kiss glances my forehead I also feel something else. A balm of acceptance. Of understanding. Of knowing me – all of me – and all of my baggage. A moment passes. A lifetime. When I resurface, my hand and the sandwich in it lie limp in my lap. He's leaning back against the pillows with his arms by his sides. His right hand picks at the sheets between us.

"You aren't going anywhere without me again." It's not a request, it's a fact. One that I'm not about to protest.

I nod, meek in a way I've never been. "Okay."

His eyebrow lifts and his mouth becomes an even more severe snarl. "And I want you to go see Leanna."

"Who's she?" I say, playing stupid. I've had this conversation with Clifton once already.

"A doctor. Our doctor. I want her to give you an exam."

"She should probably look at you too."

"A pelvic exam."

My sandwich suddenly draws my full and complete attention. I bite into it and chew, careful not to leave my mouth open long enough for him to think I'll speak.

"Hmm?" He says, not giving me the choice as he prods my waist, careful not to touch the white bandages. I want to retch up everything I've eaten.

"Okay," I murmur, "I will."

"You will?"

"Yeah."

He pauses. "You were raped?"

I smile into my food, carefully plucking a stray glob of mustard away and sucking it off my finger. I ruffle my bangs and look up at him, warm from the hair that drapes around my shoulders but from little else. "Of course I was."

His whole body seizes up. "Loredo said he wanted you untouched," he grunts out, though the words are butchered to pieces.

"You think Loredo was running the show in there?" I shake my head. "Loredo thought he'd purchased a bodyguard. What he bought was a spy. Spade called the Russians every night and I think had always been planning on offing Loredo. I just don't think he'd planned for me."

"Planned for you how?"

I swallow hard. "I really do think the *pinche culero* fell in love with me. In his own fucked way. At least, he wanted me bad enough to fuck with the cartel and the mafia. Shit wasn't supposed to go down like that."

Knox winces hard enough I know it hurts. He hisses between his teeth, kicks his legs over the edge of the bed and holds his head in his hands.

"Hey," I start, "hey…" My voice trembles and I'm afraid, not of him but of the idea that he'll leave.

"That's what Clifton said," he barks brutally. He switches back onto the bed, coming underneath the covers and I want to go to him and touch him, as much for his own comfort as for mine, but I don't. I don't know what to say. And then, with his eyes closed he reaches out to me and pulls me in. He wraps his whole arm around my head and presses me close to his chest as if he wants to absorb me into him.

"I want you to stay and I want you to be mine, because I love you and because I want to protect you."

"*Chingandos*," I whisper. My fingers are gripping his skin, the sandwich long lost in the tangle of blankets between our legs. I hold onto his sides and close my eyes. "I've never loved anybody before but I think I love you. No, shit, sorry. I'm fucking this all up. I know I do. I love you."

He sucks in a breath and kisses the top of my hair. "I know."

I laugh while hot tears swim to my eyes. I force them back. "Shit. What do we do now?"

"Now," he says, bending down and lifting my chin with his finger. He presses his lips to mine. "We get better."

I smile back, knowing that we will be doing more than just healing. We'll be waiting too. The Russians will come any day now for the man they've lost and I don't want Knox or his brothers to be in the line of fire when they do.

Dixon

There's an anvil in my brain and a hammering through my whole body. The two pains pulse out of time with one another though I'm not sure how that's possible. I thought I only had one heart, perhaps less than that, especially after this evening – or was that yesterday? Time is a vacuum in a bottle. I don't know what day it is, and I don't know what time it is either. It could be another century. The only reason I know I'm not dead is because my phone, lying just out of reach of my fingers, isn't. The red light on its face is blink, blink, blinking letting me know that someone somewhere is wondering the same thing I am: where am I?

The sound of drums grows louder, and I know it isn't coming from the bar outside of my office door. Bar. Office. I'm in Camelot and these drums are mine alone. What did I do? Drink a bottle of battery acid and wash it down with some Vicodin?

I wonder if that was before or after the fight. Must have gotten into a fight with how my back stings right between the shoulder blades. I haven't had to hit anything in a while, but it's a familiar ache. I never liked a fight like Knox does and I don't need it like Aiden, rather I was always the level-headed one, keeping my cool when the others acted like children. When they were children and impetuous and hating of everything and of one another. I taught them how to hate everyone else and how to love just us and now the glue holding our bond is broken. Now I am the hated one.

My hand fumbles across my desk as I reach out blindly. I crumple paper in my fist, knock over a tray of pens and crack my wrist on the underside of my computer monitor. I growl under my breath and exhale, keeping my eyes shut as I surrender to the sleep and sickness that's coming for me. My right hand lies splayed on the oak while my forehead rests on my left forearm. Convulsively catching air, I'm surprised when all at once my fingers find a hard, smooth surface: the glass bottle I was searching for. Taking it, I drag myself into a seated position so I can drink and when my eyes open, I look up to the sight of my brother.

The bottle in his hand is identical to mine, yet when he takes a swig his eyes are focused where mine can make out little more than the outline of his broad shape. Hazy yellow-orange light seeps in through window slats and I can see particles of dust dancing in the pattern of intermittent beams. The ceiling lights are off and I wonder how long he's been standing there, watching me in the dark.

"Bleak," I hack, clearing my throat into my fist before taking a long, deep drink.

My head spins and I sink back into my black leather armchair as the awesome force of the alcohol sings like a train through me. I watch my brother watch me for some time and as I wait for him to speak, I smooth my fingers over the chair's arm, its warmth disrupted by the chill of the nailheads. My hand, still trembling from the booze, moves in a way that is compulsive and maddening, even to me. It's the effect of his eyes. Cool and grey and unsettling.

I remember when Marguerite brought him to the house, I both hated him for his indifference and liked him for his indifference to the one the rest of them called mother. Mother. As if it's some sacred term. She convinced them of her love and they were so happily convinced of what I, to this day, still coin a manipulation in its acutest form. When she died she left me her favorite reading chair because I asked for it, knowing that I would plant it here in the office of our strip club to spite her. I wonder if she knew it too. She always knew.

"Aiden," I bark.

Expressionless, he takes another sip from the bottle in his hand. It's unmarked and clear, somehow an apt reflection of his own countenance. He's so pale, eyes the color of clear water, white hair cropped short, skin the opposite end of the spectrum from my own tarred hide. The twins might be identical but he looks nothing like his brother. He is pure ice where Clifton is only warmth, but I'm glad that it's him and not Clifton here now.

"I need you to do something for me. For us."

"I talked to Marcel. Got information on where the EMTs took the Russians. I'll hit them first then double back and find the woman who can ID you. Marcel said it was a blonde. She had a pregnant sister and both of them got in the ambulance. You got any other information for me? Any connection between her and the Russians?"

I shake my head as my fingers clench around the slim bottleneck. I see Aiden's beating me to the bottom. Can't let that happen. "No. I barely even remember the chick." Said she was an EMT though, and a medical student. I don't know why I don't tell him that. "I don't think she had a connection to the Russians."

"Doesn't matter." Aiden sets his empty bottle down on top of a tin file cabinet and a ringing fills my ears even after the echo fades. "I'll find them eventually." The guy probably gets a kick out of the challenge. He snatches his sling off of the small, padded chair directly across from me and loops it over his shoulders. Three guns hang from it, one with a silencer attachment. This isn't his first rodeo and a headcount of four doesn't make much of an addition to the tally in his ledger where he's already sporting a lot of red.

"Aiden," I say as he turns. He pauses with his hand on the knob, ice eyes flat, dead. "I have one more for you."

"Who?"

"Mer."

Aiden doesn't speak for a long moment and I am left wondering what he's thinking because there is absolutely no change to his expression. No registering shock, no eager alacrity, no disappointment. There is no change whatsoever.

"Okay." He nods once, then disappears through the door while I go back to drowning in whiskey – one twenty proof. A race to the bottom against my better self, he and I both lose.

It's been two days, but I can't get out of going to see a doctor forever. Not with Knox breathing down my neck. The kid is more vigilant than a parent. Seconds are all I get out of his sight, but I don't mind. The *idiota* is starting to grow on me in ways no one ever has. I feel bound to him and I feel that he is bound to me because of our shared experience, our twisted childhoods, our like injuries, our hands that are both broken and mended and more capable of forming fists than anything else. But we're learning other ways. Ways of affection.

My feet hang off of the end of the cushy, brown examination table, kicking absently. They are engulfed by his sweatpants which, with the giant blue tee shirt I'm wearing, make me feel like a ten year old. My fingers crinkle the paper lining the table and I'm itchy all over, and cold and hot and uncomfortable and I wonder if I really am sick or if I'm just sick with a visceral dread. My gut drops to the bottom of my oversized pants when the door opens and a short, Filipina lady walks in, eyes glued to a clipboard. So it's dread then.

"Well," Doc starts, smiling up at me in a curt, professional, *me-importa-un-carajo* sort of way that makes me respect her. "You don't have any STDs or blood borne illnesses."

"That's something at least."

She nods. "It is. Now take off your clothes and lie down on the table. You can keep that robe on and drape the blanket over your knees," she says, pointing to the piece of cardboard on the bed next to me and the one beneath it. "I'll be back in two minutes." Two minutes later, I'm sitting up on the edge of the table, ass pressed against the cool synthetic bench seat. Doc wraps a blue thing around my upper arm, pumps it up for a while, then lets it slowly deflate.

"Your blood pressure looks good. One ten over seventy." She snorts out a laugh. "And at forty three beats per minute, you've got the resting heart rate of a sea turtle. Nothing scares you, does it?" she says, and I assume that the question is rhetorical as she slips her small hands into a set of latex gloves and urges me onto my back. She prods around my boobs and armpits and I wonder what she's searching for because it hurts like hell.

"You're holding your breath," she says, "I'm hardly touching you. It hurts?"

"Like a mother fucker." I exhale the breath as she withdraws her hands.

Frowning she asks me to sit up, then pulls the tie holding my robe together. She draws it down the length of my arms. "This was supposed to just be a pelvic exam, but I think I'll need to give you the works. Let's go for an MRI. No, don't get up," she says, when I make to slide off of the table and follow her to the door, "I'm getting a chair."

"Jesus, Doc, I don't need a wheelchair."

"You do what I tell you, or I'll inject you with a dose of pneumonia."

"Just what I need right now."

She carts me back and forth from exam room to exam room. I get the full Monty – complete radiology kit, physical and a pap that's gentler than any sex I've ever had. She prattles off the results and asks me if I'll tell Knox. No, but I ask her if she will. When the grey door opens, Knox steps through on Doc's heels. He towers over her and I'm shocked at the reminder of just how big he is. He fills up most of the doorway and I feel competing flashes of warmth and ice when he looks at me. He's going to be so disappointed…

"You can take a seat here," Doc says. Knox ignores her and with a single kick-switch, he hops onto the table next to me. His hip is wedged against mine and he ducks his face until he's able to plant a sloppy kiss on the corner of my mouth. He tucks me under his arm and pulls me close and I remember that he hasn't been checked out yet. He made sure I went first.

Rolling her eyes, Doc flips open her clipboard. "Nevermind."

"What's the prognosis?" he growls, his mouth still pressed against my ear. He slides his hand into the opening along my back and wraps his hand around my hip roughly, drawing me close enough to him that pain ripples up my left thigh. "Sorry," he murmurs, though I didn't say anything. He combs my hair behind my ear and straightens. "Leanna?"

The Doc called Leanna pushes her hair over her shoulder and shakes her head, looking very composed in her straight, white coat. "I have some news on Mer's current and past health conditions that she wanted you to be aware of."

"She did, did she?" He tugs on my hand, but I don't look at him. Eventually, he draws back. Keeping my hand on his lap, he clenches my fingers but there is a breath of space between our bodies. "Tell me."

"As you might have guessed, she has two fractured ribs, which may be life threatening should she so much as lift a grocery bag. The wound on her thigh was unfortunately infected so I've razed out the infected skin and stitched her back together. Unfortunately, the scarring may be," she pauses and I swear vermillion break out across her cheeks. "Substantial," she finishes. "She will have to have plastic surgery to remove the scars fully. Currently the scar tissue spells a word. Spade," she whispers, voice wrought with disbelief.

She shakes her head quickly and rubs her rounded nose. "I'm sorry." Back to business. "Plumeria also has a severely bruised cheekbone and a muscle in her back has been torn. Once she's well enough to walk, I'm prescribing physical therapy for that. You're also going to have to go the route of the Lord and abstain from sex for the next four weeks."

Doc shuts her clipboard and holds it to her breast. "She has some minor tearing of the vaginal walls. I gave her an ultrasound to make sure there weren't any more serious concerns and luckily there aren't, but it was as I was giving her the exam that I noticed she's had Tubal Ligation, or a Tubectomy. She wanted me to let you know that she can't have children."

Silence stretches between us like a rubber band, about to pop. Then Knox clears his throat. "Leave us." Another momentary pause follows before Leanna's white sneakers disappear from my peripheral view.

I hear the door open, but before it closes, Leanna softly says, "I am sorry that this happened to you, Plumeria."

I nod, the door shuts and Knox's hand touches my knee through the mint-colored crepe paper. It's big and flat, spanning my thigh. He squeezes. "Why did you want Leanna to tell me?"

"Because I thought you should know," I mutter.

He talks over me. "Why did you want *Leanna* to tell me?"

I suck in a breath so deep I start to feel dizzy. "Because I didn't want to be the one to drive you away."

"Why would that drive me away?"

I hesitate, hating the sincerity in his tone because I know it means that he isn't listening. Glancing up at him, I hack out, "Because I'm ruined. I mean, for Christ's sake, why do you think my tubes are tied?"

His eyebrows knit together and I find myself getting sucked into his eyes, framed by the straight ridge of his brow. "Tell me."

I scoff. "I was a girl in the cartel. My dad and Loredo sold my virginity when I was twelve, and the guy paid for the surgery. After I healed up he came to do the nasty, but I fought back. Broke the guy's nose. When Loredo found out what happened to one of his best customers, he threw me into the pits and after, when I was on the ground bleeding, he told me that I could either get in line or stay in the pits forever. I chose the pits."

I sigh and clench the bench seat as hard as I can. It doesn't help. My arms are still shaking. "You walk the straight and narrow. I've been a dead girl walking since I was four and Loredo came to my house and murdered my mom and sister. This shit is too messy and I've already got you wrapped up too deep. You're better off just cutting your losses and…"

Knox places his palm over my mouth and kisses the other side of his hand. I pull in a breath through my nose and taste him in the scent. Eucalyptus, musk. Raw masculine perfection. "You deserve happiness and so long as you're mine, that's what you'll get."

"But what do you deserve?" I whisper, pulling back from his hand and gripping it fiercely between my two.

One edge of his mouth cocks up into a charmed smile. "I'd like to try to deserve you." His fingers brush across my cheek and I lean into their pressure. "You've been through more than a human could bear and have survived. But I don't want you to just survive anymore. I want you to live."

The muscles in my back give and I drop forward onto his chest, not caring that it hurts when I bury my face in his shoulder or press myself as close to him as space will allow, and then closer. My muscles burn and there's an aching in my thigh where another man wrote his name in my skin. And Knox is still here. He shouldn't be. He should be dead because of me.

"You don't care about kids?"

"Do I seem like the diapers type?"

I laugh a little bit and feel him open up beneath me. He slides his arms around me gently and pulls me onto his lap. He presses his mouth to my neck. "And no offense, but you definitely don't seem like the diapers type."

"I scare kids."

"Hell, you scare me."

That makes me laugh outright. "*Callate.*"

He kisses me again and breathes into my hair. "You're the only one I want to take care of."

"I want to take care of you too." I sweep my lips over his and he inhales deeply.

His eyes are closed and his back teeth clench and nestled on his lap, I feel the instant his cock hardens. "This is going to be a long month."

I smile, truly hoping that for the next four weeks, a lack of sex will be our biggest problem.

Aiden

The corridors are long and crowded, so I don't blend in. At six-six, two hundred sixty pounds with skin as white as my hair, I don't expect to. That's fine. I don't need to blend in now. Yet.

My Ruger shifts subtly between my shoulder blades, suppressor and booster attachments dropping the tip of the barrel to my lower back. The Ruger's a heavier weapon, but my Walther's too long to wear under my leather coat. Even so, I may be carrying, but I don't bank on killing all five of them today. I don't even know who or where two of them are. The sisters I haven't got names on, but the Russians were easy.

Rooms four sixty eight and four sixty nine. Gavriil and Timur Popov. Brothers. High up in the Russian mafia as far as I know. Heard of a Popov leading the circus this side of the Atlantic a few years back. Not sure who the heads are these days though, this side or the other.

The Popov brothers were just moved to Westfield's West Wing from intensive care as a result of Dixon's handy work. I stop by four sixty eight and lean against the wall. Doctors move quickly from room-to-room, patient-to-patient, and though the nurse's station is within sight not a single one of the three women in floral print scrubs bothers to look up at me. Not with three meth overdoses being wheeled in on separate carts. I've been waiting for over an hour for this kind of good timing.

I pull the chart from the metal tin left of the door and thumb through the pages, then move on to four sixty nine. They've got a severe concussion and a punctured lung between the two of them, not to mention a broken arm, lacerated shoulder muscles, and a couple bruised ribs. Dixon's not one to lose it. Also not one to drink himself to death though that seemed to be his MO last I saw him.

I wonder what I'll do with his request. Dixon may want her dead, but Knox seems pretty bent on keeping the woman alive. I could silence her, but where would that get us? At least, the woman could be a useful source of information – information I wouldn't hesitate to torture out of her, if that were an option – and at best, she could be leverage. Because though none of the guys want to talk about it, we've just stepped into the middle of a war. Against a mob and a cartel we're five men and an army short.

"Crash cart!" someone shouts at the end of the hall. More nurses run past me. Sliding the clipboard back into place I watch one of the meth heads starts to seize. I reach for the doorknob. It's brushed stainless steel and warm, as if recently opened. I pull it towards me and twist so that when I push the door open, it makes no sound, but I'm surprised by what I see when I get the door open two feet. I'm not surprised often.

Somebody's in here and it isn't a Russian. I draw back, furious that the nurses could have switched the boards – a mistake that'll cost lives – but when the girl looks up, her gaze holds me in place.

"*Brivyet...*" That's all I can make out in the spiel she gives me. The only Russian word I know though the girl couldn't look farther from it. Her skin is the color of coffee with too much cream and she's got darker freckles scattered across her whole face, her neck, her chest. Her wrongly colored eyes – one brown, one blue – sit far apart on her face so that she looks as open as the book in her lap.

Her eyebrows crinkle together over a flat brow bone and she says something else but I don't answer. Her knees are curled under her and she's got a purple blanket spread over them. A lamp is on behind her and in the dark room, it illuminates her hair. Falling to her waist in a single braid, her hair is violent red and burns like a torch. It completes the cacophony that is her appearance. Without setting her book aside, she unfurls and begins to stand.

"*Minya...*Alina...*sestra...*" I hear sounds but no meaning, and it isn't just because I don't speak the same language she does. It's because she adjusts her thin gold-rimmed glasses, whose wide lenses remind me of the kind the grandfather used to wear. I never knew if he was a grandfather or not, but that's what he seemed to me when I was eleven, sitting in the park watching him feed the pigeons. Watching him in his small world of happiness is the only thing I can ever remember giving me peace.

"I'm sorry," she says, this time in an accented English, "do you speak Russian?"

I don't answer her, but instead push the door all the way open. There he is. Mr. Gavriil Popov, the taller of the two brothers according to his chart and the one in the most critical condition. Slipping from her grip, the blanket pools around her feet revealing long, lean legs whose definition I can just make out through her opaque black tights.

The book falls to the ground and she jumps as it hits the tiles. She turns to look down at it and I use her momentary distraction to peel away from the door. My fierce strides eat up the length of the hallway and I take the first turn, not knowing where it goes or caring. I don't stop until I'm at my car.

I'm silent for a minute, then I beat my steering wheel until skin comes off of my knuckles. I went off-plan opening the door like that. Careless. Could have been anybody in there – other members of the mafia, members of the cartel... I didn't expect anyone to find the bodies so fast and I didn't expect her. I think the worst thing I did tonight was get distracted. I could have closed the door behind me, killed both Gavriil and the girl in the blink of an eye and walked out, though I had hoped I could just smother the fucker. Would displace suspicion for a few days, at least until I had time to go after the other brother. And now I've got a witness.

She's seen my face, she knows the mafia, and it wouldn't take a detective to figure out who I am. People know me in this town, people recognize me. I wouldn't have gone into the hospital so openly at all if Knox and his woman hadn't been here today. With their presence, mine can be written off. But this...opening the door to that room...seeing her...being seen.

I wrench my coat off and throw my guns onto the floor of the passenger's seat. I roll out my neck, crack my fists and throw the old jalopy into gear. I drive with the windows down and the clean cut of the air clears my thoughts. I'll go back tomorrow, and every other day to scope out the visitors, see if she's the only one, see how much the cartel and the mafia already know. See how much she's told them. Because there's also a chance that tomorrow, she'll be gone and she won't remember my face and I won't have to kill her.

A chance.

But I don't hold my breath.

It's been three weeks and no news. No nothing. Just Mer living in the house, occupying too much space. I can't acknowledge that Clifton and Charlie seem to like her. Feels too much like betrayal. So I content myself instead with remembering the promise Aiden made me when I was at Camelot. Though everything else from that seventy two hour period is hazy, I do remember that much. All I can do is wait for Aiden to work his way through the other names on his list before getting to her.

It's taking him a while – uncommonly long – he's been spending hours at a time at the hospital and elsewhere trying to find an in to off the morons that attacked me. That I attacked. One was discharged unexpectedly and spends his time holed up in a hotel two towns over. He's not the only Mafioso there, which makes entering the place tantamount to impossible. The other one remains in the hospital where he seems to have a constant barrage of visitors, or just one, I'm not sure. Aiden was vague, which is unlike him, but I'm not worried. He always gets the job done.

I spend more time at work than ever. Normally, I'd do all this nonsense from home but my house is occupied by a squatter I can't seem to shake, so I use the office I keep at Camelot, ass planted too many hours a day in Marguerite's chair. Between the bar brawls, some chicks doing coke in the dressing area, and others trying to do johns in the bathrooms to make extra cash, it's our place most deserving of my attention.

Monday morning is sunny for October and I'm squinting against the light that glint off of the storefronts, most of which are closed as this block caters to the after-five crowd. The after-fivers and the delinquents, two of which are stumbling towards Camelot's heavy black door, likely just as drunk as I am even though it's hardly eleven. Camelot's not open to the public quite yet but men's needs don't operate on a clock – neither thirst nor hunger – and they wrench the door open while the bell above their heads jingles.

I'm half a block away and closing, and I'm surprised when the drunks don't walk into the strip club right away but instead canter back, howling. The fatter of the two men rubs his belly salaciously as a girl walks through the door – and she isn't one of my dancers. I curse. Maybe it's just the glare or a product of the Jack and Coke I drank half an hour ago, but for a moment I hallucinate the slut who patched up the Russians well enough to cause me this extra headache.

Ignoring the drunks, she begins rifling through her purse though I can tell the act is perfunctory when she doesn't pull anything out. Instead, she waits a few seconds before looking up, this time directly at me, and I know I'm not mistaken when her skinny arms drop to her sides and her lips part. She stumbles back, nearly falling out of her heels. Paired with a short green skirt, skin tight white tank top and cropped jean jacket, I can't decide if she looks like she *should* be up on one of my stages or courtside at Wimbledon.

The slut from that night runs back into the building and the drunks, heeding her unspoken warning, beat it down the block away from me. They glance over their shoulders and I wonder what they see because they look at me like I'm a monster and I'm feeling monstrous as I follow the slut into the strip club.

I slam the door shut at my back and light turns to dark as the stark black walls and floor of the foyer open up to a massive space that is all bleak and tragic opulence. Like the floor, ceiling, and walls, the tables are black but the chairs are gold and so is the stage. Three gold trapezes hang from the ceiling at equal distances from one another. The girls swing on them naked each Saturday and when we have events but other than that, they're just gaudy decoration.

Glancing at the red velvet curtains framing the gold platform, I'm reminded that my initial vision had been a burlesque bar. However, vision in a city that lacks vision turns burlesque bars into seedy dives where whores strut naked across a stage while men that could never get this close to those kinds of women can do so now...for the right price.

Right now there are no women dancing – there's just a few guys unloading drinks behind the bar and Marcel, standing at one of those black tables while the slut speaks to him rapidly, hands making quick and frantic gestures.

Marcel has a phone in one hand and his face is wreathed in severity, but when his gaze flashes to mine the tension deflates from his arms and he laughs. "New girl nearly had me calling the cops on you, Dixon."

He takes my hand when I approach and I follow the girl with my eyes as she shifts behind him and steps away to the next table, careful to keep its width between us. "New girl?"

Marcel lifts a brow and glances back over his shoulder. "Yeah, Donnie hired her today." I don't miss the way his gaze scans her up and down. A natural blonde with blue eyes and curves in all the right places, she's the girl next door. A good hire, but not one we're making on this day or any other.

"No, he didn't," I say, pivoting then to glare at the girl around Marcel's broad body. "Get out."

Her hands hold her hips and her mouth curls down into a pout. "Who the hell are you?"

Marcel barks out a laugh, which he tries to cover with his hands. Failing, he throws a thumb in my direction. "He's the boss."

"Boss?" She shakes her head. "I met the boss earlier. He hired me."

"And he'll have to suck my cock for even talking to you." I'm not usually so vulgar, but the sight of her brings out the animal in me. She saw me at my weakest and in that moment, showed only strength. I still remember the way the blood had glittered like rubies against her white skin.

Her eyes widen, dark eyelashes arching up to touch light eyebrows. She's wearing makeup, though not enough for a stripper. Nothing about her says stripper except for the fact she was hired as one. "You're the owner?"

I nod.

Her lips form the word 'shit,' but she doesn't speak it out loud. That irks me because she reminds me of Marguerite in that moment, who hated cursing but couldn't keep any of the other brothers from it but me. I don't attribute that to her though. She taught me nothing.

Marcel chuckles. "She brought some of the fire Donnie was looking for – at least that's what he says."

"And she can take it with her." I turn away from them both and head towards my office.

I hear shuffling and a few hushed words spoken angrily before she shouts, "Hey! Hey, hey, hey, I'm sorry. I shouldn't have said what I did but I recognized you from that night off Seventh Street and it freaked me out." She hurries ahead of me and comes to a stop, holding up both hands as if daring me to run straight through her. "You can't fire me though. I've already been hired and signed a contract."

I curse silently, as she had, and stop in my tracks. My office door is just behind her. I'm so close and so far away and while I can at least respect her honesty – an honesty she doesn't try to sugarcoat – it isn't going to get her very far now. "As the owner, I have twenty-four hours to annul a hiring contract put forward by one of my subordinates if the candidate has, in some way, misrepresented themselves in their application or failed to fulfill the full terms of the hiring process."

The girl scoffs, showing contrition poorly. "And what did I do?"

"It's what you didn't." I pull out my keys and brush past her to reach the office door. Her hair smells like apple and cinnamon and autumn when she moves. I wrinkle my nose. "You didn't complete the application."

"I submitted my application online and interviewed with Donnie this morning."

"I have no idea if you can dance. You didn't complete a trial."

"A what?"

"You didn't dance for us. It's part of the application and you didn't complete it," I say, knowing full well that this particular establishment hasn't been able to conduct business that way since the previous owners lost the law suit against them for sexual harassment. Along with general mismanagement, it was one of the reasons they had to sell.

"Wait," she says as I turn the key and push open the door, the stale scent of beer clashing with that of her hair and her skin, which reek of Fall. "But I prepared a routine! Donnie just didn't ask me to do it."

That stops me dead. "You prepared a routine?"

She nods, low lights from between the window slats cutting horizontal streaks across her face and hair. For the first time, I take a moment to actually look at her. Narrow chin, heart shaped face, dark blonde hair layered beneath the light. Long lashes blink over eyes that are sapphire blue. "Yeah. I'll do it right now."

Sheer disbelief makes me smirk. "Alright, let's see it."

"Sure." She pushes her fingers back through her hair and I notice that it isn't all dry and tattered at the ends like the other blondes that work for me. Blondes are more popular with this crowd and even without having seen her dance, I know she'd do well for the business. The only reason not to hire her is because of what she knows, but if she hasn't gone to the police yet there's no reason to think she will. Maybe I should tell Aiden to forget it altogether. Maybe not. Maybe I should call him to come in a few minutes, once I have her alone…

"Now."

"Why not?" She shrugs and is pure confidence. Somehow, and maybe it's just the shadows dancing over her flesh, she looks different than she did before.

She's paved me into a corner and, unwilling to back down, I relent. Moving back out into the main room, I give her my hand to help her onto the stage. The guys at the bar cheer.

"Gentlemen, out," I bark, and the ensuing groans commence. If I'm going to torture the girl, it'll be a private show. "What did you choreograph your routine to?" My tone is mocking.

She doesn't rise to it. "Do you have Wicked Games by the Weeknd?"

The choice surprises me. Any other girl would have picked top forties and she picks something dark and twisted. "I'm sure we do." The room clears, I step into the DJ booth against the back wall and she strips off her jacket and moves towards the back of the stage. I scroll through Donnie's iTunes until I find, not the song she likes, but one she won't, then I grab the remote control. When I'm sure we are totally alone, I push play and take the cushioned throne reserved for high paying guests in the center of the room.

"Very funny," she drawls, voice ripe with sarcasm.

"You can adapt, can't you? One of the requirements of any good dancer."

I expect her to roll her eyes, stick out her tongue – something. Instead, the fixed grin she wears widens, the one that works better than any mask because I can't see through it. It bothers me that she uses the same coping mechanism I do. Only in reverse. My apathy to her cheer — I wonder which one comes out on top. I guess in a few minutes, I'll find out...

"Of course," she says with a slight nod.

"I think I'm going to enjoy this."

She winks and I'm annoyed at the sudden sensation tugging at my lips. I'm smiling against my best efforts. "I know you will."

"Then what are you waiting for? The stage is yours."

Some terrible song by Flo Rida drifts through the speakers and I turn up the volume until I'm sure the bums can hear it on the street. She backs away from the stripper pole and comes at it in a run, then she leaps. She catches the pole, legs flaring out wide so I get a full glimpse of her white lace panties before her thighs clamp around the pole six feet up.

She works her way higher and higher, then drops all at once, hair grazing the gold stage below. She plants her hands, rises up to stand and as she looks at me with flushed cheeks I'm thankful only that my mouth is closed. The girl actually knows how to dance.

I don't swallow. I don't betray any emotion. I don't want her to know just how right she was about everything and I don't want her to think that this will change my decision. It won't. It can't. Far too much is at stake for me to be swayed by the sight of her twisting around the stripper pole, hips moving with a rhythm most white girls can't touch. Worse, most strippers dance dead-eyed and make sure not to meet any of the customers' gazes directly but hers doesn't let up.

She spins, landing with her back against the pole and while her hair flies around her shoulders, settling against her cheeks, she looks at me and smiles in a way that makes me feel fully exposed even though I'm the one fully clothed and still seated.

"You know you have to take your clothes off at some point, right?" I hack out in an effort to unseat her.

She doesn't so much as blink. "I'm getting to that." She slides into a split then, moving onto her back, lifts both legs and crosses them at the ankles. Like this, I get a full view of her panties. They cup her perfect ass and if I pulled them aside an inch, I'd see pussy.

The thought makes my mind wander, wondering what it looks like. Does she have a big clit or a tiny one? What about pussy lips that I can suck all the way into my mouth? I close my eyes for a moment and in the darkness I hear the pounding of my own heart over the sound of the bass and the beat of the treble. I've got an erection that makes me feel like a boy because even though I've owned Camelot for the past nine years, I've never been affected like this by a dancer. Watching her on stage now, I realize I'm not teaching this slut a lesson. It's the other way around.

On her knees, she lowers her skirt to the stage and kicks it over the platform's edge when she stands. Pulling herself up on the pole, she bends backward towards me, her leg the only thing holding her up. Forming a perfect U, she strips her shirt off over her head and lets it fall in a loose ring around her hair.

She twists twice more around the pole and I only get a complete picture when she steps in front of it and spreads her legs. She dips her hips and I try to think of painful things, because my cock is an angry pressure against my belt and I don't have a second to rearrange it with her watching me like that. The girl's in all white lace and looks like a virginsaintangelsiren and both all wrong and entirely right standing against so much gold and black.

"Stop," I say, turning down the music. Another song has come on but I can't remember when the last one ended.

She smiles at me and swings around the pole. With her head tilted to the side, and her ankles crossed, she says, "Had enough?"

The storm in my belly rumbles hungrily. She'll pay for that one. "You're not finished yet."

"I'm happy to continue."

"You will. Down here. I need to see if you can do a lap dance comfortably," I say, words leaping from my lips before my mind fully forms the concepts. I just want to make her cringe, make her uncomfortable in the way that I am. It isn't working.

"Sure thing."

"Full nude," I add.

"I wouldn't have expected anything less. It's a strip club, after all." She winks in a way that does nothing to alleviate the tension in my groin and steps to the very edge of the stage.

Reaching around her back, she unbuckles her bra, lets it float down her arms and jumps onto the floor a few feet from where I'm seated. She's got perfect tits, but I knew that already. Full and clearly natural, they sit high on her chest. Her nipples are pink and hard already and I pray that Marcel thought to turn the cameras off because I'm a sexual harassment suit waiting to happen.

I blink longer than necessary and the momentary darkness helps sober me. I've got both feet planted on the floor and one hand under my chin, the other on the arm of the chair. I grip it tighter than I need to as she drops her panties. I don't look at her below the waist, but instead focus on her face and that brilliant, wicked expression. It taunts me, and in the game we are playing I am nearly satisfied accepting that she has complete and utter control over the situation because to do otherwise brings a sharp and cutting pain to the hardened shaft between my legs. It wants her.

"Are you going to turn the music up?" The remote control rests between my legs and she reaches for it.

That I don't react is the only thing I'm proud of in that moment. She cranks the music up – some song by Miguel – turns away from me and lifts her hair away from the back of her neck so that the whole of her backside is bare. She keeps her legs together and sinks into a low seat. Her ass meets the erection throbbing on the underside of my zipper and I curl my fingers so hard into the arm of the chair, velvet rips off around the tacks.

I want to tell her she isn't allowed to touch the clientele, but I know that my voice will break if I speak. Plus, I like the sensation too much. Enough to be reminded that she's a clear autumn breeze and I've spent the past days swimming in the bottom of a handle. She smiles at me as sweetly as a Disney princess posing for kids at Disney Land, rather than on her hands and knees on the floor of my strip club. When she rises, she loses her balance and catches herself on my chest.

"Sorry," she whispers, tone dangerously real for just an instant before it too becomes a mask. "I hope that isn't a fireable offense."

She lifts her right leg high and straddles my thigh and when I look down, I catch a flash of that pink prize before slamming my eyes shut. I want to respond to her quip, but my tongue is lodged in the back of my throat. I clear it while she continues to dance inches from me, undulating in a sexy wave. I want to touch her, but don't, and then in an instant everything changes. I don't hear the back door open, but it makes a hell of a racket when it clangs shut.

I shoot up onto my feet and the slut – the girl – falls back. She catches my arm as I cradle the backs of her elbows with my hands, which feel massive against her slight frame. Somewhere in the ballpark of hopeful, her expression is one I can't decipher and I don't have time to probe when the one person I'd wanted to show up – now the last person I want to see – strolls into the room.

"Aiden." My voice isn't my own. It's gravel, a depth that I feel rumbling through my gut.

Taking the girl by the hands, I guide her into the shadow of my body. My adrenaline is still racing, and I feel more sober than I have in days though I wish I weren't. Because it's in that moment I realize something critical: I'm protecting her. Aiden crosses his arms over his chest and remains immobile in all but the eyes, which seek to find what it is I'm hiding. I need to explain before he does something drastic. Or irrevocable.

"What do you have there?" His voice is a slow, insidious snarl.

"Aiden, turn around."

He begins reaching into his coat. "Your friend looks familiar."

"Aiden!" My voice echoes off of the ceiling and walls and I pull the girl close to me so that I can feel her heat like a blanket against my spine. "Turn around."

"No."

I clench my back teeth, knowing that he's in a foul mood otherwise he wouldn't be baiting me like this. "Hold on." I turn, shrug out of my jacket and wrap it around her mid-section. Snatching her clothes and purse off of the floor, while being careful not to step too far away from her, I lower my voice. "Go to my office, wait for me in there and don't touch anything."

She spares a curious glance over my shoulder at Aiden, runs her fingers through her hair and flushes for no reason I can identify. But she doesn't protest, even though I half expect her to. I wait until I hear the office door open and shut, then I close the distance between my brother and I by half. "She's the witness who saw me brawl with the Popov brothers, but she works here now. I'm keeping an eye on her to make sure she doesn't talk."

"You don't want her quiet?" Aiden asks, voice lifeless as he talks about lifelessness.

"She's been quiet and she'll stay that way."

Aiden stares probingly at my face for a moment before casting a final glance towards my office. I flinch towards it. "Fine. That's not what I came here for anyway."

"What is it?" I exhale, relieved in a way that I hate.

"Ollie got jumped by a group of Russians. They thought he might know where Loredo is."

"Loredo? I thought the Russians were looking for their boy, Spade."

"Not these guys."

I pause. "Any idea why?"

"No."

My mind is a fog, blood still pumping through my erection making it harder to focus. I shut the music off but that hardly helps as the sight of the stage is a better visual aid than any song. Every time I blink I see her prowling towards me like I'm prey.

"Thanks for telling me. I'll wrap up here and head to the house."

"You do whatever you want. I'm going back to the hospital. Knox, Mer, and Charlie are going down to the barn. Charlie's fighting tonight and Mer's agreed to take over the bar with Griffin's little brother as her bar back."

"And Clifton?"

"At Ollie's apartment."

"Is Ollie okay?"

"Got a broken arm, but he'll live. Seems like the Russians were just sending a message."

"Yeah, but to who?"

Aiden shrugs. "Hard to say."

I hang my head and massage the bridge of my nose. "Okay."

Aiden nods once and leaves the way he came. I wait until I hear the door slam shut before hurrying back to my office.

There's no other way in than through the front door, but there are windows, and I'm not fully convinced that Aiden wouldn't call an audible and make a decision that would mean nothing to him and might haunt me. Her pussy on my mind, her brains splattered across my desk.

I push the door open, evidently startling her because she jumps. "Dang," she exhales clutching her chest. "Is everything okay?"

"That's really none of your business," I snarl, coming off meaner than I intended. I'm pissed I stood up for her, pissed Aiden walked in on us in the first place, pissed about Ollie, about Knox and the fact that he's taken one of my businesses away from me, about Mer, most of all, the bitch who started this.

I notice my laptop sits open on my desk and I slam it shut, then pick it up and fold it under my arm. I cock my head. "Out."

Wordlessly, she hoists her purse up onto her shoulder and heads back into the club. I start to follow her, then pause as my gaze drops to her long, lean legs peeking out from beneath the edge of her short skirt. My cock is still a halfie though my mind is a million other places. Still, it's because of that halfie that I open up my personal safe – not the bar's – and peel a few hundred off in fifties from the nearest stack.

She hovers by the table closest to the door and I admire her for a moment as she's looking in the other direction. Long throat, graceful hands. Among other things. "I'm sorry, I shouldn't have pried," she says, turning.

She wasn't prying. She knows she wasn't prying. I know she wasn't prying. "Fine." I step too close to her, fully invading her space, and grab her hand. I crumple money into it. "I've got rules," I say without releasing her. "You break them, you're out."

Surprise, concern, a tilting of the head, and then, "Does that mean I'm in?" Her lips creep up into that slow smile that's nothing if not persistent. I nod once and she claps her hands together. As she bounces lightly in her heels, she teeters dangerously and I grab her by the elbow to keep her standing. "Sorry," she whispers, brushing the hair from her face. "And thank you. And…" Finally finding her fist and the cash I smashed in it, her cornflower gaze glitters. "What is this?"

"Earnings," I grunt. I'm all grunts today, no eloquence. I need a drink. Maybe drinks are my issue. Even if that's true it doesn't curb the need or the action of my hand reaching across the bar for a bottle. I pour some into my mouth as I head to the back door. She stumbles after me.

"Woah. This is seven hundred dollars."

"It is."

"I don't understand."

I sigh, exhausted, "Three fifty's the going rate for a private show. The rest is for the lap dance."

In the hallway by the dressing rooms, she stares at the cash she holds between us and I catch a glimpse of true emotion in her face the first time all day. She's desperate and it shows. Maybe more than most of the girls that work in this place. Maybe more than most of the men. Everything about her cuts into me like salt and sadness.

"Doesn't the club usually take most of this?"

"I am the club. So not today."

"Wow." She licks her lips and that cheerful smile returns, the real girl behind it erased. "Thanks..."

I cut her off. "I said there were rules. The first is never to leave the building without an escort from one of the bouncers, bartenders, or managers. A male escort. I don't even want you stepping outside for a smoke alone."

"I don't smoke," she says.

"Good. You come in a car?" She nods and moves forward as I hold the back door open for her, then steps out into the narrow parking lot wedged behind the building. Cool wind carries the scent of an arriving winter and complements the smell of her hair, which is untouched by the air freshener we use inside. I inhale deeply through my nose.

"Park here next time. If the lot's full, call into the bar and one of the boys will walk you from Mercer." She smirks at that. I ignore her. "When did Donnie schedule your debut?"

"Wednesday."

I grunt.

"Pardon me?" she asks and I try not to look at her. When I blink, I picture her twisting around the pole like a snake, or better yet, gliding between my legs on her knees. It's been too long since I've been laid. My mind flickers back to the brunette I banged in a motel a few weeks ago. I've been celibate since. I think briefly about ending the nightmare tonight with Mindy, one of the strippers from Camelot. I could bend her over my desk and screw this blonde free of my memory, the only hiccup being that I told myself when I bought the joint I wouldn't mess with any of the dancers. There's too much drama there and I don't plan on changing that because of a blonde with a tight ass and a wily smile.

I realize I haven't answered her when we reach the corner of Prospect. She hangs a left onto Eighth, catching my sleeve to stop me when I do the same. A car breezes past us — one I don't recognize. The windows are tinted and the ivory Mercedes has dealer plates. I watch it drive past as a distraction from the pressure of her hand on my arm and I wonder if she senses my discomfort because she pulls away quickly.

"Wednesday tends to get relatively busy. Most girls debut Tuesday night," I respond.

"Donnie said as much, but I have class Tuesday nights. I'm really sorry, but it's a lab and there was no way for me to get out of it."

"So you are a med student."

"Yes, sir." She pulls out her keys and it doesn't occur to me right away that this is her car until she turns the key in the lock and pulls open the door. It's nearly rusted shut and she has to use most of her bodyweight to wrench the thing ajar. When she does, it seems to hang on by threads. My guess is that the 1988 Volkswagen was most recently painted red, but in the places where rust shines through the roof I can see a melee of other colors — blue, green and yellow, all the colors of a bruise. The tires are bald and I find myself breathing hard through my nose, arms clenched tight to my sides. I'm angry. And it's what I find in the backseat that really tops me off.

"You got a kid?"

"I do," she says and she smiles that same irritating smile. The slut. The whore. The mother. I feel the erection in my pants still lingering and in my mouth, I taste poison.

"And you drive this?"

"I sure do."

"Your baby daddy lets you drive his kid around in this?" I repeat.

Her mouth twists – still not a frown. "Nobody lets me do anything, and yes. This is the car I drive."

I take a step towards her though I don't know why I bother. Slut's a slut. I shouldn't let this bit of information take me by surprise. "I took you for responsible."

Her teeth press against her lips. "You may take me sir, for whatever you like so long as I've got a job."

"You'll only keep that job if you follow the rules."

"You said so before." She throws her purse into the car and plants her hands on her hips. A slight twitch in her cheek is the only reaction she gives me, the only indication that true emotion hides somewhere beneath the surface of that freakishly effusive veneer. "Park in the lot, get an escort. Anything else?"

"No kids, no men, no drama." I hold up my pointer finger. My middle lifts alongside it. "No fucking the customers in or outside of the club. I don't care how desperate you are."

Not an inch of her moves except for her eyelids as she blinks, and somehow that small act seems to change everything about her expression. Her smile is still slight and fixed, but her gaze pans past me, seeing through me to something else. Or maybe the opposite. Maybe she sees me for what I really am. A monstrosity among men.

"I signed on to be a stripper, not a prostitute."

"I wasn't sure after your performance."

"I'm sorry, was it in some way unsatisfactory?" She glances towards her car, and I understand that she wants to get into it and get away from me but something keeps her from it: desperation. And the desperation that I'm throwing in her face now is the same one that I exploited earlier.

I take a step towards her, feeling heat in my arms that I don't often feel – an irony given that the last time I felt this way I was also with her, though the situation couldn't have been more different. Then I was trying to keep her from being slaughtered.

"You don't touch the customers. They don't touch you."

"Funny you didn't mention that earlier."

My rage spikes and I press her backwards until she's right up against the opening of her car. The position is menacing and I know if I saw us standing like this from the other end of the block, I'd call the cops or intervene myself.

"Maybe I was wondering how far a little slut like you would take it. You seemed eager enough to do anything for the right price. You still do. And I don't want any of that shit in my bar."

"I got it." Her voice is louder than it had been, and severe, and then all at once it breaks as she spits, "Is that all?" She coughs into her fist and the ball of rage and tension in my chest bursts.

"What are you even doing here? Have you ever set foot in a strip club before today?" I grab the edge of her car door and paint flakes off against my rough hands. It's cold to the touch and feels flimsy enough to snap myself.

"That's really none of your business," she says, parroting my own words back to me before reapplying that saccharine grin to her face. "Are those all the rules you have? If so, then I really should be going."

I bare my teeth but she doesn't break, so I cock my chin towards her car. She gets in and I slam the door shut before she can reach for its handle. Her ignition clicks again and again before finally catching, then she drives off. She doesn't look back – better that way. I don't need to be caught in the memories of yet another crap mom.

Sara

Sherry flips back long, vivacious curls and traps her straw between her lips. She sucks hard, though her drinks are almost empty and flashes do me eyes to the bartender. Instead of giving her anything for free, he chuckles to himself.

Amber sits up higher on her barstool and tugs hard on the wrists of her long-sleeved shirt. "My lord, Sherry, do you have to be such a tramp?"

"My lord, Amber, do you have to be such a trout?" Sherry fires back.

I laugh hard and sweep my hand back through my hair. It's greasy at the roots. I haven't had time to wash it between running from the hospital, home, and back again. This is the first night off I've had in three weeks – since Brant came into my life – and I feel guilty without him now. I just love him so much. I worry about him alone with Stephanie, even if she is Amber's little sister. Brant's not even six months. What if he gets scared without me? He's probably still in shock after losing his mom...

"Stop looking at your phone," Sherry says, slamming her hand onto the flat face of my cell just as I reach for it. "And tell me more about this new boss of yours at the club," she leers, "I still can't believe you're doing this. You just went from my most responsible friend to complete badass."

"Don't be so crass, Sher," Amber mumbles on Sherry's other side. "You know she's only doing this because you convinced her it would be more lucrative than working at some place respectable." She turns to me then and ruffles her brown hair. "At least until you pay your med school loans off and land that amazing residency at Westfield Hospital, like you know you deserve." Her plump pink lips lift and so does her margarita. Margarita Mondays at Cactus were our favorite when we were undergraduate students and even though it feels so good to be here now, I'm still feeling guilty.

I take a sip and open my mouth, but Sherry speaks first. "Fuck that. To being a goddamn stripper and proud of it!" She throws her arm in the air and margarita sloshes over the side of her cup.

"Woohoo," I cheer, laughing harder. "To being a stripper!"

"She's a *dancer*. A dancer," Amber mumbles, a flare of red igniting her cheeks. I'm glad I've come to terms with what I'm doing and why I'm doing it, because I don't have that reaction anymore. I guess, in a funny way, I've got Dixon to thank for that. I didn't think it would be so easy to take off all my clothes and dance nasty on a stranger but trying to prove something to him made it easy. What was I trying to prove? Absolutely no idea.

I drain my margarita and order a water, though what I really want is a third margarita. I suck on an ice cube, hoping to cool down because the bar is full – but not crowded – while Sherry tells me all about the Tinder date she had the day before and Amber rebukes her for it. As Amber desperately tries to steer the conversation towards her job at the physical therapy clinic, a guy slides onto the barstool beside me.

He's far from the first guy to try ruining girl's night, but his pickup line does draw my attention: "So if you work at Camelot, then you must know Dixon."

"Wow," I say turning reflexively, though the other guys I've succeeded in brushing off. "That's a lot of assumptions."

He looks me up and down, but in a way that doesn't make me feel totally dirty. Then he shrugs. "There's a few strip clubs off the block, but Camelot is the only nice one. I figure a girl that looks like you probably works at the nice one is all. The brothers run Camelot and most everything else in this town, but Dixon's the only one that spends any time there."

"Dixon," I say with a gulp. "Is he…he's the one with the uhh…"

The guy laughs at my struggle and runs his hand back through his hair. "He's tall, dark and yeah, I can see how a woman might find him pretty good looking."

Laughing uncomfortably myself, I let the curtain of my hair fall between us. On my other side, Sherry gives me a lecherous grin. "You didn't tell us the dick who made you dance for him was tall, dark, and handsome."

"Seriously?" Amber balks. "After what he did, you get *that* reaction when this nice man so much as mentions his name." She rolls her eyes. "I don't even recognize you anymore."

"Sorry, I didn't mean to get you in trouble." The man angles his body to face mine and while I'm not attracted to him, I can understand why Sherry has scooted her barstool six inches closer. Noticing, he flashes her a smile.

I make way for Sherry and a less-excited Amber to crowd in. "No, you're fine. But sorry – how do you know Dixon?"

"I don't. Just heard about him. He and his brothers own all of Seventh and most of the surrounding blocks so it makes me curious."

"He owns this place too?" I glance over each shoulder, worried I might see him here and feel like there's something else that I owe him.

He nods. "Yeah, Cactus too."

I mouth the word 'shit,' though I don't say it out loud. Instead, my hand reaches for the cross around my neck. The man's grey gaze flashes to the pendant, then he smiles at me thoughtfully. "So can you give me any insiders?"

"To be honest, no. I didn't even know his name was Dixon," I confess, shouting to be heard over the din of the music.

"Her first day is only on Wednesday. I'd say you should stop by and see her, but maybe you should stop by and see me instead." Sherry leans over my legs in order to rest her hand on his knee. Her dyed honey curls fall in a magnificent wave over my arms as I reach for my drink and try not to spill it.

Our new friend straightens up and the grin he sports lights up his pale cheeks. His hair is short, dark brown and he's got a scar that snakes back past his ear, disrupting his hairline. "That's quite the offer," he says slowly and I laugh again. When I flip back my hair, the first thing I see is

Amber, rolling her eyes, and behind her, three men watching us from afar.

"What's your name?" The man asks, reclaiming my attention.

"I'm Sherry." As she stretches out her left hand, her right snakes further up his leg.

"Oh my gosh," Amber crows.

I grab Sherry's hand and place it back in her lap despite her pouts and protests. "Sorry about that," I say with emphasis.

The man laughs. He's got an easy laugh that he's quick to share. Genuine, in a real unapologetic kinda way. "No apologies necessary. And you are?"

"I'm Sara."

"Sara, Sherry and..." He looks to Amber, who introduces herself, at which point he says, "Nice to meet you, ladies. I'm Neil."

Sherry barely lets the poor man finish. "So Neil, what do you do?"

"Nothing quite as exciting as Sara here, I'm sure."

"Bold sir," I say with a giggle – a gosh darn giggle. "Teasing me when I barely know anything about you. Tsk, tsk." I poke his shoulder. Am I flirting? Is this flirting? After my last relationship ended at the same time I took Brant, I didn't think I'd be back to flirting for a long time. And shoving my crotch in some strangers face so he'll hire me doesn't count.

Neil massages his shoulder, feigning injury. "You know what? Maybe I will come see you on Wednesday." He winks.

Even Amber cracks at that one and soon we're launched into a deep discussion of all kinds of things. I want to stay and talk the whole night away, but I can't keep Stephanie up on a school night so I head out around eleven. When Neil finds out we didn't drive, he offers to chauffeur us home. Ordinarily, I would say no, but two margaritas plus Sherry's evident infatuation dissuades me from finding the bus. Half an hour later, I'm skipping up to my front door.

It's crazy how excited I get to see Brant every time we're apart for more than an hour, and though poop and pee and tears might deter others, I'm glad enough that he's still awake. That means, I'll get to spend time with him.

"Hey!" Stephanie stands up the minute I walk through the door. She's got a crying baby bundled in her arms – my crying baby – and I swoop down on her as she issues me a whole slew of apologies.

"Stephanie, you're fine!" I laugh and kiss baby Brant on the cheek. He smells like baby powder and baby oil and diapers. He's perfect. His little caramel cheeks quiver when I kiss them again and again and finally, I pull back and he's quiet. His doe eyes blink at me. They sit too big on his face and in their depths, I can see my whole face reflected.

"Oh my god, I can't believe it. He's been crying all night. I tried everything…the bottle, the pacifier, reading to him, rocking him…"

"I know, and I am so sorry. He's like this a lot at daycare too." I hoist him up on my hip and his chubby little hands reach for my hair, trying to draw it into his mouth. I tickle the tips of my blonde locks against his own black curls, then trickle them down to his nose and mouth and neck. He giggles wildly, nearly shrieking in a delight that fills my whole body with warmth.

Meanwhile, Stephanie is staring at me with her mouth open. She has the same auburn hair her sister does, and is just as compassionate. I hate making her do this, but there is no one else I trust who has this kind of availability. At least, no one else within my price range. I hand her sixty dollars for watching Brant for the past six hours and she takes it with such a heavy sigh of relief that I hand her ten dollars extra. I can afford ten extra dollars after what Dixon gave me. I try not to think about him as I carry Brant against my chest to the bedroom. He's got his arms tucked between us and his head on my shoulder. His diaper's dry and for that I'm grateful.

I lay him down on the little co-sleeper crib extension that abuts my bed and quickly shower off, then climb into bed beside him. In the dim glow of the nightlight against the far wall, I watch him take slow, even breaths. His cheeks are round and his nose is round and his brow bone is flat and he's so freaking beautiful.

I don't know what his father looked like, but he has Lilian's lips and her same tiny ears. This little boy is the only piece of her left and I will do anything to give him the best life. Eight hundred dollars will put him into the nice daycare – the one on Stone Avenue near the mansion district – for five days a week. Even if it's only a month, it's better than leaving him with the series of sitters he's been staying with. So yeah, if rubbing my cooter all over a stranger will change my little man's odds of surviving this crazy world, I'm fine with that. Just as long as next time, it's not Dixon.

Aiden

They're looking for something. The three Russians that were upstairs have moved to the parking lot. They stand out in the open near a white Mercedes, leaving me no space to creep closer without detection. The dealer plates on the Benz don't give me much to work with either.

I glance at my watch. It's half past three and the sun has moved beyond its highest point in the sky so that I'm cast in the building's shadow. I have some time to linger in this invisibility though I know I shouldn't. I should forget about the Russians in the lot and return to the West Wing where Gavriil Popov lies awake and defenseless. I should go end it this second, plug two bullets into his skull. Bam bam. Done. I should, but I'd rather be here because he's still got a goddamn visitor. The same goddamn visitor. And I hate the way she looks at me. Such innocence. Like I could be anyone but the man sent to kill her brother.

Alina Popov. Gavriil and Timur's half-sister. She's there every single day. From noon to two on Mondays and Wednesdays, ten to three on Tuesdays, four to six on Thursdays, four to eight on Fridays, and on Saturdays and Sundays she spends most of the day at the hospital. Every other Sunday morning, she goes to church. She brings the orderlies and nurses small gifts each Saturday morning and they, in turn, let her sneak in meals from the outside. The entire unit's infatuated with her. I hear the male doctors and nurses talking about her when I snake up and down the halls – one surgeon in particular seems to have developed a particular affection for the girl.

Alina Popov. She's a law student at Echardt College of Law, a small, expensive, private liberal arts university two towns over. She drives a mint green Fiat, is a registered Democrat, participates in her university's mock trial, volunteers at a nursing home on Monday and Wednesday nights and each time she comes to the hospital, she takes time to visit the kids in the children's cancer wing. She's also a model and features frequently in fashion magazines as well as our local tabloids.

I have some information compiled on the brothers but not nearly as extensive. I don't know why. And the information I have on the Russians crowded around the car is weak. Overall, I've counted roughly nine of them who are involved in searching for whatever it is that's lost. They typically arrive in twos, though today there are three. The other brother, Timur, is here today and went into Gavriil's room with two Russians.

Alina stepped out and the surgeon with the hard-on for her used the opportunity to try to talk to her at the nurse's station. She seemed agitated, constantly glancing at the door, so I slipped into the adjacent room. Through the thin walls I could hear Russian words thrown angrily back and forth. The words were too muffled to capture on my phone. Too muffled and too brief.

Leaving less than five minutes in, they went straight to the parking lot and tore apart three cars in the lot – including the

Fiat. My hands twitched towards my guns and I found myself compelled to intervene as they threw law textbooks, tablets, and fashion magazines onto the asphalt. I didn't, recognizing that there was no reason for these acerbic feelings.

A younger man that I haven't seen before is leading the trio and when he drives off in the white Mercedes, the two remaining men climb into a second black Benz. Timur joins them and together, they head down Nineteenth in the opposite direction. I step into the center of the lot. Even in green surgical scrubs and a mask, I look out of place, so I don't linger as I canvas the items the Russians threw away.

A cell phone charger and three power banks, contents of an overnight bag – men's gym shorts, boxers, tee shirts, toothpaste – plus a dozen fast food wrappers and gas station receipts. Not much, but I do snatch the receipts from the ground. The first one's from Lexington. That's three towns over. A couple others are closer than that. Several are from in town, but over half are out of state. Well out of cartel territory. I thought they'd come for the big guy Knox killed, but if they were, they wouldn't be here now ransacking some half-dead Mafioso's truck. They're looking for something else, something smaller.

A harsh breeze blows past, scattering some of the trash. A Chik-fil-A wrapper lands near the Fiat. My feet wander towards it and though I should get back inside, my body doesn't yield to my mind's resistance. I stop at a large, leather purse fallen on its side, contents spewing out near the back left tire. A black dress lies half outside of it, along with a hair brush, a comb, a towel and a pair of panties. Also black.

I lower myself into a crouch and before I can think too much about my actions, I bring the dress to my nose. It smells like her. A concentration of rain and cardamom and some kind of flower. Christ, it smells good. I shove the dress back into the bag, the brush, the comb, the towel, the panties. I grab the textbooks and the papers and shove them in too. The Russians left the car doors wide open so I don't have trouble getting inside. I throw the bag into the trunk, lock the car and head to my own.

I drive for what might be hours or minutes and find myself at Renway Mall in the perfume department. I've smelled two dozen bottles but I can't find the one I want. "If you're not...satisfied by any of these..." The woman who's been attempting to attend to me edges back nervously when I look at her.

She points to a locked case in the corner I hadn't seen. "We've got more expensive brands, but I do mean much more expensive. They range from three hundred to over a thousand dollars..."

"Let me see."

She spritzes just two paper white tiles before I find the one I'm searching for. It's in a gold tear-shaped bottle. A large number one is scrawled on its smooth surface beneath a man's name. Christian something. "That one," I tell her.

"A sample size, sir, or the bottle?"

"The bottle."

"Are you sure, sir? It's eight hundred..."

"The bottle."

Her eyes widen and I see her look at me the way women look at men they want. Women look at my twin like that, not me, and I'm made uncomfortable by it. Her grin turns from frightened to eager and when she flips back her dyed blonde hair, I can tell she's trying to be brave as I hand her my credit card.

"No bag, no box." I hold out my hand and she places the jar of perfume in it along with a scrap of paper marked by a name I don't care about, and a sequence of numbers. Taking back my card, I turn from her and chuck the paper as I walk.

It's been five weeks since I've been at the barn, but nobody's keeping me away any longer. Cooped up in the house all day, I'm so damn bored. So. Damn. Bored. "Put that box here, kid," I shout over the sounds of a brawl. It's fresh blood night and two college kids are beating the shit out of each other. From the little I've seen of the fight from behind the bar, their forms are fucking terrible. Not like I have strong legs to stand on. Literally. The wound on my side has turned into a scar, one that spells the name of a ghost whose presence I carry with me. In the night, wrapped in Knox's arms, I hear him whisper my name.

"Mer, where do you want these?" Morgan is big and I'm sure his size is the only reason no one messes with him, because the kid's a huge softie.

"Full or empties?"

"Empties."

"Back out by the smoker's shed."

Balancing two huge boxes in his arms, he edges behind me and out of the back door just as the crowd surges towards the pit. They're pushed back by the boys standing along the pit's perimeter. Knox is among them. He came down to check on me, but he stayed to help maintain order. It's a lie, but it's what he tells me. He's worried and I don't blame him. We haven't heard from the cartel or the Russians since

Dixon's initial brush with them, though they must be looking for the men they lost. We didn't cover our tracks well. Aiden said that when he went back to recon the barn last week somebody'd been through it. Maybe more than one somebody.

They'd torn apart the house and all the shitty furniture, but didn't seem so concerned with the backyard, where there were evident marks charring the earth. Wouldn't they have wanted to know if their men had been burned or if their bodies had been buried? I don't know. I know nothing except that I want to keep Knox and his brothers living. Aiden's still on the hunt but can't get close enough to do the deed without witnesses. The thought makes me shudder. The brothers are all clean but Aiden – and now Knox – and it terrifies me that those two now fall into the same category.

"How are things going?" someone shouts at me from across the rickshaw bar.

I look up. "*Hijo de tu puta madre.* Look who's risen. How you been?"

Ollie lets his cast thump down onto the upturned crates and flips me the bird with his free hand. "Never better. I figure it's karmic revenge."

I pull a beer from the ancient sub-zero behind me and crack the top, slam it down. "How you figure that?" He opens his mouth to answer, but the crowd goes wild and drowns him out.

I smile, even though a fierce and consuming emptiness inflates in my chest, like a sad balloon. As much as being back in the barn is a relief for me, I'm still filled with tortured thoughts of Mario. I try to repress them like I do all painful things but every once in a while the husky sound of men laughing or flesh smacking against flesh reminds me of the fights we used to have when we were just two kids trying to survive our ruined childhoods. The smell of blood takes me to those moments when he would slap Band-Aids over my wounds and take me back to the ring after I lost a fight. He'd make me practice against him again and again until I never lost a fight to a bigger opponent.

He was a good big brother until he started getting more responsibility in the drug game. I refused. Loredo had me beaten for it. *Padre* had me beaten for it. Even Mario thought it was weakness that kept me from it, even though it was just indifference. He was a good big brother but a bad man, and I still loved him.

"Mer?"

I look up with a start. "Yeah? Sorry, you were saying?"

"What were you thinking about?"

"Karmic revenge. Same as you."

Smiling, he takes a sip from his drink, then inhales deeply. He shakes his head – or maybe it's a shudder. The skinny kid's oversized tee hides too much of his body for me to be sure. "Just working in this place every day, watching ugly mother fuckers beat the crap out of each other and profiting from it. It only makes sense that I get beat up by a group of ugly mother fuckers."

I laugh. "Yeah, actually I can understand that. Karma's come after my ass many times. I'm starting to wonder if I haven't started racking up some kind of cosmic credit."

Laughing with me, Ollie chugs half of his beer before setting it down. He pushes the long, oily hair from his forehead and as I turn to hand someone else a couple beers, he leans across the bar. The whole thing threatens to topple and we both overreact, reaching to stabilize it at the same time. I grin. He doesn't.

"So I actually wanted to ask you..." He licks his lips and I notice they're dry. His eyes are red and he's got a vein throbbing near his right temple. "What happened when you were alone with Spade and Loredo?"

"Woah, Ollie. Out of line."

"Sorry." He touches his hair again, slicking it back along his hairline, and polishes off his beer. "Just...did they talk...about anything?"

The aching muscle in my back spasms and I catch myself on the bar. "Of course they talked about shit, Ollie. I was there for nine fucking days."

"So did they talk about..."

"Ollie, if you don't stop talking now, I'm going to reach across the bar and break your other arm. Scale back, son." I recoil from him and return to the fridge, grab a couple more beers and pocket the cash one of the frat boys gives me. "You're three short."

I grab the kid by his pink popped collar and drag him into the bar so quickly, he crashes through one of the bar stools. A few guys standing nearby turn away from the fight to look at us. My pulse is thumping and I long to bloody his polo as placeholder for Ollie, but Knox intervenes as I should have anticipated he would.

"We got a problem here?" His face is mean and his tan skin gleams under the light. I suck in a breath and the bloodlust doesn't fade, but rather, morphs into something else. I can't believe the man is mine. *Mine.*

"N-n-no," frat boy stutters, trying to melt back into the crowd. My panties are soaked by the time Knox rights the barstool and presses the kid's torso down to it. The position might have looked erotic with Knox behind him like that, but Knox's expression is closer to impaling than it is to fucking. He looks to me, as if awaiting my command.

Maybe it's the way Knox is rocking those light blue jeans, but I go easy on the poor bastard. "Nah. He's alright."

Knox tosses the kid into the crowd without breaking the line of my gaze. He slides onto the abandoned barstool beside Ollie, then grins. "You both happy being back in this shithole?"

"Couldn't be happier." I pass him a beer and take one for myself. Holding it up, we cheers, then I tap my beer to Ollie's.

Ollie lapses into conversation with Knox while I dole drinks out to some of the other guys mobbing the bar. I shout orders to Morgan as he struggles to keep up with me and though Ollie's got me irked, Morgan and the frat boys and tonight's bloodied contestants got me grinning.

"What were you guys talking about earlier?" Knox says as I pop lids free from three beers.

"Nothing." I glance at Ollie pointedly but he's staring at the table as if he's found gold there rather than battered wood. I pass him a beer, hand another to Knox and take the third. "Ollie's trying to solve the case of the missing Russians."

Knox snorts. "We don't talk about that here."

"That's what I said." I keep my stare trained on Ollie and yes, I do mean it as a threat.

"Besides." Knox claps Ollie on the back and Ollie's entire body pitches forward. "Aiden's on it and so are the rest of us. Don't worry. There's no reasons for anyone to go after you."

Ollie mumbles an apology under his breath before sliding off of his stool. He drains his beer, sets the bottle down and makes his way out of the barn with the rest of the college kids. Regulars are the only ones who linger.

"Plumeria." Knox's voice is sharp and I turn to face him. He smiles softly, bashful in a way that makes me want to throw him across the bar. If he'll let me. Big fucker. "Are you actually okay? You're not feeling tired or anything?"

I am feeling tired, but I'm not about to tell him that. "Tired of not being back in the ring." Even now, the barren earth draws me to it as most other women are drawn to jewels and fancy things. I glance at the dirt patch. Dust rains down on it from the platform seats overhead, occupied now by Marcus and Dean and a few others representing the home team. They're laughing uproariously and I am warmed from the inside.

He pushes off of his barstool and rises to stand. "The only person you're fighting anytime soon is me and it'll be for who gets to be on top."

"Then we better get started." I follow him around the bar and call over my shoulder, "Morgan, take over for a second."

Knox laughs and shakes his head softly. "Hell no."

"To what?" I advance until he's forced to the pit's perimeter, marked only by a line drawn in the dirt each night before a fight. It's mostly faded now.

"Fucking or fighting."

"So what? You planning on losing then?" I slap him in the face lightly, but the sound still turns heads. A few of the guys start "ooh-ing" and almost everyone among the dozen or so dudes still in this dingy place turns to watch. Marcus and Dean and the rest peer down at us from the railing.

Knox's face flares a bright and dangerous cherry. "I'm not going to fight you."

I slap him again, harder this time and when he looks at me his lips are tense and his green eyes glitter ominously. I can see why he scares the hell out of people but right now, I'm racked with a different kind of anticipation. "You're going to have to if you want to make it out of here."

"You're trying to get me excited, but I don't break that easy." His gaze pans down the length of my body to reach my feet before travelling back up again. "You can't have sex…"

"For four weeks. It's been five, *cariño*. I'm done waiting." I slap him a third time – now with the back of my hand and hard enough that I leave a red imprint behind. He clenches his jaw, I curl my fingers into a fist and I aim for his lower abdomen. I fully intend to hit him, but as my hand glances his tee shirt, he takes a half shuffle to the side and grabs my wrist.

I tumble forward when he twists behind me and I would have fallen had his left arm not coiled around my body while his right came to cup the front of my neck. His right leg crosses over mine so that I can't move at all, and when I struggle I feel his erection press against my lower back through his jeans.

His breathing is hard and when he tries to speak, his voice catches. I laugh. "Fuck you, Plumeria," he growls against my ear.

"That's the plan, Knuckles."

He releases a low grunt and suddenly, I'm being hoisted into the air. He throws me over his shoulder and turns back towards the bar. "Morgan, can you lock up on your own?"

Morgan mumbles something hesitant and incoherent. Knox turns to face him and I can't see him anymore with the way my face brushes Knox's tee shirt, hair swaying by Knox's ass. I'm draped over Knox's back like a messenger bag in a way that manages to avoid crushing my injured ribs, or lighting up the healing muscles near my spine. I laugh as I bounce along.

"I'll give you five hundred dollars," Knox blurts out. We're moving now, and we're moving fast.

"Oh shit. I mean yeah. That sounds good." Morgan says, "But wait! Where are the keys?"

Knox and I are already at the door and the guys we pass on the way are cheering. "In the safe," I shout, "you know the code!"

And as Knox carries me out into the rising night, I forget momentarily about the cartel, Loredo, Spade, Ollie's nagging questions, Dixon's hate, and all the rest. After all, it's been five weeks. If they wanted to revenge against us for what happened to Spade or Loredo then they would have done so by now. We might be in the clear. We must be.

Dixon

I'm in my home office on the second floor. It adjoins my bedroom and I've been avoiding it until now for precisely this reason: Mer stands on the other side of my desk with her hands folded across her chest. She's got pale brown scars on her arms and welts on her neck that look fresh. No, not welts. Hickies.

"I know you have a problem with my being here and that you and Knox are brothers. I have jeopardized everyone's safety with my existence and honestly, I used to be sorry for it. Recently though, Knox has made me rethink the whole self-hatred thing." She laughs lightly and glances to the window that overlooks the wide front lawn. From here, you can't even see the street.

"Now, I'm just sorry. If you still want me to move out, I understand, and you and Knox can hash out the details because it's honestly not my place to negotiate between you two. I am however, hoping there might be some way we can learn how to co-exist. What do you say?"

"No." I'll be happy only when Aiden makes good on his promise, a promise I still mean for him to keep. Where the hell is he anyways? I shoot him a text to come see me and scroll through our past correspondences. Messages beckoning him or ordering him to hurt people are the only I've ever sent him, and he's never responded. He just does. Usually.

She sighs and shakes her head very softly, making me feel as if I'm being unreasonable. "Well I tried." Shrugging, she turns and stalks to the door. Even her stride is no nonsense and I imagine that she would be the kind of person I might admire if she were a man, and wasn't trying to ruin one of my brothers.

"You should have that talk with Knox then," she says from the doorway. "We can move out if it's that much of a torture for you." She disappears and I glance at my phone, hoping Aiden will text me back or better yet, appear on the other side of my desk with Mer's body in a bag and no blood for me to clean up. I don't dislike the woman, but rather, hold a deep hatred for her and everything she represents.

We. There was a we before she arrived. Now from where I sit, there's a them.

Aiden doesn't show up for another hour and when he does, he doesn't announce himself. Looking up, I see him out of the corner of my eye and jump in my seat. "Christ, Aiden. You're a goddamn ghost. How long have you been there?"

He doesn't answer me, but instead steps into my office and moves to the bookshelf against the opposite wall. He looks at the titles and says nothing for a long while, but I don't prompt him. Aiden isn't one to prompt, so I wait. I'm not one to wait and the act is painful.

"There was something else in the house."

"What?" I push my computer aside. Aiden eyes my bourbon glass and though his expression is flat, I feel condemned. I'm drunk again and though my eyes aren't bloodshot and my speech is clear, it's a Tuesday and it isn't even four pm. "In what house? Mer's?"

He nods. "And the Russians are looking for it."

I sit back and think for a moment, until it clicks. "You said something. Not someone. They're not looking for Spade or his killer?"

Aiden shakes his head.

I go to say the word "shit", but don't make my way through it, and suddenly I'm reminded of the dancer, Sara Elan. At least that was the name she wrote on her Camelot contract; she, the reason I haven't gone back since. I don't want to be thinking about her and the things I said when I was wasted, but seeing that car seat in the back of that piece of crap car infuriates me, even now. What man lets his wife and kid out...and even if the man is no longer around what type of woman...what mother...I can't head down this road. Shaking my head, I try to clear my thoughts and focus on the present.

"You got any ideas?" I ask him.

Aiden sets his hand on the corner of my desk and doesn't move. For a moment, he looks like a statue. "It's something small. At least, small enough to carry. Very valuable."

"We don't have it. Any chance the Russians think we have it?"

"More likely the cartel, but not impossible."

I sigh out a curse. "So we're nearly in the clear. We just have to keep looking for whatever it is they want and hope that either we find it or they do."

He blinks once, ice eyes clear. "We need her."

I clench my fist and, as if accepting that as tacit endorsement, he heads to the door. "But after?" My voice breaks and I sound hoarse and weak.

Aiden watches me from the doorway, then leaves. It takes me far too long to follow him out of my office and down the hall. I don't find him though. He's gone as quickly as he came. I stand in the center of the kitchen and glance around myself. I'm well dressed and clean and standing in my own home, but somehow I still feel homeless. I unbutton the top two buttons at my collar and roll up the arms. I'm restless and warmer than I should be so I head to the garage. Next thing I know, I'm driving towards town. The radio is off and I'm made uncomfortable by the silence.

The sun is shining through sparse cumulonimbus clouds and I don't know if it's the booze but everything feels somehow muted, like I'm interacting with the world through a veil. I'm stopped at a red light on the corner of Forty fifth and Owl. The music thumping in the car to my right steals my attention away from the crossing traffic and I'm fully stalled by a sight just beyond that. Literally.

A car honks behind me and my Audi lurches forward half a foot. I manage to restart it and pull over onto the curb, roll my window down and squint against the encroaching twilight for what feels like the full duration of a lifetime.

The haze of the liquor clears and I see the grocery store parking lot clearly. I wish I couldn't, but I know that these images will play tonight in my dreams. The sight chokes my throat and several times I close my eyes against it, but I don't leave until the rusting jalopy crawls out of the parking lot, a baby boy bouncing in the back seat.

Sara

I'm nervous as heck as I approach the back door, though I told myself I wouldn't be. The weather took a turn for the worse, and though last week I'd walked into Camelot wearing a skimpy skirt and tank top, over the weekend the temperature dropped below fifty. I chafe my hands together and approach the black back door and the woman standing beside it.

"Hello," I say, shooting her my warmest smile. I hold out my hand. "I'm Sara. I think I'll be...dancing with you tonight." I was going to say stripping, but catch myself.

Rather than shake my hand, the blonde lifts her cigarette. "So you're the new girl?"

There's something cagey about her, but I don't let it bother me. I just shove my hand back into my pocket and nod. "Yep. That's me. And you are?"

She scrunches her nose and straightens up to her full height. In plastic platform heels, she's almost a head taller than I am, which makes me wonder if I'm going to have to wear shoes like those tonight.

"Some of the girls were saying that you gave Dixon a private show in order to end up here. I've been here for the past four years and I didn't have to suck Dixon's dick to get the job, so don't think you can swoop in and take business away from me or any of the other girls because of it. This is a real job that some of us take seriously."

The tip of her cigarette has burned down to the filter, so she flicks it beneath the wheel of the first car in the lot – a black Audi. It was one of the first things I noticed – not because nice cars do anything for me, but because the contrast between it and mine is stark. I think back to last week when I'd left Dixon, to my most embarrassing moment of a sequence of embarrassing moments – trying to storm off and not knowing whether my car would start. It had, but barely, and I'm reminded again of why I'm here tonight. If I do well, I could maybe afford the down payment on a safer car for Brant.

Focusing hard on that rationale, I give the woman my best, most Southern grin. "Thank you. I was really just asking for your name though."

She grunts and, without another word, stalks through the back door. She doesn't hold it open for me either, but marches instead down a short hall, takes a left and disappears behind a heavy black curtain. Up ahead, another black curtain has been drawn to separate this hallway from the mayhem of the bar beyond it, and beyond it I can hear glasses clinking and men hollering and laughing.

Trap is playing, bass so loud the floor pulses in time with some great god's heart. The vibrations reverberate through the soles of my boots and I'm smiling nervously as a cool gust of air hits me, lifting my hair from my shoulders. The back door clangs shut with a racket and I turn, only to be startled by the presence of a body standing too close for comfort.

I look up at Dixon glaring down and I try to will away my body's first reaction, but my mind is weak. I'm Icarus and for all the darkness he exudes, Dixon is the sun and I'm incinerated. He's wearing dark blue jeans and a white tee shirt that he fills out too well along with the same black leather jacket he used to cover me. I wish I could forget that happened. It felt too much like genuine concern. Maybe more than that. Possessiveness. The desire to claim me. And he's just the type of guy I always wished would. Before I inherited Brant, that is. Now it's just the two of us and the good lord only knows I don't need to worry about any other boys at the moment. Or men.

I clear my throat. "Dixon, where should I…"

"I shouldn't have said what I did last week. It was none of my business and frankly, I don't care. While you're in this building you're my employee and I'll respect you as such so long as you do your job. We don't need to be friends and I don't need to know anything else about you." He licks his full charcoal lips and when they part, I see pink.

His gaze holds mine in a way that's fixed and level, even as his feet shuffle uneasily. I can't see the hall at all past his breadth. I can't see anything but him.

"Understood?" Every time the man talks it's like a punch straight to the gut. I physically flex my stomach to help steel myself against the impact of his words but they still sweep over me like a wave and I'm almost, but not quite, swept away.

"That sounds good." My pitch is higher than normal and I hope he doesn't notice. I don't want him to think he's had any effect on me whatsoever. "Thanks for letting me know. Where should I go to get ready?"

Dixon's eyelashes are naturally curled and inky black, like his eyes, which betray nothing but suspicion as they narrow against me. He nods once. "This way…"

"Oh hey, Dixon. I didn't know you were in today."

I spin and see Donnie on this side of the black curtain. He winks at me and I smile in response. He's a nice guy, if not a little creepy, but hey. I guess it comes with the line of work. "I am," Dixon says shortly.

Donnie's face falls and he pivots. "Okay then, Sara why don't you wait there and I'll be back with Marilyn to show you the ropes."

"I got it." Dixon's voice is brutal and intimidating.

Donnie gives him a surprised look before saluting and disappearing behind the curtain. "Whatever you say boss."

"So," I turn to him and rub my hands together, not so much cold as I am uncomfortable. The man just seems so flawed and scarred, but I won't be drawn into it. This is a job. Just a job. "When am I on?"

"When we're finished here." He points to the curtain separating us from the bar. "No customers come back here under any circumstances, and no men are allowed back there." He points to the second curtain to my left that the rude woman disappeared through earlier.

"Not even you?"

"Not even me. The dressing room is where you will spend most of your time though. In there, you'll find a locker with your name on it. The combination to the lock is 0-0-35-89-48."

"Wait just a second. Sorry. Let me write that down." I pull out my phone and quickly make a note of it.

As I go to put my cell away however, Dixon opens his mouth, as if he's about to say something. When he doesn't I prod, "Something wrong?"

He shoves his hands into his pockets and grunts, "That your kid?"

On my lock screen is a picture of Brant and me with our faces pressed together. In it, we're both laughing and that makes me laugh out loud then as I recall the reason. "Yeah. That's my baby boy. I took it at the park last weekend. Brant was obsessed with this woman's dog. Every time he saw it he went completely mental…" I realize I'm rambling and cut myself off with a hard swallow. "Sorry."

Dixon stares at the phone murderously until I shove it back in my purse, then says, "The dressing room is where you'll change before you go on. There are stairs that lead directly from the dressing room to the stage so you won't have to go all the way around. I don't like my dancers on the floor."

Confused by the direction of the conversation, my mind is slow to catch up. My fingers reach out and touch his arm – my polite way of interrupting – but his reaction is severe: he tenses beneath me. I jerk back.

"Sorry," I say again for the second time in sixty seconds. Some people just don't like to be touched, but with him, I feel it's a whole lot more than that. "Donnie told me that after I strip on the big stage, I'll need to give private viewings in the booths. If they're on the other side of the bar, then how will I get there if you don't want me out with the customers?"

Dixon's teeth clench and he seems angry again, though I can't possibly imagine what I've done this time. "You'll go back to the dressing room, put on one of the robes, then go to the private rooms directly. Don't waste time on the floor."

"You make it sound dangerous." I smile at him weakly.

He doesn't smile back. "Cocktail waitresses are on the floor. Dancers are on the stage or in the private rooms. You'll soon learn that dancers have celebrity status within these walls and you are naturally beautiful. You'll attract a lot of attention." His inflection doesn't carry the weight of a compliment as other men's do. Instead, he speaks as a fact – and not a very interesting one. Meanwhile, my heartbeat races. So what if a hot guy thinks I'm hot? Get it together!

"Marcel stands at the front door and watches what happens in the private rooms on his iPad. He intervenes where necessary, but it can take him a few seconds to react if things at the door are busy."

I nod, understanding what he doesn't say directly: yes, it can be dangerous. "Where will you be?" I immediately regret asking, though try to keep my expression passive so he doesn't read any expectation into it.

He cocks his head. "In the office. Working."

I smile and make a face. "I'm sure you don't watch the shows. They probably got old after the first one."

He looks surprised again, black brows arching over his forehead, the color of espresso and like an espresso, he exudes warmth and a certain lightness, as if a switch has been flipped under his skin. I tell myself to stop looking at him – focus only on his eyes, but I'm still distracted by the fire in them.

"No, not even the first was interesting. Dancing isn't my thing."

"Dancing or stripping?"

His arms cross over his chest and he stares down at me furiously enough that I want to pull away, but don't. Instead, I stand my ground because if I don't now I never will. Not when every interaction with him is pure warfare.

He opens his mouth to speak, but a woman's voice interjects, "Dixon, don't be so tough on the new girl. Even I know you like watching the dancers sometimes." The rude woman peeks out at us from behind the curtain – the one reserved for ladies only – this time wearing only a pair of thong underwear and pasties beneath an open robe. She's so *naked* and though I was wearing even less last time I was in the building, I still feel flushed.

She waltzes up to Dixon and leans against him, pressing her torso to his while she hangs off of his shoulder. "Then again, maybe it's just me."

She winks at me while Dixon's upper lip curls back to reveal white teeth. Other than that, he doesn't seem to mind her leaning on him. I doubt most men would. I wish that didn't irk me but I feel a momentary pinch of self-consciousness when I remember the last time I was here and how Dixon reacted when I had on even less in front of him than this woman does now. He was loathe to touch me, and would barely look at me. I haven't been touched by a man since I took on Brant and though it's only been about a month, it feels like years.

Dixon mumbles something to the woman under his breath and my efforts to eavesdrop are thwarted when a second voice cuts in. "You must be Sara." I turn to face an open palm and the pretty woman standing behind it. "I'm Marilyn. Sorry for keeping you, sweetheart, but Laurent was giving one of my waitresses a hard time so I had to straighten him out. Plus, it looks like you had lots of company with Dixon and Mindy here waiting on you. Now let's get you outfitted and up on that stage."

Marilyn draws the curtain back and ushers me inside the fitting room, which is long and narrow, lined on one side by a sequence of eight vanities that are exactly how they feature in fiction: exposed light bulbs surrounding gold-gilded mirrors. Everything is gold, even the short rolling seats and the tabletops. The walls, ceiling and floor are all black. All in all, it's not the hovel I expected. In fact, if you changed all the curtains to red it would kind of remind me of a 1950s burlesque nightclub.

Marilyn starts into the room after me, but before she enters, Dixon catches her elbow. "I don't want her going full nude on stage." He doesn't look at me as he says that.

"You got it, boss." Marilyn gives him a short salute – same as Donnie had – rips the curtain closed and gestures for me to follow her towards the lockers all the way in the back.

"Not that I mind but, why doesn't he want me going full nude?" I say as she pops open a locker with my name on it.

She beams and between chocolate cheeks, her square teeth couldn't be whiter. With hair cropped close to her scalp and a full set of curves, evident beneath her black jeans and black, thick-strapped tank top, she may be the most beautiful woman in the bar.

"If you keep some clothes on, more guys will want you for private dances. That's where the bar – and you – earn the most money. The bar keeps seventy percent, but still, at three hundred plus a pop, that's decent income for an hour's work. Now why don't you take off your clothes and let's see which of these will fit you."

My cheeks burn as I return from the lockers – not because I'm ass naked in a room full of six other women in robes, but because for a second I thought that Dixon might have been keeping me in clothes for more altruistic reasons. I guess not. Glancing down at the stack of clothes Marilyn's laid out on the vanity, I drag my fingers across the sequined patterns.

"These are yours," she says, gesturing to them as she sweeps her gaze up and down over my white, shaved skin. "They're brand new and should fit someone who's thirty-two, twenty-five, thirty thirty-four."

"Wow." I smile at her as I pluck a pair of gold hot pants from the stack. "You're good."

She winks. "I've been doing this for the past eight years, sweetheart. Now let's get you up on that stage before the dogs get too rabid."

And before I know what's happening I'm walking up a short flight of black stairs wearing eight inch heels, a white crop top with a deep V, and glittering gold boy short underwear. My heart is beating fast and the grin I've got on my face feels stretched like a mask, but I'm ready. At least, I think.

I push the curtain back and step out onto the stage, hands planted on my hips. I comb my fingers back through my hair as the DJ introduces me to the crowd as Sara Sweetheart. Donnie told me that most of the other girls choose stage names that aren't their own. I didn't really see the point. This is me.

The room has over thirty four-to-six-person tables, all of which are packed, as is the bar area in the back that's crowded with dozens of bar stools. Too many to count. The whole room is clapping, whistling and cheering my name. I'm nervous to speak in front of so many people, but as the music quiets and the cheering follows suit, I know I'm expected to say something. I swallow hard and approach the stripper pole, taking it in one hand.

Then I see him. All the way in the back at the mouth of the hall that leads to his office, Dixon is leaning against a wall with his arms crossed, nursing a beer. I grin a little broader and my heart does a tiny summersault that might have annoyed me if I didn't feel so suddenly sure. I'm reminded that I've done this before and I remember that instant when Dixon's stoic expression broke. He hadn't wanted to hire me, but I'd changed his mind. I did it then against an unwilling audience. I can do this now.

"How are y'all doing tonight?" I say. The men in the room respond with cheers and the whole first row – just feet from me – bangs on the bar abutting the stage. These are the premium paying customers and the ones I'm supposed to cater toward, but I can't seem to unhinge my gaze from the man standing at the back of the room who, earlier tonight, told me he didn't watch strippers dance.

"My name is Sara, I'm twenty-five years old, and I'm a Southern girl born and bred. I'm a little nervous, because this is my first time…" The men erupt again. "But I'll do my best to give y'all a great show tonight. Are y'all ready to see me dance?"

They cheer and I give them a few more sassy remarks before the music comes on and I begin. Marilyn gave me twenty minutes, but I'm only dancing for about ten when the first customer is removed from the room by Marcel. No one else seems to notice and I can't imagine why he was expelled – he hadn't been jumping at me like some of the guys sitting up front, or spraying beer towards the stage like the drunks seated at a table a few rows back. Marcel reenters the room and goes straight to Dixon who gestures to two other men in the room. Marcel promptly removes the first – he has his hand down his pants, and so does guy number two. Gross.

I finish off my routine by prowling around the edge of the stage so that men can slip dollar bills into my clothes. Most manage to do so without incident, but one guy sticks his sweaty fingers all the way down my shorts to cup my ass and another does the same to my tit. I don't make it past him before hands grab him and the other guy from behind and throw them from their chairs. This time, it's Dixon.

"What are the rules about touching, gentlemen?" he snarls, looking back at Marcel as the massive bouncer scoops the two men off of the floor and drags them to the doorway.

The kid I come to has big, wide eyes and flushed cheeks. As he rises a little out of his seat to reach money towards me, I can see he's got an erection. He's careful though, slipping the money into the strap of my boy shorts. The last guy's dollar bill I take between my teeth before sliding it salaciously into the front of my bra.

My routine is over, but Dixon's taken one of the now empty seats, so as a final number, I crawl right in front of him and place my hands on the bar – not allowed. I lean forward, hinging at the hips until I'm low enough to take his beer into my mouth – definitely not allowed. I take it deep into my throat, remembering how much fun he'd been to tease and for a moment I'm having fun myself. Surprise lights up his face as I suck his bottle off in the way I'd suck a man.

The surrounding guys have gone nuts, thrusting their bottles towards me and waving fives, then tens, then twenties, into the air hoping to claim my attention. I don't give it to them though. Instead, Dixon holds onto the bottle as I pop it free of my mouth. I slide up to standing and when Dixon reaches into his wallet and pulls out a fifty dollar bill, I turn from it proudly. Let him think what he wants about me – wasn't that what I said? Somehow now I'm determined to change the record.

I'm thrilled that my performance seems to have warmed some of the girls to me. They congratulate me when I step back into the dressing room and immediately begin asking for pointers when they see how many bills are tucked into my underwear. Apparently I got more than average.

I don't have time to count it though when Marilyn comes into the room. "Wowza, sweetheart. You have got some killer moves." She's holding a pen and pad and flips through several pages. "You have nine requests for private dances. Six for an hour, and the rest for half that. One guy even said he'd be willing to pay fifty bucks more to go first. You won't be able to get through all of them so guys will have to go see other girls or come back later in the week. This is a huge boost for the business. Dixon will be pleased."

She gestures to the robe hanging on my vanity and I try not to smile at what she's said – not the first part, but just that last bit. "Come on then. We don't have time to dilly dally. Get your robe on and head to booth three."

The girl is confident, I'll give her that much. She's also either reckless or naïve and I'm willing to bet on the latter. The kid's got no idea what she's done. The men who had front row seats to the show she just put on with my beer bottle are thirstier than ever and the moment she steps off stage a line forms at the bar and I head straight back to my office.

I open my computer and bring the cameras up. I tab over the ones that show the bar and the outside entrances until I get to the screens for private viewing. There are six rooms, but typically only three are occupied – Saturday is the only day they ever fill up. Wednesday three is the max. The booths are empty while the main act was on stage, and they remain empty for a few minutes more until men file into three of them, and then fill the rest.

The girl is single handedly bringing in double my typical weekday business and I want to feel shock but I don't. Instead, all I feel is a ringing in my chest that I had been able to fill with alcohol – until I watched her dance. I shouldn't have done that. All I could think of as I watched her spin around that pole was the incident from the other day, when I'd seen her at the grocery store.

She'd been pushing her cart, a latte-colored boy seated in the front basket shaped like a car, and she'd been pushing it fast. The kid's fists were up in the air and his tiny feet were kicking; he'd been shrieking and laughing and she'd been laughing along with him as she finally loaded her groceries and her kid into her car. She'd pushed the cart away, careful not to move too far away from her vehicle. And as she looked into the backseat window, making faces against the glass, she'd just looked so damn happy. The kind of happiness I've never known. The kind of happiness to kill for.

Watching her through my computer screen now as she enters the third room, I pinch my fingers over her face and zoom in. The smile she wears isn't the one I saw in the parking lot, but it does exude happiness. Maybe that's why the first guy she sees doesn't ask her to strip, but just to sit there and talk. I watch them for the full hour as she takes a seat beside him on the black C-bench instead of climbing up onto the mini-stage and shaking her ass on the pole, like the other girls are.

At the end of those sixty minutes, he reaches out to hug her and I grip the arms of my chair, struggling to remain in it. But rather than touch him and violate one of the only rules I gave her, she holds up both hands. A few words are exchanged between them and he reaches for his wallet but she waves her hands. It bothers me to no end that she won't take extra money from him either.

The next guy that enters the booth looks to be in his thirties. He sprawls out across the seat, legs spread wide as she mounts the short stage. I can't hear sound through the speakers, but I know when the music turns on by her body's immediate reaction. The kid can dance and my stomach pitches as her robe falls first, and then her shirt, and then her bra and panties. Private booths are full nude.

Pushing my computer away, I turn to my desktop and power it up. I try to focus on anything but the images playing on the laptop beside it but half an hour later, I've still got a blank Excel spreadsheet in front of me and I'm staring directly between the two monitors so that I can see the laptop in my peripheries.

Two more hours pass by. It's ten thirty and I should have left a long time ago. I shouldn't even be here now. I seem to be relentlessly compelled by women to do what I wouldn't otherwise. I think I've gotten ten minutes of work done cumulatively and as I power down my desktop, I turn my full attention to the laptop. I rub my face roughly and simply...give in.

I watch her twist around the pole without seeming to tire though I'm exhausted enough for us both. She dances for this new customer for about twenty minutes before all at once, she stops. The man's lips are moving, but she's standing still, unresponsive. It's the first time all day I haven't seen her smile.

Slowly, she lies down on the platform and the man shifts so he's watching her at pussy-level. He whispers a few more words, nothing happens, then her knees peel apart and she exposes herself to this stranger fully. I've seen girls do this – and more – before, but never wearing an expression like that. She's biting her lips together and her eyes are shut and even through the screen, I can feel the tension of her body. Against the stage, her palms are bearing down.

My knees crick loudly and the door slams loudly and the music is loud and so is the pulse in my ears. I see the world through a tunnel and though Mindy and Marilyn and other customers try to stop me, I yield to nothing. A gold number three hangs against a black door and as I throw it open, it cracks shut behind me. I shrug out of my jacket first, before anything, and fan it over her body. She inhales quickly and tries to sit up, but I hold her down by laying my palm gently against her chest. Through the supple leather of my coat, I can feel her heart pounding.

"Don't get up." My voice is calm though I'm not sure how. Her eyelids flutter and she nods.

I nod back at her once, then turn my attention to the man in the booth with his fly down and his hand covered in semen. I don't want her seeing that. I grab the man by the back of his coat and throw him out of the room. He crashes through the nearest table and the group of guys standing there rise angrily.

"Free drinks for the rest of the night if you take the bastard outside and beat the shit out of him."

The older men cheer and don't hesitate to carry out my request, which I'm grateful for, because I can feel her presence like a blast of sand behind me, peeling my skin clean off. I step back into room number three and close the door. She doesn't try to rise again, but merely clutches my coat to her chest and clenches her knees together. For the first time, she manages to look vulnerable. Standing over her with my hand again on her chest, I decide that I don't like that. It makes me anxious enough to want to book it back to my office, but that would require leaving her behind, which I cannot.

"Are you alright?"

She nods quickly and clenches her knees together so hard it makes mine ache. "I'm fine," she says, though the words sound automatic. She blinks a lot and very quickly. "Did I..." She clears her throat and tries to sit up again, but I don't let her. Not because of anything she's done, but because I can't move my arms. They're rock solid, just like my legs, just like my neck, just like my cock. "Was that wrong?"

Word vomit coats my tongue and I can barely speak through it. "You did nothing wrong."

She smiles at me weakly and turns her face to the side so that I can't see it fully. "I didn't know when he asked me if I was supposed to...is that umm...is it..." She just leaves it at that and I can feel her heartbeat work its way through her body and into my own. It drives me insane. Makes me want to hurt something – a compulsion I began to know only when she and I met.

"It's up to every girl to decide what requests she's willing to accommodate. You don't have to do anything you aren't comfortable with."

"Hard to know what I'm comfortable with these days..." She sighs shakily. "I better get back to it, though."

I slip my hand behind her head, shocked by the softness of her hair, and cup her neck. I help her up into a seat and pass her her robe. As she begins to lower my coat, I show her my back, giving her the privacy to change. At the same time, my phone begins vibrating in my pocket.

"You should take a few minutes," I tell her as Charlie's name flashes across my cell's screen. "You haven't had a break yet tonight."

She doesn't respond and that irks me, but not enough not to answer my brother's call. He doesn't call me much for pleasure these days.

"Hey," Charlie says the moment I answer. "You got a minute? Maybe sixty?"

I don't respond right away. When I do, I say, "Yeah. What do you need?"

"We might have found something at Mer's old place. Thought you'd want to come and check it out."

"Anything good?"

"Good may be too strong a word. Let's try interesting. Something best seen in person."

"I'll be there in forty minutes." I glance at my watch. It's eleven and the bar closes at midnight. If I leave now, I'll be leaving for the evening.

"Cool. See you soon."

"See you soon." I hang up and when I turn around she's sitting on the edge of the stage, so damn close to me I could reach out and touch her knee and I'm overwhelmed by the desire to do just that – not to abuse my position with her but to comfort her because she watches me without smiling and though I hate the forced way she usually grins, this is so much worse. It fills me with the desire to stay.

I clear my throat into my fist and look for answers in the concrete floor, stained black. Her feet swing gently, the tips of her toes visible in those ugly shoes that complete her salacious wardrobe.

"I have to leave. Let Marcel know if you have any other issues during your shift. I'm sure I'll see you sometime later in the week," I lie, because I'm going to plan my days to avoid her at all costs. There's something wrong with me. Something wrong with her for drawing out this reaction.

I turn to leave her, but her quiet voice calls, "Thank you, Dixon."

My stomach pitches and I feel hungover as I stalk down the hall and out of the back door. The air is hard and cold so I slip my arms through the sleeves of my coat, hating the way it smells faintly like her. My car is the first in the lot and I get behind the wheel and drive ten, twenty, thirty minutes... Then I pull over. I'm in the middle of nowhere, one of the only cars on the road. My dashboard lit in blue fights against the darkness of the world outside, which is impregnable with no moon.

I'm staring at my phone. I've never accessed the monitors from it before though I've always had the app. I open it now and tab through until I find her. Still in room three, she's dancing for a college boy. Meaty, I'm sure I've seen him fighting in the pits on amateur days out at my barn once or twice. The sickness in my stomach grows more intense as I watch the way he shifts around on the couch, not even trying to conceal his hard-on, but rather thrusting it towards her as she dances off of the stage and on the ground directly in front of him. Then it happens all at once: the kid reaches out and grabs her.

He wrenches her small body onto his lap, grabs her breast in one hand and with the other, covers her mouth. I slam my phone down onto the dash and rev the engine.

Before I know what I've done, I've swung a wide U-turn into the center of the street and am racing in the wrong direction.

The seconds it takes for Marcel to come into the room make me want to murder the bastard. He's supposed to be watching out for the girls. Out for her. I'd call him to rip him a new one or text Charlie to let him know I won't make it, but both would require me closing out of the app and right now I'm focused on it more than I am on the road. Marcel breaks into room three and when he escorts the girl out and spends a few minutes hammering both fists into the college kid, I feel slightly vindicated.

It takes me far longer than I'd like to get back to Camelot. The bar's closed by the time I do and the lot has mostly cleared out. Her car is still there and I feel the strangest wash of relief. Marilyn is the first person I come across when I blow through the back door. She's carrying money from the till to the safe in my office – the only other person in the whole establishment who has a key – and wears a brilliant grin.

"New girl did incredible today. Record high for a Wednesday and she didn't even get all the way through her private shows." I follow her out onto the floor, searching for Sara, though the bar is mostly empty. Just Ollie and the bartenders toasting in the back and a cocktail waitress flirting with Marcel by the entrance.

Marcel looks up and when he sees me, smiles. "What's doing, Dixon? You forget something?"

"Sara." The word rips out of my mouth before my mind can form words and thoughts. "Where is she?"

Marcel's grin is that of a wolf — cunning and full of mischief — but I don't have time to decipher that, or answer the phone buzzing in my pocket. I want to see her. Need to see her. I look to Marilyn and her eyes are wide and her lips are slack. Belatedly, she points to the back entrance.

"She worked longer than the other girls because of all the interruptions in her schedule so she's just now getting her stuff."

The world passes by in a blur until I reach the dressing room curtain and, in violation of my own rule, I throw it open and step inside. The narrow room is empty but for the body against the wall crouched by the ground. Resting on her ridiculous heels, she's tucked into a tight ball and every impulse in my body fires.

I see her playing with her kid in the parking lot, hear her speaking about Brant at the park, remember the desperation in her tone as she spoke to me after her audition. Now that desperation is on full display. She's shaking ever so slightly, head bowed over her knees, but as the curtain falls she jerks up to standing.

"I'm sorry, Marilyn, I just dropped something." She lies and she lies poorly. From where I stand, I see the way she reaches up to wipe her face.

"No you didn't."

Sara lurches forward and catches herself on the wall. "Sh…" she begins. The closest she ever gets to cursing. My heart beats faster on a cause of it. She flips her hair over her shoulder as she struggles to look at me without turning around. All at once, a fistful of bills spring from her hand.

She reaches for them, then covers herself instead because she's still only wearing gold hot pants and nothing else.

Sara staggers towards her locker but her hands are trembling too badly to manage the lock. I feel anger and poison and pure darkness sift through my veins like a serpent with no teeth or eyes or tongue. This is my bar and this dancer works for me and she's a mom and a student and a good person and desperate and I am the gate keeper and I have so much and what do I give to those around me but hate and death and grief?

She begins speaking before I do, which is fine, because I have nothing to say. "Aren't only women allowed in here?" She sniffles and her left leg trembles. She reaches down to massage it as if it's a question of sore muscles. She's really not great at pretending. "And didn't you have somewhere important to be? Did you forget something? I didn't mean to be here this late. I just took an extra break during my shift that I shouldn't have. It won't happen again…"

I take slow, even steps towards her until we're less than a foot apart. She must sense me there because she crosses her arms over her chest and stops trying to open her locker. "Dixon, I…" She quiets when I settle my coat over her shoulders and push her gently to the side.

I grab one of the vanity chairs and roll it against the wall, then guide her down onto it. She keeps her head bowed though this doesn't hide the fact that she's beet red from hairline to chest. I drape a robe over her thighs and when she slips her hands through the sleeves of my leather jacket, I reach for the zipper resting dangerously close to that pink slit

I wish I'd never seen as my lust of it makes me no different than any of the other scumbags that come into this place.

"May I?"

She grips the edges of my coat together and nods. Carefully – without touching her skin – I zip the coat closed all the way up to her neck. "That's three times now," she whispers.

"What?"

"With the coat. Thank you."

"You've worn it so many times, maybe I should just let you keep it," I say quietly as I back away from her and collect all the money she dropped.

She smiles very slightly, though it's not the same smile she wears normally. This is raw and tender and makes me want to pull out my intestines through my belly button. "Not quite the right size."

"Looks good on you anyways."

She meets my gaze a little longer then, before letting her eyes settle on the money I hold out to her. It takes her too long to take it from me. Her lips flare a bright cherry when she licks them. There's something going on in her head that I want to understand, but whatever it is, she doesn't voice it.

"You made good money today."

She nods and rubs her nose and it turns a deep pink, like the rest of her. "Yeah, it looks like it. Made almost four hundred in tips alone. That almost pays for half of Brant's daycare."

I whistle. "Must be some daycare."

"Lemon Crest," she says, voice turned up as if a question. "It's the best." She shrugs and as she inhales deeply she sits up a little straighter. Her eyes close and she licks her lips again as she folds the money in half once. "The best for baby Brant," she whispers. "It's what my sister would have wanted."

"Your sister?"

Sara shoots me a hesitant glance, then stares at her locker as if willing herself to move towards it. I breach the distance for her and open it up myself. "Sorry," I grunt, "I know all the combinations." It's a lie. The first I've ever told her. Because I don't know all of the combinations. Just this one. "Can I put your things together for you?"

She looks at me like I've just slapped her in the face and for a moment I wonder if she'll say no. Eventually, she gulps, then gulps again at the same time her carmine cheeks pale. Is she thirsty? Is she cold? "That would be…fine. Would you please hand me my jeans?" I do. I hand her a pair of flat boots along with the socks that are stuffed inside of them. Scuffed, but practical. Everything of hers is a bit like that. Worn, but well cared for. Loved.

I don't ask her any more questions or speak to her at all, so I'm surprised when she offers, "Brant isn't my biological baby. He's my sister's."

"And you take care of him now."

She nods and I focus on the floor as I hear her legs sliding into her pants. "My sister was a junkie. So was Brant's father. He OD-ed and then she killed herself and our parents died a long time ago so she left Brant to me."

The whole patchwork portrait stitches itself together seamlessly before my eyes and I feel criminal for the thoughts I'd had about her initially, and the resentment I'd harbored towards her. I say nothing this time because any words out of my mouth would be coated in an anger I don't want her to think is directed towards her. It's mine and mine alone.

"I've always been really good at saving and stuff, but it all happened so quickly." She inhales and when she breathes out, the treble is shaky enough to let me know that she's crying. I freeze because I can't bear to turn around and see it. "I just thought this would be easier."

"Being a mother?"

She laughs at that, but it's hateful and cutting. "No, being a stripper. Being a mother is the easiest thing in the world."

My stomach dips and dives and through the tumult, I struggle to speak through it. "What about your job as an EMT?"

"It pays fifteen an hour," she says quietly. "It's what I love doing, but it's not enough to cover basic expenses anymore."

"And your loans? Welfare?" I throw the words at her like bullets that she dodges.

"My school won't recalculate my financial aid award until next year now that I have a dependent and welfare gives me six hundred dollars a month. That's just enough to cover rent." Rent in a poor neighborhood. One far from here.

My eyes close and I feel my fist curl around some bit of fabric but I don't open my eyes until she whispers, "I think your phone is ringing again."

I curse silently, like she would, and reach into my pocket. "What?"

"Woah, no need for the third degree. Just checking to see if you were coming. Aiden mighta just found something big."

"Shit." I glance down at Sara and see her watching me with wide eyes, so I quickly step out into the hall. "Can you tell me over the phone?"

"I'd rather not."

I curse again. Uncharacteristic. So is the tension of a thousand steel cables in my stomach. I want to go back in there and shred through everything – burn the whole goddamn bar to the ground – and take her and her kid to a hotel somewhere nice, buy them a wait staff to just make sure they stay fat and comfortable and I want to go back to not caring about them because they're fat and comfortable and then maybe I'll be able to go back to a time before – a world in which Sara Sweetheart doesn't exist.

"Can it wait?"

"I mean, this is pretty big, D. Where the hell are you?" Charlie says guilelessly. It's that guilelessness that keeps me from lying.

"I'm still at the club," I grumble.

"At the club? You were there last time I called."

"I know."

"What's the deal?"

"No deal. Just one of the girls."

There's a pause on the other end of the line and I can feel the weight of judgment pass through the silence between us. "Wow. Can't say I'm not a little surprised. We'll give you the low down when you get back to the crib. That's where we're heading now. Warning you, even bringing the uhh…thing back to the house is a decision. One we're making without you since you aren't rocking up."

The line goes quiet and for a moment I don't say anything. I'm cold. Frozen through to the marrow despite the sweat beading along the back of my neck.

"Dixon?"

"Fine." The word comes up from my lungs with all the consistency of gravel. I grip the sides of my phone so hard I hear something in it crack. "Just handle it."

"We're on..." I don't let him finish, but hang up.

The second I turn around, Ollie's voice calls, "Everything okay, boss?"

I shrug, shake my head, cross my arms. "The guys found something," I spit through clenched teeth.

He licks his lips and leans forward eagerly. "The Russian guys?" The kid's always been scrawny, but his face has been gaunt ever since his attack. He's wasting away and it makes him look pathetic.

"I don't know, maybe." I click my tongue against the back of my teeth and hiss, "Get out of here, Ollie. You don't work here and the bar is closed."

He starts but doesn't move. Instead, he does the opposite and shuffles another foot forward. I open my mouth to tell him to fuck off, but I'm quieted by the curtain to my left opening beneath my outstretched hand. In her flat shoes now, I am reminded of how short she is. Not as short as Mer, but certainly not over five eight, a good six inches shorter than I am.

She's bundled in a sweatshirt layered with a down vest. It's deep blue and her hair looks bright white against it. It's been a long time since I've seen her in so many clothes and I can't say I don't prefer it this way. Prefer it, but also hate it.

Somehow in more clothes, it makes me want to rip them off of her because I know what all that unflattering cloth is hiding: something incandescent. I want her.

I lick my lips and bite my front teeth together. My gut is a storm raging and the muscles in my thighs, fire. All thoughts of Ollie and Charlie and whatever it is that the boys found are gone. Poof. Carried away on a breeze that tastes like cinnamon and an autumn that is over now.

"Can I take something?" I say, gesturing to the oversized purse she has draped over one shoulder. She carries a backpack in her other hand.

"What?"

"Your things. I'm assuming you're ready to leave."

She meets my gaze hesitantly, looking flustered and afraid. "I was going to ask Marcel to walk me to my car." She points absently in Marcel's direction and I feel heat rise up in my chest that warps the way I speak.

"I'm taking you home in my car." Not up for discussion and the hell Marcel or anyone else is coming anywhere near you – all things I just manage not to speak.

"You're...what?" she says slowly, as if caught in a daze which only reaffirms that I will be taking her home – not just for her benefit – but to slake my own need to do something for her.

"I don't want you driving that bucket of rust this late. You've had a long day."

She backs up when I lean in towards her and I get the distinct and harrowing impression that she's afraid of me. I had wanted her to be...once. Should she be now? My mind says yes, but is contradicted by the sudden pain in my gut.

Bile rises in my throat and I swallow hard to keep it down and to keep myself from hitting something.

"But my car. I'll need it in the morning."

If I didn't sound like a mad man offering to come and drive her around like an Uber, I would have suggested it. "Ollie," I call, voice too loud because Ollie's still standing there just six feet from us, invading our privacy. I growl, "Can you drive?"

"Well enough," he says brandishing his black cast.

"Good. You'll trail us in Sara's car. Sara, give Ollie your keys." Her mouth is twisted though the rest of her face is open enough to peer straight through. Now, it's as if I can read her soul. "You don't have to be afraid. I'm not going to hurt you." Her caution makes me proud more than it wounds me, though it does a bit of both. What does she know of me but my capacity to deprave other depraved souls?

"I...I..." She tries to tell me something that will somehow get her out of this situation, but for as much as I want her to trust me, I want her to yield to me now.

"Do you need to pick up Brant?"

She shakes her head softly. "No. Tonight he's staying at a friend's. I wasn't sure how late this would go."

I nod once. "Good. Give Ollie your keys and we'll get you home."

She nods, but like a puppy that's just learned how to shake, it's as if she has no idea what she's agreeing to. She produces her keys and I take them from her without asking and toss them to Ollie, who catches them with his left hand. "You mind?"

He stares between us and manages to look just as surprised as Sara does. "No. Not at all."

"Good."

Ollie goes ahead of us while I take her bags. She doesn't exactly give them to me, but she doesn't protest either when I grab them. I guide her to the Audi parked at an angle in the back of the lot. She seems hesitant to get inside when I place her things in the trunk and open the passenger's side door. After a short pause, however, she slides in.

I turn on the radio, but every channel plays the same series of top 40s songs we do at the club. It used to sound like white noise to me, but now I find it aggressive and grating. I turn the radio off. The blue lights in the doors near the floor cast an unnatural glow over everything in a way I think is meant to be soothing, but her anxiety counteracts that. I can feel it wedged between her hands, which are laced together tightly enough that she's white around the knuckles. Her knees are pressed together just as firmly and she stares at them or out of the window. The entire ride, she only looks at me twice.

"It's a left up here," she says. I take the turn, glancing in my rearview to make sure Ollie's still behind us. "I know it isn't the nicest place, but I had to move out of student housing when I was blessed with baby Brant," she explains, though I neither asked for nor needed an explanation. I need nothing from her. Nothing but everything.

I snort. "Most people in your situation would be resentful."

Her nose crinkles up and her eyes do too. Her make up is slightly smeared beneath her lower eyelids, but it doesn't succeed in making her look any less beautiful. "How could I resent something perfect?" She shakes her head and tells me where to park. As I do, she hesitates a moment before reaching for her stuff. "I love my son more than anything in this world. I just wish I could do better for him. I know this is none of your business and I am so sorry that I unloaded my problems onto you earlier. I can do the job. I don't want you to think I can't."

I glance over at her and with the little yellow light illuminated between us and the darkness of the outside world pressing against the glass, I want to touch her. So instead, I clench the steering wheel with both hands.

"I know you can."

She sniffles, pausing before she says, "So you won't fire me?"

"No." As if that had been among one of the thoughts on my mind.

"Thank you."

I open my car door when she doesn't and step out onto the cracked asphalt of her visitor's lot. I need her gone before I reach across the car and aggress her like so many others have tonight. I'm no better than they are. No, I'm much worse. Where they lust, I need, like an addict before their addiction.

Ollie's pulling in just now and I focus on him to have somewhere else to look. The air is cold and I'm grateful for it, even though I can taste rain on the horizon. Always hated rain and grey skies. Always hated mothers and women since that very first conscious memory I have of foster mom number one stroking my four year old body. I hated them all, until this one...

She moves to the trunk of the car and I'm drawn back to the present and to the delicate way the strands of her white blonde hair lift away from her shoulders and sweep her face. I remove her things before she can and tell her to lead the way. As I walk, I toss Ollie the keys to my car and tell him to wait.

Her apartment complex is composed of four separate housing units, each hosting about sixteen apartments. New low-income housing, but low-income all the same. Made out of cheap materials, the walls are thin and I can hear inside of each apartment that we pass. A couple shouting at one another, somebody playing video games, kids shrieking, a couple's quiet conversation. A party in the apartment right next to hers makes my teeth ache. Mostly men, and they're rowdy. The scent of weed has flooded the entire hallway. I want to throw Sara over my shoulder and back into my car, but I manage to contain the compulsion and hand her back her stuff.

"Thanks," she murmurs as she cracks her apartment door. Number 313. The gold font has been painted on and matches the looping script of the welcome mat, though every other apartment has the same boiler plate black and white plaque and none have doormats. She's tried to make this place a home. She's also trying to get rid of me.

"And thanks for the ride home." She steps inside and bars the way in with her body.

I nod but I don't leave right away. I'm standing in front of the door that's just barely caging the party. The wolf pack sleeping so close to the lamb.

"Give me your phone." She doesn't answer or react in any way and when I glance at her, she's got her lips pursed together. "Your phone," I repeat.

She looks down and begins rifling through her purse. "I know that I just begged you not to fire me and that I'll probably end up begging again before the night's over, but I'd really prefer it, Dixon, if you didn't talk to me like that."

The girl could have just as easily flattened me with an eighteen wheeler as she has with her words. "Excuse me?" Nobody talks to me like that. Nobody questions my authority. Not even pretty girls who jack up my pulse and make me want to commit murder.

Against the light she flips on beside the door, her cheeks take on a cherry glow. She swallows hard, licks her lips, then hands over her phone. She's trying to stand her ground but she can't because I have all the power and she has no weapon but the one in my gut that she hasn't yet realized she's laid claim to.

"I'm sorry," she whispers. "Nevermind."

"Say it. I won't fire you."

She lifts her gaze and beneath the smeared makeup, there are bags under her eyes. She's tired and I'm standing out here wasting her time as I dream of what it might be like if she asked me inside. An outlandish fantasy.

"You might ask for my permission to do things, rather than just order me to do them. You're my boss inside Camelot, but that doesn't entitle you to anything else."

And that's when I see it – a resurgence of the fear she'd shown me earlier. It's a residual side effect from what happened to her tonight in the bar. At least, that's what I tell myself. Because the alternative is that she really does see me as she does the rest of the disgusting degenerates that pay for her time because that's the only way to get it. Maybe worse, because in her eyes, I control her son's fate.

Rage hits me all at once and though my torso jerks forward I keep my feet planted. The beast and the gentleman rage within. She sucks in a hard breath through her teeth and straightens, but doesn't close the door when I expect her to. Is it shock?

"So this is what you think of me? That I'd force you to do something against your will?" We both hear the unspoken question I ask: does she think I'm the kind of man capable of rape?

"That isn't what I meant," she says breathily. "I just meant with the phone and the car and stuff. Little stuff..."

"I wanted your phone to give you my number so you can call me if you ever have trouble in your building with people like this," I sneer, jerking my thumb towards the apartment next to hers.

"Well I didn't know that. If you'd said that..." She's flustered and tired and the distance between us has all but disappeared. I'm standing right at her door, hands gripping the lintel.

I cut her off a second time. "I didn't explain myself so that was your first thought? That I wanted to hurt you? Maybe force myself inside your house? Why bother with all that? Why not just rape you in my car? That's why I asked to drive you home, isn't it?"

"No!" Her voice is a shout, but that isn't what shocks me. She hasn't moved away from the door. "That's the last thing I think! I feel safe around you. Safer around you than anyone. Why do you think I freaked out at the club? It was because you left! I like when you watch me strip. I was scared before but when I saw you watching I felt better. And with those guys who were touching – you stopped them – and then you helped me in the room even though I know that some of the other girls do that. I asked." She makes wild and frantic gestures with her hands, pushes them through her hair, crosses her arms, uncrosses them. "I was only trying to tell you that you could be nicer when you talk to me. You can be crass and rude and you don't ever thank the people around you."

She's breathing hard and I've stopped breathing altogether. "You never thanked me for not calling the police after you beat up those guys. One of them was in critical condition and I waited up at the hospital for almost six hours just to make sure that when I lied to the cops, it would just be to cover up for a beating and not a homicide. You don't ever say please, or would you, or may I to anyone. Even to the people you talk to on the phone, or your colleagues, or the other strippers. You don't smile. You just act like a really strict dad. You're not a dad. You're just a boss, and a brother, and I'm sure a friend to somebody somewhere but you're also kind of mean. I was just asking you to be a little bit nice…"

I reach for the doorknob and lean too much of my weight on it. Lurching forward a half step, that step places me inside her house without her permission. I want to go farther. Her words peel the skin off my flesh and incinerate it because she feels safe around me and I'm not a dad and I am mean and I don't want to be any of those things but the first. And maybe one day the second. I remember when I'd told Knox otherwise, but I was lying.

Words tangle in my throat, forming one solid mass. I'm surprised I don't choke. I'm surprised I'm able to breathe. I'm surprised that she's still standing there speechless, staring up at me with huge, moon eyes and that she hasn't started to scream. I'm in her house, but I no longer have control over my body. She mouths my name in the same way she does a curse, but she doesn't speak. I don't give her that chance.

I slip my right hand around the small of her lower back and with my left, I cup the back of her neck in the same way I had earlier this evening. With a slight pull, she stumbles into my body and Christ in heaven, her warmth feels good. I press my lips to her forehead and taste her sweet skin. She's been dancing all night but she still smells like cinnamon and tastes like a Golden Delicious.

"Thank you," I say in the millimeters that separate us. My voice is husky and deep. "Forgive me." I pull away from her in a rush and she sways forward, catching herself on the same knob I'd just used for support. This time I'm the one breathing hard and she's holding her breath. "Sara," I say and I don't wait for her to respond. I can't.

I've reached the end of the hall and have just started down the stairwell when I hear her whisper my name back.

Every step away from her, the thread is pulled another inch and by the time I make it to the parking lot, I've unraveled almost completely. I'm not conscious of the questions Ollie asks me as I drop him back at the bar, and the entire drive back to my house is a reel in matte black.

I open the door to my home, walk into the living room and am shocked to find all four of the guys plus Mer seated around the coffee table made of gnarled petrified wood. Charlie stands, flipping his black hair back and though he's Native and Mer is Mexican, they look for a moment like true siblings. I start to think that perhaps she's part of the family more than I am when the thought is gratefully cut short by the sight of what's spread open on the table: an open duffel bag and what looks like a good thirty to forty pounds of heroin wrapped neatly in clear plastic bags.

Aiden stands in the corner with his hand on the trigger of his gun. It's late now, but he's still wearing his sling and I can see that everyone else in the house is also armed. To the teeth. I'm looking at Aiden as I say the only thing that comes to me: "Sh…"

Part III
The Bag

Aiden

I've been awake all night and most of the night before, so around three pm I try to get some sleep. I lie on my bed fully clothed, two guns within reach, covers tucked neatly beneath me. The lights are all on. Hate the dark, though I've never admitted that to anyone. Monsters lived in the dark when I was a boy. They still do. That I'm now one of them doesn't change the fact that there are still others out there like me, and much worse.

I force my eyelids shut and shift against the mattress. It's hard as a rock and ordinarily, I wouldn't let myself indulge in laying on it – opting instead for the chair in the corner so if I do manage to nod off, I sleep light – but I'm strung out tonight. Running too low on fuel. Sleep. Eat. Recharge. Kill. Can't get through the first part though. Thoughts are racing back through the contents of last night. A night that sealed our fates. Our deaths.

Knox and Mer were at the barn. Charlie was out with a woman. Clifton was at the house. Dixon was down at the club. I was at the hospital. Alina Popov wasn't there – her night to volunteer – and everything was quiet. With the hospital in chaos due to a salmonella outbreak at a local high school, it would have been a perfect opportunity to end Gavriil's life. I didn't though. Not for any reason I'd like to think about.

I left instead and headed straight for the house. Something was off. The past week I'd spent canvassing what I knew of Loredo's other known hideouts: an apartment up North where he kept his mistress had been abandoned in a rush – cardboard boxes, pallets, and moving equipment left alongside piles of perfectly good clothes and plastic-covered furniture. His house in town was much the same. Another apartment out of state took much longer to find. When I broke in, I found rotting food still in the fridge and a bottle of wine on the counter, uncorked and festering with fruit flies. I scoured the place, found nothing, and when I'd gone back three days later to search again, the apartment had been ransacked.

The Russians were closing in, but I was still a step ahead of them. There must have been something we missed. I knew Mer's needed to be canvassed that night.

Telling Dixon we needed Mer was the easy part. Not sure I really intended to kill her in the first place. Not worth it. Because if the Russians didn't, the Mexicans would find ways to end her before I ever could. When they kill the rest of us. Canvassing the house was where the real work began. The thing was massive and ancient. A slave ship with no sails, full of tiny rooms and half a dozen hidden corridors. Most were easy to spot but two were tricky. *Trompe d'oeil* as Marguerite would've said. Woman's linguistic talents however, were wasted on me. By the time she got me, I was fully cooked. Numb. Broken. Hollow. Better this way than to feel for anything. It made my job easier to do.

The other brothers didn't want to spend time in Mer's bedroom. The blood-stained sheets put them off. So did the fishing line still attached to the bed's four corners. Glass covered the floor, so did bits of wood from broken furniture. Couldn't imagine what the room might have looked like before. Probably hardly more livable. Mer got ripped up in here and the brothers all knew it. Mer didn't seem to notice the shit, but Clifton had to take Knox out for a walk. Soft ass bastard.

Alone in that room with Mer, it was easier to spot the floorboard. She had been blindfolded only twice during her time with Spade, but during those moments recalled the sound of creaking hardwood. We looked together – scouring every wall and floor panel, the ceiling too – until I finally saw blood congealed around one floorboard's loose edge.

I placed the dresser on one end, using the leverage to lift the opposite edge and slide my hands into the space. I tore the floor and my palms apart trying to break through. When I did, I found a key. I found the bag it belonged to buried out in the back underneath a pile of rocks that Knox had mistaken for a burial mound. I didn't bury any bodies though. I burned them.

And here we are. A bag of heroin and five nearly dead men and one woman who died a long time ago.

Too restless to sleep, I get up at six and head to the hospital. I slip my surgical gear on in the car before heading into the building. I know the routes. I know where everyone will be and when, so I'm surprised when I don't see the surgeon with the hard-on for Alina at the nurse's station, and I'm even more surprised when I glance into Gavriil's room and Alina isn't in it.

The nurses are talking, wondering about her. Wondering about a group of men that arrived just minutes ago – about half an hour after she left. Her brother had been agitated and she'd been crying as she ran to her car. As the hard-on said, she'd looked panicked. And then the Russian goons had been upset to find Gavriil alone.

The pulse flicking through my wrists picks up its pace. I don't like this. The attention should have been on us, not on Gavriil or his sister. Why waste time on them when they could have been looking for their drugs? For Spade's killer? For me, the one hunting them? I'd meet them head on and revel in it, but Alina? She's not a part of their world. No. She's not of this world. They get a hold of her and she's dead instantly.

Nurses congregate around the nurse's station, and the hard-on keeps them entertained. Gavriil's door opens up beneath my palm and I slip silently into his room. He's got a sheet pulled up to his waist and his hospital gown on backwards so I can see his mafia tattoos. The coat of arms on his left pectoral means he's part of the royal family, so to speak. The symbols on the right mean he's killed something. I disregard the sigils in blue and red and walk instead to his IV. I touch the device that could end his life if I were to insert a single bead of air, but I don't intend to. I want to know what he's saying into his cell, and more importantly, what the female voice is telling him on the other end of the line.

"Alina…" That's the only word I make out in the ceaseless Russian stream. He says it many times, as if he's trying to convince her of something.

I can't take it anymore. I draw the blinds first, then go to lean against the room's only door. As his steel gaze flicks to mine, I withdraw the Ruger tucked in the waistband of my scrubs. He jerks forward, but when I raise a finger to my lips he quiets. I lift both palms and he shows me his own before pressing the speaker button.

"Alina," he says and the moment he so much as whispers a word of Russian I cock the Ruger's hammer. His face twitches but he switches to English, biting back a visible irritation. "I must go. Will you be okay for the next few minutes?"

Russian words rasped quickly are flung back at him. She sounds as if she's crying and my intestines flicker in my gut like water snakes.

"Hang up," I grunt, taking a step towards the plastic edge of the bed.

"Alina, I will call you back."

No he won't.

He hangs up as she continues to speak and I lower my weapon as he lowers his phone. "I thought it would be you," he says. It's strange, because he is right and because at the same time, I don't plan on giving him the release he speaks of. I'm distracted by his accent. It reminds me of her. Her voice. The sound of it – that stilted, sibilant brogue. "The doctor with no medicine…"

I pull myself back into the present. "Why were the Russians here?"

He laughs, leaning back against the pillows with his arms crossed. Like he doesn't care. Like survival or the nurse's call button is the furthest thing from his mind. "You're going to kill me. Why say more?"

"I'm not going to kill you." A lie, and then the truth. "I want to know who was on the phone."

His smile dips. He spares a glance at the cell in his lap, a brick of black against mint green sheets. "No one."

"Alina is no one?"

His eyes narrow and his body tenses up. "She is my sister. What you want with her?"

"To help her."

"You lie."

"For what?"

"I don't know."

I inhale, exhale, glance at his cell. That one act undoubtedly gives him more information on me than what I'd harvested from him. I don't care. "Is she safe?" I say, because that's the only answer I want. He doesn't speak for a moment and I advance on him, close enough to place the butt of my silencer to his temple. "Is. She. Safe?"

He's not a man easily disturbed, but he glances again at his phone in a way that makes me salivate. I'd kill him just for the wrath his delayed response makes me feel, but then I'd still be as I am now: answerless and angry. "You will not hurt her?"

"I will not."

A brief moment of silence, then: "They take her to convince me that I know what I do not."

"Take her to do what with?"

"What mafia does with pretty girls." His voice would come off as a threat if it didn't catch at the end. He loves his sister, and he's ready to die for the girl.

"Where is she? Where are they?"

The words come out of him like teeth, but he still says, "Third and Connecticut." That's all I need to know. I stow my gun where I'd retrieved it and as I turn, Gavriil calls out, "You will save her?"

Save her. "Yes. I will."

"Why you do this?" I don't have an answer, and I don't have to give that to him. I turn and as I meet his gaze he shudders visibly and glances again at his phone. "I will owe you debt. Forever."

I know this, but I don't want what he has to offer. All I wanted was the address. I leave the room and arrive at my car and am driving for ten minutes before I realize that I left Gavriil alive. Perhaps that's what I intended from the beginning. Hard to say. Hard to know anything that will happen or their consequences as I arrive at the address I was given.

Pulling over by the curb, I sit facing a dilapidated brick building. I don't know what would bring her out here. A safe house maybe? A car with clean plates? Both are worthy of a guess, but I have no information except for the little that I requested and that now, I'm starting to believe, may be worthless. Did the bastard lie to me?

My right hand twitches as I imagine ripping his tongue out through his neck, but in the next moment, I hear a voice shouting. A woman's voice. Revving my engine, I peel away from the curb in a blaze of rubber. Two blocks down, one over, I pull up onto the sidewalk and exit the car in my surgeon's outfit. There is one man that carries her. You wouldn't need more than that. She is tall, but light and delicate. The other two men stalk towards the black Bentley wordlessly, though the girl they are prepared to abduct is crying.

Her lean limbs are thrashing, pushing out and vying for anything she can catch, but she doesn't. With one hand, a man takes her wrists and uses his other to lock her knees together. She's wearing black jeans with tears at the knees and a white sweater. Her hair is the color of violence as it swings around her face.

A face that turns to me as she whimpers. "Please," she says.

I don't know if she's speaking to me or someone else, or if it would have mattered. I draw my gun and pull the trigger. The first man falls. The second turns at the same time the third does. Seeing me, he throws the girl to the concrete and her head cracks against the brick wall before bouncing on the sidewalk. She doesn't move after that.

My sternum opens and my lips tighten against one another. I feel that they're dry as the two men reach for the guns at their hips. Neither of them have time to draw before they hit the ground. Lights out. Successfully, I've killed three Russians in a day. Not the three that were on my list.

Instead, I turn towards the Popov that should have died the moment I saw her. She lies still, subtle rise and fall of her chest the only indication of life. I crouch at her side and I can smell the perfume she wears. Christian whatever. Cardamom. Lily. Something else sweet. There are three dead bodies. I need to get out of there and I need to take her with me.

I don't think. I slide my arms beneath her delicate form and lift her from the ground. I don't like the way her body feels on mine. It's too soft. Too breakable. So I hold her away from me until I reach my car. The beat up Volvo creaks as I collapse into it though it barely whispers when I slide her into the passenger's side. The seat is all the way down and she's sprawled over it.

Her face tilts towards me and her hands fold in her lap. Her breath is even and though her hair covers her lips and her right cheek, I am calmed by her face's perfect symmetry. I am calm as I pull away from the bodies and drive out towards the thoroughfare. I am calm as she exhales and inhales and exhales. My eyes drift closed, but by gripping the steering wheel harder, I revive them. Twenty minutes later and we are in front of my home. I don't know how we arrived there. I must have been on autopilot.

It takes me another half an hour to arrive at her townhouse. It's here that I don't know what to do. There's always a plan. Always a next step. But I glance over at her as the stench of her perfume clouds my entire car. As subtle as it is, I can't breathe through it. She's not awake. I reach over and check her pulse. It's even. Like her breath. As my skin grazes her skin, I notice that hers is very smooth. Her cheek. Her throat. Her hands. Her hands are cold.

I pull off a block away from her place. There are people out here, but the windows are dark and bullet proof. No way to see in so we are alone. I turn on the heat and shrug out of my coat. I lay it over her and watch how the black material completely engulfs her from chin to knees. Black coat. Black upholstery. Black windows. Black night rising. And inside her hair blazes like a standing flame. It's thick and full. The kind of hair a man would run his fingers through when fucking her. But she's not the kind of girl that's fucked, to be sure. She's the kind that's worshipped.

Her eyelashes are long... My hand stretches forward to touch one, but then I remember that she's the kind of thing I'd break simply by touching it. I fold my arms over my chest and lean back in my seat, edging away from her as far as the confines of the car will allow. I won't touch her, no. But I still watch.

Nineteen minutes later I'm interrupted from my gargoylish staring by the sound of a phone ringing. It isn't mine. I let it go to voicemail once, but pick it up the second time. It's in the bottom of the purse I collected, now lying on the floor of my car between her feet. Through a pile of cloth and bags and things, I reach the hard, curved edge of the device. The face of the screen is a photo of the Popovs. Timur on the left, Alina in the center, the man I'd just left in his hospital bed on the right. I hit talk, and lift the phone to my ear.

"Alina," he says the moment the line goes live. He says her name again and again. Russian flows from his lips, but then fades slowly. "Alina?"

"No."

"Doctor with no medicine," he says, voice ice.

"Yes."

Quiet.

"You have Alina?"

"Yes."

"She is safe?"

"Yes." I glance over at her and she hasn't so much as stirred. Her chin, rather, is drooped down. I reach over and, against the seat, lift it. Her face tilts so that it looks up towards mine and my rib cage clenches. I stare forward.

"Can I speak to her?"

"She's unconscious." When the man doesn't say anything for a moment I bite down, then spit through my teeth, "She hit her head when the Russians tossed her aside." I don't want this man to think that I hurt her. A strange compulsion. That's the first that I notice that I'm behaving strangely. I glance again to the girl.

His unsteady pitch rises. "You said she was okay..."

"She doesn't have a concussion. The fall was soft but Alina is...delicate."

He pauses and I can hear his anxiety crackle through the receiver. He says, "I want to hear her."

"She's unconscious."

"I want to hear her breath." An inkling of respect for the man surfaces like a match struck but like a struck match, it quickly dies. Fleeting, like everything. Like life. I lower the phone from my ear, turn it on speaker and place it close to the girl's face. "Alina?" Gavriil says.

As if the sound of her brother's voice animates her, she stirs and releases a small, fragile whimper.

"Alina," he repeats, but her eyelids are peaceful and the girl doesn't move.

I lift the phone to my ear again. "She can't hear you. She's unconscious, like I said."

"But she is alive." The man rasps something in Russian. It sounds like a prayer. "And…" I can hear him lick his lips and then fumble with something. A second later, I hear the crack of a bottle being opened. "And the others?"

"Dead."

Silence reigns once more and is eventually broken up by the last thing I expect. He thanks me, first in English before he says, "*Spasiba.*"

"They were your men."

"My men. Not good men. She is my sister." He lingers with a silence that I don't breach. "They rape her?"

I look at her again and lift my coat, then her sweater so I see the flat of her speckled stomach up to the belly button. "Pants still buttoned. No bruising."

He mutters another whispered prayer. "She is virgin." Of course she is. "My sister is virgin," he repeats, this time with an emphasis I don't understand until he says, "I give you lots of money to take her to her house. She lives on Magnolia by the university. You take her to her house, you put her inside and you don't touch her."

"Okay."

He guards his breath. I'd be surprised if he believed me. "Where are you now?"

"213 Magnolia Drive. Parked across the street from her place."

Silence. Lots of it. I'd bet that the man would appear stunned if I could see his face. Nothing stunning about it though. "Why you help her?"

My right hand reaches over and smoothes her sweater down and I lay my jacket back over her. It's enough and I draw away from her. "Because she looks like something pure," I say in hushed breath.

"You don't want her like other men want her," he states, but I can tell he means to ask me a question.

I exhale, sounding exhausted to myself. Sleeplessness catching up to me. "I don't take things that can't fight back. Asleep or awake she couldn't against me."

"No. She could not."

Something moves in my body and I shift in my seat. "So what I want is irrelevant." Want. Another foreign sensation grips me. Wanting is weakness. I want nothing. Never have.

I wait as long as I have to for the man on the other end of the line to make up his mind. Gavriil. This is the longest conversation I've ever had on a phone and it's with a man I meant to kill. "Will you take her?"

"Take her?" Confusion. I grip the wheel hard and I know I am a strong man because I manage not to look over at the girl sitting next to me.

Gavriil clears his throat. "Take her with you. She is not safe on her own and I cannot protect her with the Russians suspicious of me."

"No." Fuck no. The word leaves my lips before I even begin to understand the question. Gavriil Popov – one of the gangsters of the Russian Mafia operating in the United States – wants me – one of the brothers responsible for the disappearance of several pounds of his heroin – to take his little sister under my protection?

"Okay." He doesn't fight me on it and there it is again. A small match lit in the back of my mind where the blackness lives as an impenetrable force. Respect. "In the back of her phone case, she keeps extra key. Take her inside. Leave her. I will leave hospital and come."

"Where's your other brother?"

"With Erik, the boss's son. Erik knows you have what belongs to him."

The news is news. Not enough to shock me, but I'm not bored. "How?"

"Informer."

"Who?"

"I don't know his name. I am boss's nephew and threat to Erik. I am not trusted and neither is my family." He's asking me again to take her, but I'd rather pull out my own teeth. Not because I'd have to knock out Dixon, which I would, but because everything is okay now with her asleep. What would I do when she wakes? I rub my chest. No, I cannot take her. Not for her sake but for my own. She would see me and my hideousness, in and out, and she would cower in fear. To see that fear for myself would be torture.

"If he knows we have it, then why hasn't he made contact?"

"He want leverage first. That's how he work. Take something of yours that cannot be replaced so that he have upper hand, even in your territory. He knows you work with cops. He cannot afford direct confrontation. Something that belongs to you or your brothers will go missing. And soon. He only have three weeks before he must tell his father that the money is gone. Or recover it."

"Tell me how I can contact him."

"I can't do that. Already, I give you too much."

He has, but I don't ask why. I don't need to. I have leverage over him in this moment. I glance to my right as she releases another small whimper. Her lips part. They are full and the palest pink. I brush just the tip of my finger across them. Soft. Even softer than the rest of her. I am disgusted – not with her, but with my inability to resist. I'm poison and sickness. She's the most beautiful thing I've ever come this close to. I've got no business doing anything to Alina but killing for her.

"I'll take her to her room. You'll find her there. Unharmed."

"I owe you debt," he says after a moment.

"I know." I hang up with no other words exchanged between us.

Night has descended quickly in the time it took to talk to Gavriil. In the back seat, I've got several spare changes of clothes. I pull black sweatpants and a black hoodie on over the scrubs I wear, throw on a pair of sunglasses and a black baseball cap. Driving gloves are the last thing I put on before I open up the passenger's side door. From there I move quickly.

Seizing a long break in the flow of foot traffic, I wrap her up in my coat and take her in my arms to her door. The key is where Gavriil said it would be and I slip inside, kicking the door closed behind me. I'm in her house. I've seen it from the outside many times, but this is different. Flipping on a light, I move from the entry into the living room.

The whole floor is one open space – the living room is to my left, complete with a fifty-inch flat screen and built-in surround-sound, and a small dining table sits in front of the open kitchen against the back wall. It's not big, but it's decadent. I imagine that it runs her in the realm of four grand a month. With mafia money lining their pockets, I'm betting that her brothers pay for it.

I climb the stairs by the entryway to the second floor, noticing that everything is neatly decorated. Framed photos of family. A large canvas at the top of the stairs with an abstract motif. Just spattered paint, dots and lines. Art never made sense to me. There's an office to my right, books and paper spread over a drawing table rather than a desk. Bookshelves line the walls and colorful cacti sit on the windowsill above the computer.

Down the short hall to the left there's a bedroom with pressed sheets and decorations on the wall generic enough for me to know the room isn't hers. Hers I don't find until I've passed the bathroom and reached the end of the hall. The only messy room in the house. The purple bedspread is bunched in a mound in the center of the queen-sized mattress. It's four poster and the canopy overhead is printed to look like the night sky.

Stepping around half the contents of a closet spewed over the floor, I push all of the covers to the foot of the bed and lay her down. I'm heavier the moment I do, though it has nothing to do with her physical weight as I give it up. There's a tearing in my body, like stitches pulled, and I acknowledge that I won't see the girl again beyond this moment.

Gavriil will take her somewhere safe and if he does his job well, she'll relocate seamlessly and live out the rest of her life in a place no one will ever be able to recognize her unless it's off of a magazine cover. If he doesn't, she'll be dead. Either way, the intersection of her life into mine is over. Done. I pull the blankets up to her chin and do one final walk through of her room, just to be sure there aren't any Russians lurking in any crevices. I find none, but I still linger in her doorway when I should have gone.

Her key is still in my pocket. A momentary urge to keep it flits through my mind, but to what end? I go to her bedside table and am about to set it down when I see the ornately illuminated bible. Russian Orthodox. She goes to church every other Sunday, but she missed this week. A long, delicate chain lays on top of it and the thin, gold pendant is what I can only assume to be a Russian cross – three diamond shapes fanned outwards with a crescent moon at the base of the fourth and longest stem.

"*Brat?*" The whispered word freezes me still. I glance down at the bed without shifting my stance and see her blink slowly. She hasn't yet focused on my face and downstairs I hear the front door open and close.

I move quickly, dropping the key on the book and sweeping into the bathroom just as heavy feet hit the steps. I draw my gun and crack the bathroom door, angling my weapon so that I'll hit whatever heads towards the bedroom in the back. A red-headed male about as tall as I am. I mark him as Gavriil easily. I exhale ever so slightly and wait until his hand hits the bedroom door. He pushes it open, his sister's name on his breath.

"Alina?"

"Gavriil," she says, sounding teary in a way that I can't stand.

Moving quickly now, I don't stop until I reach my car. It's there that I wait. I don't leave until they do and when they do, she's carrying a medium-sized suitcase and he's carrying an even larger one. They load them into the SUV parked just a half block ahead of mine and speed away.

I wait for an hour after that and watch as her house is broken into by a Lincoln Town car full of Russians. I wonder which of them is Erik, if he's even among them. I debate killing them all for touching her things, but instead place an anonymous call to the police. The irony. Because I've got my fingers on the wheel and a gold chain, as fine as hair, clenched between them. Though they ransack the place, I'm the only thief here.

My soul is empty. The wind wouldn't even whistle as it passed through it. It always has been. But then there's that subtle tearing as I pull away from the curb, the sound of police sirens in the distance, and the cross I loop around my neck. I let it fall under my shirt and feel it press against my sternum. Goodbye, Alina Popov. A woman I killed three men for who doesn't know I exist.

Dixon is more agitated than usual. He has reason to be, but he doesn't usually let it show like this. He keeps glancing at his watch. "Where the hell is Aiden? We were supposed to move the drugs an hour ago."

The bag of heroin Plumeria estimated at thirteen and a half mil sits on the coffee table where it's been for the past three days. Plumeria's on the couch beside me, Clifton to her right. Charlie sits on the ottoman, tossing his gun up and down in the air.

"Something's got Dixon's panties all in a bunch." Charlie laughs, clearly noticing the same thing I do, though neither of us would dare speak it loud enough for Dixon to hear. "Dixon," Charlie calls, lips pulled up into a smile that I know is about to get him punched.

Dixon doesn't hear him the first time, or ignores him. He's still staring at his phone. Charlie repeats the man's name twice more before he turns. "What, Charlie?"

"I stopped by the club yesterday," he says, tossing his gun up into the air so that it spins five or six times before catching it. I hold my breath every time the weapon leaves his palm.

Dixon's voice is a short snarl. "So what?"

"I saw you got new talent."

"Leave the dancers alone." Dixon crosses his arm tight over his chest so that it looks like he's trying to keep them under control.

Charlie looks at me and sniggers under his breath, "Too late for that."

"I didn't take you as the type who goes for strippers," Plumeria smirks. I reach for her thigh and squeeze it firmly beneath my hand, wishing she was in a skirt instead of these long pants. She shoots me a wink and massages the back of my neck, which only intensifies that desire.

"Did you take Charlie as the type to have a type?" Clifton laughs. "You may be the prettiest boy in this house but your standards are erratic at best."

"All y'all are haters. Y'all know as well as I do that I get more pussy than any of you."

"No one's disputing that, Charlie," Clifton says with an exaggerated eye roll. "But what kind of pussy and whose?"

Plumeria and I laugh while Charlie tries to tell us about his hot date scheduled for tomorrow night. While he does, he tosses his gun into the air and I watch the precarious path it travels up and down and up and down.

"You're going to blow your brains out doing that," Plumeria chides.

He shoots her a salacious wink – one that he uses on women at the bars – before turning his handgun on her. My hackles begin to rise, but Clifton edges his body in front of hers before I rip Charlie's head off. He grabs Charlie's gun by the barrel and rips it away from him.

Tossing the gun onto the couch, Clifton says, "Knock it off, Charlie."

"I'm not too worried about it. If his shooting is anything like his fighting then I think I'm pretty safe." Plumeria shoots him a wink in return and when Charlie shoots up onto his feet in a mockery of menace, I can't help but laugh. Plumeria rises and they exchange a few jabs – hitting only air – before Plumeria aims her knee for his stomach and Charlie circles his arm around Plumeria's neck and collapses back onto his ottoman, dragging her with him.

She makes a choking sound that in any other moment might have made me revert to red, but watching her now, I find that the red beast has all but disappeared. He's docile now, sated. Maybe on Spade's blood, or maybe by the sound of laughter. Hers. My brothers'. Clifton's shaking his head and rolling his eyes while Plumeria fights her way free. Charlie's nearly flat on his back howling.

Plumeria stands above him and makes a more serious comment about his stance. He listens to her and it freaks me out because they don't just look, but act, like real siblings. "I'm going to get a drink," I say, patting Clifton on the arm without taking my eyes off of Plumeria.

She's in a black tank top and black cargo pants. With her hair combed back into a straight braid and a few scars decorating her arms and a few more on her face, she looks like a killer. Hell, against her, Charlie looks soft. It takes less than that to get me hard and when Clifton begins speaking, I'm slow to answer him.

"What?" I bark.

Clifton's grinning at me in an invasive, knowing way. The kid sees through everything. "I said, get me a beer too, will you?"

"What kind you want? Bud light? Natty Ice?"

Clifton shakes his head, but is still laughing. "Now you're just being mean."

I laugh in response, though I sober up as I approach Dixon. He's still pacing the hall, wearing down the floorboards. "What's up?" I say, about to move past him.

We haven't shared warm words since I brought Plumeria home. In fact, Dixon hasn't really talked to anyone. He's staring down at his phone with his jaw set. His black eyes are blazing and every few seconds his lips move, as if whispering curses to himself.

"Dixon?" I say his name twice more before he hears me. Or acknowledges me at least. "What's doing, brother?"

"Nothing," he spits. "Aiden should be here by now."

"He text you?" I glance at his phone probingly, but he shoves it in his pocket so I can't see the display. From what I could see though, looked like a black and white video.

"No."

"You late for something?" I offer slowly.

He seethes as he says, "Nothing that concerns you."

"Fuck it. Sorry I asked."

I head into the kitchen, but he blocks my path. Our shoulders brush and he takes my arm. "I..." He bites his teeth together hard and lowers his gaze. "I'm beginning to understand."

"What?"

He glances towards the living room where I can hear Charlie and Plumeria practicing. Charlie curses just then and Plumeria reprimands him for something. "Everything,"

Dixon exhales, and a small smile lifts just one side of his mouth. "Nothing. How this story began."

I go to ask him what the fuck he's talking about when the front door behind us opens.

"Aiden." Dixon straightens and turns towards our brother, the connection between us instantly severed.

Aiden is slow to close the door, as if surprised to see us waiting for him. Or at least as surprised as he ever is. The man betrays nothing.

"We're ready to move the drugs. I'll carry the bag, Knox will drive. I need you in the passenger's seat. Plumeria will drive the first decoy car. Charlie will drive the second. Clifton will head out now to the bank. Clifton," Dixon calls.

Clifton responds right away. "On it." He smiles at Aiden as he passes him in the hall. Seeing them next to each other I'm reminded, as I not often am, that they are twins. Same brilliant blonde hair. Same massive six-and-a-half-foot build. Their grey eyes are the same color but when I look at Clifton, I want to laugh. When I look at Aiden, my testicles shrivel up. I have to remind myself that though he may dwarf my height by a few inches, I'm just as meaty as he is. If push ever came to shove, I might be able to take him. If it were Plumeria we were fighting for, I would. Maybe only then.

He may be my brother, but I don't know what he's capable of, so I plan for the worse. For anything.

"I'm out of here," Clifton says. "Call you when I'm at the bank. Let you know when the box is open and I've got the key." He edges around Aiden – not even the twin will touch his brother. A man who doesn't like to be touched, I've seen the way he fucks and it's a brutal, soul-crushing thing. Lucky for the women that have to endure it, they're well compensated.

"What you got there?" Clifton smiles and just the tips of his fingers graze the knuckles of Aiden's left hand where he grips something that catches the night and turns it gold. That's all it takes. I don't know where the knife comes from, but in the next tenth of a second, the blade has drawn a sliver of blood from Clifton's throat. Aiden holds the stubby hilt in his right hand and with his left, drapes a necklace over his shoulders. He tucks it into the yoke of his shirt before I make out the mark of the pendant. From the little I glimpse, it looks like some sort of religious symbol. Knowing Aiden, probably Satanist.

"Aiden." Dixon's voice is severe, but rather than go to block Aiden, he angles his body in front of Clifton's, like a shield. "Aiden," he says again, "are we ready to go?"

Aiden nods once and stows his blade underneath his coat, but only after he wipes the blood off on his pants. The crimson is eaten up by the darkness.

"Good." Dixon licks his lips and straightens the lapel of his coat. He looks unsettled. We all are. Aiden doesn't react to much but whatever that necklace is must be important to him. Few things are – fuck that – nothing is. "Now we move."

"Wait." The words are Aiden's and everyone in the house goes silent. Clifton lowers his hand which is dabbing at the blood on his throat. "The Russians know what we have and who we are." As he speaks, he wades out into the living room. He looks at his nails as if all of the alarm bells aren't going off.

"How?" Plumeria is the one to speak.

I wonder if he hates her. I've wondered it for a while. But he speaks to her no differently than he would one of us. "Someone told them."

I suck in a short breath and I don't miss the way all eyes go to Plumeria.

"It wasn't her," I say, moving to her side though I wish I were confident enough in my brothers to remain planted. "For the past weeks, she hasn't left my side."

An uneasy silence falls and I look around at all of my brothers. Dixon's face betrays anger. Clifton's curiosity. Charlie's shock. Aiden's nothing at all. Plumeria. I can see is sweating. Finally, I give up and close the gap between us. I gather her in my arms.

"Why haven't they made contact?" Dixon asks.

"They will take something of ours. Something of value. They haven't gotten what they need yet."

"For leverage?" Clifton asks.

Aiden nods. "Yes."

"How do you know all this?" Dixon says. Aiden shakes his head, only once, but it's enough to know we don't need or want to know the answer. "Is that all?" Aiden nods and Dixon continues, the leader he hasn't been these past weeks resurfaced. "Okay. We stick to the plan. From now on, we operate on a system of hourly checks. I call Knox," he swallows, and starts again, "I call Knox, Knox calls Plumeria, Plumeria calls Charlie, Charlie calls Clifton, Clifton calls Aiden, Aiden calls me. We do this every hour on the hour. If any of you don't get a call within ten minutes of the hour, then sound the alarm."

Everyone agrees and when the room begins to break up, Plumeria no longer allows me to hold her against my chest. She untangles her fingers from mine and steps towards the black duffel on the coffee table. "I know that I'm...new here and by some of you, unwelcome, which makes my credibility shit. But if you're willing to listen, I think I've just figured out who the informer is."

I'm not shocked often, but the weight of the past hour is beginning to settle in. Rather than crumple beneath it, I turn to stone, ready to intervene if any of the brothers don't like what she has to say. We all turn to Dixon. He steps forward and I'm ready for something terse, or cutting.

Instead he clears his throat and though it seems to pain him, he speaks. "What do you know, Plumeria?"

"I think it might be Ollie." She begins twisting her hands together and she meets Dixon's gaze. Not an easy gaze to meet, she holds her ground, even if the ground beneath all of us is shaky.

"Why?" Dixon's pitch is off and his shoulder blades move down his spine as he takes a step towards her. I don't mean to flinch, but I do. Dixon notices, glances at me and doesn't move again. For fuck's sake, what is happening? He's understanding my response towards Plumeria's life being threatened, and he's listening to her.

"He asked me a few questions the other night at the barn that rattled me a little bit. He asked me about what happened when Spade and I were together. He also kept a second set of books."

"What?" I say, eyes narrowing.

She looks at me and holds up both hands. "Sorry, I really did think you guys knew. I thought you all were friends. Hell, for a minute I thought he was one of the brothers."

"Books on what?" I say, anger choking my throat. I'm not angry at her, for certain, but I'm pissed off that I was duped.

She shakes her head. "I never knew. But Mario sometimes would drop off packages and someone else would pick them up. I didn't ask what was in them. I didn't want to know. Spade dropped off a package once and I saw him with the bag on my first night in the house, but never again. I didn't see him hide it and he never took it to Ollie. He wouldn't leave me alone and he knew he couldn't travel with me back to the bar. So he just sat on it." She shrugs and the room falls silent. It's a pained sort of silence that beats with its own pulse.

"I mean." Charlie stands from where he was seated and runs both hands back through his thick, black hair. The kind women swoon over – I've seen it happen. "Not saying that I don't trust you, Mer, but maybe you don't have all the facts. Maybe we should try to investigate more before we leap to any crazy conclusions. I mean, it's Ollie we're talking about..."

"She's right." Dixon surprises me, not for the first time tonight, as he sticks up for my girl. He closes his eyes and bites down on his fist. Then he pulls out his phone. "It is Ollie. He knows we have the stuff."

"How?" I say.

"Because I told him." Dixon dials a number and lifts his phone to his ear.

He mouths the word, *shit.* Reminds me in a funny way of something Marguerite would do, though I never thought Dixon was a fan of hers. From the moment she'd taken him in at twelve, he'd been nothing but resistant. A natural of women that I don't know if he'll ever shake. Maybe a hatred. These small steps he's taken with Plumeria tonight have been too much for me to think they'll last.

The phone rings long enough for me to know it's going to voice mail. Dixon's lips are tightly pursed and his wide nostrils flare. "Ollie was at the club, asking me questions that weren't any of his business. When Charlie called to ask me to come down to Mer's, I told Ollie that you guys had found something and that it was related to the Russians. He may be a moron but even a moron can sometimes put two-and-two together and now he's not answering his phone."

He curses again in silence and answers the question we all want to ask. "I was distracted and I had no reason to suspect Ollie of anything. If I had been more open with you all, this might have been avoided. I'm sorry." Fuck me in the ass on a Sunday. I've been living with the kid for over fifteen years and I've never heard him say anything in the realm of an apology. And he's not done. "To one of you in particular."

He inhales deeply and I don't breathe at all because for a second I think he's about to come to me, which would have been shock enough, but when he takes three steps forward, bringing him directly in front of Plumeria, I nearly black out.

"I'm sorry, Mer." He holds out his hand.

Plumeria takes it. "Shit man, you don't need to apologize to me." She rubs the back of her neck and stretches out her fingers the moment Dixon releases her. She's uncomfortable with the accolade and probably as unsure as I am that Dixon still won't kill her.

He pulls back and doesn't give me time to think or react in any way. Instead, he reaches for the bag on the table, gripping the handles fiercely. "For now we stick to the plan. After we break from the bank, Aiden will head to Ollie's. Our checks will begin tomorrow at nine and will go to midnight. Knox," he says, sounding more like an authority than ever. "Expect to hear from me."

I've never respected the man more as I agree and follow him out to the car. Kissing Plumeria chastely on the lips, I then slip into Dixon's Audi. The black bag sits between us like a live explosive, and the city that looms up before us has never looked more like a battleground. I glance at the car behind me, the one in front, the brothers beside me. There's no one I'd rather go to war with.

Dixon

I didn't expect the Russians to jump us on our way to the bank, but I'm a little disappointed they didn't. I don't like waiting for them to make contact. I don't like what Aiden said earlier. Any of it. This calling system is a bullshit safeguard. We live separate lives. At any moment, any of us could be at risk.

I'm racing to the club, furious as I glance at the clock, but for all the wrong reasons. I'm anxious about the Russians and I'm curious to know what Aiden will find as he continues his hunt, but I'm fuming because it's nearly two o'clock in the morning and I haven't made it to the club yet tonight. I pull into the parking lot and the hideously conspicuous car I'm searching for isn't there. Cursing under my breath, I wonder if I missed it on the way in. Maybe she parked on Eighth.

I blow through the back door and, though it's against club policy – policy I set – I flip the back curtain open. Mindy sees me and waves. "Dixon!" She turns away from Dallas who looked like she was mid-sentence. I ignore her and let the drape fall shut, but as I turn, her voice calls out, "Hey Dixon, wait up."

Groaning as I reach the mouth of the hall, I turn away from the sight of chairs being stacked and tables, wiped down. The bartenders are where they usually are – drinking up my reserves – and Marcel is where he usually is, standing at the front door flirting with one of the dancers. Only Marilyn is running around doing any actual work.

"Yes?" I try to keep my voice even, but it comes off too low. I could tear Mindy's head off as amped as I am in that moment. I don't know where this aggression and hostility comes from but I wear it these days like a second skin, one that only fades into the background when I'm able to wrestle it into submission or when she's near. And that's why I'm here isn't it? Risking my life when I should have stayed with my brothers. For a girl. Because I remember what she said to me the last time; those acrid words that will burn for the rest of my lifetime in memory. She feels safer when I'm near, and tonight Aiden was late and I was moving drugs and I wasn't there for her when she needed me. She needed me and I failed.

Mindy is nearly my height in her six-inch platform heels, and I wonder if it's that height that gives her such confidence. She drapes her arms around my neck and I shrug her off. "I'm heading to my office," I say, turning before she can sink her talons into my coat. I hear the muted thud of her heels as she follows. "Marcel."

He pivots and takes my hand when I'm near enough. "How's it doing, boss?"

I nod and, fully ignoring the girl he's standing with, murmur, "How was…business tonight?"

"Business is over." Marcel smiles and cocks his chin towards the brunette he's standing with. "Bring me a beer, sweetheart," he coos and she scampers off.

"Any trouble with any of the girls?"

"No more than usual." His grin widens and I know he's baiting me. "Which girl do you want to know about in particular?"

My eyes narrow and I imagine I've got talons for hands and razor blades for teeth. I'm about to carve into him so deep he'll be shitting blood for weeks. "Where is she?"

Marcel's grin falters and his gaze flashes over my shoulder. I turn to see Mindy still standing there and rasp, "What do you want?"

"I just wanted to ask you a quick question." She holds up both hands and it's the first time I notice that she's wearing a thong and skimpy bikini top and nothing else.

"Wait for me by my office then. Right now I'm talking to Marcel."

She moves abruptly towards my office, though doesn't have a key so she just watches me from the shadows, her dusky eye-makeup making her look all kinds of animalistic. The woman is hungry and so am I, but she isn't what I'm looking for.

"Sara." I say her name as an exhalation, as if I've been holding it in all day.

Marcel nods, grinning at me again, only this time his expression is belittling and bordering on pity. He grips my shoulder hard. "She had to run twenty minutes early. Apparently there was an issue with her babysitter. Donnie gave her the okay. We lost a little business – you know how the boys love her – but Donnie figured you probably wouldn't be too cut up about it."

The tension in my chest I wished would release doesn't. "She have any trouble tonight with any of the guys?"

"Less than her first night," Marcel considers, straightening back up, "More than yesterday."

I ball my hand into a fist in my pocket to keep from reaching out and hitting anything. The past few nights at the club had been getting better. I'd been leaving my office only to watch her shows, just so she would know I was there, but I haven't talked to her since that night. I haven't had the courage to explain the inexplicable. I kissed her for Christ's sake. Maybe I was just too damn horny, or sleep deprived, or stressed from all the bullshit. Or maybe I just like her and I admired her for putting me in my place.

"What specifically," I choke.

Marcel tells me how he had to pull a guy off of her in the private booths and that some drunk frat boy hurtled onto the stage during her routine and pulled her top off. The other guys in the audience might have enjoyed it, but not enough to keep them from stepping up and gleefully taking over Marcel's job. The bar was in chaos and the kid left with broken bones. Apparently I'd missed an exciting night. At least that's how Marcel puts it. To me it sounds just short of harrowing.

I sigh and head to my office, needing a drink more than anything. Mindy follows me in and shuts the door behind her while I pull a tumbler out of the bottom desk drawer and a bottle of Bourbon with it.

"You want a drink?" I say, voice passive as exhaustion begins to set, moving from my sternum through my rib cage, then radiating out to the rest of my bones. I'm pissed and I'm disappointed and that rage blanket is fixed and I'm tired of fighting against it. Riding on a wave of whiskey, I let it drag me under.

"I'd love one." She comes and perches on the edge of my desk, lifting her leg just enough for me to get a perfect glimpse of her pussy. Her thong doesn't begin to cover it. I hand her a glass and she downs it as quickly as I do, so I pour us each seconds.

"Wow. This is good stuff," she says. It isn't, but I don't respond. "I'm feeling hot already. Mind if I take this off? It's so uncomfortable."

I roll my eyes. "Do whatever you want."

Mindy pulls the string ties at her neck and each hip and comes around the desk. She takes a seat on it and plants her feet on either side of my chair and there she is, fully naked with her pussy just below my eye level and her big, orb-like tits floating above me.

"So can I have another drink?" she says. Lifting an eyebrow, I pour her a third glass, but as I go to return the bottle to the drawer she leans forward and slides her hand around my wrist. She draws my hand towards her and takes the bottleneck into her mouth in a parody of what Sara did on her opening show. Shit. That memory gets me stiffer than a slugger and I feel a momentary guilt when Mindy's gaze drifts downward to the erection I'm suddenly sporting because I know she thinks it's for her.

"I know you liked it when Sara did it for you," Mindy says, rearing up and crawling down onto the floor between my legs. I can't help but think back to Sara and when she did this and how hard it had been not to touch her. Not touching Mindy is easy, though this time I actually want to. I want to stop her. "I bet you'll like it even better when my lips are around your big cock."

Closing my eyes I wonder if I shouldn't just let her blow me. I haven't been laid in what feels like a century and I've been jacking off to the memory of Sara's lap dance for the past weeks like a real classy kind of pervert. Her fingers are on my belt, tugging, and suddenly she's got the zipper down, her fingers around my shaft.

"Just let me take care of you, baby," she murmurs, and suddenly my dick is trapped between her massive tits and she's moaning like she's coming.

The phone rings and it's a necessary distraction from the sounds she makes as she stares up at me and rubs her perky plastic nipples against the length of my erection. They may even be real, but they don't look it affixed to the rest of her. Under the desk, she tries to wrap her lips around my dick as I reach for the plastic receiver, a relic from another era, but I push her aside and yank my boxers up.

"Camelot," I growl into the receiver.

The response is immediate. "Oh shi..." But the curse never finishes. My whole body bucks, my mind blanks, and I'm throttled by the sound of her voice.

"Sara," I bark. My voice is thick, throat hoarse.

She has to speak loud to be heard over the traffic in the background. "Wow, um...this is embarrassing." She hawks out a little laugh. "Sorry, I just...you weren't in today so you're kind of the last person I expected to get through to on the phone. I was hoping to talk to Donnie?"

"He's not in, or if he is, I haven't seen him." I glance down at Mindy still on the floor. Now she's lying flat on her back with two fingers jammed into her pussy all the way to the palm. I snatch her clothes off of my desk and throw them at her. "What do you need?"

"Is Marcel there?"

"What do you need, Sara?" I say though speaking through the rage blanket is difficult; it only seems to heighten the pressure in my dick. I want to tear the damn thing off for the confusion it's causing. I'm not myself. I don't know who I am, but I know what I want: to see her.

"Well if you could give me Marilyn or Donnie or Marcel's number that would also work…"

I groan and punch my fist down onto my desk. I hope she can't hear the sound it makes, but Mindy sure can because on her feet now, she jumps. "Sara, I don't like to repeat myself. What did you call the bar for?"

She quiets for far too long. Long enough for Mindy's voice to cut between us. She says, "Night Dixon. It was great spending some time with you. Let me know if you want a repeat tomorrow." She winks at me and I follow her to the door, slamming it behind her. There's no chance Sara didn't hear that and I feel oddly compelled to explain myself though there's no reason to. She has no claim over me, I think to myself, but even I know that isn't true.

"Sara." I speak when she doesn't. "Answer me."

The sound of sirens interrupt her the moment she begins to speak. When they die down, she clears her throat. "It's nothing. You're clearly busy. If you could just put me through to someone else I would really appreciate it." Someone else, she says, but what she means is anyone else. Just not me. My thoughts are white hot. The week's been too long. I'm too high strung. Everything is backwards. Mer, Knox, Aiden, Ollie, Sara.

"If I tell you I'm not busy, I'm not busy," I insist, and I'm starting to sound desperate, even to myself. Not desperate. Pathetic. "Mindy was just collecting her check," I lie, "she switched banks and had to refile," I lie some more.

"Oh," Sara says and her tone becomes just a touch lighter. Just a touch.

"So what did you call for, Sara?"

"Umm...oh. Well I was...I am having car trouble."

I'm stiff as a board and I don't just mean my dick. I buckle my pants and pull them into place, grab my coat, then start towards the door before I remember I'm on a landline. "Where are you?"

"I'm on the 401."

"What do you mean on the 401?"

"I mean I had to pull off on the shoulder. I spent the past ten minutes on the line with the towing company, but they are a man short tonight and can't come get me for another hour. Ordinarily I wouldn't mind waiting, but I've got Brant with me and he's starting to fuss because I don't have a bottle. I was really hoping that I might be able to beg Donnie or Marcel or Marilyn to come get me."

"Can you send me a pin of your location?"

"You...you want a pin?"

"Yes."

"Are you...are you sure?"

"Sara," I growl and it's impossible not to sound frustrated with her.

"Umm sure...wait! I don't have your number."

I repeat it for her three times and hang up the phone. I wait until I've received the pin before I call her back. By then, I'm already climbing the Interstate ramp. "Are you in your car?"

"Yeah. I got out to put up a couple of those cone things, but then a few different guys offered to help me…" Her voice dies and her discomfort makes my hands tighten around the wheel. Then I hear the sound of muffled whispering. She's speaking to someone that isn't me. To a child. "No, it's okay baby Brant. We're okay. Uncle Dixon's coming to get us."

Uncle Dixon. My reaction to the moniker is twofold: a hatred that the association puts me in a position of responsibility over the young one and his mother, and the fierce desire to be exactly in such a position.

"Sorry. He's not happy with me at the moment. Tired." She's moving around and as the phone settles I hear crying on the other end of the line.

"I'll be to you in five minutes. Leave me on speakerphone until then. You don't have to talk to me." I just want to be able to hear her. Even if it's only her body moving, or her light voice whispering to her kid, or her kid crying in her arms. I hear all of that and more as I cruise down the freeway, taking it at ninety even though the speed limit's sixty five.

My phone told me I'd arrive in twelve minutes. Four later, I'm slowing to a crawl on the shoulder behind a beat up old Volvo that makes my trigger hand tingle. I want to shoot the tires out so she never drives this death trap again. I leave my car and walk up to the driver's side and though I can make out the smear of shifting bodies, there's a thick fog congealing against most of the windows. I rap my knuckles on the glass.

"Sara," I say, "It's Dixon." Uncle Dixon.

"Thank the Lord," her voice calls through the doorframe. She has to shout to be heard over the sound of the infant crying. She opens the door to the backseat and the sound gets louder. Seated on the far side of the car, on the other side of a large car seat, she's got a baby in her arms. He's a golden brown color with a dusting of raven curls on the top of his head. In a blue onesie with a lion on the front of it, he's clean and smells like baby powder, even from where I stand. Yet the woman that holds him is in a sweater beneath which she wears the signature Camelot crop-top and a pair of medical scrubs. She must see me staring at her wardrobe, because she tries to balance the baby in her left arm while using her right hand to close her sweater over her exposed stomach.

"Sorry," she says, "I didn't have time to change."

"You look cold. Why didn't you turn on the heat?"

She smiles at me weakly and continues bouncing the baby on her shoulder. Brant. "The car wouldn't start at all. I've been trying to wrap Brant in a blanket, but he's being obstinate. Please, if you just could grab that car seat then I could maybe get all of his other stuff…"

I cut her off and reach into the car. My hands slide around the small child's sides and I lift Brant away from her before she can protest. I stand up outside of the car and can hear Sara scrambling over the shrill shriek of Brant's initial protest. He whines for a moment until I drape his body over my forearm, stomach facing down, and hold his head in my palm. With my free hand, I rub his back in slow circles. The response is near immediate. Brant quiets and so does Sara.

"How...how did you..." Her question fades as she leans far enough over Brant's car seat that the moonlight cuts across her face and chest. Her breasts are pushed up high from whatever ridiculous contraption Marilyn made her wear and I'm distracted by them. "Do you have kids?"

"No."

"Then how...Brant normally doesn't like strangers."

"I grew up in a foster home. Been raising kids my whole life."

"Oh." Her blonde hair blows around her face and I can see the goosebumps rise on her chest. She's still wearing makeup from the club and it shimmers in the moonlight. She's got perfect skin. It's the color and consistency of fired porcelain. I'm surprised no one's called the cops yet. A big, black man like me aggressing this poor white female with a baby and car troubles. They'd get close enough though and maybe they'd think the kid was mine. With his high yellow skin, he looks like he could be. I recoil from the thought mentally and turn towards my car.

"You got a blanket?" I say.

"Oh yeah, of course." She passes me something soft and yellow and I drape it over the baby on my left arm. I remove the carrier from her car with my right.

"Grab your things. All of them."

She starts to move quickly. Scrambling from her position in the back seat to gather things she left in the front, it takes her a few minutes to amass a bag with a bunch of baby equipment sticking out of it and a second, familiar backpack.

By this point, I've already got Brant's seat strapped into the backseat of my Audi – last car in the world I thought would ever have a baby in it – but when I go to strap him in, the kid starts whimpering and Sara grabs my arm.

"Sorry," she says in a huff, showing me both palms as if I might be mad at her. I want to tell her I'm holding her kid, and that I can feel his little heartbeat thumping against the pulse in my wrist and the heat of his breath against my palm. I want to tell her that I'm angry and it has nothing to do with her – that she's the only thing that helps cut through that curtain. I want to tell her that I'm crippled by the sight of her. I want her to know that there's nowhere I'd rather be than here with her now.

In an effort to control the rage that's made me a target of her fear and anxiety, I gulp hard and speak in a gentle, even tone. "Sara," I say, don't you dare recoil from me, "what is it?"

"Well I know it sounds insane, but please…" She wrings out her hands and is so far from the girl I first met, she's no longer recognizable. She's entirely herself. Still a force to be reckoned with, but with so many weaknesses that she's tried so hard not to betray. None greater than the boy I'm holding. "I don't know how you got him to fall asleep so fast, but I do know that if he wakes up now I'll never get him down again. Would it be at all possible for me to drive and you to sit with him in the back? I know it's illegal, but I'm literally the next exit and it's only side streets after that. I have to get up ridiculously early tomorrow and the fact that he's asleep at all is frankly a godsend. Please."

She clasps her hands together and looks like she's about to get on her knees, the sight of which would freak me out more than her plea already does. The desperation in her eyes has me headed for the backseat before my mouth has a chance to respond. Even though no one but me has ever driven this car and I thought no one ever would, I toss her the keys and she thanks me again and again.

In the back seat, I reposition Brant so he's on my shoulder now, head buried in the curve of my neck, stubby little fists clutching at the fabric of my tee shirt. As she drives to her place, I cancel her tow truck and instead, call my guy. Over the phone, I explain about the busted car on the interstate and ask him to come get it, but when I hang up, I send him a text that clarifies what I need more precisely.

"He'll have the car back to you the day after tomorrow."

"Good," she says, sparing a quick glance at me over her shoulder. Her eyes are bright and somehow her flushed nervousness makes her all the more magnificent. Not just magnificent. Irresistible. "I mean, thank you. I'm so sorry I got you involved in this. And by this I mean my whole life disaster."

She has no idea and I grimace at the thought. "I got you involved first."

She laughs at that and though the sound is light and anxious, I enjoy hearing it all the same. "I guess you did. And I guess I'm lucky I went insane that day and decided to intervene in that street fight."

"Why did you?" A question, among many, I've wanted to ask her for a while. It's a small weight off of my chest just to voice it.

She shrugs in the front seat, which is pushed so far forward I imagine how strange it will feel to adjust the position when I drive away. "It's my job. You know I'm still an EMT on Monday nights."

I didn't know that and it bothers me. "Why didn't you turn me in that night?"

She adjusts the rearview mirror so she can see me, then quickly tips it back to its original position. "I don't know," she finally says, "maybe stupidity."

"Dangerous lapse of judgment notwithstanding, I don't think I ever thanked you for that."

I catch her profile in the light of the dashboard. She's smiling. "You're welcome."

Next thing I know, she's pulling into a familiar parking lot. I'm reminded of the last time I was here and the horror she must have felt when I kissed her forehead. Tonight, I know I won't make that same mistake. I won't touch her. It's a promise I make to myself that becomes increasingly difficult when she asks me to walk Brant up to her apartment. It's the first time I'm invited inside and my anticipation is embarrassing, so I say nothing.

The front door opens up directly into her living room. When she switches on the lights, I see a beat up blue couch on the right wall. She drops all of her things in front of it. "Here. You can just bring him directly into his bed." She closes and locks the front door before guiding me around the left corner. On the right is a small, neat kitchen with black and white tiled floors, followed by a bathroom. The bedroom is on the left.

She leaves the lights off, though I can still see that the bed is made and that she's got either a lavender or pale blue bedspread. A tiny C-shaped bed is pressed against the bed's opposite side, so I have to fully cross the room in order to reach it. I whisper softly to Brant as I lay him down and I wait a few moments before withdrawing. He whimpers at first, starts to sniffle and cry, but I keep my palm pressed over his tummy and draw the small blanket up over his legs.

He stretches, looking momentarily like a tiny old man. His expression twists then and his massive, brown eyes blink open. He sees me and a small smile flutters across his face, inflating his rounded cheeks. I touch one and kiss the boy's forehead for absolutely no reason I can justify. When I pull back his eyes are closed and his breath is even. I rise to stand and when I turn it's to see Sara watching me from the doorway in a stunned, haunted way that makes me uncomfortable. I clear my throat.

Her lips move, and she looks like she's trying to come up with something to explain why she's watching me like I'm God and she, a mere apostle even though it's entirely the other way around. I spare her from the grief.

"You have an early day tomorrow?" She nods and doesn't speak. "Get ready for bed and I'll wait here with Brant." Her eyebrows draw down and the soft expression shatters into a sharpness that I should have anticipated. Quickly, I add, "If you'd like. I don't want you to do anything you don't want to."

She exhales, smiles, looks at her feet. "Alright." Then pauses. "Thank you."

She disappears around the corner and I can hear her moving rapidly. She isn't gone for long. When she returns, I'm seated on the edge of her bed and she's standing in the doorway wearing boxers and a big tee shirt. From the way she crosses her arms over her chest, I can tell that she doesn't have a bra on.

"Thank you," she repeats, "I'll show you out."

I nod. "Bye Brant." He doesn't respond and I smile again. It pleases me to see how soundly he's sleeping. I pass her as I head out into the hall, noticing and hating how she makes sure that our bodies don't touch. Still, that hatred isn't enough to make me angry. Her presence is a soothing balm and I'm grateful that she stops me before I reach the door.

"Dixon?" she says.

I turn to see her standing in the center of her living room. She's not wearing shoes, and her arms are exposed and her neck is long and lean and she doesn't have any makeup on. She's not the same girl she is on that stage. She shouldn't be on that stage dancing. Stripping.

"Yes?"

She smiles and makes a face, balls her hands into the hem of her tee shirt, the one with the hospital's name on it – Westfield – then huffs, "I was just wondering…hoping really, that I might ask you out for dinner sometime this weekend."

Did she just slug me over the head with a baseball bat? No, I'm still standing. "I don't date my employees," I say mechanically because I don't know what else to. I don't have anything else.

"Sorry." She shakes her head and blonde hair flops down over her cheek. "That was super inappropriate. I feel bad for asking. Sorry again, I..." The first wave of lust is her soft acquiescence, the second is her self-flagellation, and the third is her simple beauty. But it's her desire that tips me.

I take the step that brings her right beneath me, slip my finger underneath her chin and tilt her face up. I'm going to kiss her again, but this time it won't be for curiosity. It will be for need because the simple truth is that I do need her. I need her in order to breathe evenly. I need her to quench my thirst.

Sara

I don't expect him to kiss me – I really don't – but I don't push him away when he does. Instead, like the girl that I am, I swoon. I am Scarlett O'Hara and Elizabeth Bennett and Jane Eyre and Catherine Earnshaw and he is him. Dixon. I've wanted him for a while and despite the cold rejection I just endured I want him still.

And I don't just want him. I want him to want me back, but I know that's stupid. I'm a stripper and a student with a baby that she can barely take care of and he's a bachelor who owns most of the city – the only world I've ever known. But when he presses his mouth to mine he doesn't kiss me like I'm worth any less. Rather, he kisses me once and then pulls back. He licks his big, soft lips as if tasting them, and meets my gaze. He looks between each of my eyes. The rest happens in the span of a moment.

His left hand slides around my back and lines my spine, which is good because without it, I would have fallen. His lips part and his tongue invades my mouth, tasting all of me and with a force that demands I fight back and stand my ground against it. I hook my arm around his neck and suddenly my feet no longer touch the ground and Dixon's falling back like I've just pushed him.

He hits the wall and he slides his hand along my thigh, all the way up my boxers so that he's fully cupping my right ass check. If he moved his pinky over an inch, he'd be inside of me and Jesus, I want him to be. Men never interested me too much, but he interested me from the first moment I saw him beating on those two other men, even the drunken mess that he was. He'd been jumped. I'd suspected as much when I saw those guys walking down the block towards him. What I hadn't expected was my body's physical response towards him, to do something, to save those guys – and not just to save them: to keep Dixon from harm. I'd wanted to protect him.

My lips find Dixon's ear and I suck the lobe hard into my mouth. He grunts and pulls at the hem of my shirt. Before I know what's happened, it's flying over my head and he's lowering me onto my carpeted living room floor. He rips off his own jacket and it lands on the couch with a soft thump before he takes off his tee and comes at me. My breasts arch up and meet the wall of his chest. His mouth finds mine and I swear, as he massages the thick length of his cock against my pussy through the fabric of my boxers and his jeans, he whispers my name between us. It sounds like a plea.

"I want you inside of me," I moan.

Dixon releases a roar before rising up onto his knees. He's a big guy. Huge. And corded muscles ripple down his stomach and make me feel soft all over. Soft maybe, but also beautiful. I've never been stared at like that before by anyone. Not the sleazy guys that come to Camelot, not my past boyfriends, not boys at bars. He's looking at me like I'm the single most perfect thing that's ever existed. And I feel that I am, for just one ephemeral moment. Then he rips off my boxers and kisses his way down my body.

"Dixon," I cry out as his lips pull on my nipples at the same time that his fingers slip inside of me. "Sh..." I start to curse and for some reason that makes him laugh. I don't think I've ever made him laugh before and I want to know how I've done it, but he doesn't give me the time to ask.

I'm dripping wet and his mouth on my tits sucks relentlessly. My back arches as his thumb joins his pointer and middle finger. He rubs my clit with it while the other two pump in and out of me. I wanted to last longer than this, but I'm not going to. The orgasm hits me and I scream his name loud enough I know the guys next door will hear it. Maybe that had been his plan.

I'm panting and whispering his name, trying to sit up when I see him working with his belt. "Dixon, fuck me," I say. I'm not usually so crass but he doesn't seem like the type for love making and I don't care enough to mess with the semantics.

I reach for his cock, but he holds me down by the chest. He kisses me hard and his body smothers mine to the floor and I can feel the smooth skin of his erection against my stomach seconds before he whispers a curse between us. His whole body stiffens and he breathes hot air against my throat as, seconds later, his semen spills over my abs, my thighs, and my pussy.

"Sorry," he chokes, moving off of me slowly.

I struggle for words. "It's...it's okay." I prop myself up on my elbows to look at him on his knees, but that's as far as I make it. My head is spinning. He doesn't move either. My leg kicks – an involuntary reaction – and his broad, flat hands cup me underneath each knee. He spreads my legs apart and

I gasp as he looks at his own semen spread over my body. The white milk of his orgasm drips from my stomach to the shaved section around my most intimate part. My clit is covered in it and I can feel it sliding over my pussy lips and inside of me. It's all over my thighs.

My head falls back in wanton rapture as he spreads my legs wider. He slides another finger inside of me and I collapse, unable to hold myself up a second longer. He uses his cum as a lubricant and draws patterns over my clitoris with two hands now instead of one. It takes me less than sixty seconds to come for him and it's only as I lay there wasted and spent that he stands up.

"Wait are you…are you leaving?" I pant, unable to catch my breath or form rational words or complete sentences.

Dixon nods. "I'm sorry," he says.

I really do curse. Not out loud though. Just to myself. "So you haven't changed…your mind?"

It takes me the full length of the inhale and the one after that to climb to my feet. As I do, I'm unsteady. Dixon flinches towards me, looking very much like he wants to touch me and I can't make any sense of it. This is clearly a once off thing for him, but he's looking at me as if he wishes it were more than that. Funny, since he's the only one between the two of us holding the brakes.

"No," he says and his voice is thick. I have a hard time looking at him with the way he's staring. So intensely, but I don't know what to make of it.

"I…I'll show you out. I just…let me get a towel first."

"Take your time," he whispers and I've never heard anything more belittling.

Back in the living room, I've got a towel wrapped around my body but his cum still lies thick over my belly and legs. He's fully clothed though, wearing that vacant mask he's so fond of. I was reading into things I shouldn't have been reading into. He told me what he wanted and it isn't me. It doesn't matter that tonight I found out Brant likes him. I already did. And I shouldn't have let him drive me home because now I don't just feel *like*...but more than that. This is the kind of thing that might have distracted me for a minute before Brant, but I no longer have that luxury.

"So bye then, I guess." I inhale deeply and try to plaster on a smile, but it fits all wrong. I let it fall and watch him from the corner of my eye as he reaches the door. "One last thing." Oh my lord. I can't believe I've gotten myself into this situation. That I have to do this. That I have to beg once more. He pauses with one foot in, one out, and I debate how painful it would be to swallow my own tongue.

"Yes?"

"I know that I have no right to ask you this, but if you could not tell your brothers about this until Saturday, at least, I would really appreciate it."

"Why?" His eyebrows pull together. He clears his throat when I meet his gaze.

I frown, anger licking the back of my neck and causing the hairs there to stand on end. "Is this some sort of game you guys have going? Because I don't really care if y'all think of me as a slut for messing around with more than one of you, but if you guys are trying to pass me around and take turns, I'll have you know that isn't just going to fuck up my body. You guys are messing with my head." And my heart.

I wait for a second and because he's staring at me like I've just turned into a fish before his eyes. Then I shout, "I like you, okay. And for a second I deluded myself into thinking you might like me back, which is why I didn't say yes right away when he asked me. I wanted to see if you'd go out with me first, but you won't, and I don't need him knowing that he was only my second choice." He still hasn't said anything and his body has grown so still I start to panic. In my panic, I keep talking though I should have shut up thirty seconds ago.

"It's not fair to him and it's not fair to me either. I haven't gone on a first date in months and I have tomorrow night and all day Sunday off and like my friend Sherry says, I have to remember how to have a life sometime. I mean, I went from being a med school student living and partying in the dorms with tons of friends and cash to spend to being a young mom living in low income housing who has to strip in order to get by each month. I've got to get back out there and when he introduced himself as your brother I thought he seemed cute and nice so why not give him a chance? I just had to check with you first about dinner…"

I rub the back of my neck and I have never been hotter. In a half-whisper, I curse. "Why am I rambling? Why am I always rambling in front of you? Just…if you could not say anything. That's all I wanted to ask…I don't want him to think I'm a slut…"

"Who." His voice is the blunt tip of a pencil breaking against a desk. It cracks and crackles and I don't miss the violent twitch of his neck. I'm startled into asking him to repeat himself, though I've heard him quite clearly. "Who the fuck asked you out?"

I clench my arms to my sides and the front of my towel fans open. Embarrassment doesn't begin to cover what I'm feeling. I'm gutted. "Don't curse at me, Dixon."

"I'm sorry. I'm sorry." He holds up both hands, but he's leaning against the doorframe and his teeth are clenched together and his fingers curl around the doorknob and I get the impression he's going to tear it off. He's angry again and I've got his cum on my stomach and tomorrow I am going on a date with his brother. "Please tell me which one of my brothers asked you on a date."

I have a hard time choking through the first syllable and an even harder time with the second. "Charlie," I finally manage.

Dixon's eyes close. "And you're going?"

"You said no." I shrug. "And nobody else asked."

Dixon's lips murmur something too quickly for me to make out. Then he backs away from the door and looks down the hall, towards my neighbor's apartment. They're still partying – or at the very least smoking weed – even now.

"Lock the door. I want to hear it click." He inhales through his nose as I approach the door, obeying his command without protest only because he looks like he's about to lash out and eat me. "Please," he whispers when I draw close enough to touch.

I nod and shut the door between us. It freaks me out when I don't hear his boots plodding down the hall but I'm too nervous to look through the peep hole to see if he's still there. A part of me wants him to be and an equally large part of me doesn't want to see him ever again. I rinse off my legs and crawl into bed beside Brant, happy to see him still soundly sleeping even as I lay awake, waiting to hear the sound of boots in the hall. I'm asleep before I ever do and awake too soon after that.

The day passes in a blur. I try to forget about what happened last night, but only succeed when I get an unexpected phone call at noon. From that point forward, I'm too steeped in shock to focus on the A- I get on my immunology exam or the previous evening's activities with Dixon. My heart is pounding and the grin on my face must be jarring because that night as I enter Camelot's dressing room, Marilyn sees me and takes a step back.

"Woah. Somebody's having a nice day."

I nod and fight not to laugh, but in the end girly giggles bubble up and out of my throat. "Yeah I am. I got some crazy news from Brant's daycare. They said that they processed my paperwork incorrectly when I submitted it last week, but that we're eligible for a scholarship. Full ride and they're even going to include their nannying service free. That means that I don't have to ask friends to watch him these crazy hours anymore. They will watch him anytime and one of the women lives right around here so I can drop him off and pick him up before and after my shifts and come visit him between classes. He's with her now and she's so wonderful. An older woman, she seems to really like kids. I was worried she'd be put off by the crazy times but she says that Lemon Crest pays well enough and that she enjoys the company. I mean I just…can't believe this." I lift a hand to my forehead and plop down on my vanity seat. A couple of the other girls who'd been half-listening wander off. Mindy rolls her eyes.

Marilyn just laughs. "Looks like the good lord sees you out of the corner of his eye. Either that, or you've got a generous benefactor here in this world." She winks at me but a second later, starts handing me clothes and puts me to work.

I'm surprised to see Dixon standing where he usually is as I begin my routine. I'm even more surprised by who else is in the audience. As soon as my number is up, I run back into the dressing room, throw on a robe and beg Marilyn for five minutes before I hit the booths. From the hallway, I jump up and down until I get Sherry's attention. She grabs Amber's hand and Amber grabs the last member of their little trio before all three of them crowd around me in the hallway.

Dixon's response doesn't slip by me. On the contrary, I feel like anytime he's within a football field's length from me, he wins at least thirty percent of my attention – usually more – and now he's coming towards us.

"Neil," I say, hugging him with one arm. "I can't say I'm not totally mortified you're here but it is good to see you. Did y'all run into each other?"

"No!" Sherry answers as Neil opens his lips. He cracks a knowing smile and watches Sherry with a fondness that warms my belly. "I actually got his number the last time we ran into each other. You remember," she says without taking a breath. "I asked him to get drinks only about a dozen times but nothing and then all at once last night I get a call super late asking if I was free this evening and guess what I said?"

"Yes?"

"Yes!"

Amber rolls her eyes and manages to squeeze past Sherry for a hug. "She said yes," Amber sighs into my ear.

I laugh. "So it would seem." Stepping back, Amber looks so out of place in here with her cashmere sweater buttoned up to her throat and her dark brown hair parted down the center. She's not the kind of girl I imagine most men look twice at, but somehow I find her insanely beautiful. Either way, I'm both grateful and saddened by her presence in this place. She reminds me more of the type of girl I used to be while Sherry, on the other hand, fits in perfectly. In platform wedges with a skin-tight strapless dress wrapped around her body, she's loving it.

"So Neil," I say, turning to him finally. His gaze, which had been trained on me but not on my face jerks up suddenly and I tighten my arms over the short robe I wear. "How are you enjoying the venue?"

"Well, I can't say it's the casual drink Sherry promised me, but it's definitely something different."

"Hey, you wanted to come here," Sherry says, throwing her hands on her hips in mock anger. It doesn't last long. Within the span of a blink, she's all over him again.

He laughs and I can't imagine anything sounding more genuine. Here is a guy who wears his entire personality on his sleeve. Nothing like the brooding jerk standing just six strides behind him. Nothing at all. "No, I'm kidding. I'm glad I got to see you dance."

"Strip," I correct.

He concedes. "Strip. You actually seem like you know what you're doing." He glances over his shoulder at Chantal, now on stage. I'm more interested in Dixon standing by the door to booth six with his gaze pinned on me. He makes no effort to disguise it, and it kind of freaks me out.

"Sherry and I took a pole dancing class last year. I actually really liked it."

"She rocked and I sucked." Sherry's mouth turns down into a pout before her bright red lips cock back up. She leans into Neil's shoulder and rubs her palm across his chest underneath his open jacket. "Though I bet you wouldn't mind seeing me up on that stage just once."

Neil kisses Sherry's forehead much in the same way I'd kiss Brant's and for a moment, I wonder why he's with her at all. He seems to like her, but not as anything more than a friend. Then again I thought Dixon was into me, so I'm really no authority on the matter.

"Maybe we should leave it to the professionals, sweetheart," he drawls, bending down to kiss her again.

"Sara," Marilyn's voice snaps behind me, "you're slowing down the show, baby girl. Paying customers are waiting."

Heat ravages my face and I go to respond, but another voice cuts in. "Marilyn, push Sara's first hour back."

I'm grateful for his intervention, but I'm more grateful that he didn't use the word customer or client or john – any one of which Marilyn might have. I don't mind when it's just me, but I still prefer that my friends maintain their own private delusions about what I do for a living.

Marilyn makes a face, then pops her head back into the dressing room at the same time Mindy comes out. Once again, the girl's robe is open and she's wearing only a string bikini beneath it. Her eyes fix on Dixon's face and I fight back the memory of what it had been like to hear her voice on the other end of that call last night. He'd said it had been for paperwork and I'm inclined to believe him for no other reason than the fact that he hasn't lied to me yet. At least, I don't think. At the same time I have no reason to be jealous. He owes me nothing.

"Hey Dixon." Mindy speaks his name as a sultry moan that makes me want to scratch her. I'm not prone to violence, so that's really the best that I can come up with. And in any case, I don't, opting instead to turn back to my friends and try to make up an excuse as to why I have to be going, but Dixon intercedes again.

He clicks his tongue against the backs of his teeth and swivels, putting Mindy at his back. It also places him directly beside me. "Will you introduce me to your friends?"

No. Why would I? "Uhh…yeah. Sure. This is Amber and Sherry. I've known Sherry since we were toddlers. Amber I met in college and this is Neil, Sherry's date. Everyone, this is my boss, Dixon." Remain professional, I tell myself, though it isn't easy. I'm torn by the conflicting desires to jump him and jump his bones.

Sherry's grin spreads so as to consume her full, smug face and even Amber's lips part. "*The* Dixon?" Sherry is gawking and my intestines are knotting themselves around my lungs.

I exhale painfully. "Mm hmm. Yep. The one I told you is my boss." Though I told her much more than that and the fact that she's bringing it up now makes me want to punch her square in the boob. I smile, though it feels brutal on my face.

Neil is the first to laugh, though he straightens and holds out his hand rather than comment. "I've heard a lot about you. Owner of this, and many other fine establishments downtown."

Dixon looks at Neil's hand and for a moment, I don't think he'll take it. When he does, I exhale, relieved. "Where you from, friend?"

"Damn. You're good." He grins. "Been hiding it for years. What gave me away?"

"The Rs. Accent's hard to make out, and I can't place it. Where are you from?" Dixon's face is severe.

Neil drops his hand and shoves it in his pocket and I'm surprised because I hadn't noticed an accent. Listening for it now, I can almost make it out but it is still too subtle to be pinpointed. "Germany. That's a good tip. I guess it's something I'll have to work on."

Dixon doesn't say anything and another uncomfortable silence ensues. I go to break it, but Dixon turns to me first. "How do you know him?" He speaks like Neil isn't even there.

"He's Sherry's date," I say, flushed and flustered, "He's cool."

Dixon grunts, stares at me for a few moments more then turns to my friends. "Nice to meet you." He shakes Sherry's hand, then Amber's. Amber is still staring.

"Lovely to meet you as well, Dixon," Sherry muses, lifting her hand to Dixon's mouth and forcing him to kiss it. I grab her arm and step between them, to spare him. "We've heard so much about you."

"Good things, I hope."

"The best." Sherry winks at me and the urge to strangle her rises. "She told us that you were even nice enough to drop her off at her place the other day. Even had someone trail y'all in her car so she would have it the next day."

"Oh my lord." My voice is a shout though I don't mean for it to be. "It was so great seeing y'all but I really have to get back to work."

As I move forward to hug Amber first, Dixon sweeps his hand underneath my hair and places it on the back of my neck. The gesture sends chills all the way through me that melt when I turn to look at him. He's smiling, and I get the distinct impression that he's teasing me.

"There's no rush. I'm enjoying getting to know friend's of Sara's."

The pressure of his thumb on my skin makes my knees feel like putty. I'm no longer strong beneath his touch, but worried. I feel for him and the way he's looking at me now makes me think that he feels something in return, which I know is false. I begin to wonder if the man feels anything. I force myself to pull back.

Dixon's smile fades, but he's distracted and reaches into his pocket. "Sorry folks, I have to take this." He holds up a finger and takes a few steps away from us while Neil asks me about my work and if I'm enjoying it.

"Oh umm...yeah. I guess. It pays the bills." I shrug, answering Sherry's next questions about my schedule though my mind is someplace else. I'm listening as Dixon speaks into the receiver.

"I'm here," he says. "Good. You? Good." Then he hangs up and dials another number immediately. "You good? Good." Then he hangs up the phone and turns to look at me and I'm caught staring at him and fumbling over Amber's next question.

"Oh. Where am I off to next?" Crap. Not a question I want to answer. I make a face and try to think of a lie but Amber's not an easy girl to lie to. "I was about to go to the…"

"Office." Dixon's voice cuts in and when I look up, he's standing right next to me though I hadn't heard him approach. "If you'd grab your things actually, that would be great. Just your backpack. Not everything." He turns again to my friends and feigns a whisper. "Don't worry, she's not in trouble." He winks at Amber and she smiles back at him meekly, looking strangely star struck.

"Okay," I say slowly, wondering where he's going with this. I've got clients to take care of and he knows it. Still, I reach forward and embrace Sherry and Neil. I hug Amber last. As I untangle my short arms from her lanky ones, I squeeze her shoulder. "Y'all are sweet coming here to see me, but you really don't have to stay."

Amber sighs and as she looks around, she seems one part grateful and one part reluctant. She drops her pitch and says into my hair. "Are you sure you're safe working here?"

"Excuse me," Dixon's voice rings above us and it's slow and deep and soothing. "I know you weren't talking to me and it's not my place to answer for Sara, but I can promise you that while I'm here, Sara's safety is one thing you can be sure of."

Amber smiles, but it doesn't reach her eyes. She crosses her arms and turns to face him fully, looking momentarily like a librarian and a tigress. "I'm sure that's true, but you can't possibly be here every time Sara works."

"I've missed one of her shifts, but I won't miss another. That is a promise. I don't break my promises." He holds out his hand, as if offering her something – more than he's ever given me and yet it's somehow in my name and in my honor.

Amber takes it. "I'll hold you to that, sir."

"I'd expect nothing less of a friend of Sara's." Amber smiles and Dixon looks at me. "You getting your things?" No. I'm spellbound. Stunned. Electrified in place.

"Sh...sure." I wave bye to all of my friends and reenter the dressing room. Mindy, who I hadn't realized had been there throughout our entire conversation, follows me in.

"You think that because Dixon stands up for you, you're something special, don't you?" she says, her voice chasing me to my locker. Her robe hangs open to reveal her carmine chest. She's so red and splotchy, I wonder if she's on something because she hasn't been dancing. Or she's just furious.

Trying to ignore her, I mumble, "I don't know what you're talking about."

"Don't bullshit me," she sneers, "Sara fucking sweetheart. You have no idea what you're doing in this place. Dixon is mine."

Anger. I drag my backpack out of my locker and shove the rage way down. No reason to rise to it, least of all when the girl has three inches on me and at least fifteen pounds. "I think you may be delusional. Dixon doesn't date employees."

"Is that what he told you? Because that wasn't what he told me last night when I was in his office." Her lips curl up into a carnivorous grin and her hands roam over her skin. She touches her tits, and then her pussy. "That's right. Dixon wanted it all. And he got it. He hadn't even zipped his pants yet when you called him."

I tell myself I don't care, but it doesn't erase the sensation of my stomach dropping to my feet and then through the floor beneath them. "I have to go to his office." My ears are ringing as I push past her.

She calls after me. "Have fun on his desk. That's where he had fun with me."

I rip through the curtain door, shocked to find that though my friends have left, Dixon is still standing just inside the hall, not yet out on the main floor. He looks at me expectantly when I approach. My vision is off and my heartbeat is thumping erratically. It must show because he asks me if I'm okay.

"I'm fine."

He makes a face and offers his hand. "Can I take your bag?"

"Why?"

"I thought you could do some of your school work in my office. I bought your first hour."

I want to ask him why, but I'm starting to understand the reason. He's been messing with me this entire time. Pushing my buttons. Trying to see what I would do for him. I wish he'd come off that way from the start. Then, I'd have known how to handle it – but to wheedle his way into my heart and affect its beat isn't just disgusting, it's cruel.

"It's fine. I've got it."

His hand falls to his side and clenches. His eyes flash over my shoulder and I can smell Mindy seconds before she breezes past me on the left. "Hi Dixon. Let me know if you'd like me to join y'all later."

She winks at him, and then again at me before stepping out onto the main floor though she isn't supposed to. She does a couple ass shakes for Dixon and the customers – more for the former than the latter – before entering booth number two. The guys seated nearby cheer and I forget that even though I don't see Mindy's appeal, I'm not the audience she caters to. Dixon is though. A man with eyes and a dick. A big, beautiful dick. And he didn't even want to have sex with me, but with Mindy he was all for it...

"Shall we?" Dixon says, holding out his hand again as if with the expectation I'd take it. I don't.

"Fine." I step out onto the floor and when guys look up and start to cheer, Dixon brushes up beside me so close our arms touch. I hate how much I love his warmth and break away from it the moment I'm inside his office. It's quiet in here. My eyes flash to the desk. It looks the same as it did last time I saw it but I don't dare approach. I move instead to the circular table in the corner and set my backpack on the plastic chair beside the wall. I open it up and pull out my books and computer.

"You have a lot of work?" I can see him in my peripheries, seated on the edge of his desk, his left foot propped up in the guest chair. Is that how Mindy sat when he had sex with her?

"Yes." But that's not the reason I'm working so diligently.

He quiets in that off-putting way he does before asking, "Is something wrong?"

Only everything. "No."

"I don't like when I'm lied to." He clicks his tongue against the backs of his teeth. "And that's twice now," he hisses. "You were fine a few moments ago and now that we're alone, you look upset. What is it?"

I unglue my gaze from my computer screen, which is blank. The page I've opened to in my Biology textbook is also for the wrong unit. I feel purely angry, but not at him. Well, not only at him. I'm an adult woman and a mom now, I should be able to control my emotions better than this.

"I don't understand you at all and frankly it's starting to get to me so I'd really just prefer it if you either fired me or treated me like you treat every other girl that works here."

Dixon rubs his thumb against his fingers, and I imagine sand dripping through his hands. There's something cautious and calculating in the gesture, as if he's conjuring up each word to speak it exactly as he wants. "I've tried."

I take an opposite approach and react viscerally. "What is it about me that makes you so angry?"

At once, he breaks into a smile of all things. I'm about to shake apart and he's sitting there like I've just said something funny. "I'm angry because of how distracting I find you. I can't help but be interested in you in ways I'm not normally interested in women," he sighs.

To that I roll my eyes and return my focus to my text book, successfully bottling my irritation. For the moment. "Yeah. Just me and Mindy."

"Mindy?" Don't answer, don't answer, don't answer, I coach myself. My resolve holds but only until he says, "What about Mindy?"

"I didn't realize that when you said you didn't date your employees it didn't mean you weren't willing to do other things with them, like you did with both me and Mindy last night. You hooked up with her just minutes before I bared my soul to you like a lunatic and asked you on a date. I know you're out of my league. At one point, I probably wasn't, but now I most definitely am so it's easy for you to take advantage of a girl like me. Girls like us, I should say."

I turn to my computer and start to type. The words are complete jibberish but I can't look at him because I can feel the anger radiating out of him and I can't stand up to it. I'm going to lash out and get myself fired and then where will Brant and I be?

Too much time lapses. I have nearly a paragraph written and when I glance at my open Biology book, it's to see that I've copied down the words verbatim. Then his voice cuts through the quiet cleanly. "I was going to ask you out tomorrow night."

"Well I can't go. I told you. I'm busy."

He laughs. I don't know how it's possible but it seems that the angrier I am, the happier he is to delight in my misery. "I can't believe this." He smiles up at the ceiling and massages his head with his hands. His hair is shaved short on the sides, but is longer in the middle, forming a Mohawk I've never seen on a black guy. It's sexy as hell and I hate it.

"You're the first girl I've asked out in my entire life and you're rejecting me because of Mindy." He shakes his head and when he looks at me one half of his mouth is cocked up into a smile. His teeth shine brilliantly. "I didn't fuck Mindy."

"I don't care."

"You're lying again." Only this time, he doesn't look so mad. He looks curious.

My heart races and I wonder if I've started to sweat visibly or if it's all in my head. Has Dixon finally driven me insane, once and for all? "You lie to me all the time," I blurt.

"When have I ever lied to you?"

"It's not what you say. It's what you don't." I brush my hair back and as I turn to face him, my robe slips open. I don't try to cover myself. He's already seen everything because I've already debased myself to my lowest point. "You don't tell me anything about anything, your motives least of all. You do all this stuff that makes it seem like you like me, but when you're near me, you're hot or cold and nothing in between."

"What am I now?" His dark eyes glisten in the harsh overhead light and I can see the muscles in his back ripple through his white tee shirt. It offsets the color of his skin and I know that the girls were all swooning over Charlie when he came in the other day, but in my book that man's got nothing on Dixon. I clench my knees together and hold onto the edge of the table because otherwise, my legs might spread wide apart and I might fall out of my chair and onto the floor so he can take me wherever he wants.

I stammer, "I don't know anymore. I've honestly stopped being able to tell the difference."

"Go out with me tomorrow night."

"I have a better idea. Why don't we call Mindy in here and whoever else you'd like and we can all fuck you and keep our jobs and you can get everything you want all at once." I stand up, rip off my robe and toss it onto the floor at his feet.

Finally. The revenge of his rage slips across his face, turning it to stone. "Do you want to see the tapes?" he says.

"What?"

"Footage from last night. It'll prove that I didn't sleep with Mindy."

I gulp. Because my answer is yes, but what I say instead is no.

He growls and his left leg twitches and I can see that it causes him great pain to remain seated. Why he does baffles me. "Then what do you want? What can I do to be worthy again in your eyes?"

"Reverse time!" I throw my hands to the side, this slow descent into madness fully complete. "Unwind the clock to the moment we first met and decide whether you want me or not. This has been torture enough."

"So there's nothing I can do now to change your mind?" He blinks and I fight the urge to hit him. How can he be so calm as I split apart?

I shake my head, blonde hair flying around my shoulders. "No. My emotional response towards you is too high. I have to hate you. Because if I don't hate you then I'll fall in love with you and I can't be in love with someone who decides whether or not they like me back at the drop of a dime. I need someone who either says yes or no when I ask them out, not both. My heart can't afford that. My kid can't afford that." I'm trembling now. All over. I shake my head and start to pack up my things. "Please tell Marilyn I'm sorry but I need to leave. I'm not going to be able to go dance for anybody right now."

"Good." Dixon moves towards me and I think he'll intercept me for a moment, maybe stop me from leaving, maybe take advantage of me now when I'm at my most vulnerable. He does none of that though. Instead he reaches into his back pocket and pulls a small stack of fifties out of it. He grabs my wrist and forces the money into my hand. "I didn't just buy your first hour tonight. I bought all of them. I also called the hospital and asked them to put you on EMT rotation. At least until you start your residency. All of the hours you currently spend at Camelot you'll be spending at your old job starting next week."

"You did…what? I can't afford that. You knew I couldn't afford that. How could you?" I can feel tears welling in my eyes and hysteria knotting my throat.

He's still got my hand crushed in his, but he softens his touch and his tone so that he's as close to gentle as someone like him gets. He says, "I know. Which is why I'll be supplementing your income."

"What?"

"I worked out an arrangement with the hospital. I'll be supplementing your wages through the hospital so it'll come to you in a single paycheck. You don't need to worry about interacting with me anymore, which it clearly seems like you aren't interested in doing." He looks at the contact between our palms as he speaks, which is good because then he doesn't see me staring at his face, slack-jawed.

"You…you're seconding me to Westfield?"

"Essentially." He pauses, "They were thrilled to have you back. Apparently you're very good at what you do. Not that that's a surprise. The hospital director himself told me that he was eager for you to complete your studies. It seems very likely they'll make you an offer."

"You met with Gerald?" I don't know why that's my first question when there are so many others.

"I did."

"When?"

"When I had time." He reaches forward and touches my face with his free hand. I jerk back. "Just an eyelash," he whispers, "make a wish."

I see my black eyelash resting on the tip of his pointer finger and I want to scream and cry and hug him and hit him. I shake my head and quickly turn back to my things. "I have to go." Hoisting my backpack onto my shoulder with my right hand, I try to wrench my left away but he holds me in place. I know why. It's because I don't have a grip on the money.

"Take it," he says and when he inhales a breath, his chest swells and I'm both aroused and afraid. "I don't care if you want nothing to do with me so long as you take this money and show up to your shift at the hospital next Wednesday. I don't want to see you in here again."

I breathe in, then out, and nod. I drop my gaze and he releases me when my fingers curl around the cash. My mouth opens to thank him, but I can't get the words out.

"I don't want your thanks."

I nod again and heat washes over me. I'm embarrassed and heartbroken and so dangerously close to love. No one's

• 294 •

ever taken care of me before. Ever. My head and heart hurt. I don't know what to think. Is this still him manipulating me? If so, it's the most elaborate and expensive hoax I can think of.

"I should go," I repeat.

"Don't think you're walking out of this bar in that robe."

I forgot I was still wearing it. "Oh yeah. I think I might have left some stuff in my locker," I grumble.

"Let's go." He walks me back to the dressing room and waits outside while I pull on a pair of jeans and an ugly grey sweater, then he walks me to the back door. "Your car," he says abruptly, surveying the jalopy-free lot, and I think it's the first time either of us has remembered that my car's still in the shop. "Jay called me today to say he'd have it for you Sunday morning. Sorry if that's an inconvenience."

"No I mean…that's fine. I mean, I owe you." More than I already do. Which is infinite.

Dixon grits his teeth and pulls the door shut behind him. It closes with a loud clang. "That's what I was afraid of. I don't want you thinking you owe me anything regardless of whether or not you're mine."

I don't try to hide my surprise, but turn to him and say, "Mine?" I think he's misspoken and will somehow offer an explanation, but instead what I get is a brutal narrowing of his eyes.

"Mine."

I steel myself against the invasion. "I don't belong to anyone."

He scoffs and looks me up and down. Even though I'm fully clothed in front of him, it's like I'm completely naked.

Worse, actually. Even naked I feel more confident than this. "Not yet. Charlie'll take one look at you tomorrow night and be in love by the morning."

"Love?" I balk.

He growls and takes a step off of the crumbling stoop. "In a manner of speaking." Reaching into his pocket he withdraws his phone and presses a few buttons, keeping his eyes trained on Eighth Street as if waiting for it to vanish.

"Well," I blurt, sounding too loud and too weak and too much like a kid, "the only person I love is Brant and he'll probably be the only person I ever love so I don't really care what Charlie thinks about me."

"Fine."

"Fine."

"Fine," he grunts again with emphasis. "Your Uber is here." He points towards the street and sure enough, a Toyota Corolla is sliding up to the curb at the far end of the parking lot, hazard lights blinking.

"Uber?" I say, stupidly.

He stares at me with something other than contempt. It's as if for a single moment, he cracks wide open and I can see into the depths of him and he's so dang beautiful. I want to cry and when I turn away, and then back again, he's no longer looking at me but down at his phone as if there's someone there that's so interesting and he's so interested.

He clears his throat. "I didn't want to offend you by offering to give you a ride." He wouldn't have offended me but he'd have no way of knowing that. I nod, but I still don't move towards the car he's called for me. "You should go," he says parroting my earlier words back to me. He glances down at my coat hanging over my arm. "You're cold."

I am. But that's not the reason I've got my fists bunched under either arm. I start to curse and when I do, he grins for a moment before fighting it back. I want to ask him about that, but what the heck can I say at this point other than, "Bye."

"Goodbye, Sara." I hate the sense of finality I hear in his tone.

Fuck you, Dixon. I love you, Dixon. "Bye." I head to the car, open up the backseat and toss my stuff inside. Dixon's still standing on the back stoop, his phone in his hand though his arms are down at his sides, hanging there limply. His gaze follows me and is filled with alarm, like he's seeing a ghost. The wind pulls my hair in front of my face, and I push the blonde strands back as I stand there, watching Dixon over the frame of the door while the Uber driver asks me if I've forgotten something.

"Dixon," I say, as if he isn't already looking at me, "Brant really likes you."

Dixon makes a face. I wonder if he's unhappy I said that. I don't know why I said it. "Tell him goodbye from me."

I open my mouth to curse again, but don't. Instead, I get into the car and let the Uber drive me home.

Dixon

The house is so loud that I can't remember a time when there was silence. With the bag out of the house everyone seems to be back to normal. Back to normal. I can't remember what that was like. Knox and Mer are fondling each other underneath a blanket on the couch to my right while some shitty movie drones on in the background. Explosions, screams, superheroes, and one-liners that I think are meant to be funny. I don't see more than that, and I don't realize they've changed the title until more credits roll in.

Mer gets up first, ripping the blanket off of her lap and exposing shorts that are too short. Maybe a pair of Knox's briefs. Not that it matters. She isn't my type. I have a type now. I didn't have a type before. Mer's got braids down the back of her head. When Knox stands, he reaches for them, like he's going to grab a fistful and force her into submission. The thought might have made me smile wickedly if I could feel my face. I'm a whiskey bottle in and two blunts deep and I no longer find Knox and Mer's relationship grating. It's become torture to me, so I work hard to focus instead on the films that continue to run on an endless stream. If I hadn't been so cold, so callus, such a wounded disaster I could be sitting on this couch next to my girl too.

Mer ducks under Knox's next parry. She slaps his cheek and I don't recognize my brother. He looks wholly consumed. I could've been electrocuted, branded, shot and lit up like a torch right next to him and he'd have never taken his eyes off of her. I wonder if that's how I appear when Sara's in the room.

My mind drifts. She'll be getting ready now. Maybe just out of the shower. Maybe already in her clothes. I wonder what she'll wear for him. My brother. I didn't listen when he came in earlier to tell Knox his plans for the night and get Mer's approval, but instead turned the volume up on the TV to the point that it's now deafening. Mer glides towards the hall and there's a cunning and carnivorous gleam in her eyes that even I can translate. Knox responds to it like a lion to a lioness in heat and lunges for her. She darts out of the way and moves down the hall until I can no longer see her. She's begging to be chased and he does.

Clifton steps into the room as Knox steps out. A second later, there's a bang. "What the..." Clifton plops down onto the sofa where Mer and Knox had been. There's laughter from down the hall, followed by another loud thud. My guess, the end of the chase. "So what are we watching?" Clifton's voice draws me into the present.

My gaze swivels back up to the screen. Who put that there? Looks farther away than I remember it. Everything looks so far away. My hand stretches forward and fumbles over the edge of my glass. Pushing it aside, instead I grab the bottle. Something amber colored. Could be rum or whiskey or something else. Anything else. I pour some of it down my throat and shrug.

"You eaten anything today, man?"

I shrug again.

Clifton makes a face and swipes one of the other bottles off of the table. Cracking it, he takes a sip. "Cheap shit." He grimaces. "You trying to die or just forget about something?"

I feel the rumbling in my chest before I realize I'm making the sound out loud, like an animal. That's what I feel like right now. Maybe less. I feel worthless. Like nothing. Clifton looks away with a small shake of his head, one whose intentions I don't understand and I don't like it. I feel words swimming somewhere in my chest, but as I attempt to cull the right ones to challenge my brother, a door opens and shuts and the sound of hard-soled shoes cleaves through everything.

"Alright, that's it folks. Wish me luck on my date." He steps into the living room looking like a goddamn Casanova. Navy blazer over another navy shirt. Light blue jeans to keep the ensemble just this side of casual. He's soaped up, washed, smelling like a pimp, even from here. When he runs his fingers through his hair, holds out his arms and takes an extravagant turn of the room, Clifton begins a slow clap.

"Nice digs," Clifton says with a grin that sends a renewed rush of blood thundering through my temples. "Looks like you're actually trying with this one."

"As opposed to the three other chicks you took out this week." I didn't see Mer or Knox walk back in, but there she is, framed by Knox who's silhouetted by light from the hall. He's got his arms wrapped around her. I hate the gesture. I hate her. I hate him. I hate me. But right now, I hate Charlie most.

Charlie points his finger at her. "Don't hate the player. Hate the game."

"So is that what this is? Just a game?" Clifton rolls his eyes when Charlie holds up both hands, as if in surrender.

"Whatever it is, it's a hell of a time." He winks, then tucks his right hand into his breast pocket. He heads for the door and my legs turn to cement. "Don't wait up for me, ladies and gents. If I have anything to do with it, it's going to be a long night."

And it likely will be, because a guy like Charlie is not just what she wants, but what she needs. Someone whose interest in her is straightforward. Someone handsome and rich and uncomplicated who will like her but not love her that she can have a nice time with. I could never fill that role not least because she can't have a nice time with me. That much she made abundantly clear.

The door opens and closes and the alcohol in my stomach climbs up the back of my throat along with a healthy heaping of bile. I wonder how much more I'll need to drink before my body gives up and gives out because the one thing I cannot do is be awake when Charlie returns in the morning.

"You okay?" Clifton is staring at me. Mer and Knox are both staring at me. I close my eyes and flare my nostrils in an attempt to breathe through my nose. I think it'll help me calm down, but each breath that comes is shorter than the last. My senses are all finely tuned, each tendon taut, each muscle strained. I'm waiting for the same sound I'm hoping to drown out with the sound of the television…and there it is.

The sound of Charlie's Porsche engine revving explodes through my temples and though my torso is lead and my legs are concrete, neither stop me from flying off of the couch, through the living room and out of the front door. When I slam both palms down onto the trunk, he brakes right away and rolls down the window. His first two moves are his first two mistakes.

Ripping up on the emergency brake, Charlie throws both hands into the air. "What the fuck, dude?"

Rather than answer, I reach into the car and unlock the door — if his shoulders were narrower, I'd have ripped him right out through the window. I have him by the back of the neck and I drag him up the stoop and into the house. I throw him down and he crashes through the hall table before meeting the floorboards. A glass vase shatters and the beads inside of it scatter.

He clutches his right elbow and curses in an endless stream, but I don't give a shit that he's hurt. He's got every intention of taking Sara out, making her laugh, treating her well, getting her drunk, and fucking her right. All things that she deserves and all things I should have done the first moment she walked into Camelot looking for a job. What did I do instead? I drove her away because I was scared. Petrified. I'm not supposed to be scared of anything. I'm supposed to be taking care of my brothers and I can't even take care of myself.

"Look at me," I growl and when I take another step towards Charlie, a heavy arm locks around my neck.

Clifton pushes me into the wall face-first and I'm too slurred and drunk to fight back without killing someone, or myself. "We are looking at you, Dixon," Clifton grunts, teeth clenched as he resists my resistance.

"If Charlie leaves this house, I swear..." I don't finish the sentence, because nothing comes to mind besides drinking myself into oblivion.

Clifton eases up, but only slightly. "We know, man." He's still got my tee shirt in his fists and his forearm across the back of my neck. "We know..."

"Took you long enough to admit it," Charlie spits. The way my face is angled, I can just see Mer grabbing him under the arm and helping him back onto his feet. Standing, Charlie straightens out his jacket and throws up his hands. "Jesus, man. How far would I have had to go before you admitted it to yourself? Did you want me to actually fuck her first? Not that I would have minded, but...woah!" Charlie backs up and I'm shocked when Mer edges in front of him. She angles her body to the side, but I never get that far. Clifton holds me back.

"If you..."

Charlie cuts me off. "I fucking won't, man. Who the fuck do you think I am? You're my goddamn brother and you're in love with the girl!"

Love. What? I start to curse, just like her, but I also start to canter back. Clifton's there again, this time to catch me. "Dixon? Dixon, hey. Hey!" He pushes me against the wall, this time using it as a brace as he settles me onto the floor. I place my elbows on my knees and let my head hang between them.

"Love," I groan, voice so gravelly I barely understand it.

"Yeah man. Love." I see Charlie's shiny Oxford wing-tip nudge the side of my shitkicker. "And right now she's waiting for your sorry ass. I thought one of y'all was supposed to be watching him."

"Don't worry, all the bottles in the kitchen were watered down," Knox says.

I shake my head and tilt it back to face the many faces staring down. "Bottles on the table...from my room." I cough into my fist while the world above me swirls in and out of focus.

"For fuck's sake, Knox. I thought you were his brother. Didn't you think he might have kept shit in his room? *Pinche idiota.*" Mer leans into him while Charlie turns to Clifton.

"Shit. I'm supposed to meet this bi...chick...woman..." His gaze finds mine and the brown pools fill with panic. He holds up his hands and edges backwards abruptly. "No offense. I'm just trying to figure out what the hell we're going to do now. This wasn't the plan. You were supposed to stop me half an hour ago and you weren't supposed to be fucking wasted. Jesus, Knox. You had one job..."

Knox throws his arms in the air and Mer pushes on his chest when he starts to crowd the narrow sliver of hallway between Charlie and me. "What the hell was I supposed to do? Big brother's got his door locked. There's no way to get in there."

"Alright, enough with the excuses." Clifton slides his hands under my armpits, clenches his teeth together and drags me to my feet. I'm shaky, and it isn't because of the booze. I'm petrified. Scared as hell of what's happening to me. What is happening to me? I don't know, but everyone else seems to. "Snap out of it. You've got a date to go to."

"Date?" I wipe the back of my hand across my mouth and try to take a step, but as my adrenaline crashes the floor disappears from beneath me. I lurch forward and catch Charlie's chest with my shoulder. Clifton's cursing endlessly in my ear.

Then Mer's voice. "Dixon, can you hear me? I know that even talking to you will probably piss you off but do I have your permission to go into your room?"

"No," I moan. Bile pitches in my stomach and swims up my esophagus and into my mouth. I swallow it down and I can hear people speaking to me, but I'm too focused on what Mer just asked. Why is she speaking to me directly? She never has before, at least not unsolicited.

"What?" I choke.

"Knox here." He grabs the back of my neck and forces me to look at him. He slaps my cheeks. "Stay awake there, buddy. Mer wants to go into your room because she's trying to help you, for fuck's sake."

"Help me?" How the hell could she help me? No one helps me. Least of all a woman.

"Yeah. Help you." He squeezes my pressure points until the idea of pain fires into my mind. I don't feel it though. I feel nothing. Not the skin of my fingers or my brothers' hands keeping me upright. "You look like hell and you smell like shit. Mer's a chick…"

"Sort of," Charlie chides. Mer lunges at him and he cracks up when she smacks her hand across his thigh.

Knox ignores them both and adds with a smile, "She's a woman and she can help you if you're going to see Sara tonight." His gaze hits mine and I fail to find understanding. For the first moment. Then I lurch half a step forward so that Mer comes into view. Behind Knox's body she looks quite small, but I've seen what the muscles that ripple down her arms can do.

I nod once. "Go."

She balances on the balls of her feet. With her arms crossed tight over Knox's tee shirt she looks uncomfortable. "Shit, man. I know I'm not welcome here, but I was just trying to…"

"No. Go to my room."

Her eyes widen and she glances around, braids whipping over her shoulder. When none of my brothers contradict her, she whispers, "You serious?"

I nod and Knox backs up, dragging Mer with him. "Be quick," he tells her, squeezing her ass hard when she turns from him and breaks out into a light jog. "And pick out something that normal girls would like."

"I know what I'm doing, *puto!*" Just before she disappears around the end of the long hallway, she looks at my brothers standing around me and says, "Run a rag over his face and neck so she won't be able to smell too much of the booze bleeding through his pores. And get him to brush his teeth."

I'm walking or falling into the kitchen and onto one of the bar stools. Clifton's pressing water glasses into my hand and somebody's lifting my shirt off over my head. A cold, damp rag comes over me and I hiss. Trying to pull away from it,

I'm at the sink and someone is forcing a toothbrush into my hand. By the time I finish scrubbing up, Mer is back.

She's got a tee shirt for me. It's black with little grey dots that are hand stitched into the heavy cotton material. I know that it's mine but for the life of me, I can't remember buying it or ever wearing it before. She sprays cologne in my general direction while I punch my fists through the sleeves of the leather jacket she hands me. Pants off, the jeans she gives me are dark grey. Charlie adds oil to my hair and brushes it up into shape so that the short fade doesn't look so schizophrenic. Suddenly they're all standing away from me, as if to review their collective masterpiece.

Clifton is first to say, "Not bad."

Charlie whistles. "You might just be able to pull this off."

"But we don't have time to chit chat," Mer snaps, none too apologetically. "You're supposed to be there in five minutes."

"The Uber's already here." Glancing at his cell, Knox moves forward to the front door. He pulls it open and cold air rushes into the house. "Come on. Your chariot awaits."

"You got your wallet? Your keys?" Charlie asks.

I reach into my pockets at the same time that I take a step forward and the dual action proves to be too much because my right knee buckles and my body embarks on a short and dangerous journey to the floor. Simultaneous curses reign. It's Charlie who grabs me this time. Charlie and Mer.

"*Dios mio*, you weigh a goddamn ton," she says, transferring my weight to her other, bigger half. Knox grabs me and he and Charlie help me to the door. "Where are you going?"

"With him, I guess."

"On his date?" Mer curses. "You and Clifton can't go alone and Charlie, you can't go at all. Give me thirty seconds to grab a shirt."

Clifton laughs. "A group date, it is."

"Why can't I go?" Charlie whines.

"Because if you even look at Sara," Knox says as he helps me out of the door and into the cool, dark night, "I guarantee that Dixon will rip out your throat."

As we reach the Lexus parked in the center of the driveway Charlie shouts, "How do you know?"

"Because that's what I would do." Knox laughs. Mer grins and I can see a surge of lust color her expression crimson. I don't know what it would do to me if Sara ever looked at me like that. Like she wanted me more than anything else.

"Don't forget to check in," I grumble. Charlie nods and retreats into the house. As he does, he pulls his cell phone out of his pocket, I'm sure to call any number of other women who he's got on retainer. Just another reminder of why I'm doing this. I may not be enough to deserve her but she sure as hell deserves better than that.

In the Uber we sit three in the back. Me, Knox, Mer and in that order. I keep the window cracked despite the protests of my brothers. I'm burning up, charcoaling from within. She was supposed to be with Charlie alone and now I'm about to rock up with two of my brothers and Mer. As if I weren't terrifying enough. As if she didn't already hate me. I never want to arrive. Can't get there fast enough.

My palms are sweaty and my breathing is shallow and weak. We cross the city in its entirety, the lights on Seventh Street flashing past. Looks like a torch compared to the darkness surrounding her complex though my brothers don't comment on it, or on the state of the building as we pull into the lot. Suddenly my body has become a battlefield. My mind is clear with the desire to act, but I can't move. My fingers fumble over the doorknob and from the other side of the car, I hear Mer curse. Her door opens and suddenly she's standing in front of me.

"No, you stay," she says as Knox tries to slide out after her. His lips clench together, and he looks at me, then at Mer and back again. "What the hell do you think will happen?"

"Dixon," Knox growls.

I meet his gaze bluntly and say, "She gets hurt while she's with me and I'll give you my life."

The severity of his face releases, he slouches back into his seat and he crosses his arms over his chest. He nods once, but Mer doesn't see it. She's already wrapping my arm around her neck and leading me towards the building. I tell her where to go and she guides me up the stairs and down the hall to Sara's door. My mouth is dry as ash. I can't lift my fist. What the hell am I doing? She's going to take one look at me and slam the door shut and I don't want or need Mer with me there to see it.

Mer rolls her eyes and zips her coat up over the low-cut, long-sleeved shirt she's wearing. Her braids, she flips over her shoulder. "*Dios mio*, wait here."

She releases me and my back finds the wall a short ways down the hall. Standing in front of Sara's neighbor's door, the scent of weed thickening my already cloudy thoughts, I'll be out of sight, which I'm grateful for, but I won't be able to see her either. I lick my lips and watch in horror as Mer's knuckles crack against the cream-colored door. It swings open almost immediately.

"Oh." I hear her voice, tinted by surprise and my heart races faster. "Hello."

"Hi," Mer says, sounding more human than I've ever heard her. "My name is Mer. I date Knox, one of Dixon and Charlie's brothers." She holds out her hand.

Sara's porcelain palm stretches out to meet it tentatively, still cautious. Good girl. "Hi. Sorry, I'm just…is there something wrong. Is he hurt?"

He. The word rings repetitively, filling up all the silence surrounding her voice. Which one of us is she thinking of, is she concerned about?

Mer laughs and shows Sara her palms. "They're both fine. Well, one is more fine than the other."

"What happened?"

"Well, one of them happened to ask out a girl the other one is in love with so that one went on a bender then attacked the other one when he tried to leave the house. They're both fine though, physically at least."

I could kill Mer. Kill her and kiss her in the same second for having the balls to say what I couldn't. Sh… What the hell is Sara going to say? What is she going to do? My fists are shoved into my pockets and I clutch hard at the material as if it'll keep me from falling over. I'm swaying, even though my back is flat against the wall, spine stiff, shoulders knotted. She still hasn't said anything, and my whole world is crumbling to the ground. Rejection has never come easily to me and this is the first time I've been rejected by something I want.

"He told you that?" That's what she says. I expect something more, but why I do, I don't know. Her skepticism is the least that I deserve.

Mer shrugs both shoulders to her ears. "Why don't you ask him? He's right here."

A pause. Then, "Here?" Her voice catches, and the word comes out butchered. I've never heard her anything less than eloquent.

"Yeah I mean, right here." Mer jerks her elbow towards me and glances vaguely in my direction, as if there were somewhere else she'd rather be. I can tell however, that she's loving this. I would too if I were her.

A pale hand stretches forward into the light. That hand is all I can see of her. "You mean, he's in this hallway?"

"Yes."

"Like right here? He can hear everything we're saying?"

"Yep."

Her face peeks around the doorframe and her expression is one of shock as she takes me in. "Sh..." She jerks back up to standing and disappears from sight.

Mer laughs. "So I'll wait at the end of the hall, maybe give you two a few minutes to chat. But essentially, I'm here because we didn't want to ruin your night. You asked for a night out and that is exactly what we plan to provide. We just weren't quite sure if you would feel comfortable going out with just Dixon alone in his current uhh...state."

Sara drops her pitch, but not low enough because I can still hear it. "How bad is it?"

"Fine," I blurt out, voice raw from all of the liquor. I stand up and away from the wall and Mer lurches towards me when I try to take a step. This is embarrassing, because I want to shove her off, but have to use her as a crutch instead.

"I'm fine," I repeat, blinking quickly. Everything is blurred — except for her. Sara, I can see in total clarity.

She's standing just inside her apartment, arms crossed tight over her chest and the outfit she's wearing makes my mouth water. She's got on skin tight jeans and a royal blue shirt cut low enough I can see the swell of her cleavage. Her blonde hair falls around her shoulders in loose waves and the makeup she wears makes her look like she belongs in front of a camera, not staring at me with concern — or is it fear? revulsion? — in the middle of this dimly lit hall.

"You don't have to come," I say. "I just know that you got a sitter for Brant and you don't get many nights off...wanted you to have a good time." At least this was what Mer and my brothers said earlier.

The real reason I'm standing here is because I'm too weak to resist her. Never more so than now. She looks perfect enough I want to reprimand her for not wearing a trash bag out with my brother. She put herself together like this for him.

Her blue eyes beam up at me and she shifts a couple inches closer. Glancing at Mer, she says, "I'll come out with you guys, but may I talk to Dixon for a second? If he's okay to stand, I mean..."

"I'm fine," I repeat, but neither woman is listening to me.

Mer edges me back until I'm against the wall. My head swims rapidly for a moment when I try to break free of her grip and stand on my own, unsupported. The effort is futile and when the world finally settles around me, I'm leaning where Mer put me. Sara is standing just out of reach and Mer is at the end of the hall, waiting and watching like a good babysitter. My core is fire and though I know Sara just agreed to come out with us and I should be happy about it, I'm still embarrassed to hell.

I expect her to lay into me, tell me off and reassure me that her feelings towards me could never be anything other than hostile, but when her lips part the guarded expression she wears falls. She reaches towards me and I'm stunned by the pressure of her hands on my face, my forehead, running underneath my collar to feel my chest.

"Sh…" she breathes, never finishing the word and I smile because of it.

"I'm sorry," I whisper.

"Your skin is fire, your pulse is fast and your eyes are bloodshot. How much did you drink?" I shake my head and her eyes narrow. "Don't lie to me."

"I drank as much as I could to forget you were going on a date with my brother."

The words don't seem to faze her. She repeats, "How many?"

"Two."

"Two what?" Color rushes to her cheeks and I want to move closer to her, but know that wouldn't be welcome right now.

"Two bottles."

Her dark eyelashes arch up to her forehead. "Oh boy." She exhales heavily. "That explains it then. Whiskey?"

"How'd you know?"

"Everyone knows you're a whiskey man." She pulls her arms back and crosses them, hands balled into tight little fists. The gesture only succeeds in pulling her tits closer together. I focus on her face with renewed intensity and she sucks in a breath. "You told them you loved me?"

I shake my head. Can't meet her gaze. "Didn't say anything. They just knew." I clear my throat. "I spend every day I can with you and am pissed off all the days that I don't."

She swallows and I see all of her limbs reposition themselves very subtly. "You seem pissed when you do."

"I'm an asshole."

She laughs. "Yeah, you are."

"But you're still here."

"What do you mean?"

"I mean…" I lick my lips and though it takes all of my concentration, I manage to bring life into my back muscles and stand up on my own. "You could tell me to leave anytime, close and lock your door."

She glances back, and edges in that direction. I've done something to anger her again. It's not the first time I've seen this response. "How could I do that to the man who's given me so much?"

"Is that the only reason?" Because I pay for the privilege. Just like all the other scum.

She nods. I grit my teeth, collapse back against the wall, and call for Mer. As she looks up and starts towards us, Sara grabs my arm.

"No, wait!" Mer stops in her tracks. Sara turns to me. "Wait. I didn't mean that. I mean...I don't know what I mean. You've just been so hot and cold to me that up until Mer knocked on my door, I thought you were trying to dick me around."

"I never meant that." I rub my face hard as the alcohol wages war with my rationality. "I just...never been in love before. It hurts here..." I touch the center of my chest.

I've never been good with emotions, and have never had to articulate them. Marguerite used to try to coerce the thoughts out of me, and while she never succeeded, I'm standing in front of a woman who's never even asked trying to force her to understand my perspective.

"When you're not around it hurts here." I take her hand and force it to my chest, under my jacket, and I lock it there beneath my palm.

Sara looks directly down and shakes her head. She doesn't say anything and it worries me because she's the type of woman who always speaks her mind. I say her name and she punches me in the shoulder with her other hand.

"You are such an asshole," she says and it's the first time I've ever heard her curse but I'm not given time to dwell on it when she lifts up onto her toes and presses her mouth to my lips.

She kisses me hard and my whole body reacts. I hold her there against me – my hands on her hand and around the broad of her back – and I commit the sensation of her body's curves against mine to memory, just as I have our every encounter leading up to this. Her lips are fire and so deliciously soft. I'm not used to kissing women like this – as if to stop kissing them would be to die. I want more than her mouth though. I want her to want me back.

I wrench away from her, holding her shoulder at arm's length – her arms, not mine. "Do you..." Do you have feelings for me? Tell me now, otherwise to keep kissing you will be to break me entirely. "Do you want to come out with me?"

Sara inhales deeply and smiles. "Yes. I'd like that."

Nodding, I release her arms and as she separates us by another step, I whisper, "I won't let you down again. Ever."

There's that blush again, swirling across her chest in shades of carmine. "Says the man who's so drunk on my doorstep he can hardly stand or speak."

"I'm sorry," I say, smiling for the first time this evening. For what feels like forever. "This is...not how I wanted this to go."

She smirks and the atmosphere between us is lifted, made lighter by something that I don't understand but that I want to know intimately. "How did you want it to go?"

"Any other way."

She laughs quietly and shakes her head. "Alright, well why don't we get on with it then and see where the night takes us? After all, I'm training to be a medical doctor. What kind of doctor would I make if I let you go out into the world like this and fend for yourself?"

I let her slide up against me and pull my arm over her shoulder. She walks me to Mer who then takes most of my weight and helps me out to the car.

Mer sits on Knox's lap and we drive like this to Mercury — a bar we like two towns over, one we don't own so we don't feel any responsibility for the clientele. Knox and Mer head to the dance floor immediately and Clifton cozies up to a blonde at the bar. At a table, just the two of us, Sara sips on a gin and tonic. She's got the straw trapped between her teeth and she's laughing at something a couple on the dance floor is doing. The smile on my face makes my cheeks hurt because they've never been in this position for so long.

I drink water. Tons of it. Because I refuse to still be hammered when it's time to take her home. I wait for that time. Wait for it on the edge of my seat. I want to play the gentleman. I want to give her my elbow if she stumbles, give her my jacket when she's cold. I want to open the door for her and kiss her on the cheek and promise her that I'll be over to make it up to her tomorrow. To her and Brant.

But she doesn't ask to leave and pretty soon it's nearing two am.

Her eyebrows lift and she suddenly balks. "Oh my gosh, is that Clifton with a prostitute?" That drags me out of the spell I'd been under. She's a vision in blue.

Reluctantly I turn my head, following the line of her finger until I see a tall, modern day Viking trailing a pro with short, auburn hair. "Woah," she says, and I see why a second later. At the bar, a second man who looks daringly close to the first tries to catch the Viking's attention, without success.

"Clifton's twin brother, Aiden," I say. "Hard to tell them apart from here, but when you get close enough, you'll see the difference."

"What is it?"

How do I put gently that one's a loveable teddy bear and the other, a sociopath with a penchant for killing? "Aiden's not like his brother. Don't make the assumption that he is. Ever."

"Why didn't he come here with us?" Sara asks, looking puzzled.

I grimace. "Not much for socializing."

"Sure seems like he's socializing now." We watch them disappear through the door to the bathrooms. He won't fuck her in there though, but rather take her to the alley. Even in winter, outside in filth is the only place he fucks women. The man hates himself as much as he hates everything else around him.

"It was Aiden and not Clifton who interrupted us the first time we met. I don't want you around him alone."

I look back at Sara and though her lips twist down at the corners, for once she doesn't protest. "Okay."

"Hey, lady and gent...well, lady." Clifton chuckles as he approaches. "Let's say we continue this party at ours? I think Knox and Mer need to get out of range of pubic eyes."

Feeling more sober now I open my mouth to tell him that Sara probably wants to go home, but it's Sara who speaks. "That sounds like fun," she says with a shrug, pulling her purse off of the bench seat beside her and over her shoulder.

I fidget with my jacket uncomfortably. "Are you sure?"

Her cheeks are flushed, eyes glossy, but she seems coherent and clear. "Sorry. I don't mean to intrude."

"You're not intruding," I say before she's finished and she smiles at me broadly.

She shrugs and takes a sip of her drink, sucking in dredges of melted ice cubes and air. "Okay then. It's a plan."

She takes my hand when it's offered and I lead her back to the car. The five of us who'd gone out together pull into the driveway and it's strange watching her pass across the threshold – a barrier I've denied so many others. Not just women, but everyone. That's all I ever wanted was to keep people out. And now I want to share everything with her.

Clifton pours drinks and Mer and Knox don't last long. Watching their inability to keep their hands off one another makes me roll out my neck, wring my hands, cross and uncross my legs. Makes it difficult to remember to be a gentleman when I glance at Sara seated next to me on the couch. After a while, Clifton leaves and it's just us and the throbbing in my body grows more intense. I lower the volume of the music playing.

"Do you want me to take you home?" I say, throat dry. Scorched. I drank too much, stared too hard, acted too out of character. I don't know who I am anymore because ordinarily, denying a woman would be easy. Denying a woman I wanted because I didn't feel good enough, on the other hand…well, I'd never been in this position before.

She blinks up at me, runs her hand back through her silky hair. The way she's seated, twisted towards me on the couch causes the cleavage I'd been trying to ignore all night to rise higher on each inhale. "Do you want to take me home?"

Sh... I clear my throat. "I know what I want to say, but what I want to do is something else entirely."

"Well why don't I make it easy for you?" She sets her glass down on the edge of the table and slides her hand across the couch towards me. I watch it hungrily.

"How will you manage that?"

"I might start by asking you to show me your room."

The heat in my chest swims down to the rod hanging between my legs. Leading the way there, I feel like I'm in high school again. Sober now, I can't fully recall the moments that led to this. What state of utopia did I have to be in to secure her tacit endorsement, even enough to hold my hand, which she is.

"This is it." I turn the key in the lock and open the door to my most sacred space – a space I was denied as a boy: my own. It's entirely different than the rest of the house, and not just because it's four times bigger than any other room. It has its own living room, couch, TV and fireplace while the bed sits against the opposite wall against a half-partition. It's bigger than her entire apartment and the blush on her face looks to me like one of embarrassment. My gut softens, and grows cold.

"You don't like it," I say, knowing that's not the reason she takes a tour of the space. She keeps her hands to herself, as if she's not worthy to touch any of my things. It makes me want to shatter them.

"No, I just...you have so much. I probably wouldn't have let you into my apartment if I'd known you live like this."

"I'm glad you didn't then." I inhale and breach the distance between us by half, but I won't go farther. Can't.

Not when I'm this in love with her. Another step forward and I'll need to keep her forever. "It's just stuff. What you have in your house is more meaningful."

"You mean Brant?"

"Yes. He's part of it."

She glances down. "I didn't think you liked kids."

"I like your kid."

As she exhales, she shivers from head to toe. "Oh lord."

"What's wrong?"

She bites her lips between her teeth and the red in her cheeks holds. Sanding between the couch and the bed she looks so small against such ubiquitous and superfluous luxury. It's meaningless without her.

"Sara, what is it?"

Her gaze hits mine and is enough to knock me backwards. I imagine myself falling, like a set of dominoes though I haven't moved. "Shit," she says.

Her arms drop to the sides and her purse hits the floor with a thump and a clatter. She's moving swiftly towards me and my mind screams that this is a trap. It is. Because when her hands hit the wall of my chest and sweep around my sides, wrenching me in, I'm standing upright as I fall for her.

She squeezes my waist and pushes up on her toes and her lips meet mine and every muscle in my body reacts. My arms circle her body and I crush her to me, lifting her from the ground in the same motion. I cup her ass, squeezing it hard and she breathes hard against my mouth as we come together in the middle of my room. She tastes like lavender and butter and I melt into her. Her hands move quickly over my face and neck and arms. She grips my shoulders, slips her fingers underneath the edges of my shirt, and as I collapse down onto the edge of the bed she rips it off of me. She's got my belt in her fists and my erection kicks violently towards her.

"Easy," I hiss, taking her two hands in one of my own and stretching them above her head. I lie her down, sliding my other hand against her stomach, beneath the edge of her blue, blue shirt, one that has nothing on the color of her eyes.

She gasps and her eyelids flutter. "Please," she begs, "I've wanted this for so long."

I can't believe that, but I want to. I kiss a circle around her belly button before covering my body with hers. My right hand shoots down the front of her jeans and I cup her core through her panties. They're soaked and I'm unraveling. "Jesus," I murmur.

"Christ," she mimics.

I taste her cheek, her jaw, her throat, and then I feel my way down the front of her G-string and run my fingers over that soft, supple section, loving the reaction that I win from her. The sudden surge of air that sweeps into her lungs, and as she expels it, my name. She comes for me the first time, and everything kicks into high gear after that. Her pussy is pulsing around my fingers as I draw her shirt over her head and wrench off her jeans. She rips my belt free of the loops and I push her all the way onto the bed. My hand around the back of her neck, I stare deep into her eyes as our two bodies come together at the hips.

We release a shared moan and goddamn, she is tighter than a vice. Moving slowly at first, I soon pick up speed and glide in and out of her relentlessly, the pressure enough to shatter. But she takes it with deep moans. Her porcelain skin is splotchy, red flowering under my palms as I squeeze her breasts and twist her nipples between my middle finger and my thumb. I kiss her lips, taste her cool breath.

"Sara," I whisper.

"Dixon," she whispers back.

Her lips part and her eyes close. Her nails bare down into my shoulders and watching her come for me, I lose control. The orgasm folds over me like the dawn, tackling me from behind. I worry I'll crush her beneath me, but she only wraps her arms around my shoulders and her legs around my waist. A few moments pass before my length hardens inside of her again, without waiting for either of our heartbeats to settle.

"Sh..." she says and I release low laughter between us as slide my hand beneath her lower back and lift. She gasps.

"I'm not finished with you by a long shot," I growl into her neck, knowing that nothing I could have ever done in a past life would have made me worthy of her. So as my lips pull at hers I vow that I will treasure every minute of this life that I have been given because every minute with her is a gift.

Aiden

I wake though I never really fell asleep. My eyes were open the whole time, though I wasn't conscious of what I was seeing. Now, I want to close them, but I remember what can happen in the dark. Even just the darkness of an eyelid. All the lights in my room are on and though there are no mirrors here, I catch my reflection in the glossy surface of the dresser. I've got bags like bruises under both eyes and I'm unshaved. My lips are dry and I imagine that if a stranger saw me standing beside Clifton right now, they wouldn't even know we were brothers, let alone twins. I'm meat and ash and he's sunlight. I remember thinking that the first time I met him. He'd called me brother. I hadn't seen the resemblance.

It's three am. I get up and go to the gym.

My bare feet pound down on the treadmill. Music blasts into the room through the ceiling and walls. Rakim, Bob Dylan, ocean sounds, Faith Hill, Local Natives, Tupac, Mozart. No theme, artist, band, genre, consistency. Just sounds. I like sounds second to silence but these days silence gets my mind wandering and there's only one thing to dream about.

The cross that does not belong to me thumps against my chest beneath my shirt. I looked for her. Thought I'd return the cross. Swore I would. Hacked her accounts. Email, Instagram, Snapchat, Facebook, Twitter. All active but no posts, despite fans flooding her DM. All of her messages went ignored, including those from photographers and clients from fashion magazines and well-known brands. I gained some insight from an email sent from her law school study group wishing her the best with her grandmother's illness, but it still didn't help in tracking down where Gavriil had taken her.

Sweat runs down the back of my shirt as I force myself to shut down all thoughts of Alina. Concentrating instead on the sound of Death Metal blasting through the speakers overhead, my mind finally drifts. I think of nothing. Some indeterminate amount of time passes before the door behind me opens and shuts. I know it's Clifton when he doesn't announce himself.

He stands directly behind the treadmill and when I don't step down or slow, he says, "I don't know how you live like this." He has to shout to be heard. "Daft Punk's shaking the whole damn house."

Glancing at the treadmill dashboard, I hit the red button. Fifteen and a half miles will do. I step off the treadmill and silence the surround sound. I toss Clifton the remote and he hands me a bottle of water.

"You look like you need it. You're raining, man. How long you been down here?"

I take the bottle from him and crack the lid, emptying most of it down my throat. "An hour." I shrug. "Maybe more."

He makes a face and leans in towards me, then sniffs like a dog. "Funny. After an hour of sweating like this I'd have expected the smell to have worn off."

He's talking about the perfume I sprayed on my wrist earlier that day. The smell of it helps me nod off. These days, it's the only thing that helps me sleep at all. I say nothing and he shrugs. "Nothing doing, just doesn't seem like you. Wanted to know what was keeping you up."

"Nothing from the Russians yet." I don't know if it's a question or a statement. I just want him to shut up.

Clifton shakes his head. "Nothing yet. And Ollie's completely MIA."

"Unlucky for him."

Clifton clenches his teeth together and gives me one of his stern glances, full of condescension that I don't feel, or respond to. "He was our friend, man."

"Yeah. Our friend." The word means nothing to me. "Which is why I'd have killed him outright instead of torturing him."

Clifton shakes his head. "You've got no soul, brother."

I don't contradict it.

"Are you even happy here with us?" he asks as I brush past him and head to the door.

Happy. What's that?

I cross the full-sized basketball court and my feet echo as they slap the glossy wood. Tossing the crushed plastic to the side, I step back into the house. I move quickly to avoid Clifton, whose footsteps I can hear chasing me down the hall. I pass Dixon's closed door, then Knox's, which is open.

"Shit," a woman's voice says. Mer's. I glance up and she's standing in the light of the bathroom wearing nothing but a pair of Knox's boxers. I reach into the room to close the door at the same time that a body tackles me from the side.

"What the…" Clifton says from the end of the hall. He's running, but I've backed Dixon into the wall hard enough a picture frame falls and shatters. I elbow him in the ribs and he hisses, relaxing his hold enough for me to twist out from beneath him and sweep his feet.

On the ground, Dixon shouts, "Don't!" He glances at the door, and holds his hands up like he might stop me through will or kinetic energy. "I know what I asked you to do, but don't do it."

I smirk. Funny. He thought I was going to kill her then. "I was shutting the door."

"What the hell is going on?" Mer's wearing a tee shirt now that drapes to her thighs and stands in the open doorway. Her arms are crossed and her hair falls around her shoulders in glossy waves.

"Dixon thought I was going to kill you."

Mer looks at me, then at Dixon. He's still on the ground and makes no move to get up. "And you tried to stop him?"

Dixon doesn't react, except to clench his teeth.

"Why would Aiden try to kill Mer?" Clifton asks behind me. It doesn't take as long as it should for Mer to figure it out. Unsurprising. A girl in the cartel, I'm likely not the first bastard who's tried to kill her.

"Because you asked him to," she says, voice passive except for the slight hiccup at the end. Trying to be strong but love's made her weak.

I don't respond to that, but step over Dixon, leaving the three of them in muted silence. I'm in the kitchen, making a sandwich, when Clifton curses long and loud. "You're a selfish fucking bastard."

There's commotion before Mer cuts in. "Hey. Hey! *Gillopas,* it's done. It's over. I'm still here and Dixon clearly doesn't feel the same way anymore if he tried to stop…" Their voices dissolve to white noise and I find myself again drifting in and out of this perpetual state of hallucination, a sandwich in one hand and in the other, a stolen cross.

Sara

"Sh…" my voice is a silent curse as I drift awake.

"What's wrong?" His voice comes as a shock because it's so close and because it means that last night wasn't a dream.

I shake my head and bury my face into my pillow, not wanting him to see how haggard I likely look. "Nothing's wrong." In fact, everything is pretty perfect. "Just achy all over. In a good way." Not to mention a little hung over.

He laughs under his breath and his hand finds the back of my head. Fingers gently comb through my hair. It's tangled. "That can't be good for me then." As he speaks, he shifts across the mattress and lines my body with his.

Against my rear, I feel the pressure of his erection and I emit another half-curse. He laughs again, the sound a deep rumble I can feel against my back, through his chest. He sounds so satisfied and I feel hopeful in ways I haven't felt in a long time.

I roll over so that we lay face-to-face. Kissing his shoulder, I work my hands around the thickness of his erection, loving the way his eyes close and his whole body tenses. He whispers something that I don't quite catch, but it sounds sensual and dangerously like my name, and his whole face is contoured in a profound rapture that I'm not worthy enough to break.

So instead, I straddle his hips and lower myself down onto his shaft. My whole body buzzes pleasantly and when Dixon asks me if I'm okay to do this, I tell him the truth: "Never wanted to do anything more."

He smiles and his teeth are bright white as they clench together. His large, flat hands roam over my breasts, cupping my neck and drawing me down to him. I come first, which is good because after he comes and pulls out of me, his semen is everywhere – my thighs, my pussy, the sheets, the pillows, the duvet – and I remember that we willfully forgot to wear condoms again. He seems to have the same realization I do as he collapses down at my side, like all of his muscles have been liquefied.

"Are you on the pill?"

"Nope." I groan, "I'll have to pick up Plan B from a pharmacy."

"Shit," he grumbles, "I'm sorry. I should have…"

"It's not your fault. I thought about it last night but I just…" My voice trails off. I'm too winded and windswept to be talking right now, because every word out of my mouth is going to be embarrassing. "Never mind." I shake my head and turn my face away from his.

He doesn't press me. Just lays there in silence. I glance over at him and he's staring at the ceiling until all at once, he looks at me and says, "I love you."

"Sh…" I start to curse and stop myself and he grins.

"I think that's what I first fell in love with."

"What?"

"That sound you make when you're about to say shit, but don't." He slides his palms beneath his head and glances down the length of my body, as if he's either the happiest or the proudest man in the world. Maybe both.

I gulp hard, wondering if this is what he tells all the women he sleeps with…but somehow, I don't think so. "I love you too," I say.

That seems to shock him because he sits up, then collapses back onto his elbows. His full lips hang suspended, forming a loose O. Then he licks them. "I didn't need you to say anything back. If it makes you uncomfortable…"

"I've loved you since I first saw you." He stares at me skeptically and I can feel myself blush as heat begins to build in my chest. "It's true so stop staring at me like I'm lying to you."

"I don't think you're lying," he says after a moment. "I don't think you ever do. I just know I don't deserve it and I'm grateful, just so grateful for you." He leans over me and plants a kiss gently on my forehead before taking my hand in his.

He laces his fingers through mine and I stare at the contact. "I think you might. You're not just paying for my school. You're paying for Brant too, aren't you?"

He hesitates before he redirects and I know I've got my answer. "Speaking of Brant, shouldn't we be collecting him about now?"

"We? And don't think you're going to get out of answering me." I'm shaky, but with him watching me like that, it helps me feel sure. He looks at me like no one's ever looked at me before. Like I'm the only thing in the world.

Shaking his head, he sighs, "Looks like we've made a hell of a mess, and I don't just mean the sheets." He slides off of the bed and, standing at its foot, hooks his hands around my ankles. I laugh as he drags me to him with a swift jerk. He scoops me up and carries me to the bathroom where we make love again without a condom because that option's already come and gone. By the time we make it to the car, I'm spent.

We pick Brant up first and Dixon walks with me to the door, then leaves Mrs. Petersen a generous tip. She doesn't complain about the late arrival after that. We stop by a pharmacy next and Dixon pays for the Plan B – as well as a box of condoms, for the next time, he says. That keeps me grinning because I had hoped there'd be a next time.

The breakfast place he picks is kid-friendly and Brant is pleased as a peach the moment he's got Cheerios in front of him, and stuck to most of his arms and face. Dixon laughs as he eventually gives up trying to keep Brant clean and lets him do whatever he wants, which had been my plan to begin with.

The light glints off the glossy wooden tabletop and when I glance up, I see that the sun's out. Winter's upon us but with my boys laughing as they are and the sun shifting in between the blinds like a coy dancer, I imagine that it's summer and that we've reached nirvana and that everything in the world is just right. Dixon catches me smiling and leans across the table to kiss me. He kisses me so deeply, I have to push him back before we make a scene because he's so tall it makes the table between us seem like nothing.

Massaging his thumb across my cheek he asks for the check, then looks to me and says, "I better get you home." He plants his elbows on the table and takes another sip of his coffee. As he sets it down, he grins and ruffles Brant's hair. "I think I got some Cheerio in that last drag."

I laugh and lean over to kiss my baby's chubby chestnut cheeks. He howls with laughter as I near his neck and I notice that the sound is infectious. Several of the people in here are staring at us and I wonder for the first time, if they don't think Brant is my baby and Dixon's. The thought fills me with pride.

"You were saying," I blurt in an effort to distract myself from the pleasant and tingly sensation that thought brought on. Dixon grinning at me in that funny way he has been the past twelve hours certainly isn't helping me much. On the contrary, the space between my legs is soaked and I'm not wearing any panties, but the same jeans I was wearing the night before and one of Mer's camis underneath Dixon's coat.

Trying to harvest whatever we'd been talking about earlier, the conversation takes an abrupt left turn. "Thank you," he says.

"For what?"

"For the first time we met. What you did."

My fingers pluck a piece of fruit off of my plate and I chew thoughtfully. "You're welcome."

"Who were those guys anyways? Did you know them?"

Dixon looks away from me and shakes his head. "No. Just some assholes."

"Yeah I'm sure you did nothing to deserve it."

"Nothing at all."

I roll my eyes. "What on earth were you doing that drunk, alone, in the middle of the night on Seventh?"

Dixon winces. He doesn't answer right away and that concerns me. His gaze passes to Brant and he uses his thumb to wipe a smear of lord-only-knows-what off of my baby boy's cheek. "I don't have an alcohol problem, if that's what you're asking."

"Oh. I umm... I hadn't really thought of that. Guess that makes me a lousy doctor."

He smiles though there's no feeling in it. "I don't have healthy coping mechanisms though I'm working on that. And I'm a fairly private person."

No kidding. Man was shut tighter than an oyster. Too bad I was such a sucker for pearls.

He continues, "When Knox brought Mer home, it ticked me off. Was the first time any of the brothers had invited anyone to live with us. I didn't handle it well."

I gulp. "Wow. That explains a lot. And last night?"

"Don't make me spell it out for you." When I don't prompt him, he breathes through his mouth like a horse. "I was jealous."

"Jealous enough to beat up on one of your brothers?"

"Nearly ripped his car door off."

I roll my eyes. "Just what a girl loves to hear." Except, it is.

Dixon's fork maneuvers past mine to attack a piece of pineapple. I fend him off with my knife. He grins and clears his throat, changing the subject. "And thank you for the second time we met, too."

"Second time?"

"I think most guys would consider themselves pretty lucky to get a lap dance on their first date from you." He exhales and reaches down to adjust his belt. "Christ, we need to get out of here before I lose it at this table."

"You looking for a private showing?" I tease.

"Not looking. Begging," he answers without an ounce of humility.

"I hate to be the bearer of bad news, but I must warn you that they don't run cheap."

He huffs through his nostrils in a brutish, animalistic way that cranks up the heat between my thighs and makes me truly regret goading him. "Name your price and I'll pay it so long as it's mine and only mine."

My voice softens. "You know it is."

He doesn't say anything for a moment, then all at once jerks up to standing. He offers me his hand and with his other, collects Brant in his arms. "You're going to move in with me one of these days."

"Coming from the guy who just told me he tried to drink himself to death when Mer moved in?" I laugh, though his expression remains sober enough to shut me up. "You're serious."

He comes up behind me as we reach the door and jerks my body to his. "Have I ever lied to you?" He whispers in my ear, low enough that the sound sizzles.

"No," I whisper, only answering that last part because the first is too distant. His hand snakes down the front of my jeans but I push away from him as a group of three older women head down the sidewalk towards us.

"I'm a good southern girl, Dixon," I say, and I have no idea what I'm responding to. It doesn't seem to matter because Dixon's eyes are fire and I'm grateful for the biting wind because it helps settle the more ravenous impulse bubbling inside of me too. I've never felt like this before: so lustful.

On the drive home he takes a call from Aiden before placing another call immediately to Knox. He evades me when I ask him what the terse, clipped calls were about, much in the same way he evaded me when I asked him why Clifton had been so cold to him this morning when we'd been about to head out. He makes a face and tells me not to worry. Then we're driving into my apartment's parking lot.

I don't notice something is off immediately, but when Dixon looks over at me with a huge grin on his face and my heart lurches along unapologetically I know to be wary. "Looks like Erol's finished with the repairs." He honks twice and I notice the car parked in my spot for the first time. But the car isn't mine at all.

Dixon pulls in beside it and gets out. He greets the guy around the rear of the vehicle and as I step out into the cool air, keys exchange hands. "Erol, this is Sara and Brant. Sara, this is Erol, the genius who managed to entirely repair your piece of sh…" He pauses and laughs when my scrunched up face turns towards him. I can't decide if what I'm feeling is more horror or confusion.

"Pleasure to meet you Sara, Brant." The man tilts his head down, fingers lightly brushing the brim of his baseball cap. "Car's all ready for ya." He speaks in a gentle southern lilt, one that reminds me of home. "Hope you like how she purrs."

"I think it'll be a refreshing change from the sound her car used to make." Dixon places his hand along the back of my neck and gives me a gentle squeeze. My jaw is just hanging open. I don't say anything. "Sara?"

"I...this...you..."

Erol laughs and starts to turn. "I'll leave y'all. Got to get back to the lot."

"Thanks again. You need a ride?"

"No, Jason's coming to pick me up. Should already be on the corner at the entrance." He gives a small salute before leaving us in silence.

Dixon breaks it. "So?"

"So you..." I hoist Brant higher up on my hip as Dixon dangles a set of keys in front of me. One of the fob kinds with only two buttons because everything else is automated. "I can't believe you did this."

"In a good way, I hope." He wears a smile, but I can see that he's actually nervous and not just my heart but my whole freaking chest melts. I'm a puddle on the ground but Brant's spontaneous laughter solidifies me.

Brant furls and unfurls his fingers as he stretches towards Dixon and Dixon reaches for him. "May I?" he asks.

And the whole perfection of the day is complete. My eyes water and I quickly nod and hand Brant over. He shrills with happiness when Dixon bounces him high in his arms. "If you hate it, I can get you something else but I can't have you driving around in that piece of..."

"No. I just...I could have never afforded this car in a million years. It's a BMW." Bright red, and new. It's a BMW. Easily the nicest car in the lot. That worries me a little, but not as much as it should. I'm just so overwhelmed by the thought of having a car that'll consistently start.

"You alright?" Dixon comes to me and wraps his arm around my shoulders.

I bury my face in my hands and nod. "I can't believe this."

"I hoped you'd like it."

"It's a bit flashy," I sniffle.

He laughs loudly and ruffles my hair. "I know. But so am I. Hang around with me and you'll end up in labels and rocks so big they weigh you down."

I roll my eyes. "Lovely."

"You want to take it for a test drive?"

"Only if you promise me no rocks, no labels, no nothing."

"The first two we may be able to compromise on, but nothing? Not on my life."

I couldn't have imagined driving anything like this before getting behind the wheel, but afterwards, couldn't imagine Brant's car seat in anything else. Dixon got the model with all these kid-friendly custom features – seatbelt made for clipping in a car seat, extra leg room for the expandable versions, kid control windows and locks, and a steering wheel that only unlocks with my fingerprint. As I pull back into the lot into my parking spot, I kill the ignition.

"I just..." I bow my head and a wave of sadness grips me. "I don't think I'll ever be able to repay you, but I want you to know that I'm going to try."

I've barely finished speaking when he leans across the center console and presses his mouth to mine. "You can pay me back in anything but currency." His gaze sweeps the length of my body, coming to rest on my breasts, which aren't anywhere near visible underneath his oversized jacket.

A nervousness tickles my heart, but the expression on his face makes me smile. I coil my arms around his neck and lean into his cheek. I kiss it and whisper against his flawless espresso-colored skin, "You said you wanted to watch me touch myself this morning. Maybe I'd be willing to give it a try."

He groans as I slide my hand over the bulge in his jeans, then grabs my wrist. "You're aching for punishment aren't you?"

"No. Just aching to punish you." I slip out of the car on a laugh and, grabbing Brant, let Dixon follow us up to my apartment.

After the car, the help with Brant and with my own finances, not to mention after seeing his place, it really is difficult to say no when he asks me to move in for the third time as he's standing on my doorstep. He's glaring at my neighbor's door and I wonder if it's the smell of weed that bothers him so much.

"They're harmless," I say, pushing open the door and heading to the couch. Brant's blanket is spread out on the floor where a coffee table should be and I place him on it. The moment he's so much as out of my grasp, Dixon comes and covers my body with his and I am laughing as I poorly defend myself against the onslaught.

"No, no, no. I can't do payment now. You have to leave."

"Why?" He says, straightening up and rubbing the bulge below his belt buckle.

"Don't whine. I've got to get some homework done. Seriously, I am so behind and I have an eight am class tomorrow."

"I'll just sit here and play with Brant then."

I laugh. "You will not just play with Brant. You will distract me at best."

"At best I'll do a lot more than just distract you."

I'm still laughing as he lets me push him to the door. He kisses me and has only barely broken the kiss before he asks, "When will I see you next? Your answer better be tomorrow."

"Monday is always really crazy for me. I have classes in the morning and lab at night. Tuesday should work though. Just two classes in the morning, then the whole afternoon off since I don't start my shifts at Westfield until Wednesday." He draws away from me so I lean forward and place both hands on his chest. It's so warm. I can feel the heartbeat pulsing under his skin. "I'll miss you until then."

"You'll have little to miss. I'm going to call you every hour on the hour until I see you again." He covers my palms with his and, lifting my hand, kisses each of my fingertips. As I stare into the darkness of his chocolate eyes I wonder if he's serious.

"I'm serious," he says.

I pull away from him and huff, "You're crazy."

I feel a subtle tension eke out of his gaze, which pans past me and looks to Brant. He doesn't contradict my accusation but instead smiles and says, "I'll talk to you in an hour."

"Okay."

I watch him head down the hall away from me – and Brant – and my chest fills with sadness. This is the honeymoon phase right? Where everything is picture perfect. Seeing him leave feels sacrosanct.

As he gets to the mouth of the stairs, he turns back and points at my chest. "You had better pick up."

I stick out my tongue. "I will."

He leaves with one last smile and a lingering look.

"So how are things going between you two?" I say the moment Sara gets up and heads to the kitchen for more beers. She's staying overnight again, this time with Brant, and even with the baby in tow Dixon couldn't look more goddamn pleased. He fucks her with his eyes as she walks and I have to clear my throat and repeat myself a couple times before I think he hears me.

He rubs his face roughly. "Sorry. Yeah. Things are going good. Too good. I know it's only been two weeks but it feels like it's been longer than that."

Knox throws his arm over my shoulder and wrenches me in for a kiss that's so hard, I have to fight back. As I do, he coos, "I know what you mean."

Dixon looks at his near-empty bottle and sets it on the floor. When the baby crawls towards it, he lifts the kid up and onto his lap, as if he's done this a thousand times before. Makes me feel even shittier about my lack of a maternal instinct. Since I first met the kid a few days ago, I haven't touched him once and Sara sure as hell hasn't asked me to. As a good mom, I think she can sense my aversion to the idea of motherhood. ESP must be one of the perks.

Not that he isn't cute or anything. The kid could go Gerber with his mulatto skin and head of inky black curls. He's got light brown eyes too. Pretty eyes. The eyes are the only thing about him that give any indication he isn't Sara and Dixon's kid. Dixon's eyes are so dark they're nearly black and Sara's are as blue as the ecstasy pills Loredo used to traffic. Drugs have been on my mind these days. This never-ending game of telephone between me and the Brothers. Every hour on the hour. It hasn't failed yet. But when will it end? Somehow I get the feeling that when it does, I'll wish I'd never asked.

"I owe you guys one hell of an apology," Dixon says abruptly. He looks at me first and with meaning before flicking his gaze to Knox.

Knox shakes his head and reaches over me to slap Dixon on the knee. "Don't sweat it, man. Hard to explain how it feels to fall hard unless you've done it yourself."

Dixon doesn't smile, but again looks at me. "I owe you more than you think."

He knows that I haven't told Knox and I won't, but it's still a power imbalance that I don't think he's accustomed to feeling. I could tell Knox and ruin the relationship he has with his brother irrevocably but I wouldn't. I never would. I put all their lives at risk. No hit would have ever been out on my life if I hadn't introduced chaos into theirs. And the Mexicans have been so quiet. I wonder if there's a war raging further north that we haven't heard of yet because the Mexicans aren't like the Russians. There's no waiting like a viper for the right time to strike. There's only now.

Aiden never did find Loredo's right hand, the fucker who escaped. Maybe he did die. Only I somehow get the feeling he didn't. The helpers never get their comeuppance. They live in the shadows of monsters and when those monsters fall, they scurry to other shadows like cockroaches destined for survival.

Sara returns with a beer in each hand. She hands two to Knox and me and when Charlie enters the room with two more, he pawns one off onto Dixon and the second, he empties. I can't help but notice that Dixon's grip tightens around Sara's shoulders as she takes her seat beside him, holding a glass of water in place of alcohol. He glances up at Charlie in the way a kitten looks up at a cobra. I muffle my laughter in my beer, but Charlie still hears it.

He kicks the edge of my foot as he struts past, as much a peacock as ever. "What's so funny?"

"Besides that outfit? Where the hell do you even find a silver shirt?"

He holds out the lapels of his jacket and does a slow turn for us. "Where ballers buy shirts, baby."

"Bold," Knox says with a nod.

Charlie's unfazed. Rather, he dusts off the sleeves of his eggplant-colored blazer and heads to the door. "Going to meet up with Portia so I may be slow to respond to calls today, if you know what I mean."

"Not an option," Dixon shouts over his shoulder. "Every hour on the hour."

I add to the chorus. "You ignore my call, I'll whoop your ass like I did last week."

Charlie waves his hand into the air, shrugging us off. "Yeah, yeah." The front door opens and shuts and I laugh quietly.

"Kid's a real killer," I muse. "Not many men could pull off silver and purple at one in the afternoon."

"Sh..." Sara starts to say shit, but doesn't quite finish. Instead, she's up on her feet, setting her beer down and scooping up her baby. "I completely lost track of time. I need to head to my shift. It starts in an hour and I've got to go home and change, then drop Brant off at the sitter."

Looking forlorn, Dixon stands and starts after her. They say their goodbyes and suddenly Knox and I are alone. It isn't often that we're alone these days so I work hard to maximize any free moment we get together. "So," I start.

"So what should we do for the next few hours before we've got to be at the barn?" I hear the salacious lilt on his tone and I lift mine to match it.

"I've got some ideas." Rising up onto my knees, I take his earlobe into my mouth and purr, "Mini golf."

"Again?" He says on a laugh, wrapping his arms around my waist.

I let him manhandle me for a moment, then take my knee to his chin and roll off of his lap and onto my feet. He kneads his jaw as he rises with me and I hold up both fists, backing away from him. "I sort of missed out on that whole childhood thing. Mini golf last week was a lot more fun than I thought it would be."

"You embarrassed?"

It took his asking for me to realize it, but I am embarrassed. "No."

Shit-eating doesn't touch the grin he's wearing as he saunters over and wraps his arm around my neck. "You're so fucking cute." He kisses the top of my head, then my lips more deeply. "Come on, put your shoes on. I guess we're going mini golfing."

Sara

I'm in complete panic. I've got less than half an hour to get to my shift and I'm not close to changed yet. It took far too long to get Dixon off my doorstep. He's a pesky fellow, I think to myself, a grin on my lips. I laugh and Brant, seated on the floor on his favorite pink and blue blanket, looks up at me. He grins this gummy little grin and laughs shrilly before shoving the plastic pretzel in his hand into his mouth. He's teething. The happiest little guy I've ever seen with the white caps of little teeth sprouting into his smile.

I stare at him for a second longer than I have time for and sigh, "How did I get so lucky to have you and Dixon in my life?" For a moment, I imagine that this is what princesses must feel like.

There's a knock on my door. Dixon probably forgot something, or is just gambling to see if he can get away with bothering me for a few more seconds. He always can, because I'm too weak to say no. I'm light on my feet as I approach the door and when I wrench it open, I'm startled as it springs back when the chain catches. Standing there is a white male with light brown hair and blue eyes and a subtle scar marring what would otherwise be a near perfect face. Perfect, but not the one that I dream about.

"Oh hey, Neil. What are you doing here?"

"I'm sorry," he breathes and there's a tension in his forehead that transforms his face. He looks worried, and it's that worry that keeps me from trying to shoo him away. "I didn't know what else to do. It's Sherry."

"Oh my god, what happened?" Everything in my chest shudders to a stop and I forget all about work and any other obligations that I might have had. The warmth that had been sitting so high in my ribcage freezes over and my bones turn to splinters underneath my skin.

"It was an accident. I'm worried though..." His voice trails off and he glances at the chain between us.

"Oh sh... Sorry. Just a second." I close the door, rip back the chain and hold it open. But then Neil's face softens, the anxiety gone from his expression as his shoulders roll back and his mouth relaxes into a natural frown. Suddenly he isn't the man I saw that one night at the bar, or the sweetheart who showed up with Sherry on his arm at the strip club or the concerned friend he appeared to be seconds ago. He's a stranger I've never met before.

"Neil?" I question.

He raises a hand, tips his fingers towards me and from around the corner, two men I hadn't seen hiding against the wall loom into view. They tower over me and walk into my apartment like I'm nothing more than an obstacle to be trampled. I stumble back the first step, almost fall, and just manage to catch myself until the first goliath lifts his hand and hits me.

He strikes my right cheek so damn hard it whips my whole head around and my body follows. I fall, chin landing inches away from Brant's kicking feet. He releases a blood-curdling scream that ricochets throughout my whole body, forcing it up and off of the ground even as the whole world spins.

Adrenaline keeps the pain at bay and my fingers graze Brant's belly. I go to scoop him off of the ground until the goliath's hand grabs me by the hair. I kick at his legs, but when my heel finally connects with flesh, he growls close to my face and wrenches my head so far back I can't breathe. Brant's screams in my ears are the only thing keeping me from passing out entirely. If I pass out, he'll be alone with them.

"Sasha, *vtsavay*." The voice is Neil's but the language is not one that I know and I don't have time to try to puzzle it out when I'm hauled to my feet and slammed against the wall. The man who has me wraps both hands around my upper arms so hard I'm sure they'll bruise if they haven't already. His eyes are light and his eyebrows pull together angrily above them. They are so light that they blend in with his skin which is paper white everywhere except for the mouth, which moves towards mine hungrily. I scream and Brant shrieks as the man's mouth – and body – presses me so hard to the wall, my lungs are crushed beneath his porcine weight.

Wet lips wander the length of my neck before his hulking presence lurches away from me. More words are rasped between the men and when I blink next, Neil is holding a gun to the goliath's head. "We don't hurt mothers," he says in English this time before turning his gaze down to Brant. He bends down and picks up my wailing baby and I freeze from head to toe. A cold sweat covers every inch of me.

I whisper, "Neil…"

"Erik," he answers, and as he speaks, he presses a soft kiss to the top of Brant's head. Brant screams harder, chubby arms reaching for me, straining against the cage of flesh that holds him.

I lick my lips, heart bruised from pounding so hard against my sternum. "Erik." My voice comes out as strong as I intend it and I'm glad for that. "Give me back my baby."

He smiles and looks like a schoolboy, so coy and so beautiful. Also insane. His eyes hold a fire he'd been hiding and it terrifies me because I imagine that this is a man who could and would do anything. Who is he? Why is he here? How did this happen? I have no answers. Only fear and a tattered hope that mother really does mean something to him.

Erik steps forward and I don't move except to lift my arms, wincing from the dull pain in my shoulders where the other man held me. Erik hesitates before placing Brant into my hands. "I am terribly sorry about this," he says without sounding sorry at all.

"Are you going to hurt us?" I ask him the only question that matters as I rub Brant's back softly. I shh in his ear, though it doesn't help at all. Brant is terrified, shaking violently, and so am I.

Neil – Erik – laughs and traces his finger down the side of my face. As he reaches again for Brant, I twist towards the wall, shielding the baby. "Sara Sweetheart. I did so enjoy watching you dance."

"You didn't answer my question." My voice hitches and my throat has gotten so dry I cough when I mean to swallow.

"I won't hurt you or your baby until he comes with what I need. If he gives it to me, your baby may just survive." He doesn't say anything about me.

"He?"

"Ohh, don't be shy. I know how much he cares for you."

"Wh…who?"

Erik takes a step into my vision and I twist again, holding Brant directly between my chest and the wall. I close my eyes against Erik's stare because it's suddenly wild and frightening. I feel, rather than see, as the cold barrel of his gun slides against my temple. "I don't like playing this game, Sara Sweetheart. I'll give you to the count of three to say the name of the man who wrongs me, who loves you. One…"

"Dixon," I scream, knowing there is only one man he could possibly be talking about. There is only one man who's ever told me he loved me. Who I foolishly thought actually did. How could he though, if his actions would lead to this? "Do you mean Dixon?"

"*Suka, blyad,*" he slurs withdrawing his weapon, and it leaves a chill behind in all the places it touched me. "She gets it gentlemen." Light laughter fills the room and at the sound of bodies hitting my couch, I remain planted, facing the wall, eyes shut, Brant screaming.

"I'll be back in an hour. Keep her here until I give the signal. I need to make sure the other package is secure." My front door opens, but doesn't shut right away. Right before he leaves, he utters, "Don't fuck with the mother or her baby. Yet." Alone now with these two other men, I understand two things: I'm going to be killed, and Dixon put me in danger.

"Hey girl," the goliath shouts, "shut the baby or I shut the baby. Get beer for us and remote control."

It takes me some time to coerce my legs into obeying the commands I give them. Instead I am too wrapped up in the sound of the men speaking amongst themselves. Vaguely, I remember Dixon asking Erik about his accent at the club. He'd said German. My history teacher in ninth grade was German though and this definitely isn't that. Something Eastern European perhaps? Russia's the only country that comes to mind but I've never met a Russian before. Also, it doesn't matter. What matters is that I never asked Dixon about his businesses and he never shared any reason for me to think being with him was a risk.

Looking back on it, I feel foolish. His house, all of his money, his stuff? He must be involved in drugs or something much more sinister. And he never shared. Why would he? He's a criminal, and involved in dealings with men like this. No wonder he had so much to give me. All of it was blood money and like an animal I moan, wounded. I realize now as I turn towards the bedroom that I don't know the man I love any more than a stranger.

"Girl! Where you go?" The smaller of the two men says. If the first is a goliath, this one is a hawk. He holds his long aquiline nose pointed in the same direction as his gun: towards me.

Shuffling Brant to the edge of my body furthest from them, I gather my breath. "The bedroom. Where Brant's things are. I need to get his binky if I'm going to keep him quiet."

The goliath starts to stand but the hawk threatens him with the butt of his gun. Words pass between them before the goliath falls back to the couch and rubs his crotch. The hawk comes after me, following me as far as the bedroom door. He leaves it open and waits for me on the threshold. I quickly cross the room and, on the other side of the bed I see that I've placed my plastic box of medical supplies right next to Brant's day bag.

The blue box is non-descript – no red and white emblem – and I wonder if he'd even notice if I grabbed the wrong one. Even if he did, couldn't I just pawn it off as panic? But what if he doesn't believe that? What if he thinks I'm planning something? Am I? I have no idea what I'm doing. All of my thoughts are a red hot blanket that screams survival.

"Girl," the hawk barks.

I grab the blue case from the ground and shuffle out of the bedroom and into the kitchen. I set the box down by the sink, underneath the bar ledge where the two men can't see it. Then I turn to the fridge. I grab a bottle for Brant and put it in the microwave before reaching in and plucking out two beers. I set them by the sink while the hawk settles onto the couch beside his larger, more lecherous counterpart. The man's eyes remain fixed on my face, more guiding than following my every movement.

As the sound of the microwave blares in the background, I readjust Brant on my hip and pop the lid to the box. Inside are rolls of white bandages, sterile white and blue gauze packets, plastic vials of every kind of pill imaginable and there, nestled between them, three medicine bottles and six unopened syringes. The microwave dings behind me and in one motion, I grip Brant fiercely in my left hand and with my right, release one of the syringes and grab the clear canister of a benzodiazapene.

I make sure everything is open and all wrappers are tossed before I turn around and take Brant's bottle from the microwave. Brant goes onto the counter, bottle nipple pressed between his lips. I tip the syringe full of sedatives upside down at the same time the goliath lumbers up off of the couch. He stretches his arms high above his head, easily grazing the low ceiling with his hands. He starts towards me and I throw up into my mouth.

I thought my heart had been at maximum speed before but this is different. This is enough to make me start breathing through my mouth, and then stop altogether. My hands are shaking violently as I inject two doses of Lorazepam into each beer bottle. It's meant to be an anti-anxiety drug, but in this quantity, I wonder if it'll be enough to kill them. I hope it is because the alternative is that I'm found out and if I'm found out, then it's over. I snap the lid shut and push the blue box aside just as the goliath reaches the other side of the counter.

"Girl. Where is beer?"

I set his beer on the counter and grab Brant, clutching him as close as possible while the goliath brings the beer to his lips and empties half the bottle down his throat. It pulls free of his full lips with a loud popping sound. "You good girl." He pauses to take another sip. "Maybe I don't let Erik kill you. Maybe I take you instead. If you good then I keep you for a long while. If not, then I give you to my brothers to sell. You fetch good price."

I shudder and he seems to delight in that. He slams his empty beer onto the counter and reaches across the sink for the second one. Sh… That amount of tranquilizer would take down a boar. This is bad. Really bad. Because if he stands here all day watching me I won't have time to make another cocktail for his buddy before he drops like a log.

"Don't want to save one for your friend?" I say, voice sticky, arms starting to strain under Brant's blossoming weight. He's quieted since he's been given the bottle, but I continue to press soft cloths delicately to his cheeks. His eyes swim with tears and his tiny nose is red.

Sweat pools on the back of my neck and drips down my spine. The bear doesn't seem to see it. He winks at me and laughs. "No friends in *Russkiy mafiozi*."

The guy on the couch says something tersely in Russian before tilting his gaze to me. "Bring me a beer."

I nod and say nothing. Turning back to the fridge, I keep it mostly closed and, while my nerves vibrate loudly in my brain, sounding like an electrical storm during a tornado, I force my hands to steady as I reach for the beer. I pull back, but as I do, notice the Senokot I keep for Brant. It's kids' strength and a syrup. He'll surely notice that.

I gnaw hard on my bottom lip until I hear the collapsing of weight onto the couch and the bunched nerve bundle in my lower back gives just a little. I dose the beer with the Senokot and walk it over to the two men seated on the couch. The hawk snatches it and I try not to pay attention as he takes his first drag.

"Disgusting," he says, spitting over the side of the couch. He reads the label and thrusts the base of the bottle towards me. "What is this?"

"It's a craft beer," I answer in my smallest voice. "An IPA."

The goliath nudges him in the ribs and the hawk rolls his eyes but continues drinking. "American beer tastes like shit always."

"Sorry." My voice warbles.

I take a seat on the only other chair in the room – some decades-old LaZBoy monstrosity Amber's parents tossed. I expect Brant to be sated on milk, but when I look down at the bottle, he's hardly drinking. Coercion doesn't work either. He won't have it. His eyes are red and his cheeks are flubbery and soon he starts to stink. I change him in the bedroom fifteen minutes later, when the hawk begins to squirm. He holds his stomach while the goliath leans his head onto the back of the couch. As if to disguise the fact that he's sleeping, he lowers his shades.

I'm in the bedroom with Brant, he in a fresh diaper, me sweating through all my clothes, when I hear the hawk finally go into the bathroom. I'm freezing though my apartment's always too warm and I head to the open bedroom door. I peek out and around the corner and see the goliath with his head fully reclined at the same time I hear the sound of shitting coming from the bathroom behind me. I don't hesitate.

The keys to my – to Dixon's – car have been in my pocket for the past hour. So has my phone. It's rung a dozen times and I've gotten a few text messages I haven't dared glance at for fear they'd take the device from me. I'm surprised they didn't. Are they that confident, arrogant, cocky? Or is there something they know that I don't. Maybe it doesn't matter. Maybe anyone I could call already knows. Maybe they're all dead. Maybe they killed Dixon before they came for me and I'm just too stupid to realize it yet.

Fear grips me as I cross my living room, this time for more than one reason. And I hate that I'm so afraid for him when I should hate him. He did this to us – to Brant. I grip the doorknob and slide back the chain, praying desperately that the door doesn't stick like it usually does. For once, luck is on my side and the door opens soundlessly. I slip out into the hall and walk to the top of the stairs. From there, I run.

Dixon

I'm laughing at something Knox said when Clifton walks through the living room door. He looks up and, seeing me, pivots to the kitchen. Knox calls after him and when Clifton's only response is terse and uncharacteristically cold, Knox mutters, "Something's off with that guy."

Mer and I exchange a meaningful glance but neither of us responds. It's hard for me to believe she hasn't said anything yet and harder still for me to understand why she hasn't. She should hate me and yet she shows me an allegiance that is more than I deserve and more than I could ever deserve from her.

I, on the other hand, am shut tighter than a nun's legs because I don't know what it would do to Knox, his knowing what I had planned. I know what it would do to me if I discovered he'd been out for Sara's blood. I'd have to take his and it would have been deserved. Owed. My blood is the least I'm going to have to give and for every minute that I say nothing, I feel the penance grow. I clear my throat, working up the nerves to say something, to end the guilt hanging over me like the blade of a guillotine.

I open my mouth but before I can speak, Mer cuts me off. "Get me a beer too! Hey, what time is it?" She lowers her voice and speaks directly to Knox. Her dark chocolate eyes pan to mine once and they are full of a knowing that fills me with guilt, both for what I had been about to say and more for what I didn't.

"Quarter to five," Knox says.

He shows her his watch and she murmurs, "Almost time for check in." She glances at me and winks as if there's nothing wrong between us. In Mer's eyes, I see that she's already forgiven and forgotten.

"I wouldn't forget," I say cryptically, meaning something else. She doesn't answer.

On the couch, Knox slips his hand around Mer's waist and pulls her in close. He stands, dragging her with him. "No time for beer, little one. We've got to get to the barn."

"Barn's closed tonight, *estúpido.*"

He snarls into her mouth and kisses her. "What day is it?"

"Sunday," she answers. "So closed. So beer."

"Fucking hell. I thought it was Tuesday."

Mer laughs into his lips. A few moments later, Mer mumbles about the beer Clifton was meant to be fetching. At the same time, the front door opens. "There's a car swerving down the driveway. Gunning it," Clifton shouts, reentering the room with his hands empty. "Could it be them?" He doesn't wait for a reply, but runs into the hallway and turns left, towards the basement steps. "Aiden!"

I'm on my feet and striding towards him fast, the length of my legs eating up the distance. Behind me, Knox and Mer are both running to their room to grab weapons. "What kind of car?"

His brows are drawn in concern and his hands hang like a gorilla's on either side of his torso. He's a big guy and for a moment, looks like he's forgotten he hates me. "BMW M3 series. Red."

I see the door in front of me, closed against an invasion and am suddenly running towards it. I barrel out onto the driveway as Sara's car screams to a stop. She kills the engine and I stalk around to the driver's side door, wanting to rip it off the handle. It opens as I reach for it and she steps out into the narrow space between us, her body a wall, arms wrapped around Brant, shielding the crying baby. He's got no car seat and no blanket, she's got no purse and no coat. She's shaking badly and when the wind whips the strands of flaxen hair away from her face, I take in the welt below her right eye like a punch to the groin and all but collapse. Against her cream colored skin, the welt stands out in violence. Shades of red skirt its outer edges before hardening to a deep crimson, purple at its heart.

I reach for her arms and pull her half a step towards my chest. "Sara…"

She winces dramatically and I release her. "Sh…" She hisses. I look down and beneath her short, white sleeves, there are finger-shaped bruises on her arms.

I reach for her hair, whispering her name again only this time it's my voice that comes out unsteady.

"Don't." Her eyes hit mine then immediately shift away, down to the gravel beneath her feet and she doesn't move except for her trembling.

The wind pushes the scent of vanilla towards me, that and the smell of encroaching winter. As a kid, I hated that smell because it reminded me of Christmases I'd never have, shared with families that I'd never know. I never thought I could hate a smell more than that until I smell a man's cologne wafting from her clothes. One that I don't wear.

"Sara." My teeth crunch together so hard I imagine they'll splinter. "Who did this?"

"Why don't you tell me?" Her face tilts towards mine and her expression is incriminating, but not as incriminating as the finger I've got pointed at myself. "They were after you."

My insides shred themselves apart and I have no words to express to her. My mouth hangs open and eventually, I manage to thrust aside the sting of her derision and speak. "Russians?"

She nods, shrugs and clutches the cross at her throat as if in attempt to leach its strength. "Maybe. Probably." Tears surface on her lower lids which, like her chest, takes on a carmine hue that usually would make my dick stir. Now it might as well be steeped in bleach.

"Don't touch me," she whispers when I reach for her waist. I ignore her and wrench her to my chest anyways because the thought of her meeting those Russian fucks makes my testicles shrivel up and the blood in my veins turn to ash. Brant's body, squirming between us stills as I knead the delicate baby hairs along the back of the boy's soft skull.

Sara's breathing hitches and I know she's fighting hard to keep it together, but she isn't strong enough for this. Neither am I. I never thought they'd go after her. It never even crossed my mind. Why would they when she knows nothing? Why didn't I give Aiden's words more consideration? He'd said they'd take leverage from us to tip the scales of power and I'd cut the heart out of my own chest with a butter knife if it meant Sara and Brant were returned to me safely.

As soon as she stops protesting and melts just a little into my arms, I hold her away from me and sweep her face, inspecting its surface without breathing. My thumbs sweep beneath her eyelids and she flinches when I get to her cheek.

"How badly did they hurt you and Brant?" I ask, hating and fearing the answer.

She seems startled, because the cover of her anger slips out of place and for a moment she looks purely petrified. "I…" She shakes her head and looks down at her baby boy. He's no longer crying. "This is the worst of it. Just hit me when they came into my apartment and shoved me against the wall. One of them wanted to do more but Neil…Erik told them not to touch me because I'm a mother."

"Erik?" The voice comes from behind me and my spine stiffens because I had not heard his approach. I turn to see Aiden standing just a few feet away, arms crossed over his chest. The look of boredom perpetually plastered across his lifeless mug manages just a slight change when his dark blonde eyebrow lifts. Mer, Knox, and Clifton stand between Aiden and the door to the house, giving us the space that Aiden didn't feel was necessary.

"Yes." Sara nods and a look of understanding passes across Aiden's haggard face, causing it again to flatten. It's the first time I really notice how tired he looks.

Against his whitewashed skin, blue bags stand out beneath bloodshot eyes. A single vein screams in his neck and another pulses along his left cheekbone. Meanwhile, his body is fuller than I've ever seen it, likely from the hours he's spent locked away in the gym these past weeks. You can hear music screaming through the house as he lifts during the day, and again at night as his feet pound on the treadmill. I never thought to ask him what was up, if he was okay, if there was something I could do. I just took from him, and took, and relied on him because I'm a selfish prick and I don't deserve an ounce of respect or admiration or love or happiness from any of the people around me. It takes me until then to realize I'm more monster than good.

Clearing my throat and brushing aside the mounting sense of contrition and shame that's building up in my right temple like a tumor, I grunt, "What is it?"

Aiden shrugs, frowns, seems to consider saying nothing at all, then uncrosses his arms. "Erik is their leader. Cousin of Gavriil, one of the guys you sent to the hospital."

This comes to me as news, but I shove away my curiosity for a moment and target the more important questions. "How did he know where she lived?"

Aiden looks at me as if I'm dumber than a box of hair and I curse as the latent realization dawns on me. I hug Sara with one arm, wrapping it tight around her shoulders so I can feel her heartbeat through her chest. It's pounding too hard and too fast. Or perhaps it's my own heart that sounds like war drums in the wake of an attack.

"Ollie," I whisper. Cold wind rips into me.

Crushed against my body, Sara shudders. "It might not have been. Erik drove me home the night I first met him. He hit on me at a bar. That's where he met Sherry. He's known where I lived for weeks."

My mind goes blank for a moment and I hold onto Sara's open car door for support. My kneecaps have been shot and my legs are crumbling beneath my weight. He knew where she lived for weeks. He knew to target her. He knew that she would be leverage for me even before I did. He knew I loved her when I'd still been committed to hate.

"This is good news," Aiden says, and for a moment he might have been speaking Mandarin.

Clifton, who's edged closer, says, "How the hell do you figure that? She could have been killed for Christ's sake!"

Aiden shrugs and it takes the weight of the girl leaning against my right side to stop me from throwing myself at him and tearing him apart as proxy for the men who brought her harm. "He failed to take Sara, so he has no leverage." He tilts his head to the side and looks past me, at her. It's the first time he's even acknowledged her presence. "How'd you escape?"

Sara's whole body sways forward and she nearly tumbles out of my grasp. I slip one arm around her ribs and with the other, take the baby. He lays his head on my shoulder, warm breath blowing softly against my neck, as it should be. As it always should be.

"I drugged them. Might have killed one. I don't know." She buries her face in my side and I feel her tears begin dampening my tee shirt. I need to get her inside. "I asked what they were going to do to us. Erik said he'd let Brant live but that he was going to kill me no matter what. I had to do something."

"Good," Aiden says, entirely oblivious to the state she's in and the equal devastation rattling through me. Or he just doesn't care. The bastard doesn't care about anything.

Anger hits me like a train on the tracks and I roar, "Why are you even here?"

Aiden blinks once, then again. "Nowhere else to be."

My left foot shoots forward, but Clifton skirts his twin and comes directly in front of me. "Forget him," he says, "you need to get Sara inside. She's got to be freezing."

Giving Aiden a wide berth, we start towards the door, moving one step at a time and slowly. Clifton's at her other side and on the house's brick stoop, Mer's face has fallen. Her typically tawny skin is whitewashed and pale. She looks like she's about to be sick and flinches away when Knox reaches for her.

In the living room, I place Sara on the couch and Brant's limp body beside her. He curls into himself immediately and as I rise to get a blanket for him, Clifton's got one already along with a glass of water. I wrap the baby up while she drinks like a woman tasting water for the first time and as I watch her, the thought of her being gone from my life makes it hard to look anywhere else. It's as if I hope to prove by sight that she's still here, with me. I touch her knee so that the sensation of sight is accompanied by another, but she pulls out from beneath my fingers.

"Where are you going?" Knox says and out of my periphery, I see Aiden leaving the room, hands down at his sides.

"Gym," he says.

"For fuck's sake, brother, can't you show even a thimble's worth of concern? She's practically your sister."

Aiden looks at Sara on the couch, then at me and starts to turn, but Sara holds his attention. "Wait. You...you said that if I'm safe they wouldn't have leverage." He doesn't answer. She gulps. "There's more."

"You should take it easy," Clifton says. "We can go over the details once your heart rate settles…"

"No, this is important." She gathers her breath and places a hand to her chest. "There were three men, Erik and two other guys. He left me alone with them and when he left, he said that he was going to secure the other package."

Aiden's jaw clenches. Knox's face falls and he glances in Mer's direction, as if somehow worried she'd be taken out from under him. Mer's eyes widen to saucers and her parted lips roar, "Fuck!"

A string of Spanish curses follow her down the hall as she runs, returning moments later with the phone to her ear. She drops down to her knees, pressing her forehead to the rounded corner of the coffee table's edge.

"He's not answering," she says, though through the speaker, we can all hear the calls go directly to voicemail. "*Hijo de tu puta madre.* Charlie's not picking up."

"Find my phone." The words rip out of Clifton's mouth as he launches himself towards the stairs to the study, Aiden hot on his trail. I want to follow him, but Sara's by my side, breathing hard and demanding answers.

"Dixon, what the hell is going on? Who were those guys? Where is Charlie?" The tears she'd been trying to hide fall now ceaselessly.

Kneeling before her, I grab the leather couch in each hand on either side of her shins. I kiss the tops of her knees, noting that they're softer than the leather beside them, and bow my head over her legs. "The story is complicated. Best you know as little of it as possible. I don't want you tangled up…"

"Tangled up? Do you call what happened to me and my eight month old baby today tangled up?" Her voice lurches along like a bad drunk until it collapses. She covers her mouth with the back of her hand and shields her face with her hair. She releases a sob as she says, "Neil…Erik…whoever broke into my house today because of you. What did you do?"

I clench my teeth together and crush the fabric of the couch so hard, I worry I'll tear it free of its lining. "I know I owe you an explanation…"

She scoffs, "You owe me a lot more than an explanation. You put me and my baby directly in harm's way. We could have been killed."

The words slam into me and I canter back. The cabinet of DVDs appears before me and I slam my fist into its ebony surface. Dust flakes to the floor, covered in blood from my knuckles.

"I know," I say, trying to marshal the volume of my pitch because it's too loud and my anger isn't directed at her but at me. "And the thought kills me. If anything were to happen to you, I'd take out everyone responsible."

"Including you?"

I look up at her and my heart breaks. Hatred seeps through her pores as she passes one hand over her baby's face. I put him at risk. Anyone who does that is demonic in her eyes and I deserve no less than the way she's looking at me.

"Including me. I'd be following you to the grave right now if they'd taken you from me. I love you."

"Don't talk about love," she spits, voice warbling, "and don't touch me." She holds up her hand and like a sorceress, it holds me in place. "You don't have to tell me why this is all happening, but you also don't ever get to touch me or Brant again."

And my heart breaks all over again.

I don't have the vocabulary required to convince her this will all be okay, and that she's overreacting, because it won't be okay and she isn't overreacting so the words simply don't exist. "Sara, I..."

"We have a location on the phone. They didn't turn it off so it's likely they want us to follow." Clifton bursts into the room, a sling on his shoulders like the one Aiden wears as a second skin. Aiden appears behind him like a more monstrous shadow, mirroring the first image. For each of Clifton's weapons, he carries two. He has a knife under his right arm and two on his belt, Rugers decorate his shoulders and sides like Christmas ornaments, two with silencer attachments, and when he turns to swing on his jean coat with the white wool lining, I catch a glimpse of a string of hand grenades strapped beneath a floating Steyr machine pistol.

Clifton holds a Beretta and a Glock towards me and when I glance to the right, I see Sara's face has gone completely white. Any chance of salvation for me is gone in her eyes, so I don't bother trying to make it right. I grab the guns, adjust them to my hips and take a mini-Kel-tec 9mm and strap it to my ankle – not the most useful place for it, but it's the backup for my backups in case everything goes to hell, which it very well might.

Straightening, I look to Sara. She watches me like she's never seen me before and I know that there will be no coming back from this. I go to her and grip the back of her head, wrenching her into a kiss that's rougher than it should be.

"I will fix this," I say as I release her.

She gulps, licks her lips, then blinks very rapidly. "It won't matter."

"I know."

Sara

Dixon breaks the kiss before I do and my whole body sways forward, as if he's pulled something right out of me. It doesn't matter. Had I just said that? Because as I watch him gather with his brothers and Mer in the front entryway, my whole body spasms. I want to call the police, call Dixon back, tell him I'll do anything to keep him here. Sell my soul to the first demon who asks for it.

Instead, I say nothing and listen to their debate as to who will stay and watch me and Brant. I reach for my baby, resting my hand on the soft blanket that covers him and, feeling his heartbeat through it, I remember that everything I do is to protect him. Dixon will do what he has to, to make sure Brant stays safe. I just pray that safety doesn't cost him his life.

A momentary and uncomfortable silence looms, but is broken quickly by Mer. She clears her throat. "You don't have to ask. I'll stay with her." This isn't the Mer I once knew and suddenly before my eyes, they all change. I know nobody in the room.

The silence persists and Mer takes a step back, coming towards me. She clips the gun in her hand to the belt at her waist. Two more guns sit beside the first. "You don't have to worry, D. Nobody's going to touch her unless they kill me."

"Fuck. Now you're worrying me. I'll stay with them." Knox reaches for Mer, but she dodges his hand.

"As much as I want you to, you can't leave them hanging. The Russians mob deep. You need manpower. Fire power." She sucks in a breath that expands her chest. Her shoulders roll back and I feel momentarily inferior. I'm no woman like that. I doubt she would have cried if she'd been confronted by those two thugs. Then again, I wonder if she's ever had a gun pointed directly at her. Ever been afraid for her life in the way I was less than an hour ago.

Knox growls, closing the space between them. He grabs the back of her neck and I just barely hear him grumble, "I don't know if I can leave you. Maybe you should come. Maybe you both should come."

He glances at me and I gasp at the same time Dixon and Mer speak together, "No." Mer ducks her head and gently peels Knox's hand from her arm. She drops it like a hot stone. "I...I can't..." The word blusters out of her, the wind felt throughout the house and it's cold. Frigid. Goosebumps break out on my skin and I start to stand. Shit.

Shit. Shit shit shit.

I've never heard Mer cry before.

Knox's emerald eyes go wide and his fingers skim his cropped hair. He's shaking as he suddenly rushes in on Mer with enough violence to make me think momentarily that he'll hurt her. But that's not violence I see, just their own form of disastrous and perfect affection.

"I'm sorry," she says and her throat is cinched shut, so that her pitch comes out real high. "I'm sorry, I just can't see the Russians. When I do, I think of him." She inhales once and untangles herself from Knox's grip.

He holds her cheek in his hand and stares deeply into her eyes. His teeth are clenched. "They won't ever touch you again." Again. What does he mean by that?

"I know...I know..." She nods and is again the woman I remember. It frightens me the way she does that. Two Mers, swapped seamlessly. She inhales, exhales and says firmly, "I know. I just don't think I'd be much use to you around them. Any of them."

"It's understandable," Clifton says, ever the diplomat. "And you both will be fine here."

He turns to the other two men standing near him. Aiden's already at the door, staring out at the driveway with apathy. His hand rubs a space at the center of his sternum, tugging on his tee shirt so that I see the outline of a pendant at the end of a long chain. He never seemed like the type of man who'd wear jewelry. Again, I'm revisited by the idea that I know none of these people in anything but face and name.

Knox and Mer kiss for a moment that lasts lifetimes. Dixon looks at me and I hold his gaze. I wonder what expression I must wear because his response is a grimace that presses his full lips to a thin line. It frightens me in ways I never thought he could. Everything about the world suddenly frightens me.

Then the front door opens and they leave. I hear an engine rev and go to the window only to see a massive black Lincoln shooting down their driveway like a rocket. They make a turn where the driveway bends and are swallowed up by grass that's forever green, untouched by the nearness of November. I swallow my heart to keep it from exploding through my mouth the moment Mer slams the front door closed. Locks click into place, but I don't feel any more secure. I turn to Mer for reassurance, but she doesn't so much as acknowledge me. She's got her back plastered to the front door and her chest is surging with each breath that she takes. My adrenaline kicks up and sweat breaks out along my hairline. The doctor in me takes over and I start towards her with quick, short steps.

"Mer, you've got to breathe. You're hyperventilating." But she isn't just hyperventilating. She's having a full blown anxiety attack.

A sob roars out of her mouth, echoing around me. I touch her arms, but she pushes me off and races down the hallway into the hallway bathroom. She leaves the door open and I arrive behind her just in time to hold her hair off of her neck as she pukes.

I hold my finger to her pulse and let her vomit, having seen it all before but never when I wasn't able to look at it objectively. My heart is wrapped around hers and right now we're both way too out of control. I try to think of something nonchalant I can say, but nothing comes to me. I can't think. Dixon left and Mer's protecting me and I left Brant on the couch. What if he rolls off? What if he hits the coffee table? I close my eyes and take the advice I just gave Mer. I breathe.

"Four seconds in, four seconds out. Breathe," I say, once the dry heaving has stopped.

Mer's breath still comes unevenly. She starts to choke and, fighting for breath, she coughs so violently it shakes her whole body. Until now, I'd never fully realized how small she is. She's shorter than I am, but far meatier, with a woman's shape and muscles that mean business. She's my protector but now I'm protecting her from herself.

I blurt, "Dixon told me you and Knox had a fun time at putt-putt the other day."

Mer's laughter echoes inside the basin. She laughs, chokes, sobs, then sobs some more. This cycle goes on for the next ten minutes before she collapses backwards onto her ass. Her left hand goes to the gun on her hip while her right goes to her forehead. Beads of sweat drip down the sides of her face and plaster her dark hair to her skin. I wet a towel with cold water in the sink and wipe it across her cheeks, forehead and neck.

"Thank you." Her voice is gravel, throat torched. She takes the towel from me and drags it across her mouth. I reach around her and flush the toilet. "Thank you," she says again, "thank you." Her face twists, her lovely lips clamping together. She squeezes her eyes closed and curls her knees tightly into her chest. "Fuck," she breathes, struggling to maintain her even inhalations. "Fuck." Tears stream down her face and I've never seen anyone more beautiful crying. On her, tears become something for the poets.

I say nothing, but drop down to my knees and take her hand. She grips it back fiercely and when her eyes open she blinks at the contact. The white tiles beneath and behind her scream order, but the two of us are only chaos. White tiles, plush black hand towels, stainless steel fixtures. A weeping woman with a pistol at each hip and me, the terrified mother hovering over her.

Reaching above her head, Mer drags the last remaining hand towel off of the heated rack. She presses it to the front of her face and inhales, exhales, inhales, then chokes on a quick, jerky sob.

"I know you blame Dixon for all of this," she whispers, "but it's not his fault." Her gaze is bludgeoning and her hand tightens around mine. Somewhere in between the syllables, I sink down onto my haunches at her feet. She bows her head over my hand and brings it to her chest. She releases another sob. "*Maldita sea. Dios los salve...*"

"What do you mean, it's not his fault?"

"*Por favor perdoname*," she says. "It's my fault. Everything is because of me."

And with no prelude, she launches into an explanation of how she was the daughter of a Mexican cartel boss who was killed by a Russian mobster who then imprisoned and tortured her, and how Knox and his brothers took her in and saved her life.

She tells me how they found a black duffel bag filled with over ten million in heroin and how they hid that bag in a safety deposit box at the bank and how now, the Russians have taken Charlie in order to get their heroin back.

Part IV

The Exchange

Knox

We're silent in the car. Each of us thinking about what lies ahead, and what we left behind. All but Aiden, perhaps. From his position in the backseat, he stares listlessly out of the window, pupils large and unfocused, nearly obliterating all of the grey. I wonder what he sees, where he's at, wishing I could see the same things and join him there.

As it stands now, all I think about is Plumeria and the look she'd had on her face. The admission that she couldn't face them had hollowed her out and ripped straight through me like a baseball bat through glass. My stomach pitches and I'm revisited by images of her tied to that bed, Spade menacing over her body. She's fighting. She's always fighting. But she'll be done today. I'll make sure of that.

In just under an hour we're gliding over gravel. The sound of crunching beneath the Hummer's tires is familiar. So is the tree line which conceals the horizon in strokes of ash, pine, and hickory. The pale disc of the moon hangs directly above us. It's almost full tonight. I glance up at the sky, seeking stars as I exit the car. There are none, and the wind is a sword but I unzip my jacket so my weapons remain in reach.

We'd locked the barn when we'd last closed up, but I don't imagine it had been difficult to break in. The door hangs open, orange light streaming out and illuminating the swatch of dried pine and leaf-covered soil that is the only welcome mat this place has ever known. Avoiding the light, we walk around the side of the barn, approaching the smoker's entrance in silence, with no plan but the one: trade the key Dixon carries for our brother. My fist clenches, twitching reflexively towards my weapon. The belief that he's still alive is not a certainty, but a hope. Red flutters over me and it's harder to fight through than it was before, not with thoughts of Plumeria and Charlie so close to the surface.

Stepping through thickets and thorns, we make our way towards the side door, hanging crooked on its hinges, while sounds of discord within fill the encroaching night with pain. The shouting grows louder still as Dixon approaches, but he doesn't open it. Instead, he gestures with two fingers and we all draw in close and peer through gaps in the slats that form this, and most other sides of the shabby space we call ours. I press my cheek against the sliver of space where the door meets the lintel at an angle.

Scanning the scene quickly, I clench my teeth. Plumeria hadn't been kidding when she'd mentioned our need for firepower. We're fucked. With a quick tally, I count eight of them on my first pass before I notice two others lingering beside the front entrance, automatic handguns at the ready. Ten then. No sign of Charlie either. Instead, the eight are grouped in the center of the space, between the smoker's entrance and the bar. Six of the men are standing, but they're too busy restraining two redheads on their knees to have noticed us.

The prisoners are screaming, fighting against their bonds. The taller of the two manages to surge up and onto his feet, dragging a man on each arm before one of them punches him in the right rib. He buckles around the blow, falling back and clutching his side. From his mouth, he's bleeding, but he doesn't appear to notice. His whole body's straining towards the large metal bin Plumeria and I use as a backup beer cooler. From what I can see, liquid is sloshing over the side. Water, maybe. Don't know why water would have anyone this pissed but the man is fuming, face nearly as red as his hair.

A Russian wearing a grin and a tan jacket barks an order and a bald man reaches into the water and withdraws a black duffel bag. The redheads anxiously settle against the straw-covered ground. Words are exchanged and tan jacket's smile slips. He snaps his finger and baldie throws the bag back into the pool. The redhead shouts Russian words at the same time something huge hits me from behind.

The weight crashes into me like a car. We've been ambushed. How could we have been ambushed? We were careful. We know the area, would have heard something slinking towards us into the woods. My body hits the wall of the door and the boards shiver beneath my weight. As I hit the ground, I reach for the 9mm lining my coat. I withdraw it, click off the safety and aim up. I wasn't far off when I'd thought this was an ambush. It is, just not by the Russians.

"What the fuck?" I mutter, stowing my gun and lurching onto my feet to help Clifton restrain his twin. Aiden's lost his goddamn mind. I've never seen emotion in him like this before. I've never seen emotion in him period and now Clifton's got him in a headlock, but he's still reaching for his weapons, as rabid as a caged wolf so I grab his arms and pin them to his sides.

Dixon is the last of us to react, turning with a slowness that's seen only in film as the whole world comes to a standstill. The birds chirp in the birch tree high above us, the grasshoppers sing far below. There are lightning bugs lighting up the density of the forest in the distance and in front of me, one of my brothers has the other by the throat.

Aiden's face darkens to the color of a plum while the vein beneath his left eye throbs with its own pulse. He's saying words, but I can't hear them as he wrenches against my hold, kicking me hard enough in the shin that if I hadn't slipped on dried leaves at the last second, I think he might've broken it. Instead, his boot catches me in the thigh and I hiss as I hit the soil, knowing it'll leave one hell of a bruise. Dixon tries to take over for me, but when he gets close enough, Aiden grabs the front of his shirt and drags him until they're chest-to-chest, nose-to-nose.

"Stop him or I will," he rasps, voice acidic and scalding. Spittle flies from his lips as he uses Dixon's weight to throw Clifton off balance. They hit a tree and Clifton releases a quiet "ooph" that, against the silence that's fallen, echoes like a machine gun.

Dixon plants his feet and raises his arm at the same time a voice calls through the door, "Don't be afraid, we don't bite."

Dixon hits Aiden with all the force he's got, his whole torso hurtling forward, propelled by the slight shift in his footing. Dixon's fist hits Aiden square in the mouth. Aiden's head snaps back, his lower lip splits, and blood weeps down his face but when he straightens it's only to continue fighting towards the door. He doesn't even wipe off his chin. It's like he doesn't notice the blood, or any of us.

Dixon advances on the door, a last look of warning on his face that I remember seeing many times when we were much younger. He doesn't have time to tame the beast we didn't know we brought with us, but opens steps inside the barn like a dignitary going to meet another. I follow him and Clifton and I share a look trying to determine how to proceed. We keep Aiden between us – me in front, Clifton bringing up the rear – but the moment we pass into the light, I wonder if I haven't hallucinated the past few seconds.

Aiden is cold once again as he plants himself at my left shoulder. His face is emotionless, cruel eyes open and hollow. His bloodied lips are pursed rigidly and I fight to understand what changed. Still eight men in the center of the room, two by the door, tan jacket standing slightly apart, an ice bucket on the ground and beside it, a duffel bag and two redheads writhing.

Stepping within fifteen paces of the nearest man, Dixon speaks first. "We didn't come here to watch you torture one another, Erik. Thought we'd wait it out." He sounds equal parts maniacal dictator and bored algebra student and I am grateful that he's here speaking for us. I wouldn't be able to speak in such a stilted, calm manner. Hell, if I had anything to do with it, I'd probably have come in guns blazing alongside Aiden.

Tan jacket – Erik – steps forward, away from his men and towards Dixon. He wears an immaculate white polo under the leather and has his hands clasped carelessly behind his back. "Looks like you had some trouble on the way in."

He cocks his chin at Aiden who still doesn't react. If he's breathing, I can't see it in the movement of his chest. He is Michelangelo's David, frozen in time in all but the eyes. He's glancing again and again down and to the left. Towards the bag.

Dixon shrugs. "Some of us were more eager than others to end this."

"End this?" Erik laughs and it's full of violence. "Why end it when we haven't even gotten started?" His English, like his Russian, is flawless and I'm not surprised he was able to fly under Sara's radar, and Dixon's.

"You came for the drugs. We have them."

One edge of Erik's mouth lifts and he muses, "You're lying."

"Am I?" Dixon reaches into the front pocket of his black pants and pulls out a densely packed brick of heroin. The plastic spirals through the air, meeting Erik's palm.

"Alright then." Erik pops the bag open and places a pinky to the powder and then to his tongue. "Now the rest of it."

"In a safety deposit box. We don't carry that kind of merchandise with us casually."

Erik's grin broadens. "You come to play ball and tell me now that you've only got a brick of my shit and a code to a safety deposit box?"

"A brick and a key." He flashes the silver object but doesn't hand it over. "This opens a box at First and Mutual. You give me back my brother and I'll tell you which one."

When Erik laughs again I imagine cutting his tongue off with the clean edge of the hunting knife tucked against my left ribs, and forcing the thing down his fucking throat.

"Take the offer. Give us our brother," Dixon says. "We're not a part of this, so this is the only offer we'll make."

"Brother?" Baldie sneers, then speaks to the others in Russian. Even though I understand fuck all, it's clear he's trying to make a joke. The others look to Erik, rather than respond.

Erik says something to the man and he winces, then kicks the duffel at his feet. My attention follows Aiden standing right next to me. His right foot shoots forward about a centimeter, but enough for me to know something's up. I've got no fucking clue what it is, but Aiden's staring at the bag like someone's thrown his heart and brain inside of it. Aiden must know something I don't. Maybe...fuck.

The thought comes and escapes my mind in seconds. There's no way Charlie could be in that bag. Near six feet, one hundred seventy pounds, it isn't big enough for someone his size. Hell, it's not big enough for an adult-sized human. I just want to get this fucking over, and get the fuck out and get my fucking brother, then go home to Plumeria and fuck her just to know we're both alive.

"I have no desire to offend by presuming he isn't your kin. Kin often don't share resemblance." He glances to the larger of the two redheads on the ground as he speaks. "And as much as I admire your tenacity, I can't just give you back your brother in exchange for the drugs. Not after everything else you've taken from me."

"If you're referring to Spade, it wasn't us that killed him..."

"Don't you dare lie to me." Erik's expression shifts, becoming something maniacal, and when he snaps the two goons by the front door go to the bar. One of them drags my brother out from behind it. The other, the Mexican I thought I killed. Both have been torn to shreds.

I bathe in red when I see the blood on Charlie's rumpled suit jacket – the one Plumeria had teased earlier – and his torn pants. The blonde Russian grabs Charlie by the neck and drags him up onto his knees. My nose twitches, so does my mouth. I'm biting down so hard, I wonder if, when my teeth shatter, they'll impale my brain. Charlie's face has been slashed from right temple to left jaw bone. His chin bows to touch his silver shirt. It's scarlet now. So is his whole face, his throat, his matted hair. He's lost a lot of blood and is barely conscious.

Dixon says nothing and Erik makes a face, a mockery of sadness. "Your brother had a little accident. Ran right into my knife." He pulls a blade from behind his back and takes slow steps towards my brother. When he reaches him, he pulls on Charlie's hair so that his face lifts towards the light. "Pretty boy had a few other accidents too."

Charlie's jaw clenches and blood and spit dribble down his chin. He says something I don't catch and Erik hits him with the butt of his knife and the angry wound on his forehead reopens like a mouth. Charlie falls back and Dixon takes a step into the loose circle so many bodies have formed.

"Return our brother and we'll give you your key and go home."

"Is this you lying to me again? Because we picked up your little runaway less than a day after you butchered Spade. He was a good fighter. One of my best. This little shit told us that it was one of you who killed him. With your bare hands." Erik's eyes sparkle. "I didn't bring you here just to get my money back. I came for a little sport. I want to see what the hands can do that slaughtered Spade and if you do live up to your legend, I'll even throw in a reward. Vlad," he barks and the bald guy grabs the duffel bag and drags it forward.

I hear Aiden inhale beside me and am distracted from Charlie's mangled face by the sensation of Aiden's shoulder jerking forward to hit the back of mine. I grab his wrist and squeeze hard enough that it should have crippled him. It doesn't. His grey eyes burn like coals, looking nothing like his brother's. The man who isn't capable of anything besides ambivalence is looking at the duffel bag like he's being flayed and gutted. Not an expression unlike that which the two captives wear.

The shorter of the two prisoners rears up, kicking back hard into the dirt and throwing his full bodyweight towards the Russian called Vlad. He hits Vlad hard enough in the stomach that the man drops the bag and doubles over with a pained sigh. The redhead then wrenches the black bag's double zipper down. Bound hands are the first thing I see. They're a pale brown – somewhere between my skin tone and Plumeria's – and covered in hundreds of freckles, like her face. She's beautiful, even with wet hair plastered to her neck and cheeks and duct tape covering her mouth. I glance to my left as Aiden's body slumps against mine. His eyes have never been so big and he inhales between his teeth. He looks... Hell. The guy looks relieved.

The redhead holds her shoulder and the back of her head. He's speaks to her rapidly and she nods, chest convulsing as she fights to simultaneously breathe and cry. Then a clacking sound fills the space, followed by the sound of a gun's hammer cocked.

"Enough." Erik points his weapon at the bag and Aiden breaks forward on a snarl. Erik fires and Aiden comes to a quick and sudden stop. The sound carries in the space, echoing where it has no right to echo. The duffel hits the ground and I can no longer see the girl's face, but it's the man the bullet was aimed for.

The redhead wavers on his knees for a moment before the crater carved into his right temple begins to pump and spurt and ooze. He lilts to the side without ceremony just a few feet away from Charlie and I'm reminded how quickly a life can end. We've got to stay calm if we want to get Charlie out of here quick enough to keep him alive – all of us, including Aiden.

The other caged redhead is screaming. "What have you done?" He continues on in Russian and Erik responds by lifting his weapon – not at him, but at the black bag on the ground. I grab Aiden by the back of the coat and by the arm to stop him from lurching forward and reaching for the gun at his belt.

Aiden rears up and when his gaze turns falls on me and *sees* me, for what is probably the first time, I sense a threat. He's going to kill me.

"Gavriil, are you finished?" Erik roars into the calm.

The man on the ground – Gavriil – says nothing, but his broad chest heaves as he looks down at his knees. His eyes are closed and he speaks English with a thick accent, and slowly. "You punish us for the sins of our fathers."

"No. You murdered three of my men against direct orders to stand down so I am going to kill you and give your sister to the brother that kills Babic. If Babic wins then I'll sell her to the highest bidder, though I truly hope he doesn't. Babic needs to learn his lesson after letting you escape on his watch."

One of the men – a shorter man, but meaty and layered with heavy artillery – steps forward and cracks his knuckles. He glances at me, then at each of my brothers. Trying to size us up. Wondering which of us killed Spade, and will become his opponent.

"So now you will watch them fight and after, I'll tear all of your fucking families apart!" Erik roars. His hair shoots away from his face and he is glaring at Gavriil in a way that makes me wonder if he's even here today for us, or the drugs. He's unraveling and I know, without knowing what they are, that the rifts between those two men run deep. But that isn't what concerns me.

I'm more preoccupied by the fact that Gavriil is ignoring Erik just like Erik is ignoring the rest of us. Instead, his hot powder blue gaze is trained on Aiden in a way that is steadfast and resolute, as if in his mind he's decided something of grave importance and Aiden is staring back with a knowing that says that whatever it is Gavriil has decided, Aiden has decided something too.

"So which one of you was it?" Erik says. "Don't be shy. Come on!"

That's my motherfucking cue. I take a step forward to kill another Russian, but as I do, Aiden's arm rips free of mine and he shoves me so hard I lose my balance. I stagger back while he moves forward as if he's been waiting for this moment all night.

"This isn't his fight," I say, surging forward against Dixon's outstretched arm. He catches me and shoves me back.

"It is now," he hisses.

Aiden shrugs out of his jacket and when it hits the ground, the weapons lining it clatter against one another. The Russian he's up against kicks aside the mutilated arm of the Mexican man they tortured. They've had weeks to work on him and it shows. Now he's missing a hand and a foot and the bloody stumps have been seared shut to keep him just alive enough. Sick bastards.

The ring hasn't been drawn tonight and this pit was never meant for fights to the death and this isn't Aiden's fight but he's moving like he's got everything on the line even though he has nothing and cares for nothing and never thought of Charlie as a brother. What moves him now? I don't know but I'm one-part guilty, three-parts grateful as he rolls his shoulders back and glares across the fighting pit at Babic.

Erik is grinning as the dust settles and decisions are made by a few men in the room. I'm not one of them. "Excellent," he says, stepping out of the circle so that the duffel bag, the mutilated Mexican, and the brain-dead redhead rest on his right, Charlie on his left. What are you fools waiting for?"

Stowing his gun behind his back, he claps his hands twice. But as Aiden takes two steps towards the fighter, bullets pierce the front of the barn and hail down on us as swift as a summer rain.

Aiden

The first shot skims the top of my right thigh. It burns but isn't the reason I drop into a crouch. The fighter is still coming at me. He tries to kick me while I'm down, ignoring the gunfire shredding the front wall to splinters. The other Russians have unloaded their cannons and duck behind the crude bar and any structural beams they can find, returning fire.

I grab the fighter's leg as it comes towards my left side and revolve him around my torso so he fits over my body like a backpack. He's dead in seconds as the shots intended for me find his body. I drop the weight. Diving left, I flatten myself to the ground as two Russians fall. Spanish words penetrate the seconds it takes for the machine guns outside to reload. The diversion the Mexicans had been looking for. No wonder they didn't come for us. For them, it wasn't about the drugs, but retaliation.

I'm deaf from the sounds of shooting and adrenaline keeps my heartbeat hard and heavy. Faster than usual. Charlie is close to me and I stretch forward until I can close my hand around his boot. I should move – pull him towards me – but my gaze searches past him. At the sight of the bag, my fingers twitch. She's behind the stainless steel bucket for now and Charlie's out in the open. The odds of her survival are greater than his. I know this. But I still don't move.

"Aiden!" Knox's voice reaches me through the chaos and I grab Charlie and wrench his limp body along the ground.

A bullet grazes my ear, but misses. So does the next. I keep Charlie flat, using my body as a shield against the gunfire, and push him towards the side door where Clifton stands with his twin Sig Sauers out, firing. Covering me. At the door, Knox puts away his Smith and Wesson and drags Charlie out into the dark.

I turn from my brothers while Clifton's voice chases me back into the light. "What the fuck are you doing?"

Ignoring him, I pull out my Ruger and point it at the Russian hiding behind a cluster of beams. He has the spot I want, so I shoot him and as he falls dead, I take it. The Russians are scrambling now, heading out of the back door. Erik's helping two other Russians restrain Gavriil, because he had the same idea I did, only his restraints are physical and more effective. The veins in his neck are the same color as his hair as he plants his feet in the ground and screams her name. The one that haunts me like a shadow in the daylight.

Bullets pound into the wooden post at my back. I wait for the sound of empty machine gun barrels clicking before soaring out into the open space. I reach the bag in eight steps and grab the rubber handle before dragging it and myself behind the bar. The bag is open, so I close it, but not before her eyes see me. A spike of cold stabs my lungs and I don't breathe as I pull the zipper to cover her face, speckled not just in freckles but in blood. The blood makes me hungry to kill something, to bury my fingers in eye sockets and watch the jelly squirt up around my thumbs.

I hack out my next breath because it doesn't want to come. The next comes easier. It's better when I don't see her. Makes it easier to think. To ignore the weight of her petrified stare because I know she's not just scared, but scared of me. I glance to my left and right. There are no easy exits from the bar with hellfire ripping through everything, including sound. The easiest way out would be through the back, but it's occupied by Gavriil's breadth.

I hate the way he watches me. His eyes are orbs. He's taken a bullet to the shoulder and another to the hip, but his lips are slack. Like he doesn't notice the gunshot wounds, or the men holding him. He's watching me like I'm worthy of something. I frown. Impossible for something worthless to be worthy of anything.

"Alina," he shouts over the chaos, then he says more words to her that I don't know. With one last glance at me, he nods and lets the Russians holding him drag him backwards through the door.

Another shout lights up the barn, this one more familiar. "Fuck you Aiden!" It's Clifton's voice. He sounds like he's in pain. I glance around the edge of the bar to see him firing automatic pistol machine guns in each hand. The returning fire lulls. I don't waste the seconds. I hug the bag to my side, keeping it away from the incoming bullets. I reach Clifton before I'm hit in the calf. My left side twitches and I miss my next step, but keep upright and catch myself on the frame of the door at the same time a second bullet hits me in the shoulder. Clifton surges up against me, shoves his shoulder beneath my arm and kicks the shattered door closed.

"You're hit," he says, breathing hard and pushing his blonde hair back. He's got blood on his palm. I wonder from what.

I glance down at his pants and see the shimmer of slick crimson against matte black. "You too."

"Only once though." He stretches an arm forward. "Let me carry it."

I grab his throat and push him towards the tree line. "Keep moving."

He glares at me. Or maybe that's surprise I see on his face. I don't give a shit, but fall in line behind the others as we take off into the woods. Dixon and Knox carry Charlie. There's a dull pain in my leg, beating like a heartbeat, but I don't slow and I don't drop the bag, just transfer it onto the other shoulder.

Clifton keeps pace with me though his face twitches a couple times and once, he groans. A few minutes in, Knox pulls out a phone. He's talking, but my focus on the tree line breaking up before us drowns out his words. The crunching leaves beneath my feet go quiet as they turn to gravel and then eventually crumbling asphalt. I feel shifting in the bag I carry, but ignore it.

The thought of her awake makes me ravenous. I don't want to see her face. Don't want to watch her watch me. We move down the old country road, heading away from town. Headlights flash in the distance and as the car reaches us, it spins a full circle, peeling tar as it gains traction. The passenger door flies open.

"Get in!" Mer is in the front seat. The back door opens and Sara's got a box of medical supplies at her feet and gloves on. They look afraid. I don't care. Instead, I throw open the trunk and the moment I toss the bag inside and climb in after it, Dixon's Cadillac rockets down the street. I barely get the trunk shut.

Behind the wheel, Mer curses. Sara shouts orders in medical terms I don't understand. Gauze packets fly. Plastic rips. Charlie moans. I stare at the black bag beneath me.

Everything is quiet.

I see my right hand stretch towards the zipper like it's alien. My hand and the zipper both. The air is cold against my skin and I get goosebumps.

I shiver as my thumb presses against the metal clasp. The black window to my right reveals a nearly full moon and a starless sky. There's smoke on the horizon. They burned the barn, probably with bodies inside. At least, that's what I would have done. Bodies and corpses both. Seconds more and hers would have been among them. And that's only if they hadn't scavenged the place first and realized what they had.

Now the bag is soaking wet between my legs and the tarpaulin is porous, and rough against my palms. She doesn't move beneath it. How long did they have her underwater? I wasn't gentle enough with her when I pulled her out of the building. Maybe this motionlessness is my fault. Fuck me. What if she's hurt? What if she's dead? And I'm sitting here with my fingers on the clasp, too fucking pathetic to know for certain. Holding my breath, I drag the zipper down.

Fingers and a face. So goddamn beautiful.

I inhale in a short burst, completely filling my lungs, then hold steady. She doesn't move. Her glossy eyes are open and they're wide and watching me. Red hair, dark like cherries, sticks to her skin. She's pale. I wonder if it's cold or fear. I reach for the ties on her wrists, but she flinches back, knocking her head against the floor of the trunk.

She starts to breathe harder, nostrils flaring since she can't breathe out of her mouth. It's duct taped. The rest of her is bound in a series of intricate knots so that she's fully submissive. I wonder what the other men did to her. How many of them raped her while Gavriil watched. The thought makes me want to go back to the barn and kill anything that breathes.

Abruptly, I sit up. I brace one hand against the back of the seat, the other on the window. It's cold underneath my palm and fog forms around my fingers so that when I lower them, I see them lingering there in relief. Alina releases a desperate moan in the back of her throat and tries to shuffle backwards, away from me though there's nowhere for her to go. I grab the front of the bag and wrench it back to where it had been. I need to see for myself what they did to her.

I pull out my knife and she stops resisting. She watches the path the blade takes to her skin and closes her eyes. A tear slides through her eyelashes over her cheeks back into her hairline. She thinks I'll hurt her. Torture her, maybe. Why wouldn't she when I'm nothing more and nothing less than monstrous?

The cool balm of self-hatred blows through me as I touch her throat. She's softer than anything I've felt before. And I'm disgusting. Fated. Diseased. Nothing that she needs right now or ever. I slice the rest of her bindings and as they drop free of her skin into the black bag cocooning her, I finally reach for her mouth.

The duct tape leaves sticky residue on my fingers as I reveal her full lips. They're pink and slightly enflamed. I trace their outline with my thumb and she jerks back. It amazes me that she doesn't scream. Her mouth is soft and full, like I've reached into an expensive pillow and pulled out its insides. Her lips part underneath the pressure of my finger and warm breath spills out onto my palm. I wrench back.

There's a throbbing in my gut that hadn't been there before and a pain below that. I glance down and see the bulge, feel the heavy head of my dick crushed by my belt. Fuck. I want to cut the thing off because there's nowhere for me to move that she won't see it. I look down at her, waiting for the scream, her struggle. I'm left waiting. Her brown and blue gaze switches across my chest, moving lower and lower.

She inhales. I inhale her perfume and the erection gets harder. She keeps her hands clasped between her breasts and I don't move. The car carries on and there are city lights flashing through the tinted glass but everything feels like it's at a distance. There's just me and her and my fucking hard-on between us. After a while, she starts shaking. Not knowing what else to do, I reach into the bag and pull her legs free. She's wearing jeans, boots and a black long-sleeve shirt that clings to her skin. It's all soaked and soaking the car around her, seeping into my clothes and pants at the knees. I have nothing to give her.

"Sara," I grunt. The cab quiets except for the sound of Alina's chattering teeth. This is the first time I've ever said Sara's name. The first time I've acknowledged her existence.

She leans over the back seat and looks down. "Sh…" She looks at me. "Who is this?"

"Irrelevant."

"Well is she good or bad?" The simple question startles me and I glance at Sara's face for a moment. She pulls back as if that's too much and Dixon hugs closer to her side. He stares at me with menace and warning. Clifton's staring too. So is Knox. So is Mer from the rearview mirror.

"Good." Purely good.

Sara blinks, then shakes her head and leans closer. "Other than the hypothermia that's about to set in, what are her other injuries? Knox," she shouts, "crank the heat all the way up."

Hot air blasts from the vents and I sit away from her, giving Sara the space to lean over the back of the seat. As she does, I murmur, "You hurt her and I take it out on you ten times."

"Hey!" Dixon roars and the whole car swerves.

There's scrambling, shouting, moaning, until Sara says shrilly, "I'm not hurting anyone so there's no issue here. I just need to know where else she's hurt because if she isn't, I have to help Clifton and Charlie."

I glance down at Alina, but she doesn't give me any sort of answer, or even any indication she's heard me. She just blinks slower and slower. Her gaze never leaves my face. "I don't know."

"Ask her," Sara orders but I don't and she turns back to the others while Alina and I watch one another in silence. Soon the car makes a left and begins to slow.

Sara is one of the first out of the car. She's got her hand pressed to a piece of white plastic against Charlie's ripped open face. I glare at her through the open back door.

"Help her." My voice isn't up for discussion.

Sara holds up a blood-soaked hand. "I'm sorry," she says, "but Charlie takes priority. If she isn't bleeding then you just need to get her inside and get her warm." Her voice fades along with the others' until the front door shuts and Alina and I are alone.

The sounds of chaos subside until there's just silence. I can't hear her breath, but I can see it cloud in the darkness. Grunting, I throw open the trunk. A burst of frigid air claims the last of the warmth, but as I reach for Alina to carry her out of the car, her right leg bucks and she kicks me in the center of my chest with enough force to surprise me.

Those seconds give her the time she needs to scramble out of the opened trunk. Her feet hit the ground and she takes off running. I follow but I'm half a hair behind and I don't see what she's doing until she's done it. She sprints around the car, throws herself onto the driver's seat, presses a button and locks all the doors. The trunk closes itself and I'm left standing at the window, inches from her but separated by glass, fuming.

I can see everything. Her panic. Her fear. Her wet hair dragging around her shoulders as she ducks beneath the steering wheel. Her shaking fists punching the admin console once, twice, a third time before it pops free. She rips on the wires and tries to fuse them together. It won't work though. This car, like all the others we own, lock up the second the console is opened. The ignition turns and she presses her foot on the gas, but the wheel remains fixed. The ignition roars but she can't move. She starts to cry. The sight of her tears moves me to homicide.

I prowl around the car slowly, feeling the air move through the damp spots on my shirt and pants and all the places where bullets ripped through my clothing. I've got blood on me and remember for the first time in a while that I've got a hole in my left leg and right shoulder. Doesn't matter. I don't matter. Only she does. I curl my right hand into a fist and catch it with my left, then crush my elbow through the passenger window. Alina screams as I reach in through the broken glass, knuckles and arms shredding themselves on the shards. I reach the lock at the same time the driver's side door opens.

She sprints into the night like I knew she would and she isn't quicker than I am, even with two bullets lodged somewhere in my muscles. She hasn't even hit the line of the yard before my arms wrap around her and I pull her against my body, back flush with my chest. She screams and I clap a hand over her mouth, while her boots kick uselessly against the wall of night.

I drag her towards the warm orange glow of the porch, and then inside the house. She's light in my arms and it would take a lot more than this resistance to pry her from me. Maybe the end of the world. Or for her to ask.

My room is the safest in the house, so that's where I take her. The last place I want her. I release her as I pull the door shut behind me and she bounds out of my arms. I see why. She's got my HK45 trapped in her trembling left hand. Her eyes are sharp but her lips are turning blue. Her shoulders curl inwards, she sways on her feet and she staggers back and forth a few inches at a time, unable to maintain her footing.

"Move out of the way." Her voice is hoarse and when she coughs her whole body shakes. She's about to drop the gun, so she lifts her left hand up to meet her right. Even then, she doesn't manage to hold it steady. "Move!" I don't. She doesn't come any closer either but closes one eye and tries to center on my chest. "*Bajalsta,*" she says.

"I don't know what means."

"Please," she begs. Tears pool in the bags beneath her eyes, but even they aren't enough to move me. "Get out of my way. Let...let me pass."

I take a step towards her and as I do, slowly remove the sling I'm wearing. "You're going to have to pull the trigger." I set the sling and the guns hanging off of it on top of the chest of drawers to my left.

"I will! I will do it," she says, each word a gasp. She isn't getting enough air and though she wasn't shot, she's shivering like she's been wounded. I don't understand. She is fine. There's nothing wrong with her.

She whispers a name then, and wipes her face on the inside of her arm. "*Moy boch...moy brat...*Timur." Her brother. Her brother's blood coats her face and the exposed bit of her chest. She licks her lips. I wonder if she tastes him. I wonder if he is the source of her pain. I wonder if that is the human response because there is no one for whom I would weep.

I shuffle a few inches closer and she shrieks, "I will shoot you!"

"Then do it." I take a large step, she shouts, and I realize that this is the first conversation we've ever had as the sound of the gun goes off between us.

Sara

I'm grateful there's so much to concentrate on because that focus the only thing that keeps me alert, and from screaming. Inside, my heart beats quickly. I'm terrified. I've only ever seen wounds like this in the ER where I've had unlimited equipment at my disposal and trained doctors to guide me. Here, in this basement I've got limited supplies and am meant to be everything from triage nurse to plastic surgeon.

"I'm sorry," I whisper. "Does that hurt?"

Charlie's on Percocet, but he's still awake enough to both see and feel as I stab the massive needle into the wound on his face. This is about the twelfth time I've injected the local anesthetic. He glances at me, but his lids are drooping. I've got him hooked up to an IV and a blood bag. A negative. His blood type. They all know their blood types and they've got a fridge full of bags for emergencies. Now I understand why I've never been in their basement before. I probably would have run out of here screaming bloody murder on my first visit if I'd ever thought any of this was needed.

The cot Charlie's on is hospital-grade. There's another empty one beside it though Clifton preferred to sit on the high stool, closer to Charlie. His pant leg is cut open to the groin and he's got a compress against his thigh. The bullet's lodged in there deep and from what I gathered, it fractured against his bone which means I'll have to spend who knows how long digging out the pieces. I refuse to look up at him or I'll get distracted. There's enough pressure as is with Dixon, Knox and Mer all watching me.

"Charlie, can you hear me?" I whisper when he doesn't respond.

It takes him a few moments, but eventually he nods.

"Good. If you can't feel this," I say, pressing near the cut on his forehead with tweezers. "Then I'm going to start stitching you now." He closes his eyes and tilts his face towards me and I know that's all the consent he's able to offer. I rip open a hospital-grade suture kit and stand up from the stool I'd been seated on. Then I get to stitching.

"How many was it in total?" Dixon asks after what feels like eternities.

"Twenty eight surface. Nine deep. I just hope it'll be enough." And that it'll be clean. I glance down at Charlie on the bed and wince. He looks monstrous. Brad from plastics would have probably been able to do a better job. "He'll probably need to go see a plastic surgeon," I say quietly. "I did the best I could…"

It's Knox – not Dixon – who clamps a hand down on my shoulder, spinning me to face him. He wrenches me into a hug and whispers, "Thank you."

Mer stands slightly back and when her gaze hits mine she mouths the same. She wrings out her hands and the words come tumbling out of her. "I am so sorry I did this to Charlie, and to all of you. I deserve nothing but…"

Knox stares at her looking stressed and torn and I know that he'll say something, but not anything that will help her feel better. The look on her face is one of complete and total self-hatred. Only Aiden ever looks like that and it wounds me and I want to tell her it will be alright but the words on my lips and Knox's are stalled when Dixon gives Mer a light slap.

"Dixon," I say at the same time Knox shouts, "Hey!"

Dixon ignores us both. He grabs Mer's chin, stares into her eyes and says hotly, "Don't you ever apologize again for any of this. You are Knox's partner, Charlie's sister, Clifton's sister, and Sara's friend. You are my sister and each one of us would die on the cross for you a thousand times over, just like I know you'd do for them."

Tears fall from Mer's eyes and she nods mutely, wiping the tears free with her sleeve. He releases her chin and grabs the back of her head, then pulls her into his chest. She releases a quiet sob and Clifton, Knox, and I go to them. We all hold one another for a while before a slight croaking wakes us.

"Don't...forget...me," Charlie says and as the group of us breaks, we're laughing. It's a hysterical laughter to be sure, light and muffled and starved and desperate but also relieved. Relieved we're all still alive and that we're all together and as we go to Charlie's side, he takes Mer's hand. "Sis, stay with me?"

"Forever," she whispers. Knox kisses the side of her head and I am honored to watch Mer's self-hatred release.

I turn to Dixon. He's watching me like I'm the messiah and all the angels. Catching my gaze, he clears his throat and looks at Clifton. "Is there anything I can do for Charlie while you're working on Clifton?" Dixon asks. "Should I go pick up Brant?"

I nod. "That would be great." My voice comes off unsteady. I'm not used to seeing this group of hardasses so emotional. It moves me. Quickly, I speak through the desire to cry, "I'm sure Sherry's at her wits end." The reason Mer and I dropped Brant at Sherry's was twofold: to make sure that Erik hadn't dropped by, and to tell her not to make contact with him in person. "Sherry's not good with kids."

The corner of Dixon's mouth twitches. "So I gathered." I hate the sight of that smile. It makes me want to smile too. It also makes me want to tell him that he's forgiven. "I'll go to yours first and pack up as much of your stuff as I can. You'll need to stay here. While I'm gone maybe Mer, you can make up the guest bedroom?"

Mer and I both agree. Dixon nods and as he turns to leave, Knox follows. "Four hands work faster than two."

"You don't need to come with me, brother. Stay with Mer."

"The house is a fucking fortress and as much as it kills me to leave Plumeria and Sara and Clifton and Charlie here, I'm not letting you go by yourself. I'll come along. We'll be quick. By the time we get back, Sara will have finished cleaning up our brothers. We're not doing her any favors by crowding the infirmary."

Dixon makes a face, then bows his head. "Brother," is all he says.

He angles his body to the side and opens up the basement door. As Knox follows Dixon up the stairs, I move towards the long stretch of stainless steel countertop. I grab several different types of tweezers and a scalpel and usher Clifton onto the remaining cot. He refuses Percocet, but takes the local anesthetic with a grimace. Soon, I'm rooting around in his leg like an archaeologist on an expedition. He twitches several times but doesn't complain.

While I work, Mer takes the now free stool Clifton vacated. She stares down at Charlie with pure love, and just a drop of horror. He's sleeping now. The wound bisecting his face is severe, and watching her distracts me because it gets me thinking about all the ways I could have done better. Had my hands been shaking? Maybe I used too many stitches. Maybe I could have...

"Mer," Clifton says and I'm distracted. She looks up at him slowly, wide eyes glazed. "No one blames you."

She blinks softly and a tear rolls down her left cheek. "I know."

"We love you. Charlie still loves you."

She smiles weakly. "So much more than I deserve."

"No." This time the voice is my own. "Exactly what you deserve."

"Thanks," she says, and as a nearly silent afterthought, adds, "*mi hermana...*"

My chest swells with warmth despite the overpowering scents of rubbing alcohol, iodine, and blood. Leaning over Charlie's body, she grips his arm firmly and whispers in his ear. Charlie's leg twitches and I wonder if, even in sleep, he hears her.

I pull myself back to the present and bend over Clifton's leg stretched out before me on the cot. "Everything okay?" I ask. I'm talking about the pain, but he doesn't seem to notice me working on him. "Clifton?" His unfocused gaze shifts from the closed basement door to my face. His eyebrows are drawn together and the sternness of his expression doesn't suit him. "It's quiet."

"What is?"

"Everything." He cocks his head towards the door. "Knox and Dixon left, but I haven't heard anything from Aiden. I don't feel good leaving him alone with that girl."

"Who is she?" Mer whispers.

"I don't know."

"I do." Setting my tweezers down, I reach for the scalpel. One last piece of shrapnel is lodged right next to the bone that my tweezers are too bulky to reach. I glance up for a moment, distracted from the task by the sensation of Clifton's clear gunmetal eyes watching me. "She's Alina Popov."

"Who?"

"A model."

Clifton clicks his tongue against his teeth and bumps his fist against the cot. "From your magazines?" I nod and he glances again at the door. It's closed, and now that he mentioned it, the silence does seem oppressive. "I knew I recognized her face."

"Yeah she's half-Russian, half-Tunisian and lives on the Echardt campus. Goes to the law university out there." I blush a little bit, feeling like a stalker, and glance back to my equipment and Clifton's exposed thigh and the task at hand. "She's in all of the local gossip mags. She's a saint, volunteers, is involved in all these education initiatives. Not to mention, everyone suspects she's connected to the mafia so it gives her street cred..." Holy shit. My voice fades. "She's with the mafia?" Clifton grimaces and his lack of answer is answer enough. I shake my head when he says nothing. "The magazines love her. Everybody loves her."

"How would Aiden know that? He's not into any of the celebrity shit," Mer murmurs.

As I begin excavating the last shred of shrapnel, Clifton's hands clench around the hospital bed. It isn't because of the pain, that much I know, because his eyes aren't focused on me, but on some point in the distance. He reaches up and ruffles his blonde hair forward. "Aiden knows a lot he doesn't let on and he knows a lot more about Alina Popov and her family and the Russian mob in general that he isn't sharing. What I want to know is who is she to him? I've never seen Aiden act like this before."

No one contradicts him. The little I know of Aiden – and it isn't much – is that he hates people, places, and things. This family, these men, are maybe the only creatures in existence that he tolerates but I saw the way he was in the car, that panic in his eyes. It was enough for me to know for certain that he wouldn't hurt Alina Popov, that he wanted her alive.

"You finished?" Clifton says as I pull the last bit of metal free.

I nod and drop the scalpel, the tweezers, and the last bullet shard into the metal tray beside me. "Now for the fun part."

"Let's hold off. You have any more of those blood clot packet things?"

I stand from where I'd been seated and go to the cabinet. There, I find the last of the packets. "Why don't you want me to stitch you?"

"It's not like that," he says, glancing at Charlie after I do. "Aiden needs you more than I do."

"Aiden? But the girl seemed fine."

"Not her. Him. He's been shot. I think a couple of times."

"What?" I say at the same time Mer says, "Fuck." I continue. "Why didn't he say anything?"

To this, Clifton gives me a pointed look, but he doesn't get the chance to respond when a popping sound, like a flare going off, reverberates through the whole house. Clifton launches off of the cot and onto the ground, leg crumbling slightly beneath his weight. He reaches the door and for the gun still strapped to his halter at the same time.

"Fucking hell. If he hurt her I'm going to fucking kill him. Finally…" He says that last bit as a hiss, swallowed into his mouth so I'm sure I wasn't meant to have heard him. I did though.

I grip the handrail in a sweaty palm as I reach the stairs. I don't want to, but I start up after him. Mer pulls out a weapon and the sound of her flicking off the safety behind me is the only sound she makes. I hold my gauze packets to my chest like a shield as I follow Clifton onto the ground floor, afraid of what I'll see.

A fucking *desmadre*. That's what this is and though I still feel responsible for it, I can also feel the weight of Dixon's hand striking my cheek. I cling to that ephemeral pain and the memory of the words that accompanied it. I would die for each of these brutal bastards and Sara and I get the feeling that they'd all do the same for me. Hard to imagine that now though seeing Sara in front of me in the hall, her white skin smeared with red, tips of her hair dyed pink while Clifton bangs on the door in front of her, looking even worse for the wear.

We're clustered in the corner because even though everybody else lives down the hall to the right, Aiden had to choose the smallest room in the farthest recesses of the house. And now he's got a girl in there. A pretty one too. Fuck, the damn near prettiest girl I've ever seen. I only got a glimpse of her, but she's enough to turn a woman and she's definitely turned Aiden...into something.

I didn't even realize what was happening – that the brute had brought home a reluctant guest – until I asked Knox where Aiden disappeared to while we carted Charlie into the house. I'd asked him if that was a good idea – leaving Aiden alone with someone who looks like that –but there hadn't been time for Knox to respond as Sara issued orders left and right to help Clifton and Charlie. I didn't think she had it in her, but adrenaline and the fact that she's evidently very good at what she does must have erased any lingering hesitation she had. She's a battlefield doctor, and easily the most useful person in the house.

Clifton holds out his hand and Sara comes to a stop. He edges forward, the barrel of his Smith and Wesson pressed against his right cheek. His left hand reaches for the knob and I step in front of Sara with my Glock at the ready. I don't know what we're ready for. But we're ready. Or something like it.

"Aiden," he says, knuckles rapping against the door for the second time. No one answers him, but through the walls I hear muffled murmuring. "Aiden, I'm coming in."

He gives no more warning than that, twists the brass handle and pushes the door open wide. I drop into a crouch and aim my gun for the body across the room, but his back is to us and he doesn't turn around.

"What did you do with the girl, Aiden?" Clifton says, cocking his gun's hammer.

"Fuck off," Aiden grumbles. His head is bowed. He speaks again but this time not to us. "Open the door." His tone is as hard as diamond and cruel, like it usually is. "Alina, open the fucking door."

His boot indents the wood when he kicks it and behind me Sara drops one of her gauze packets. She struggles to pick it up. Aiden's got blood in his hair, blood on his torn shirt and on his pants. I can't tell how much of it is his or if any of it is. He moves like he's uninjured with ferocious, lethal gestures.

"She alive?" Clifton lowers his gun and clips it to his belt, then limps across the room towards his brother.

"Get out."

Clifton edges around the foot of the bed against Aiden's direct order. I step inside the room, but only just. The lights are violent — bright white bulbs instead of a more forgiving orange — and though there's a tab to lower the brightness when I reach for it, I see that it's been taped in place. An involuntary shiver runs through me and rivals the warmth at my back. Sara is so close I can feel her breath on my shoulder. She releases a sharp little yelp and points at the floor.

"*Guácala.*" I make a face. There's blood everywhere.

"Aiden?" Sara says, voice cracking. "Are you injured?"

"Get the fuck out," he barks over his shoulder, a rabid boar, a caged beast. He pounds the side of his fist on the bathroom door. "Alina." His voice has begun to rise and my right knee threatens to give out. I've never heard him yell before and the sound is fucking blood curdling.

Just behind Aiden now, Clifton claps him on the shoulder. "Aiden, let Sara look at you…" Without giving Clifton the time to finish his statement, Aiden turns, grabs his twin by the throat and shoves him back. The whole wall shudders beneath the weight of Clifton's body.

"I said leave." Aiden's skin seems to sizzle like a sidewalk in the sun. He's got what's either densely congealed blood, dirt, or brain matter spattered across his shirt and darker streaks of blood weeping down his right leg. He favors his right arm, but has no problem pummeling Clifton with his left.

I raise my gun as Clifton fights to pry his brother's fingers away from his throat, but Aiden isn't fazed. On the contrary, I can see him squeezing harder and harder.

"Sara," I rasp, but when I turn she's gone. Hell, I don't blame her. "Aiden, let go of him!"

He doesn't turn. He doesn't even blink. Clifton's dropped his weapon somewhere along the way which means that it's up to me now to kill his brother. Fucking *cabrón. Carajo. Chinga tu madre.* "Aiden, *lo juro por Dios,* don't test me. I will pull the fucking trigger. One," I start to count.

As Clifton's face turns from white to red to purple, Aiden looks at me and says, "I should have killed you when he asked." I lick my lips, knowing that if he had come for me I wouldn't have stood a chance. That thought terrifies me, but not half as much as his interest in this girl does. Whatever she did to attract his attention, I pity her for it.

I have no response, other than to flip off the safety and squeeze the trigger tighter. The gun in my hand is about to pop off, but Aiden's life is spared by Sara, the only one who seems to be perpetually saving lives in a house full of murderers. She doesn't give me the chance to respond – or kill anyone – when she flies into the room with a box of medical supplies in her arms.

I reach out to catch her, but she bullets past me and heads straight for the homicidal maniac and a half-dead Clifton hanging from Aiden's hands against the wall. As if she doesn't even notice them there, she walks straight towards the bathroom door with purpose in her step. Aiden's gaze follows her as she swivels past him. All at once, he drops Clifton and moves to bar her path with the full breadth of his body.

"What are you doing?"

Sara looks up at him. Straight up. He and his brother are the same height but he looks so much taller. Like three of him would fill up the whole goddamn room. And Sara looks so small. I swear to God if he touches her…I keep my weapon level and trained on his chest. I'm not a good enough shot to maim him, so if I pull the trigger, it's likely he'll die.

"I'm not here for you," she says. Her pitch is high and breathy and is the only thing that betrays her fear. "Seeing how things are going it's probably safe for me to assume you haven't gotten her out of those clothes like I asked. And given your bedside manner it's not a shock she locked herself in the bathroom. She's probably freezing and hysterical."

She glances back at Clifton, limping slowly up off of the floor. He massages his neck and coughs several times while the blood filters from his forehead to his chest, snaking past the collar of his destroyed tee shirt.

The chill in Aiden's expression lingers and he remains fixed in front of the door. He glares down at her, eyes narrowed slits, shoulders tense and full, hands balled. And then a small, soft, almost inaudible sound breaks up the silence: a whimper. I can hear it, which means Aiden can definitely hear it, but I knew that already. His whole damn body reacts. His neck twitches and he glances over his shoulder. Then he steps to the side to let Sara pass.

"You hurt her and I'll…" he says as Sara reaches for the door handle.

"I know. I heard you in the car." She glances up at him, gulps and says weakly, "I won't. I won't hurt her." She knocks on the door and when there's no answer, tries the knob. "Alina?"

Russian words float through the wood. They're pitchy and Aiden's whole body jerks. "Open the fucking door." He slams the flat of his hand against it and more whimpering follows.

Sara steps away from the door and gestures at the knob. "Open it," she says to Aiden. "She's not going to open it for us."

It takes him a half second to react. Likely, he's surprised by her. Hell, we all are. Aiden's hand molds around the knob and when he presses forward with what looks like the smallest amount of energy, the whole thing crumbles under his touch. Wood shards fall to the ground as dust.

He stands aside to let Sara move forward and plants himself in the doorway so that none of us can follow her in. Like this, I can see the reflection of his face in the mirror. It's brutal and haunting in all but the eyes. He glances around the frame of the door, seeing something I can't, and for just a moment those gripping grey eyes…well, they soften. Or maybe it's just a trick of the light.

"Hey, hey." I can hear Sara's tenderness and I wish it were closer, that I might feel it too. "My name is Sara." Clack, clack. Her box of supplies opens. "You're Alina Popov. You're in a bunch of the tabloids and fashion magazines I read. I'm a doctor. Well, I'm an intern, a paramedic, and a med student. So I'm going to be a doctor. And I'm just going to give you a little something to calm you down before we get you out of those wet clothes and into something warm and dry…"

There's a woman's shriek followed by commotion. Sara calls my name and I start forward while an unfamiliar voice cries, "*Nyet! Nyet. Bajalsta, nyet.* No drugs...*bajalsta...*"

I dip beneath Aiden's arm and surge into the bathroom at the same time the future unfolds before me: Sara's got a syringe in hand, the cold, wet stranger dressed in black is wedged between the wall and the toilet and right now she doesn't want the drugs Sara's offering and Aiden is looking at her like he's going to make sure that Sara bends to the girl's will. Alina.

He rips a gun off of his back and when he steps towards Sara, Clifton drags himself forward, but Clifton's no match for Aiden and neither am I and very soon, Sara is going to meet a short sweet end.

"No!" My voice stalls the moment just long enough to keep Sara alive. "Sara, put the needle down *now*." Sara looks from the girl to me to the needle in her hand, finally up to Aiden. She's squatting but the sight of Aiden throws her back onto her ass against the shower door. The needle tumbles from her hand.

"See? She's not going to hurt her." I take a step back and put my body between Aiden and Sara and the girl using the toilet as a shield. Heat radiates from Aiden's body, from his expression. The bathroom is tiny and I'm very close to him now. Close enough to touch but I don't dare.

"He's not going to hurt you," I say, angling my body to the side so I can speak to Alina directly while keeping an eye on Aiden. "Nobody's going to hurt you."

She shivers so aggressively it looks like her long, lean limbs will fall off and then she'll disintegrate, becoming nothing more than a smear against all that marble. She places her elbow on the lip of the toilet and covers her face with her hand. Behind those long, slender fingers, we can all hear her crying.

When Aiden starts forward, I brace my shoulder against his chest and dig the balls of my feet into the cold stone floor and he'd have still taken me out if it hadn't been for Clifton's arm circling Aiden's neck. Alina hiccups and starts crying harder, flinching away dramatically when Sara extends a tentative hand.

"No one fucking touch her," Aiden spits. He's foaming at the mouth and I know that the outcome of all of our evenings depends on the next few seconds, which is why I leave it in Sara's hands. She opens her mouth to speak and I nod vigorously, urging her on.

"I'm not going to hurt her, like Mer said," Sara says too loud, like she's incapable of controlling the volume of her pitch. "But I...I need Mer's help to undress her and get her into clean clothes. Can she borrow some of yours, Aiden?" Sara always knows the right thing to say because the murder clouding Aiden's face clears, albeit slowly. In one motion, he twists from Clifton's grip and shoves his brother backwards and onto the bedroom floor.

Aiden stands there for a moment, allowing long, labored breath to pour in and out of his lungs. He looks to his feet, and then flinches towards the girl as she moans. "Touch her only to change her." His voice is a quiet command.

Sara nods. "I won't do anything else."

"What does she need?"

For the first time in minutes, Sara exhales. "Just some...some sweatpants and a tee shirt. A sweatshirt if you have. Just something comfortable and warm."

Aiden leaves and returns with what Sara asked for. Everything is large and black and sure to engulf Alina. For as tall as she is, she sure is thin. Aiden stands in the doorway with his arms crossed and watches as Sara and I approach the girl in the corner. Behind him, Clifton's got his gun in hand and the safety is off. I gulp hard, sweat beading along my hairline and running down the back of my neck as I wade towards this beautiful Russian girl across the bathroom floor like I'm crossing a field of landmines.

"Alina?" Sara squats down in front of the girl. Several times, she glances over her shoulder, blonde hair swinging as she tries to gauge just how close she is to death. "I swear on my baby boy's life that we aren't here to harm you in any way. We're women after all and dating two of the men who stay in this house."

It doesn't seem to appease Alina because she shrieks when Sara touches her ankle. Aiden's body bucks, but he catches himself on the sink instead of coming towards us. "Let me go. *Bajalsta.*"

"Alina, you know that there are other bad men looking for you and that no one in this house will hurt you. You are safe here. What are you afraid of?"

"Sell me..." The words are slight and squeezed out between pursed lips.

Aiden slams his fist on the mirror, sending a crack rippling across its surface. "No one's going to fucking sell you."

"What interest could we have in your body?" Sara says on top of Aiden's voice. She throws him an irritated glance, but doesn't go so far as to rebuke him.

"Money," Alina moans. She's buried in her knees so that all I see of her is the top of her head, hair frazzled and the color of cranberry. "Always money."

"Have you seen this house? They don't need more money, sweetheart." Sara smiles and for a moment the expression manages to appear foreign. I can't remember the last smile I saw even though it couldn't have happened more than a few hours ago. Might as well have been lifetimes.

Alina starts to weep again and this time when Sara comes towards her and touches her shin, she doesn't scream or fight or flee. Sara glances at me with a sense of urgency – as if this is the only moment like this we'll get – so I follow her lead and reach into the narrow hovel and scoop Alina up by the armpits.

Her skin is cold enough for me to want to cringe away from her and for her to cringe away from me. She hisses through her teeth when we deposit her on the top of the toilet seat and drape towels over the mass of her hair. She's light. Scary light, even in all the wet clothes. Long and lithe and lean. Her face tilts to the side, neck like a string with no tether. I hold her head upright and she cries into my palm.

She says, "Gavriil," and then "Timur," and then more words in Russian.

When Sara pulls Alina's damp shirt off over her head and hands me a towel, I'm distracted from the task at hand by Aiden grunting, "Don't look. Close your fucking eyes."

I don't understand what he means or how I'm meant to change her with my eyes shut, but when I turn, I see Clifton standing beside his brother, expression too lax for me to think he's only there to keep us alive. He's gotten a glimpse of the girl and for just a second both men have never looked more alike. Like they've both been hit with fairy dust and can't remember where they are. Then Clifton looks up as Aiden shoves him back through the door.

"I can't leave you inside alone with those women," Clifton snarls, surging back across the threshold.

"You don't have any other choice, brother." Aiden sneers.

"Aiden." That's all the warning Clifton gives before he shoves his way past his brother's body. Maybe this type of shit would have flown in Dixon's suite, but in here there's a standing shower with a glass wall a toilet and a sink. Nothing else. So when Aiden retaliates, Clifton's spine meets the towel rack. The whole thing comes down with a clatter and Alina releases a small, sad cry. In a dry tee shirt with a sweatshirt that entirely engulfs her, she leans into Sara's body and hides her face in the darkness of her stomach.

"*Stup*," she moans and Aiden freezes with his fist cocked.

He turns towards her and damn he's close – just about against my body and close enough to her that her bunched knees are separated from his thighs by less than two feet. Aiden looks down at the gap, jaw relaxing for the first time in minutes – hours, years – then at her face.

So slowly that time itself seems to hold its breath, she twists out from the safety of her sleeve and Sara's shirt to look up at him. No force on earth could have had the same effect: He staggers back and Clifton catches him. "Woah, Aiden."

"I'm going to strip her out of her pants now," Sara says, and with implication. She gives Aiden a vicious glower. Truly, a mother.

Aiden isn't alarmed by it, but finds his footing and shoves his shoulder against Clifton's. "Turn around," he orders, "and close your eyes."

Clifton shoots Aiden a fiery look, but he doesn't resist this time. In the mirror, I see pale eyelids close over warm grey. Aiden does not do the same, but watches with clinical focus as I help Alina stand while Sara undoes the buttons at Alina's waist. He's leaning on his brother and when Alina's pants come down his injured leg bends. Clifton's legs plant into the ground like the roots of trees as Aiden slumps further onto him, a vicissitude of weakness and resistance. Blood puddles around his feet and I wonder if that's why his face goes grey.

I step in front of Alina as Sara pulls down the girl's underwear, shielding her from Aiden's gaze. He clears his throat behind me. "Sara," he barks.

"Yes?" She looks up and hands me a towel when Aiden doesn't immediately speak. I wrap it around Alina's waist and do my best to hold her up with one hand and with the other, dry her frozen, trembling thighs. Red flowers everywhere I touch and she doesn't stop crying.

Aiden cocks his head and Sara comes towards him – closer than I would have dared. He whispers directly into her ear, so low I can't hear what he says.

"I'll find out." She nods, returning to Alina's side, and helps me help the girl into sweatpants before taking a towel to her hair. Flakes of ice cling to the waist-length tendrils. Sara tries to comb her fingers through them and after a few minutes, manages to get Alina's hair into two French braids.

"Not sure how you handle this all on your own," she says lightly as we lead Alina out of the bathroom and into the bedroom. Aiden backs up in front of us, dragging Clifton with him. Both boys hover on the other side of the bed as we slide her into it and beneath the covers. Her bottom jaw continues to rap against the top and she hasn't stopped shaking. This time, I start to think it's more than just the cold. I stand back, wanting to give her and Sara space.

Sara leans over her and brushes her delicate fingers over the girl's speckled forehead. "Your hair kind of reminds me my baby's. His name is Brant. He's mixed too, though I'm not totally sure with what. When I don't brush his hair out it goes poof." She holds her hands out wide. "Completely nuts." She smiles down at the girl who does nothing but shake, and frowns.

Using her most placating tone, she eventually draws the blankets down from Alina's chest. Alina covers her face with her hands and I look at the wall switch, still taped. Aiden hesitates towards it, but in the end, remains where he is with his arms crossed over his chest and brow furrowed furiously. He looks pained and it has nothing at all to do with the wound in his leg or the crimson crust decorating his tee shirt's right shoulder.

"Now Alina, will you just tell me if this hurts?" She lifts the hem of the girl's sweatshirt and it doesn't take a genius to decipher what she's searching for as her fingers probe Alina's lower abdomen. She doesn't respond except to shake and cry. "How about here?" Sara moves down towards Alina's hips.

Alina kicks her legs, throwing the sheets onto the floor and curls onto her side. "I wasn't raped," she moans. "I'm still...still virgin. I...I still make you millions..." Her sweatshirt lifts – she's got freckles on her back – and her accent only serves to make her even more exotic. From the little I know of the sex trade, she's exactly right. Some freak would pay premium for her.

"Hey," Sara says. I grab the blankets and help tuck them around Alina gently. It does no good. "Hey, I told you, no one is here to sell you. I just wanted to be sure there was no internal bleeding. That you are okay."

"I'm not okay." Her tone rises and she buries her face directly into the pillow. "Timur," she shrieks and her body spasms. A sob roars through her and Sara stands back with her hands on her head.

She's got tears glossing her eyes and I'm worried for her in ways I wasn't. The night has been too overwhelming and little Alina is too much. "I've got to give her something." She speaks to Aiden. I would too. "I need to stitch you and Clifton, but I can't leave her here like this. Not like this...Just let me get the sedative. It's mild. She'll fall right asleep with no side effects."

"*Nyet!* No needles. No...no needles," Alina moans, shifting to try and get away from Sara.

Aiden surges up to the edge of the bed, but doesn't cross the divide as if he's just met a Plexiglas wall none of the rest of us can see or touch. "No needles."

Sara cries out, but I speak before she does. "What about something herbal?"

"What?" Aiden says.

"Herbal," I repeat. Sara looks confused, her face all scrunched up. "Don't make me spell it out for you, kids. I mean weed. There's loads of it around the house. I can roll her a jay right now and...and Charlie even has oil. Just a couple drops of that in some hot tea and she'll be out like a light. No needles involved."

Aiden glances to the bed as if awaiting a contradiction that doesn't come. She's just crying. Sara leans in close and repeats my proposition. "How does that sound?" She asks, stroking the girl's hair lovingly.

Silence descends over the world like a thick pall. Then a century later, the girl nods.

"Aiden will you take her to the porch? I'll grab the medical stuff from downstairs and stitch you guys up while she smokes. Mer, you get whatever you need. Can you also turn the floor on before we get there so there's plenty of heat?"

The smoker's porch is insulated and the floor is heated. Makes for a lovely oasis even in winter. I nod and start off towards it, but just before I hit the hall I hear Sara repeat her demand of Aiden.

"Aiden, will you take her?" I glance over my shoulder to see hard ass, hard headed fucking Aiden staring at little trembling Alina with nothing short of pure fear.

Aiden

"I'll take her," Clifton volunteers. I turn and jam my thumb deep into the wound high on Clifton's thigh. Clifton roars and hits me in the face. It's the only way to knock me off him. As he hits the ground, I bring my bloodied finger to my mouth and drag my tongue across it. "What the fuck?" He shouts up at me. "What has gotten into you? You're a goddamn lunatic."

I know.

I don't contradict him, but move towards the girl like all my joints have fused together. I'm stiff as a goddamn board as Sara makes space for me to take Alina's arm. Sitting upright, Alina falls into me. Her whole body hits mine and for a second I wonder if I'll be strong enough for this even though she weighs next to nothing. Her fingers paw across my tee shirt to find my far hand. The other, I drape over her back because there's nowhere else to put it. Her face comes against my tee shirt and I tighten my stomach. She whispers the names of both of her brothers and I walk stiffly, her feet stumbling over mine as she moves at this awkward pace I've set.

Clifton stands at the door massaging the growing welt on his right cheek and a ripple of fire rockets across my lower back when I hear him follow. I saw the way he looked at her in the bathroom and don't want him near her. He looks at her like he's consumed. Fascinated in ways I thought only I was. Nothing special, I remind myself. Just another fan. A faceless aggressor. The bastard who pulled her body out of a bag. Not her brother.

Down the hall, to the left. The French doors are flung wide open and music drifts softly through the opening. Something R&B by an artist I can't name, but that I enjoy. The singer's deep, effeminate voice helps soothe me. I keep my right arm fixed beneath Alina's clenched hands and my left fingers on her waist so that she doesn't fall. A glass table is framed by two wicker couches and two wicker chairs.

Mer is seated on the far end of one couch. When she sees us, she stands. "I have everything rolled and the tea is ready. I'm not going to stay though. I'd like to be with Charlie."

I don't care, so I don't respond. Instead, I pause as I reach the edge of the hardwood and step onto the natural stone. It radiates heat. Clifton says something. Mer passes me as she heads towards the stairwell at the end of the hallway. Alina presses herself closer against my chest.

Wanting only to get away from her, I take another step while she teeters on the threshold. Her hands are still clenched around my right forearm and my left continues to hover lamely over her spine. She hisses the moment her feet touch the porch floor and steps back. Her body wavers as she's separated from me. Clifton is quick to come up behind her and a low growl purrs out of my throat as I move back to her side. I glare at Clifton and he returns the expression. I want to hit him again but Alina's got my arms and my attention.

She moans. "Ouch." She takes a few soft steps, and moves nowhere. "It hurts."

"Step on my feet." The words come from deep within me and they're the first I remember ever saying to her. I know I've shouted at her before, but now I speak.

A balm eases through my chest, erasing the fire that had been there. She glances up at me quickly, sniffles, then looks down. She eases her bare toes over the tops of my boots. They're freckled too. Her toenails are painted pink and she struggles to balance just holding my hands. I know I'm going to have to wrap my arms around her waist. I am gutted as I do.

I slide my palms around my sweatshirt, focusing only on the cotton and trying to ignore her weight, and her smell. Even in all my shit, she still smells strongly of her perfume. Cardamom. Rain. My eyes close and I inhale. I try to hold my breath but can't. She smells too good. My hands hold her harder against me. She hardy expels heat and I know she'd warm more quickly if I kept her close. The thought makes me twitch. Hell, spasm. I practically throw her down on one side of the couch.

She sinks into the cushions and I move as far away from her as the sofa will allow. I don't know why I don't take the chair. Clifton seats himself on the couch across from her, but not before he hands her a blanket. I hadn't seen him holding it. He helps fan it over her shoulders and wrap it around her back. She thanks him in her shaky pitch. The first time she's ever thanked any of us for anything and it's Clifton. I hate that. I hate him. And before now, he's never inspired anything in me but apathy.

I'm behaving strangely. I know I am and I'm equally aware that I can't control the compulsion, the rage, the docility – they're all there broiling on the surface, emotions I thought I'd kicked like a habit worse than heroin. I'd had them beaten out of me when I was young. I don't know how old. Never had a birthday. Only reason I know how old I am is because of the fucking doppelganger sitting across from me. From her.

The bastard who coerced me off of the streets and into this pathetic, patchwork family picks up the tea and passes it across the table, then the jay, then the lighter. At the same time, Sara bursts into the room. It's not the first time she's kept me from fantasies of killing him.

"Here. I have everything." She dumps what's in her arms onto the floor and begins rummaging through it. "I only have two more of these so I need to assess which of you is in worse condition. The other can wear these for now."

"I'm fine," I grunt, gaze pinned to Alina seated not three feet from me. It's too close. Never thought we'd have to be this close with both of us conscious.

Alina's body is curled tight, but her face is angled my way. She reaches up and touches her mouth. I can tell it's sticky by the way she swallows. I grab the mug of her tea from the table and bring it to her hands. My body moves without conferring with my mind. My mind is a mud slab in the rain. Clean and worthless.

She gasps a little, and looks up at me through her dark brown eyelashes. She seems surprised and stares at my face for a moment longer before her gaze pans south. She's taking me in, assessing me, and I feel like a fucking fool when the prickle of a dangerous heat creeps across the back of my skull. This is a different kind of fire. Not the one I know that accompanies homicide. But the one I felt when I was ten. I had a crush on my foster sister. So the eldest foster boy in the house raped her, then burnt her alive.

"You...you...are shot." She points at my leg and takes the tea in two hands. I keep my own fingers around the base, because she doesn't hold it steadily. When she lowers it from her lips she licks them and looks at me again. The color in her cheeks blazes a stronger red.

"*Spasiba.*" Tears fall from each of her eyes at the same time, as if choreographed, and a shiver twists my spine.

"Aiden, can I look at your leg please?" Sara is kneeling in front of me with a pair of scissors in hand.

I don't kick her. I don't send her away. But I look at Alina. She's watching Sara in a curious way. Then she looks at me. "Are...are...are you hurt?" Alina says. She hiccups, gulps, shakes again.

"No."

"But you bleed." Her accent is strong and exquisite. I want to hear her speak all day. She takes another sip of tea and I realize I'm staring.

"Fine," I bark, turning my gaze back to my shredded pants.

Sara moves quickly, first slapping the bandages on Clifton before returning to me. "Where are you hit?"

She cuts her way up the length of my right pant leg until she reaches my thigh and picks cloth out of the wounds with tweezers. I twitch several times involuntarily, but the pain is nothing but a sensation to be endured. I don't let her stab me with her morphine or her local anesthetic and I don't take Percocet pills from her.

"For heaven's sake, Aiden. It's cringe worthy watching you take pain this way. At least smoke with Alina."

I glance to my right. Alina is watching me. Has been watching. She starts when we make eye contact and a little bit of tea slops over the side of her glass. She stretches forward and tries to pick up the jay from the edge of the table. Her fingers are clumsy though and the Zippo falls. I snatch for it, but I'm too far and Sara yelps when I move so suddenly.

It clatters over the ground and when I straighten back up, my arm brushes Alina's shin. I see her face. Her full face. For the first time since the car. She looks at me with that watery gaze. Her rounded cheeks are flushed. The tip of her nose is pink. Her mouth is a deep, dark cherry. Like her hair. I hand her the joint and then the lighter, but she takes neither. Instead, she clutches her tea closer to her chest and curls even tighter in on herself, like she's afraid. She should be.

"What?" The word releases from my chest though I hadn't meant to say anything.

She flinches. Clifton hisses my name. Sara orders me to stay still. Then Alina licks her lips and they manage to look hotter and redder from where I sit. I remember the last time I'd touched them. I shouldn't have, but my fingers never forgot their softness.

"Can you…light for me? *Bajalsta*," she whispers. I close my eyes for a moment, leg kicking mechanically as Sara stabs my calf with her thin, curved needle over and over again. I could listen to her speak Russian endlessly. These few words here and there are a sacred torment because they are so rare.

"I can do it," Clifton says. "He doesn't smoke…"

I've got the joint in my mouth before he's finished and pull once, twice, a third time deeply into my lungs before passing it to her. Her fingers brush mine and I flinch back, putting more of the couch between us. Space has been shrinking between us as if the couch is getting smaller. I'm not sure how. She sips on the joint slowly, struggling to inhale. Eventually, the process becomes easier. I can see the tension in her shoulders loosen. Her eyelids begin to droop. But she doesn't stop shivering.

The joint passes from my hand to Clifton's to hers three times and she's still shaking visibly. It starts to grate on me like a high-pitched whistle with no source. Sara finishes patching up my leg, then my shoulder, and applies large white strips of gauze to both before moving on to Clifton. I use the opportunity to get up and go to the linen closet in the hall. I return with a full comforter and coil it around her body, working diligently and carefully to make sure not an inch of her except for her face and fingers are exposed.

"*Ogromnoe spasibo*," she says, watching me as I sit back down. There are tears glossing her eyes again and I don't understand what I've done to warrant that. She takes a few puffs from the end of her joint before passing it to Clifton.

There's a rattling in my stomach and a pounding in my chest. It sounds like a train crushing itself against a wall over and over again. The sincerity in her tone makes me want to kill her because there's a sudden violent emotion clogging my throat that I can't speak through. Or breathe through. I'm suffocating slowly.

"Can I sit closer to you?" she says. She's looking at me but I can't imagine she's speaking to me. Evidently neither can Clifton or Sara. They've both frozen and stare in my direction and I am embarrassed and ashamed and overwhelmed.

"No," I choke.

She doesn't look surprised or disappointed. Across the table, Clifton clears his throat. "You can come here." He holds out his arm and beneath him, Sara's mouth gapes.

The breath jerks into and out of my lungs. I look to Alina. She blinks several times, managing to look halfway dazed. Then, "Oh…okay. *Da, spasiba.*"

Pure ice blasts through me that succeeds in momentarily dousing the fire in my arms. I don't kill Clifton, but watch as Alina ambles awkwardly off of the couch. I don't help her though I want to. And I do want to. Watching her walk in short, pained steps, likely burning her feet on the floor that's fire to her but warm to the rest of us is the most painful thing I've ever done. I don't feel the bullet holes or the blue stitching zigzagging across my shoulder and leg, but I feel each twitching of her expression as if it were my own.

"Here, take my hand," Clifton says.

She looks up, trips and falls as she reaches for him. Bundled in so many blankets that her shape is impossible to define, she crashes onto Clifton's couch. No, onto his lap. His cheeks glow as she apologizes.

"Nothing to be sorry for, little lady." He makes space for her but not enough of it so when she settles between his body and the edge of the couch, she's fully tucked against his side, beneath the curve of his arm.

"You can relax," he says, "don't be afraid to lean on me."

"*Spasiba*," she whispers. She shoots a furtive glance in my direction, frightened at first, and after a moment of holding my gaze, which must be pure hate because that's the only thing I feel at all anymore, the fear seems to fade away as if watching me calms her. I understand nothing but the rage I feel towards my brother as she relaxes her head onto his shoulder.

Jealousy. I have heard of the emotion but have not experienced it before this. Perhaps a shadow of it when the doctor drooled over her in the hospital, but this is magnified and concentrated and dangerous for everyone in the room. Because Clifton looks like the better version of me. He acts like the better version of me. He is better than me in every way and is, undoubtedly, better for her.

Alina's eyelids begin to droop. With eyes closed she buries her face further into Clifton's chest. Clifton inhales deeply and as he exhales, reaches over and gently rubs her shoulders. She releases a small satisfied moan and I look away.

"She asleep?" Sara whispers. Done with Clifton, she packs up her bag.

Clifton leans around the girl's now still form and smiles. "I think so." He takes the tea from her hands, which are limp and resting in between folds in the blankets, and sets it on the table. "I think I'll take her to bed."

"Wait." For a moment I think Sara will tell me I should be the one to do it. I shouldn't be. Clifton is softer, safer, more handsome, gentler. I'm disgusting. A monster. "I know it sounds rude, but wake her up first. With how anxious she is about all of us, we shouldn't move her without warning. She won't recognize her environment and it could be enough to set her off, or make her run."

I look down at the wound travelling across my leg. The blue stitches against my white skin form a series of Xs, like a map of the New York underground. Red flakes and pink smears cover everything. Most of me. I'm a blood-soaked nightmare and she's an angel wrapped in a white sheet. I hear but don't watch as Clifton wakes her and she responds in tentative whispers. I don't move as he lifts her from the couch. At least not at first.

Sara follows him out of the room and I'm in a trance as I wade down the hall after him. After her. Sara turns as we reach the basement steps and the urge to go to the gym and run a hundred miles grips me. I can't run though with my leg all fucked. I can't lift with my shoulder fucked either.

Maybe I'll load all the weights onto the bar anyways without warming up and see if it'll crush me. Maybe it'll cut off the wind to my throat, or sit on my chest until I can't breathe anymore. They'll find me tomorrow covered in Russian blood and bruising and at my funeral no one will show up besides Clifton who will tell the congregation of ghosts that I had a hard life but was a decent man. A decent man. Decent men don't look like me. Decent men don't kill and enjoy it.

I stand outside of the open guest bedroom door, looking in as Clifton unwraps Alina from the comforter I gave her and helps her into the bed. He draws the blankets up to her chin and tells her that he's just next door, out and to the right, if she needs anything anytime, day or night.

She says, "*Spasiba*," and nods understanding.

But as Clifton turns to leave, her gaze flicks past him. She sees me and her eyes are demanding, but I don't understand what she wants. Probably for me to leave. So I turn from her and head to the basement and as I hit the steps, I am the ghost of my better brother.

Goodbye, Alina Popov.

Sara's apartment was empty. No bodies to be found. Sherry was a wreck when we reached her, nervous for her friend, but after a cup of tea and reassurance from me, she calmed down. Brant seemed pleased to see me and I hold him in my arms as I walk through the front door of the house. Knox carries two huge garbage bags filled with Sara's stuff – clothes, schoolbooks, and medical supplies. Under my arm, I have her laptop.

"Where do you want these, man?"

My chest is hollow and my heart hangs on a noose in a cavern of empty space. "Guest room."

Knox gives my shoulder a knowing squeeze as he starts down the hall to the left. Two guest rooms sit side-by-side. The first is full with our house's newest guest. Her body is so still as Knox pops open the door and peeks inside that I have to assume she's sleeping, but I can't be sure. She could be dead.

The next room will be Sara's. I hold my breath as Knox knocks, then opens it. He flicks on the lights. The bed is made, and the room is empty. The bathroom door is open and full of shadows but no bodies.

"She's not here, man," Knox says, turning to me. "She in your room?"

The thought seems ludicrous, but I nod, unable to come up with another answer. I follow Knox to my room. He knocks, but again there's no answer. As was the case with the first two rooms, he waits a few seconds, then opens the door. The lights are on inside and the bathroom door is open. Curlicues of steam wrap around Sara's body which is covered by a towel and nothing else. She looks up from where she stands in the bathroom doorway and, seeing us, gasps.

Knox looks immediately at his feet, drops the bags inside the room and beats a quick retreat. "Thanks again for everything, Sara."

He's smiling and I can hear laughter on his tone as he moves down the hall, clapping me on the back. He glances over his shoulder at me once and laughs outright. I probably would too. I feel stunned, like I've been clipped by a bullet in the chest hard enough to spin my whole body around.

I step into the room and close the door behind me, then place Brant's squirming body in the center of the king bed. Sara walks up to its other side and kneels in front of Brant. He beams at her and when she reaches for his stomach, wraps his little hands around her fingers.

"Thank you for getting Brant," she says. Her skin is flushed from the shower and the ribbons of her hair curl around her shoulders.

I clear my throat. "Thank you for saving my brother."

She flicks her blue gaze up at me and shakes her head. She doesn't smile. "I just hope I did enough."

"You did enough." My chest is tight and constricted and I shift my weight between my feet then glance at the door. "Your apartment was empty. We brought some of your things. Do you want me to help you put them away in the guest room?"

"No," she says softly. "I'm tired."

I nod. "Understandably. We can move you and Brant in there tomorrow. I'll sleep in there tonight."

I head to the door, but the moment I move, Sara stands up. The hand she's got around the top of her towel – the only thing holding it in place – falls, and her nakedness hits me like an assault. She's a fucking vision. I don't dare move because if I do, it'll be to devour her.

"You don't have to do that." She comes around the bed and is standing in front of me.

What is happening? I'm not sure. But I'm too weak to ask and sever the connection between us. She lifts the hem of my shirt and I let her bring it up over my head. She touches my neck and her fingers wander over my pecs to my abdomen and then to my belt. She flips it free and pulls it off in a single motion, then moves to the zipper.

I'm still frozen where I stand even though I'm fully naked and so is she. She starts to kiss me. Her mouth following the same trajectory her hands had. She pulls my nipple into her mouth, then bites the skin below. Biting and kissing and licking and sucking until she reaches my thighs. She's on her knees now and I catch myself on the bed. Brant's fallen asleep in its center and I don't want him to wake and see this so I lower myself beneath its edge and roll onto my back. Her lips find the head of my erection and I give myself up to the sensation, fully surrendering to the pleasure she wants to give. I'll take anything and everything she's willing to offer.

"Please, baby," I murmur, but there is no end to that sentence. I am hers.

Her hands massage my balls and her tongue works the base of my dick while her other hand folds around the tip. My mind is a haze as I live in nirvana for the next few minutes. Eternities pass before I crest with violence. I flip her body over and straddle her face and press my dick into her mouth until I reach the back of her throat. She opens for me, gag reflex massaging the head of my cock and a momentary guilt grips me but isn't enough to keep me from pressing even deeper into her. I meet her gaze as the orgasm tackles me from behind.

She looks up at me and I watch her swallow, feeling every sensation as she milks me with her tongue. My legs go straight and I roar into the floor as the last of the cum spills from my dick and onto her mouth. She licks it off and the urge to cover her in my semen comes over me, like I'm marking her as mine, as if it would come with a scent and a smell that would be a warning to other men. She gasps as I pull free of her lips and tries to rise up onto her elbows. I hold her down. Grabbing my belt from the floor, I take her hands and bind them together around the nearest foot of the bed.

"Keep your legs spread," I say in a gruff voice, rougher than I wanted it. "Wider." I press her thighs apart with my palms until she's fully spread-eagle and bared before me. That pink slit that I want to write my name into in saliva and cum. I want to impregnate her. I want her to carry my child. I want her to be my wife. I want to grow old and die with her.

"Don't move," I warn.

I don't waste the time teasing her, but pull her clit into my mouth, sucking hard enough for her to moan as the line between pleasure and pain blurs together. I slip a finger inside of her as moisture drips down my chin, letting me know just how ready she is for me, then a second, then a third, then a fourth. My lips and tongue work her clit and I pound my fingers in and out of her until she releases a breathy scream. She tries to bring her legs together as the orgasm comes, but I hold her in place with my elbows. Her pussy grabs my hand, trying to force it out as the tremors of her orgasm subside.

"Dixon," she moans, "oh sh…" She starts to squirm but I keep her knees pinned where they are. The juice of her orgasm drips out of her cunt and I lap at it like a dog. "I'm so sensitive, Dixon, I can't…"

"You will," I tell her.

I bite the skin on the inside of her thigh and she kicks involuntarily. "Dixon, I don't know…"

"Shh. You'll do what I say. And now I want you to come again for me."

I hold her down and press my tongue to her clit. It's swollen and throbbing. My hand in her pussy begins pumping in and out. Two fingers again as I prime her and warm her up. "Come now," I bark as her body starts shivering and the muscles in her thighs begin clenching and releasing.

She moans deeply as she does. I look at her face and her eyes are unfocused, her chest is heaving and her arms are clenched. She's spent. Tells me she can't go anymore, but this isn't about her. This is about me and I'm nothing if not selfish. I pin her body and tell her to beg for me. She begs. I tell her to scream for me and she screams.

I bring her to orgasm three more times with my mouth before I take her limp thighs between my hands and spread them around my hips. I fuck her half a dozen times. She isn't moving by the time I'm finished. Her mouth forms a small smile and her eyelids are hooded. She's got my semen all over her body, but mostly inside of it. Deep inside. I pull her breast into my mouth and bite her nipple. She writhes and pulls at the bindings still wrapped around her hands.

"Won't do you any fucking good," I whisper against her mouth. "You're mine." My dick is growing hard inside of her again.

"I know," she says.

"You aren't going anywhere." Can she hear the desperation in my voice? The plea behind the threat.

"I know." She smiles and her eyes open long enough for her to focus on mine. "I'm not."

My voice catches and breaks. "What changed?" I push her hair back from her eyes as tears come to mine. I'm fucking wasted. Spent. Physically and emotionally. But to have her like this is putting sight before a blind man. Without it, I'd live in the dark forever.

"Mer told me what you did for her. What you all did for her. I shouldn't have jumped to conclusions. I should have known you wouldn't put Brant or me in danger without a good reason. Mer seems like a good reason."

I blink down at her, wondering if Marguerite had been right all along. Maybe there really is a god. If there isn't, I can't think of another reason this is happening to me now after all the carnage I've inflicted. Well, I can think of one reason. Mer. Mer, who I tried to have killed. Who at this moment, is saving my life.

"I love you," I say, gliding my hips back and thrusting them forward again, hard. Too hard for her, but she takes it, and doesn't complain except to gasp.

"I love you...you too," she says as I pound into her again. I pull my cock out of her wet pussy and come on her chest, stomach and face before waiting a few minutes more and sliding into her again. "Don't stop."

I don't plan on it. "I want you to drink it again," I tell her.

"I want to drink it. Come here, baby."

I pull my cock out of her and watch her lick her juices and mine free. The sight is too much: Her, covered in the product of half a dozen orgasms, hands bound, submitting to me fully in every way. Her heart. Her body. I want to crush her to my chest and bury her in there so she'll always be close. Instead, I bury my shaft in her pussy and come one final time, angling her hips up and pounding down while my thumb works her clit like a button.

She comes for me and I come for her and we lay there for a moment, side by side trying to catch our breaths and failing before I untie her hands and carry her to the shower. She lets me wash her and I wonder if she can tell how much I need this because even though her pussy is red and swollen, she lets me press her against the shower wall and fuck her once more.

I kiss her neck. She wraps her arms around my shoulders and that night when we fall asleep with Brant beside us, I reach over her body and hold his little hand and I understand the difference between what I have with my brothers and what I have with Sara and Brant. This is what Knox meant. This, right here in my arms, is my family. And nothing will ever threaten that. Not anymore. Not even me.

Three months later…

Sara

The sun is shining and Dixon and I are on the floor of the covered porch, Brant sprawled out on a blanket between us. "I can't believe how big the little guy is," Dixon says, grinning like a fool. It's that grin that makes me feel hopeful and less nervous. I've got news and I don't know how he'll take it. That's why it's been two weeks and I haven't said anything. I've just been pretended to feel ill whenever I've gone out drinking with Mer and the brothers.

"Babies do that, you know," I muse.

"Do what?"

"Grow."

Dixon lunges across Brant's body and tackles me with a kiss. Brant squeals in delight beneath him. "You think you're pretty clever, don't you?"

"I did learn something in medical school." I laugh lightly and squint against the sun shining in through the windows. I take a sip of the water in front of me and Dixon stares for a moment up at the sky through the glass. It's cold today, but the floor heaters are on and I'm toasty warm in just a sweater and leggings. "Everything okay?"

He shrugs, returning to the present. I know he's had a lot on his mind with the current RussianmafiaMexicancarteldepositboxstillfullofheroin situation. It hasn't resolved itself, though it would seem that we're out of the line of fire for the time being. At least most of us. Dixon has been open with everything since that night at the barn, but that doesn't mean that Aiden's been open with him.

In fact, Aiden's been cagier than ever. We assume it's because he's trying to keep distance between us and the ones that are hunting Alina. Recognizing her connections, her fame and her beauty, someone is going to want her back – and I don't mean her brother. Aiden won't stand for that though. His connection to the girl is astounding at best, but I don't dare ask Aiden and it's not something Dixon or any of the other brothers understand.

Dixon shakes his head and looks again to Brant, who is currently using Dixon's knee to try to stand. He makes it upright for a few seconds before plopping back onto his bum, and on the second try manages a few steps. "So damn proud of you, kid," he says and I'm not sure whether he's talking to me or Brant, but I blush all the same.

"I'm sure Brant's proud of Uncle Dixon too. Just like I am." I look down at the red-and-black checkered blanket beneath us and gulp. "So I…"

"I…" Dixon says at the same time I do.

I smile. "Go ahead."

Dixon's squinting at me hard. He's shaved his head and it makes him look meaner, which is hard for me to fathom with the way he cradles Brant so tenderly. "What's a guy got to do to get you to stop calling me that?" He takes a sip of his beer and sets it down, then rubs his hand over Brant's curls.

"What?"

"Uncle."

Dismay swells in my chest, and falls into my gut as ash. "Oh. Sorry. I didn't know it bothered you."

"It does."

My fingers instinctively slide over my stomach. Sh… "What do you want to be called then?"

I clear my throat and try to remain optimistic, or at least accept the finality of what's happened to me and what we'll need to do to move forward, be it together or apart. The thought makes me want to weep. I love Dixon and I'd want him to be a part of his child's life. Otherwise, that means I'll be raising two fatherless kids alone. Maybe this is my fault. I should have asked him the moment I found out. I never took that Plan B pill way back when. Any of those times. Too much was happening and I forgot. It's a lousy excuse, but it's the only one I have…

"Dad."

"What?" My voice isn't my own. Brant has waddled from Dixon's arms to me and even when he reaches up towards my neck and pulls on a lock of my hair, I don't move.

"Dad. I'm getting tired of this uncle crap." He winks at me and tears immediately blur my vision.

I choke, "You…you want to be called dad?"

"What the hell else?" I laugh and rub my eyes, hoping to keep him from seeing the emotion in my expression. Then I laugh. When I look up he's grinning. "So? What's a guy gotta do?"

Marshalling it for a moment, I say shakily, "Well I would have kind of expected a ring before making any dramatic changes to your title."

Dixon smiles at me gently. "You mean, like this?"

He glances down, reaches into his pocket and pulls out a small box in cobalt velvet. Without prelude, he tosses it to me and I catch it in my left hand. "I...I...." Brant is chewing on my hair right now and it doesn't make any difference.

Dixon cocks his chin towards the box. "Just open it."

I do and a banded sapphire shines up at me. It catches the light and looks like a drop of rain, solidified. "I..."

"So what do you say?" This time Dixon's voice dips and when I glance up at him, he looks away. His nervousness is what breaks me.

"Shit." Wrapping one arm around Brant, I throw the other around Dixon's neck and I kiss him with every bit of worry that I had in me so that by the time I break the kiss, there is only love left. "I love you so much."

He laughs and there's a gloss to his eyes that makes tears fall from my own. He pulls me against him fully. "Is that a yes?"

"Yes," I say. "Of course." He removes the ring from the box and, reaching around both my body and Brant's, finds my hand and slides the sapphire onto my finger.

"Do we have a deal then? A ring for a title change?"

I'm laughing and crying and can't control the words that come out of my mouth as I stare at his dark hand clutching my fingers and the little mixed boy sitting between us shrieking with laughter. He could have been ours.

"Yes. Of course. It's just...you'll also be a dad. An actual dad. I found out two weeks ago and I didn't tell you because I was nervous and..."

He takes my chin and tilts it up, then breaks my sentence with a kiss. "I know." His hand slides over my belly and he grips the back of my neck in a way that's possessive and sure enough for the both of us. "I've known you were pregnant for the past week. You're a shit liar, Sara."

"Is that why you proposed?"

He kisses me again, this time lingering even longer. Long enough for me to feel his erection through his jeans. I rub my hip against it and he grunts. "I've had the ring for six weeks."

My pulse is schizophrenic and Dixon struggles to wipe the tears away from my cheeks before the next ones fall. I kiss him hard, first on the mouth, then against the throat. "Are you excited to be a father?"

Dixon lifts Brant from my lap and kisses his round, quivering cheek. He meets my gaze, grins and says, "I thought I already was."

Continue reading for a sneak peak of

THE HUNTED RISE
BROTHERS, VOLUME II

Aiden

"What do you mean, she won't eat?" Clifton is trying to reason with Sara as if she is the problem.

Sara shoots Clifton a frosty glance and tugs on the hem of her shirt. "I mean we're nearing seventy two hours and she refuses to do anything besides lay in the bed or the bath. She won't talk to anyone." She does not attempt to make eye contact with me for more than a few seconds. That's why I stand behind my brother. He says what I'm thinking in the way I wish I could say it. I was never meant to take care of the girl, I was only ever tasked to keep her alive. Now my only task – the only thing I've done right in my entire existence – is being put at risk. By Alina. Unlike me, she can do no wrong and yet, I could kill her for this.

"Have you tried…" Clifton starts. My fist meeting the wall cuts him off. The drywall buckles and paint flakes off around my hand. "Fuck Aiden, another goddamn wall? You know Dixon's going to make you pay for that."

I don't give a fuck about the wall. I glare hard at Sara. "How am I supposed to know what's wrong when she won't speak?"

Sara and Clifton share a glance. There's something I don't understand and I feel stupid. I am stupid. I'm dense as a goddamn wall and I have no business taking care of perfection with a face. I hit the wall again. "What?"

Sara jumps. Clifton holds up both hands and turns to face me. People around me are constantly making this gesture. I wish I knew what it meant. "Easy, brother."

"How many times do I have to tell you not to call me that?" I surge towards him and he plants his feet, preparing to take the full weight of my body.

"Sh... Stop! Just stop it! Stop it, stop it, stop," she huffs. "I can't deal with you two flying off the handle every time we talk about Alina. I need you to calm down and try to be helpful. Both of you," she adds as an afterthought. Always the lady and it pisses me off. I want to stab her and for the tenth time in the past three minutes, my hand twitches for the butterfly knife in my back pocket. "And if we're going to keep talking about this, may I suggest we do so outside? Just our luck, she'll choose this moment to wake up and hear everything we're saying." Clifton glances over his shoulder, like he's being stalked, and we both follow her outside.

"Then tell me," I rasp as I walk, "why the fuck is she doing this?"

"Because she's bored. She's lonely, she's scared. She wants to go buy things to make her feel better being here but you have her confined to the house. She's a prisoner here." Sara bites her bottom lip, wrenches open the glass patio door and takes a step into the breeze. It's cold outside, but it's sunny so I don't bother with a coat. Shrugging on a heavy flannel, Clifton tells me I'm crazy. I tell him to fuck himself.

"I'm not supposed to keep her happy. Just safe."

"Well that's one approach," Sara mutters. Her sarcasm and her condescension don't go unnoticed and when I stand taller she takes another step away from the house. Clifton licks his lips and shoves his hand through his hair. It's longer than it should be. He's also growing a beard. I wonder if it's so people have an easier time telling us apart. I'd want to distance myself from me if I were him too.

"I think what Sara's trying to say is that this isn't working."

"I may be stupid but I'm not deaf." I kick a stone and watch it skate over the grass. It needs to be mowed. Normally, that's a me task but I've been busy ignoring and neglecting Alina. I frown so hard I feel it in my bones. The sudden urge to kill something sweeps me. It's accompanied by an equally strong desire to collapse. My legs feel funny. I wonder if I'm getting sick. I never get sick. "Sara," I bark.

She flinches again and bundles her sweater more snugly around her arms. "If this is you asking me to do something, then I think you could strike a different tone."

"Sara," Clifton says. His voice is gentle, but firm. "Please."

She blinks at him quickly, then looks at me, then back at the house. Dixon's just appeared behind the glass carrying Brant. I can see him pretending not to watch us, but even his presence eases Sara because she releases her arms and relaxes her shoulders back. Not that his presence would do her any good. She doesn't answer soon and I could snap her neck before Dixon ever drops the babe and gets the glass door open.

She sucks in a breath. "For starters, I would take her to whatever stores she wants to buy whatever she needs to feel comfortable and safe in the house. Stick to her like white on rice, for sure, but you need to get her out doing stuff that is normal for her, otherwise she'll never be okay staying here."

"Fuck if she's comfortable staying here," I roar. A flight of birds takes off from the Crabapple behind me. They squawk up into the clouds and disappear. Birds are the animal I hate most. They are the only ones that I envy. "She's not supposed to be comfortable. She's supposed to be in her room, safe, where no one can touch her."

"Brother," Clifton tries. The sun catches the grey of his eyes, eyes that are much darker than mine. The only physical difference between us. "Listen to her. She knows what to do to help Alina."

"No," I spit.

Sara groans and shrugs her shoulders, like her bones can no longer support their weight. They sag down her back and she looks defeated. "She's not going to stick around. She'll either try to run and someone will find her and murder her, or she'll die right here in this house with you lording over her. How will you feel knowing that you helped kill her?"

"Aiden!" I hear my name at the same time as the gunshot. It whizzes past my ear and when Clifton throws me back, I look up to see Dixon cradling a sleeping baby in one hand. In his other, he holds a long-range pistol with a booster and silencer attachment. Well, that's one way to keep me from killing his girl.

His girl. The sound echoes through my skull, forcing me to imagine for one harrowing moment what it would be like to use that term to describe the woman I'm killing. The one I'm in love with. The only thing on this earth that I'll ever love, including myself.

"Alright fine! Are you happy now? I'll take her fucking shopping." I storm towards the house, cracking dead twigs under my boots for no other reason than to fulfill my desire to break something.

Sara tries to edge in front of me. Clifton holds her back. "Before you can take her anywhere, you need to get her some food she likes. Russian food. I already looked up the best places in the city. Three of them deliver, and the rest all do takeout."

She digs in her back pocket, then hands over a slip of paper. I rip it from her grasp and read down the list of names. Vizir, Kishlak, Mari Vanna, Alasha, Madeni…There are ten names on this list. She's circled some and I place an order at Alasha. It's the first call I can remember placing to anyone but Dixon in the past decade and a half. The woman on the other end of the line asks me what I want. I tell her one of everything, read her my credit card number and hang up. I'm standing outside of Alina's room.

"Alina." I bang on the door. "Let me in."

There's no answer.

"You're going to have to eat." I keep myself from cursing. It isn't easy. I want to tear through the wood and hurl myself at the girl with every intention of violence, but I know what will happen when she does open the door and I do see her – the same thing that happens every time: I fall the fuck to pieces.

"Alina, open the door. You will eat." Statements don't work, neither do threats, so I try pleas. "Goddammit, Alina. Do you want to die? I told your brother I'd keep you safe." Then coercion. "I'll take you shopping, alright? Just eat something. Alasha delivery will be here in half an hour. Sara says to try to eat bread or soup beforehand so your stomach doesn't hurt. Alina? Alina."

She still hasn't said anything and I'm hot. The hallway is shrinking around me and I can hear other people in the house, but they don't come into the hall. They've learned from their past mistakes, which is a fucking pity because I could use someone right about now to be the punching bag I use to unleash my hate.

"Alina! Open the door, or I will." My hand closes around the knob and twists. Bloody hell. It's unlocked. My mouth dries up. Sweat beads along the back of my shaved head. I lick my lips and step inside her room without her permission.

The bed is empty. The closets are empty. The bathroom is empty but the window in the bathroom – barely bigger than an air vent – is open. Alina is gone. My blood turns to slush and for a moment, the world ceases to turn.

Also by Elizabeth
Population series
A dystopian romance

Lawlessness, violence and desperation are all that is left of the world following the coming of the Others. Abel exists only within the boundaries that her rules allow – rules that she created to keep her alive. But when her best friend's daughter is taken by the Others, she can't keep playing by the rule book.

Instead, she must begin a life defining journey that will test her survival techniques and bring all of her instincts into question. When she finds herself allied with one of the Others, Abel must confront foreign concepts like allegiance and desire and trust as he challenges her ability to find what she has always feared: hope.

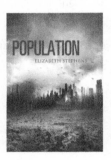 

To read a preview of Population, a science fiction romance series, sign up to become an Advanced Reader for Elizabeth's upcoming novels, or read her short stories visit

www.booksbyelizabeth.com

•   •   •

Made in United States
North Haven, CT
09 July 2024

54573631R00275